The
Tale
of
Genji

Translated with an Introduction by
EDWARD G. SEIDENSTICKER

VINTAGE BOOKS
A DIVISION OF RANDOM HOUSE
NEW YORK

MURASAKI SHIKIBU

The
Tale
of
Genji

First Vintage Books Edition, February 1985
Copyright © 1976, 1985 by Edward G. Seidensticker

Library of Congress Cataloging in Publication Data
Murasaki Shikibu, b. 978?
The tale of Genji.
Reprint. Originally published: New York:
Knopf, 1976.
I. Title.
PL788.4.G415E5 1984   895.6'31   84-40519
ISBN 0-394-72921-8

The woodcut illustrations reproduced in the text were first published in 1650
in the *Illustrated Tale of Genji (Eiri Genji Monogatari)*. They are the work of
Yamamoto Shunsho, a Kyoto artist who lived from 1610 to 1682
and who is best known for his work in lacquer.

Cover art (front and back) are details from the four panel Tale of Genji Screen
illustrating an episode from the chapter ''A Meeting at the Frontier'' by Tosa
Mitsuyoshi (1539-1613). Courtesy of The Metropolitan Museum of Art,
Fletcher Fund, 1955.

9876

Contents

Introduction to the Vintage Edition

This book, which contains a dozen chapters from early in *The Tale of Genji,* is about a quarter the length of the complete edition. The last chapter is the seventeenth chapter of the original. Chapters 2, 3, 6, 15 and 16, which stand apart from and have no effect on the main narrative, have been omitted.

Because Arthur Waley originally published his translation in six volumes, fairly regularly spaced over the years, the impression seems to be widespread that *The Tale of Genji* is a series of independent but related novels, like the Barchester novels or the Palliser novels of Trollope. This is an error. The six-part division is entirely Waley's, having no relation to the original, which is divided only into fifty-four chapters, and which is a continuing story. Waley's abridgment, which includes only the first nine chapters of the complete *Genji,* was published in a separate volume as if it brought the action to some sort of conclusion. It does not so serve. It merely takes the story an arbitrary distance and no further.

This selection is perhaps equally arbitrary, but it also has behind it the assumption that it would be well to get as far along with the story as possible, while keeping the selection to a manageable length. For this reason certain chapters not essential to the main, continuing story have been omitted. It seemed obvious that the beginning should be at the beginning, since the opening chapters are the only ones that do not depend on others for thorough understanding.

The ninth and last chapter of the shortened Waley version is inconclusive. It brings no resolution, for instance, of the political conflict between the factions of the Left and the Right. That conflict comes to a climax and resolution in the following chapters, treating Genji's exile and return. Chapter 17, with which this new version ends, may seem equally irresolute. In fact, however, what may be read as no more than a trivial dalliance for the diversion of a child monarch is an intense political struggle—ending with victory for Genji. Thus we see him fully rehabilitated, back from exile and deeply involved in affairs of state.

The second chapter (the fourth of the original) stands apart like those here omitted, but I have included it for two reasons: it is far superior to any of the deleted chapters, and it does come to affect the main narrative, because the daughter of "the lady of the evening faces" presently emerges from obscurity to assume an important role. The careful reader will see that only it among our dozen is closely akin to the deleted chapters. Added annotation was needed to clarify references to these chapters, and the last three pages, which harken back to the second and third chapters and seem to bring the cycle to a close, have been deleted. Nothing has been required by way of explanation or excision in the other eleven.

Offered the prospect of emendation, I was able to find and correct a number of errors from the original edition.

Not much can be said with certainty about *The Tale of Genji* except that it is a very long romance, running to fifty-four chapters and describing the court life of Heian Japan, from the tenth century into the eleventh. Very probably it was completed in something like its present form during the first quarter of the eleventh century. Except for fragments, the earliest surviving texts are from upwards of two centuries after the probable date of composition, and so textual problems will always remain to delight and occupy scholars; but the *Genji* is probably the work of a single hand, that of a court lady known as Murasaki Shikibu, with possible accretions during the two following centuries, not of sufficient magnitude to change the shape of Murasaki Shikibu's original. At least one chapter is widely thought to be spurious, and two others are also suspect. It is possible too that chapters have been lost, but that the work consisted of more than fifty chapters by the decade of 1020's is apparent from the *Sarashina Diary*, written in the mid-eleventh century by another court lady.

Precise information about Murasaki Shikibu is equally scant. We do not know her personal name, though scholars have delighted in speculating upon it. In Heian Japan it was bad manners to record the names of wellborn ladies, except, curiously, imperial consorts and princesses of the blood. Of the sobriquet by which she is known today, the second half, Shikibu, designates an office held by her father. Murasaki may derive either from the name of an important lady in the *Genji* itself or from the fact that it means "purple," and *fuji*, the first half of her family name, means "wisteria." She came from a cadet branch of the great Fujiwara family, which ruled the land in the name of successive emperors through most of the Heian Period. She and Fujiwara Michinaga, the "grand chancellor" who dominated court politics in the early eleventh century, had a common ancestor in the paternal line six generations back, but her branch of the family had by the time of her birth fallen to the second level of the court aristocracy. Her father occupied modest positions in the capital and twice served as a provincial governor.

Provincial governors are generally treated with contempt in *The Tale of Genji*. Their layer of the aristocracy did more for the literature of the day than any other, however, and the usual view is that it was an uncommonly fine day, and that the *Genji* itself is the supreme masterpiece of Japanese prose literature. Why the literature of mid-Heian should have been dominated by women is another problem that exercises the scholars. Possibly it has something to do with the fact that Japan seems to have been relatively free of the harem politics that so beset other Oriental countries, and talented ladies of leisure therefore found other outlets for their energies. It may have to do also with the fact that they were less conventional than men.

She was married in 998 or 999 to a distant kinsman. Since there are reasons for believing that she married rather late for the time, it seems likely that she was in her early twenties. Of her childhood we know little save what she herself has told us. A famous entry in the journal (perhaps "set of memoirs" would better characterize it) called *Murasaki Shikibu Diary*, which describes events at court from late 1008 to early 1010, tells how her father, observing her capacity for learning, lamented that she had not been born a boy. Her father became governor of Echizen, on the Sea of Japan almost due north of Kyoto, the capital, in 996. She probably went there with him, returning shortly before her marriage. Her only daughter was born in 999, and she was widowed in 1001.

She went to court, in the service of the empress Akiko or Shōshi, sometime around the middle of the first decade of the eleventh century. The *Murasaki Shikibu Diary* has to do chiefly with the birth of two sons to the empress, events of political importance, since she was the daughter of Michinaga and through his royal grandchildren Michinaga got an unshakable grip on the imperial house. Both princes subsequently became emperors. In her "diary" Murasaki tells us that she came to court on the twenty-ninth day of the twelfth month of the Oriental lunar calendar, a date which would convert to early the following year under the Western calendar. Unfortunately she does not tell us which year. The lunar years 1005 and 1006 seem the most likely.

Akiko was widowed in 1011. There is documentary evidence that Murasaki Shikibu remained in her service for perhaps two years thereafter, but the dates of her retirement from court and of her death are not known. One can visit a spot in the northern environs of Kyoto that is described as her grave; and the marvel is that it might just possibly be. Some argue the absence of her name from documents where it might well be found as evidence that she did not long outlive Akiko's husband, the emperor Ichijō. Others argue, more subjectively but no less convincingly, that the last chapters of the complete *Genji* suggest a sadly wise and aging author. If we assume that Murasaki Shikibu died in 1015, then the probability is that her life lasted barely four decades.

The *Murasaki Shikibu Diary* suggests strongly that at least a part of her great work had been written when she entered Akiko's service. Perhaps she began it in the early years of her widowhood, and perhaps, since there must have been scores of women with equally compelling political and economic claims and since the grand ladies of the day thought literature important, her book was the occasion for her being summoned to court.

The action of the *Genji* covers almost three quarters of a century. The first forty-one chapters have to do with the life and loves of the nobleman known as "the shining Genji," Genji or Minamoto being the name given him as a commoner by his father, an emperor. Genji is born in the first chapter and is fifty-two by the Oriental count in the last chapter in which he figures. Three transitional chapters, the chapters most likely to be spurious, come after his death. The hero of the last ten chapters, Kaoru, who passes in the world as Genji's son but is really the grandson of his best friend, is five at the time of Genji's last appearance and twenty-eight in the last chapter. It has long been held by Japanese scholars that Murasaki Shikibu first thought of her romance as historical, set perhaps three quarters of a century before her time. If the historical setting were detailed and consistent, then of course she would have brought it gradually from the mid-tenth century to her own day; but it is not. All that can be said is that a vaguely nostalgic air hangs over the narrative and that the setting is vaguely antiquarian. One of the things the *Genji* "means" is that the good days are in the past.

Murasaki Shikibu had a rich tradition of Chinese historical writing and Chinese and Japanese lyric poetry to draw on. As for prose fiction, she had little more than the beginnings the Japanese themselves had made in the tenth century; prose fiction is not a genre the Chinese much admired at the time, or were very good at. Interesting beginnings these were, and, in a fragile way, beautiful beginnings; but little in them seems to anticipate the appearance of a romance which is more than a romance, in that it shows believable people in real situations. When romancers of the tenth century attempt characterization, and it is of a rudimentary sort, they write fairy stories; and when they write of such matters as court intrigues, the characterization is so flat that it can hardly be called characterization at all. The diaries of the tenth century may perhaps have been something of an inspiration for Murasaki Shikibu, but the awareness that an imagined predicament can be made more real than a real one required a great leap of the imagination, and Murasaki Shikibu made it by herself. Though numbers of romances from the tenth century are known to have been lost, the evidence is that the important ones survive.

No sensible critic or scholar would argue that nothing at all was done to change Murasaki Shikibu's manuscript during the two centuries and more between its composition and the date of the earliest texts; and many have argued that the last chapters are by someone else entirely. The scholarly argument against such an ascription seems less persuasive than the intuitive one: it may be difficult to imagine a single genius building so much on so slight a foundation; but it is almost impossible to imagine a second genius taking over without preparation at such a high point in the development of the first. The historical fact is that whoever wrote the *Genji* had no successors, and so the theory of mass genius has very little to support it. Later romances are by comparison rather poor stuff. In sum: changes and additions in detail may have come later, but the narrative points essentially to a single author working over a long period of time, herself (few would dispute the use of the feminine pronoun) living long enough to have immediate knowledge of the shadows that fall over her book, shadows that come with age and experience, and working to the end.

This translation has been based chiefly on the text in the *Nihon Koten Bungaku Taikei* series, the uniform edition of the Japanese classics published by the Iwanami Shoten. The editor, Professor Yamagishi Tokuhei, has used a manuscript copy from the Muromachi Period in the Aobyōshi or "Blue Book" line of texts, deriving ultimately from the work of Fujiwara Teika, the great poet and scholar of the twelfth and early thirteenth centuries. Two other texts, both with detailed commentary and complete rendition into modern Japanese, were regularly consulted: the *Genji Monogatari Hyōshaku (Annotated Tale of Genji)* of Professor Tamagami Takuya, and the Shōgakkan text, only some two thirds of which had appeared when this translation was completed, under the editorship of Professors Abe Akio, Akiyama Ken, and Imai Genei. Both are based on Aobyōshi manuscripts. Three other modern translations, by the poetess Yosano Akiko and the novelists Tanizaki Junichirō and Enji Fumiko, were consulted from time to time.

The word "translations" seems appropriate, despite the fact that the Japanese use one word for rendition of a Japanese classic into modern Japanese and another for rendition of that same classic into a foreign tongue. In some respects the speech of western Japan, in which the tale was written, has been astonishingly conservative. A character will sometimes make a remark which one might hear on the streets of Kyoto or Osaka today. The conjugated parts of speech, however, the verbs and adjectives, have been considerably simplified, so that fundamental signals as to agent and object which were once conveyed through conjugational refinements must now very often be conveyed by other means, such as explicitly stated subjects. What this means in practice is that for Westerner and modern Japanese alike Heian Japanese takes a great deal of getting used to and can often be very obscure. One must be very alert indeed when the most important facts are conveyed by subtle shifts in honorific level, and probably only to someone who has not known anything else can the effort be other than taxing and arduous. To Murasaki Shikibu a translation into modern Japanese or a foreign tongue would probably have seemed rather inelegantly and unnecessarily specific. It was certainly not impossible in Heian Japan to come right out and name one's agents and objects, but it was considered better form to let elaborately conjugated verbs and adjectives convey the information obliquely.

Very good critics have commented upon the astonishing ''modernity'' of the tale, and have called it the first great novel in the literature of the world. Orientals have objected to the statement, on the grounds that the use of such Western terms as ''novel'' is ethnocentric. Yet there is surely nothing wrong with calling an Oriental work a novel if we know what we wish to convey by the term, and if our intent is to praise.

We may think of the novel as the form of prose narrative in which the emphasis is upon characterization rather than upon plot—on believable characters in believable relationships. If this definition is accepted, then the *Genji* is a very good novel indeed, the best one the Japanese have produced down to modern times. The characterization is remarkably vivid even in the early chapters selected for this book. Large numbers of characters are kept distinct from one another with remarkable skill.

When the *Genji* is compared with Proust in this regard, and the comparison has long been popular, it seems apt. In other respects the two are far apart, and the *Genji* reveals its Japanese origins. It is loosely constructed and inconclusive, and it is strongly lyrical, especially in its treatment of nature and the fusion of man and place and season, of foreground and background. It is a happy combination, then, of what can seem ''modern'' and immediate to the reader from a far-distant land and century, and what must necessarily seem alien and exotic, though not in an unpleasant sense.

There was still the problem of making the ''alien and exotic'' aspects accessible to the Western reader. Among the most difficult has been one which would not occur at all in translating a Western novel, what to call the characters. In the original only underlings, such as Genji's factotum Koremitsu, have names. The major characters are known by a series of shifting sobriquets or designations having to do with their station in life or with some incident or some brief passage in the narrative. Sometimes the relationship between the character and the sobriquet is tenuous. Thus Aoi, one of the ''names'' of Genji's first wife, means really ''the lady of the 'Heartvine' chapter,'' for it is in that chapter that she dies, and the chapter title derives from a poem which is not by the lady herself. Certain of the sobriquets have become standard over the centuries, so that when any modern Japanese wishes to refer to Genji's first wife he calls her Aoi. To refer to the characters as they are referred to in the original by a shifting series of sobriquets and designations would have led to great confusion and probably to unreadability. The fact that it did not, apparently, have that effect on the original audience is beside the point. The Western tradition requires that fictional characters have solid, unshakable names.

The obvious solution is to adopt the traditional designations and, for instance, call Genji's first wife Aoi. I did so in this translation. It leads to strains, however, especially when a traditional designation anticipates an incident later in the action.

The principal east-west streets of the Heian capital were numbered from north to south, with Ichijō, or "First Avenue," at the northern limits of the city and Kujō, "Ninth Avenue," at the southern. The streets most frequently mentioned in *The Tale of Genji* are Nijō, Sanjō, Gojō, and Rokujō, or "Second Avenue," "Third Avenue," "Fifth Avenue," and "Sixth Avenue." Genji's residence is on Nijō, which ran along the south wall of the palace.

Only a few of the puns in which the poems abound are explained. Explanation has seemed necessary when the absence of it reduces a poem to nonsense and when, as with "Heartvine" (the chapter from which Genji's first wife takes her "name") and "Channel Buoys," a pun is given great prominence as a chapter title. Punning is probably the single most common rhetorical device in the poetry of early and middle Heian. Some of the puns are so common that the introduction of one image into a poem will immediately introduce a second. A pine tree, for instance, usually brings with it a suggestion of unrequited love, of waiting and yearning, for *matsu*, "pine," means also "to wait." Mention of the long summer rains usually does double duty, having reference also to a time of sad, brooding tedium. Falling rain or snow is also the passage of the years; autumn is also surfeit or neglect; a fisherman is also a nun; the river, barrier, and gate of Osaka suggest a meeting, as does the province or lake of Omi; an iris is also discernment or a pattern; a rat is also a root and a cry; an imperial progress is also a deep snow; to pluck, as of plants, is also to heap up or accumulate, as of years; to cut off is also to depart; a letter or other specimen of calligraphy is also a trail; a wild goose suggests also evanescence or transience.

New translations of great classics need not seek to justify themselves. There have been translations of very great writers by very great writers, and they have been superseded. Since there is probably no such thing as a perfect translation of a complex literary work, the more translations, one would think, the better. Arthur Waley's translation of *The Tale of Genji* has been so important to me over the years, however, that I feel impelled to remark briefly on my reasons for undertaking a new translation. It was my introduction to Japanese literature, and its power upon repeated readings—I could not give their total number—has continued to be so great that the process of preparing a new translation has felt like sacrilege.

Yet the fact remains that the Waley translation is very free. He cuts and expurgates very boldly. It may be argued that he tidies things up by cutting, and therefore "improves." In some cases he probably does. One shares his impatience with clothes and meals and ceremonies, and may sometimes wish that Murasaki Shikibu had shared it too. On the whole, however, his excisions seem merely arbitrary.

More complex, and perhaps more interesting, is the matter of amplification. Waley embroiders marvelously, sometimes changing the tone of an episode or the psychological attributes of a character. Perhaps here too he sometimes "improves," but the process of amplifying and embroidering is continuous, and one is very reluctant indeed to conclude that Murasaki Shikibu has the worst of it all the way. What I am saying, essentially, is that however wonderful may be the effects which Waley achieves, and I for one have always found them very wonderful, his translation seems rather less straightforward than the original. Murasaki Shikibu's language is often slow and stately, but she moves from one detail or incident to the next in a brisker fashion than Waley. One is often astounded, turning from him to her, at how little she has to say. It is her matter-of-fact quality—if I may call it such—that this translation seeks to imitate.

A final word: the reader may be discouraged to learn that the tale gets better as it goes along, and that later chapters are often better than the ones included here. But while there seems no point in seeking to obscure this undeniable truth, it is certain that even the early chapters are better fiction than anything preceding them and most things following them in the body of Japanese prose narrative. If the reader is encouraged to go on to later chapters, this book will have had the best effect it could possibly have.

Miss Odagiri Hiroko read most of the translation in first draft, comparing it with the original and pointing out errors and omissions. Professor Ikeda Tadashi did the same with the chapters not scrutinized by Miss Odagiri. I am very grateful to them indeed. Messrs. Charles Hamilton and Eric Johnson read and commented upon the whole of the translation, and Miss Choo-won Suh, who typed the final version and of course read the whole of it, did very valuable service as editorial consultant. Parts of the translation were read by Messrs. Robert Brower, Don Brown, George Kerr, and William Sibley. I am very grateful to all of them, and I am very grateful too for the spiritual and material support of the Center for Japanese Studies and the Horace H. Rackham School of Graduate Studies at the University of Michigan.

EDWARD SEIDENSTICKER
August 1984

Principal Characters

AKASHI LADY. Daughter of a former governor of Harima. Mother of Genji's
     only daughter.
AKIKONOMU. Daughter of a former crown prince and the Rokujō lady. Consort
     of the Reizei emperor.
AOI. Genji's first wife. Daughter of the Minister of the Left and Princess
     Omiya.
EMPEROR. (1) Genji's father, whose abdication is announced at the beginning
     of the "Heartvine" chapter. (2) The Suzaku emperor, Genji's brother,
     who succeeds to the throne in the "Heartvine" chapter. (3) The Reizei
     emperor. Thought by the world to be Genji's brother, but in fact his son
     by Fujitsubo. Succeeds to the throne in the "Channel Buoys" chapter.
EVENING FACES, LADY OF THE. A lady of undistinguished lineage who is loved by
     Tō no Chūjō and bears his daughter.
FUJITSUBO. Daughter of a former emperor, consort of Genji's father, and
     mother of the Reizei emperor.
GENJI. Son of the emperor regnant at the beginning of the tale.
HYŌBU, PRINCE. Brother of Fujitsubo and father of Murasaki.
KOKIDEN. Daughter of the Minister of the Right. Wife of Genji's father, sister
     of Oborozukiyo, and mother of the Suzaku emperor.
KOREMITSU. Genji's servant and confidant.
MINISTER OF THE LEFT. Husband of Princess Omiya and father of Aoi and
     Tō no Chūjō.

MINISTER OF THE RIGHT. Father of Kokiden and Oborozukiyo. Grandfather of the
    Suzaku emperor.

MURASAKI. Daughter of Prince Hyōbu, niece of Fujitsubo, and granddaughter
    of a former emperor.

OBOROZUKIYO. Sister of Kokiden.

OMIYA, PRINCESS. Genji's paternal aunt. Mother of Aoi and Tō no Chūjō.

ORANGE BLOSSOMS, LADY OF THE. Sister of a lesser concubine of Genji's father.

REIZEI EMPEROR. Thought by the world to be Genji's brother, but really his son
    by Fujitsubo. Succeeds to the throne in the ''Channel Buoys'' chapter.

ROKUJŌ LADY. Widow of a former crown prince, Genji's uncle. Mother of
    Akikonomu.

SUZAKU EMPEROR. Genji's brother. His reign begins in the ''Heartvine''
    chapter.

TŌ NO CHŪJŌ. Son of the Minister of the Left and brother of Aoi.

Chapter 1

The Paulownia Court

In a certain reign there was a lady not of the first rank whom the emperor loved more than any of the others. The grand ladies with high ambitions thought her a presumptuous upstart, and lesser ladies were still more resentful. Everything she did offended someone. Probably aware of what was happening, she fell seriously ill and came to spend more time at home than at court. The emperor's pity and affection quite passed bounds. No longer caring what his ladies and courtiers might say, he behaved as if intent upon stirring gossip.

His court looked with very great misgiving upon what seemed a reckless infatuation. In China just such an unreasoning passion had been the undoing of an emperor and had spread turmoil through the land. As the resentment grew, the example of Yang Kuei-fei was the one most frequently cited against the lady.

She survived despite her troubles, with the help of an unprecedented bounty of love. Her father, a grand councillor, was no longer living. Her mother, an old-fashioned lady of good lineage, was determined that matters be no different for her than for ladies who with paternal support were making careers at court. The mother was attentive to the smallest detail of etiquette and deportment. Yet there was a limit to what she could do. The sad fact was that the girl was without strong backing, and each time a new incident arose she was next to defenseless.

It may have been because of a bond in a former life that she bore the emperor a beautiful son, a jewel beyond compare. The emperor was in a fever of impatience to see the child, still with the mother's family; and when, on the earliest day possible, he was brought to court, he did indeed prove to be a most marvelous babe. The emperor's eldest son was the grandson of the Minister of the Right. The world assumed that with this powerful support he would one day be named crown prince; but the new child was far more beautiful. On public occasions the emperor continued to favor his eldest son. The new child was a private treasure, so to speak, on which to lavish uninhibited affection.

The mother was not of such a low rank as to attend upon the emperor's personal needs. In the general view she belonged to the upper classes. He insisted on having her always beside him, however, and on nights when there was music or other entertainment he would require that she be present. Sometimes the two of them would sleep late, and even after they had risen he would not let her go. Because of his unreasonable demands she was widely held to have fallen into immoderate habits out of keeping with her rank.

With the birth of the son, it became yet clearer that she was the emperor's favorite. The mother of the eldest son began to feel uneasy. If she did not manage carefully, she might see the new son designated crown prince. She had come to court before the emperor's other ladies, she had once been favored over the others, and she had borne several of his children. However much her complaining might trouble and annoy him, she was one lady whom he could not ignore.

Though the mother of the new son had the emperor's love, her detractors were numerous and alert to the slightest inadvertency. She was in continuous torment, feeling that she had nowhere to turn. She lived in the Paulownia Court. The emperor had to pass the apartments of other ladies to reach hers, and it must be admitted that their resentment at his constant comings and goings was not unreasonable. Her visits to the royal chambers were equally frequent. The robes of her women were in a scandalous state from trash strewn along bridges and galleries. Once some women conspired to have both doors of a gallery she must pass bolted shut, and so she found herself unable to advance or retreat. Her anguish over the mounting list of insults was presently more than the emperor could bear. He moved a lady out of rooms adjacent to his own and assigned them to the lady of the Paulownia Court and so, of course, aroused new resentment.

When the young prince reached the age of three,* the resources of the treasury and the stewards' offices were exhausted to make the ceremonial bestowing of trousers as elaborate as that for the eldest son. Once more

---

*All ages are by the Oriental count, not of the full years but of the number of years in which one has lived. Thus it is possible to have a count of three after a full year and two days, one at the end and one at the beginning of another year. All ages are either one or two above the full count.

there was malicious talk; but the prince himself, as he grew up, was so
superior of mien and disposition that few could find it in themselves to
dislike him. Among the more discriminating, indeed, were some who marveled that such a paragon had been born into this world.

In the summer the boy's mother, feeling vaguely unwell, asked that
she be allowed to go home. The emperor would not hear of it. Since they
were by now used to these indispositions, he begged her to stay and see
what course her health would take. It was steadily worse, and then, suddenly, everyone could see that she was failing. Her mother came pleading
that he let her go home. At length he agreed.

Fearing that even now she might be the victim of a gratuitous insult,
she chose to go off without ceremony, leaving the boy behind. Everything
must have an end, and the emperor could no longer detain her. It saddened
him inexpressibly that he was not even permitted to see her off. A lady
of great charm and beauty, she was sadly emaciated. She was sunk in
melancholy thoughts, but when she tried to put them into words her voice
was almost inaudible. The emperor was quite beside himself, his mind a
confusion of things that had been and things that were to come. He wept
and vowed undying love, over and over again. The lady was unable to

reply. She seemed listless and drained of strength, as if she scarcely knew what was happening. Wanting somehow to help, the emperor ordered that she be given the honor of a hand-drawn carriage. He returned to her apartments and still could not bring himself to the final parting.

"We vowed that we would go together down the road we all must go. You must not leave me behind."

She looked sadly up at him. "If I had suspected that it would be so—" She was gasping for breath.

"I leave you, to go the road we all must go.
The road I would choose, if only I could, is the other."

It was evident that she would have liked to say more; but she was so weak that it had been a struggle to say even this much.

The emperor was wondering again if he might not keep her with him and have her with him to the end.

But a message came from her mother, asking that she hurry. "We have obtained the agreement of eminent ascetics to conduct the necessary services, and I fear that they are to begin this evening."

So, in desolation, he let her go. He passed a sleepless night.

He sent off a messenger and was beside himself with impatience and apprehension even before there had been time for the man to reach the lady's house and return. The man arrived to find the house echoing with laments. She had died at shortly past midnight. He returned sadly to the palace. The emperor closed himself up in his private apartments. He would have liked at least to keep the boy with him, but no precedent could be found for having him away from his mother's house through the mourning. The boy looked in bewilderment at the weeping courtiers, at his father too, the tears streaming over his face. The death of a parent is sad under any circumstances, and this one was indescribably sad.

But there must be an end to weeping, and orders were given for the funeral. If only she could rise to the heavens with the smoke from the pyre, said the mother between her sobs. She rode in the hearse with several attendants, and what must her feelings have been when they reached Mount Otaki?* It was there that the services were conducted with the utmost solemnity and dignity.

She looked down at the body. "With her before me, I cannot persuade myself that she is dead. At the sight of her ashes I can perhaps accept what has happened."

The words were rational enough, but she was so distraught that she seemed about to fall from the carriage. The women had known that it would be so and did what they could for her.

A messenger came from the palace with the news that the lady had been raised to the Third Rank, and presently a nunciary arrived to read the

*To the east of the city.

official order. For the emperor, the regret was scarcely bearable that he had not had the courage of his resolve to appoint her an imperial consort, and he wished to make amends by promoting her one rank. There were many who resented even this favor. Others, however, of a more sensitive nature, saw more than ever what a dear lady she had been, simple and gentle and difficult to find fault with. It was because she had been excessively favored by the emperor that she had been the victim of such malice. The attendant ladies were now reminded of how sympathetic and unassuming she had been. It was for just such an occasion, they remarked to one another, that the phrase "how well one knows"* had been invented.

The days went dully by. The emperor was careful to send offerings for the weekly memorial services. His grief was unabated and he spent his nights in tears, refusing to summon his other ladies. His serving women were plunged into dew-drenched autumn.

There was one lady, however, who refused to be placated. "How ridiculous," said the lady of the Kokiden Pavilion, mother of his eldest son, "that the infatuation should continue even now."

The emperor's thoughts were on his youngest son even when he was with his eldest. He sent off intelligent nurses and serving women to the house of the boy's grandmother, where he was still in residence, and made constant inquiry after him.

The autumn tempests blew and suddenly the evenings were chilly. Lost in his grief, the emperor sent off a note to the grandmother. His messenger was a woman of middle rank called Myōbu, whose father was a guards officer. It was on a beautiful moonlit night that he dispatched her, a night that brought memories. On such nights he and the dead lady had played the koto for each other. Her koto had somehow had overtones lacking in other instruments, and when she would interrupt the music to speak, the words too carried echoes of their own. Her face, her manner— they seemed to cling to him, but with "no more substance than the lucent dream."†

Myōbu reached the grandmother's house. Her carriage was drawn through the gate—and what a lonely place it was! The old lady had of course lived in widowed retirement, but, not wishing to distress her only daughter, she had managed to keep the place in repair. Now all was plunged into darkness. The weeds grew ever higher and the autumn winds tore threateningly at the garden. Only the rays of the moon managed to make their way through the tangles.

The carriage was pulled up and Myōbu alighted.

The grandmother was at first unable to speak. "It has been a trial for

*A poetic allusion, probably, but the poem cited by the earliest commentators is otherwise unknown, and therefore suspect.
†Anonymous, *Kokinshū* 647:

> Reality, within the depths of night,
> Has no more substance than the lucent dream.

me to go on living, and now to have one such as you come through the dews of this wild garden—I cannot tell you how much it shames me."

"A lady who visited your house the other day told us that she had to see with her own eyes before she could really understand your loneliness and sorrow. I am not at all a sensitive person, and yet I am unable to control these tears."

After a pause she delivered a message from the emperor. "He has said that for a time it all seemed as if he were wandering in a nightmare, and then when his agitation subsided he came to see that the nightmare would not end. If only he had a companion in his grief, he thought—and it occurred to him that you, my lady, might be persuaded to come unobtrusively to court. He cannot bear to think of the child languishing in this house of tears, and hopes that you will come quickly and bring him with you. He was more than once interrupted by sobs as he spoke, and it was apparent to all of us that he feared having us think him inexcusably weak. I came away without hearing him to the end."

"I cannot see for tears," said the old lady. "Let these sublime words bring me light."

This was the emperor's letter: "It seems impossibly cruel that although

I had hoped for comfort with the passage of time my grief should only be worse. I am particularly grieved that I do not have the boy with me, to watch him grow and mature. Will you not bring him to me? We shall think of him as a memento."

There could be no doubting the sincerity of the royal petition. A poem was appended to the letter, but when she had come to it the old lady was no longer able to see through her tears:

> "At the sound of the wind, bringing dews to Miyagi Plain,
>   I think of the tender *hagi** upon the moor."

"Tell His Majesty," said the grandmother after a time, "that it has been a great trial for me to live so long. 'Ashamed before the Takasago pines † I think that it is not for me to be seen at court. Even if the august invitation is repeated, I shall not find it possible to accept. As for the boy, I do not know what his wishes are. The indications are that he is eager to go. It is sad for me, but as it should be. Please tell His Majesty of these thoughts, secret until now. I fear that I bear a curse from a previous existence and that it would be wrong and even terrible to keep the child with me."

"It would have given me great pleasure to look in upon him," said Myōbu, getting up to leave. The child was asleep. "I should have liked to report to his royal father. But he will be waiting up for me, and it must be very late."

"May I not ask you to come in private from time to time? The heart of a bereaved parent may not be darkness, perhaps, but a quiet talk from time to time would do much to bring light.‡ You have done honor to this house on so many happy occasions, and now circumstances have required that you come with a sad message. I have lived too long a life. All of our hopes were on the girl, I must say again, from the day she was born, and until he died her father did not let me forget that she must go to court, that his own death, if it came early, should not deter me. I knew that another sort of life would be happier for a girl without strong backing, but I could not forget his wishes and sent her to court as I had promised. Blessed with favors beyond her station, she was the object of insults such as no one can be asked to endure. Yet endure them she did until finally the strain and the resentment were too much for her. And so, as I look back upon them, I know that those favors should never have been. Well, put

---

**Lespedeza japonica,* often called bush clover.

†Anonymous, *Kokin Rokujō, Zoku Kokka Taikan* 33903:

> Ashamed before the Takasago pines,
>   I would not have it known that I still live.

‡Fujiwara Kanesuke, *Gosenshū* 1103:

> The heart of a parent is not darkness, and yet
>   He wanders lost in thoughts upon his child.

these down, if you will, as the mad wanderings of a heart that is darkness."* She was unable to go on.

It was late.

"His Majesty says much the same thing," replied Myōbu. "It was, he
says, an intensity of passion such as to startle the world, and perhaps for
that very reason it was fated to be brief. He cannot think of anything he
has done to arouse such resentment, he says, and so he must live with
resentment which seems without proper cause. Alone and utterly desolate,
he finds it impossible to face the world. He fears that he must seem
dreadfully eccentric. How very great—he has said it over and over again
—are the burdens we bring from other lives. One scarcely ever sees him that
he is not weeping." Myōbu too was in tears. "It is very late. I must get back
before the night is quite over and tell him what I have seen."

The moon was sinking over the hills, the air was crystal clear, the wind
was cool, and the songs of the insects among the autumn grasses would
by themselves have brought tears. It was a scene from which Myōbu could
not easily pull herself.

> "The autumn night is too short to contain my tears
>   Though songs of bell cricket weary, fall into silence."†

This was her farewell poem. Still she hesitated, on the point of getting
into her carriage.

The old lady sent a reply:

> "Sad are the insect songs among the reeds.
>   More sadly yet falls the dew from above the clouds.‡

"I seem to be in a complaining mood."

Though gifts would have been out of place, she sent as a trifling
memento of her daughter a set of robes, left for just such an occasion, and
with them an assortment of bodkins and combs.

The young women who had come from court with the little prince still
mourned their lady, but those of them who had acquired a taste for court
life yearned to be back. The memory of the emperor made them join their
own to the royal petitions.

But no—a crone like herself would repel all the fine ladies and gentlemen, said the grandmother, while on the other hand she could not bear the
thought of having the child out of her sight for even a moment.

Myōbu was much moved to find the emperor waiting up for her.
Making it seem that his attention was on the small and beautifully planted
garden before him, now in full autumn bloom, he was talking quietly with
four or five women, among the most sensitive of his attendants. He had

---

*Another reference to the Kanesuke poem.
†The bell cricket of the Heian Period seems to have been what is today called the pine cricket,
Madasumma marmorata, and the Heian pine cricket has become the bell cricket.
‡"A sad message comes from court to join the sadness already here."

become addicted to illustrations by the emperor Uda for "The Song of Everlasting Sorrow"* and to poems by Ise and Tsurayuki on that subject, and to Chinese poems as well.

He listened attentively as Myōbu described the scene she had found so affecting. He took up the letter she had brought from the grandmother.

"I am so awed by this august message that I would run away and hide; and so violent are the emotions it gives rise to that I scarcely know what to say.

> "The tree that gave them shelter has withered and died.
> One fears for the plight of the *hagi* shoots beneath."

A strange way to put the matter, thought the emperor; but the lady must still be dazed with grief. He chose to overlook the suggestion that he himself could not help the child.

He sought to hide his sorrow, not wanting these women to see him in such poor control of himself. But it was no use. He reviewed his memo-

---

*By Po Chü-i, describing the grief of the T'ang emperor Hsüan Tsung upon the death of his concubine Yang Kuei-fei. Uda reigned in the late ninth century and died in 931. Tsurayuki and Ise were active in the early tenth century. The latter was one of Uda's concubines.

ries over and over again, from his very earliest days with the dead lady.
He had scarcely been able to bear a moment away from her while she lived.
How strange that he had been able to survive the days and months since
on memories alone. He had hoped to reward the grandmother's sturdy
devotion, and his hopes had come to nothing.

"Well," he sighed, "she may look forward to having her day, if she
will only live to see the boy grow up."

Looking at the keepsakes Myōbu had brought back, he thought what
a comfort it would be if some wizard were to bring him, like that Chinese
emperor, a comb from the world where his lost love was dwelling. He
whispered:

> "And will no wizard search her out for me,
> That even he may tell me where she is?"

There are limits to the powers of the most gifted artist. The Chinese
lady in the paintings did not have the luster of life. Yang Kuei-fei was said
to have resembled the lotus of the Sublime Pond, the willows of the
Timeless Hall. No doubt she was very beautiful in her Chinese finery.
When he tried to remember the quiet charm of his lost lady, he found that
there was no color of flower, no song of bird, to summon her up. Morning
and night, over and over again, they had repeated to each other the lines
from "The Song of Everlasting Sorrow":

> "In the sky, as birds that share a wing.
> On earth, as trees that share a branch."

It had been their vow, and the shortness of her life had made it an
empty dream.

Everything, the moaning of the wind, the humming of autumn insects, added to the sadness. But in the apartments of the Kokiden lady
matters were different. It had been some time since she had last waited
upon the emperor. The moonlight being so beautiful, she saw no reason
not to have music deep into the night. The emperor muttered something
about the bad taste of such a performance at such a time, and those who
saw his distress agreed that it was an unnecessary injury. Kokiden was of
an arrogant and intractable nature and her behavior suggested that to her
the emperor's grief was of no importance.

The moon set. The wicks in the lamps had been trimmed more than
once and presently the oil was gone. Still he showed no sign of retiring.
His mind on the boy and the old lady, he jotted down a verse:

> "Tears dim the moon, even here above the clouds.*
> Dim must it be in that lodging among the reeds."

Calls outside told him that the guard was being changed. It would be
one or two in the morning. People would think his behavior strange in-

*"Even here in the palace."

deed. He at length withdrew to his bedchamber. He was awake the whole night through, and in dark morning, his thoughts on the blinds that would not open,* he was unable to interest himself in business of state. He scarcely touched his breakfast, and lunch seemed so remote from his inclinations that his attendants exchanged looks and whispers of alarm.

Not all voices were sympathetic. Perhaps, some said, it had all been foreordained, but he had dismissed the talk and ignored the resentment and let the affair quite pass the bounds of reason; and now to neglect his duties so—it was altogether too much. Some even cited the example of the Chinese emperor who had brought ruin upon himself and his country.†

The months passed and the young prince returned to the palace. He had grown into a lad of such beauty that he hardly seemed meant for this world—and indeed one almost feared that he might only briefly be a part of it. When, the following spring, it came time to name a crown prince, the emperor wanted very much to pass over his first son in favor of the younger, who, however, had no influential maternal relatives. It did not seem likely that the designation would pass unchallenged. The boy might, like his mother, be destroyed by immoderate favors. The emperor told no one of his wishes. There did after all seem to be a limit to his affections, people said; and Kokiden regained her confidence.

The boy's grandmother was inconsolable. Finally, because her prayer to be with her daughter had been answered, perhaps, she breathed her last. Once more the emperor was desolate. The boy, now six, was old enough to know grief himself. His grandmother, who had been so good to him over the years, had more than once told him what pain it would cause her, when the time came, to leave him behind.

He now lived at court. When he was seven he went through the ceremonial reading of the Chinese classics, and never before had there been so fine a performance. Again a tremor of apprehension passed over the emperor—might it be that such a prodigy was not to be long for this world?

"No one need be angry with him now that his mother is gone." He took the boy to visit the Kokiden Pavilion. "And now most especially I hope you will be kind to him."

Admitting the boy to her inner chambers, even Kokiden was pleased. Not the sternest of warriors or the most unbending of enemies could have held back a smile. Kokiden was reluctant to let him go. She had two daughters, but neither could compare with him in beauty. The lesser ladies crowded about, not in the least ashamed to show their faces, all eager to amuse him, though aware that he set them off to disadvantage. I need not

---

*Ise, on "The Song of Everlasting Sorrow," *Zoku Kokka Taikan* 18158:

> The jeweled blinds are drawn, the morning is dark.
> I had not thought I would not even dream.

†The Yang Kuei-fei affair was the immediate cause of, or perhaps the pretext for, the disastrous An Lu-shan rebellion.

speak of his accomplishments in the compulsory subjects, the classics and the like. When it came to music his flute and koto made the heavens echo —but to recount all his virtues would, I fear, give rise to a suspicion that I distort the truth.

An embassy came from Korea. Hearing that among the emissaries was a skilled physiognomist, the emperor would have liked to summon him for consultation. He decided, however, that he must defer to the emperor Uda's injunction against receiving foreigners, and instead sent this favored son to the Kōro mansion,* where the party was lodged. The boy was disguised as the son of the grand moderator, his guardian at court. The wise Korean cocked his head in astonishment.

"It is the face of one who should ascend to the highest place and be father to the nation," he said quietly, as if to himself. "But to take it for such would no doubt be to predict trouble. Yet it is not the face of the minister, the deputy, who sets about ordering public affairs."

The moderator was a man of considerable learning. There was much of interest in his exchanges with the Korean. There were also exchanges

*In the southern part of the city.

of Chinese poetry, and in one of his poems the Korean succeeded most skillfully in conveying his joy at having been able to observe such a countenance on this the eve of his return to his own land, and sorrow that the parting must come so soon. The boy offered a verse that was received with high praise. The most splendid of gifts were bestowed upon him. The wise man was in return showered with gifts from the palace.

Somehow news of the sage's remarks leaked out, though the emperor himself was careful to say nothing. The Minister of the Right, grandfather of the crown prince and father of the Kokiden lady, was quick to hear, and again his suspicions were aroused. In the wisdom of his heart, the emperor had already analyzed the boy's physiognomy after the Japanese fashion and had formed tentative plans. He had thus far refrained from bestowing imperial rank on his son, and was delighted that the Korean view should so accord with his own. Lacking the support of maternal relatives, the boy would be most insecure as a prince without court rank, and the emperor could not be sure how long his own reign would last. As a commoner he could be of great service. The emperor therefore encouraged the boy in his studies, at which he was so proficient that it seemed a waste to reduce him to common rank. And yet—as a prince he would arouse the hostility of those who had cause to fear his becoming emperor. Summoning an astrologer of the Indian school, the emperor was pleased to learn that the Indian view coincided with the Japanese and the Korean; and so he concluded that the boy should become a commoner with the name Minamoto or Genji.

The months and the years passed and still the emperor could not forget his lost love. He summoned various women who might console him, but apparently it was too much to ask in this world for one who even resembled her. He remained sunk in memories, unable to interest himself in anything. Then he was told of the Fourth Princess, daughter of a former emperor, a lady famous for her beauty and reared with the greatest care by her mother, the empress. A woman now in attendance upon the emperor had in the days of his predecessor been most friendly with the princess, then but a child, and even now saw her from time to time.

"I have been at court through three reigns now," she said, "and never had I seen anyone who genuinely resembled my lady. But now the daughter of the empress dowager is growing up, and the resemblance is most astonishing. One would be hard put to find her equal."

Hoping that she might just possibly be right, the emperor asked most courteously to have the princess sent to court. Her mother was reluctant and even fearful, however. One must remember, she said, that the mother of the crown prince was a most willful lady who had subjected the lady of the Paulownia Court to open insults and presently sent her into a fatal decline. Before she had made up her mind she followed her husband in death, and the daughter was alone. The emperor renewed his petition. He said that he would treat the girl as one of his own daughters.

Her attendants and her maternal relatives and her older brother,

Prince Hyōbu, consulted together and concluded that rather than languish at home she might seek consolation at court; and so she was sent off. She was called Fujitsubo. The resemblance to the dead lady was indeed astonishing. Because she was of such high birth (it may have been that people were imagining things) she seemed even more graceful and delicate than the other. No one could despise her for inferior rank, and the emperor need not feel shy about showing his love for her. The other lady, with the backing of no one all through the court, had been the victim of a love too intense; and now, though it would be wrong to say that he had quite forgotten her, he found his affections shifting to the new lady, who was a source of boundless comfort. So it is with the affairs of this world.

Since Genji never left his father's side, it was not easy for this new lady, the recipient of so many visits, to hide herself from him. The other ladies were disinclined to think themselves her inferior, and indeed each of them had her own merits. They were all rather past their prime, however. Fujitsubo's beauty was of a younger and fresher sort. Though in her childlike shyness she made an especial effort not to be seen, Genji occasionally caught a glimpse of her face. He could not remember his own mother and it moved him deeply to learn, from the lady who had first told the emperor of Fujitsubo, that the resemblance was striking. He wanted to be near her always.

"Do not be unfriendly," said the emperor to Fujitsubo. "Sometimes it almost seems to me too that you are his mother. Do not think him forward, be kind to him. Your eyes, your expression: you are really so uncommonly like her that you could pass for his mother."

Genji's affection for the new lady grew, and the most ordinary flower or tinted leaf became the occasion for expressing it. Kokiden was not pleased. She was not on good terms with Fujitsubo, and all her old resentment at Genji came back. He was handsomer than the crown prince, her chief treasure in the world, well thought of by the whole court. People began calling Genji "the shining one." Fujitsubo, ranked beside him in the emperor's affections, became "the lady of the radiant sun."

It seemed a pity that the boy must one day leave behind his boyish attire; but when he reached the age of twelve he went through his initiation ceremonies and received the cap of an adult. Determined that the ceremony should be in no way inferior to the crown prince's, which had been held some years earlier in the Grand Hall, the emperor himself bustled about adding new details to the established forms. As for the banquet after the ceremony, he did not wish the custodians of the storehouses and granaries to treat it as an ordinary public occasion.

The throne faced east on the east porch, and before it were Genji's seat and that of the minister who was to bestow the official cap. At the appointed hour in midafternoon Genji appeared. The freshness of his face and his boyish coiffure were again such as to make the emperor regret that the change must take place. The ritual cutting of the boy's hair was per-

formed by the secretary of the treasury. As the beautiful locks fell the emperor was seized with a hopeless longing for his dead lady. Repeatedly he found himself struggling to keep his composure. The ceremony over, the boy withdrew to change to adult trousers and descended into the courtyard for ceremonial thanksgiving. There was not a person in the assembly who did not feel his eyes misting over. The emperor was stirred by the deepest of emotions. He had on brief occasions been able to forget the past, and now it all came back again. Vaguely apprehensive lest the initiation of so young a boy bring a sudden aging, he was astonished to see that his son delighted him even more.

The Minister of the Left, who bestowed the official cap, had only one daughter, his chief joy in life. Her mother, the minister's first wife, was a princess of the blood. The crown prince had sought the girl's hand, but the minister thought rather of giving her to Genji. He had heard that the emperor had similar thoughts. When the emperor suggested that the boy was without adequate sponsors for his initiation and that the support of relatives by marriage might be called for, the minister quite agreed.

The company withdrew to outer rooms and Genji took his place below the princes of the blood. The minister hinted at what was on his mind, but

Genji, still very young, did not quite know what to say. There came a message through a chamberlain that the minister was expected in the royal chambers. A lady-in-waiting brought the customary gifts for his services, a woman's cloak, white and of grand proportions, and a set of robes as well. As he poured wine for his minister, the emperor recited a poem which was in fact a deeply felt admonition:

> "The boyish locks are now bound up, a man's.
> And do we tie a lasting bond for his future?"

This was the minister's reply:

> "Fast the knot which the honest heart has tied.
> May lavender, the hue of the troth, be as fast."*

The minister descended from a long garden bridge to give formal thanks. He received a horse from the imperial stables and a falcon from the secretariat. In the courtyard below the emperor, princes and high courtiers received gifts in keeping with their stations. The moderator, Genji's guardian, had upon royal command prepared the trays and baskets now set out in the royal presence. As for Chinese chests of food and gifts, they overflowed the premises, in even larger numbers than for the crown prince's initiation. It was the most splendid and dignified of ceremonies.

Genji went home that evening with the Minister of the Left. The nuptial observances were conducted with great solemnity. The groom seemed to the minister and his family quite charming in his boyishness. The bride was older, and somewhat ill at ease with such a young husband.

The minister had the emperor's complete confidence, and his wife, the girl's mother, was full sister to the emperor. Both parents were therefore of the highest standing. And now they had Genji for a son-in-law. The Minister of the Right, who as grandfather of the crown prince should have been without rivals, was somehow eclipsed. The Minister of the Left had numerous children by several ladies. One of the sons, a very handsome lad by his principal wife, was already a guards lieutenant. Relations between the two ministers were not good; but the Minister of the Right found it difficult to ignore such a talented youth, to whom he offered the hand of his fourth and favorite daughter. His esteem for his new son-in-law rivaled the other minister's esteem for Genji. To both houses the new arrangements seemed ideal.

Constantly at his father's side, Genji spent little time at the Sanjō mansion of his bride. Fujitsubo was for him a vision of sublime beauty. If he could have someone like her—but in fact there was no one really like her. His bride too was beautiful, and she had had the advantage of every luxury; but he was not at all sure that they were meant for each other. The yearning in his young heart for the other lady was agony. Now that he had come of age, he no longer had his father's permission to go behind her

---

*Throughout the tale, lavender (*murasaki*) suggests affinity.

curtains. On evenings when there was music, he would play the flute to her koto and so communicate something of his longing, and take some comfort from her voice, soft through the curtains. Life at court was for him much preferable to life at Sanjō. Two or three days at Sanjo would be followed by five or six days at court. For the minister, youth seemed sufficient excuse for this neglect. He continued to be delighted with his son-in-law.

The minister selected the handsomest and most accomplished of ladies to wait upon the young pair and planned the sort of diversions that were most likely to interest Genji. At the palace the emperor assigned him the apartments that had been his mother's and took care that her retinue was not dispersed. Orders were handed down to the offices of repairs and fittings to remodel the house that had belonged to the lady's family. The results were magnificent. The plantings and the artificial hills had always been remarkably tasteful, and the grounds now swarmed with workmen widening the lake. If only, thought Genji, he could have with him the lady he yearned for.

The sobriquet "the shining Genji," one hears, was bestowed upon him by the Korean.

Chapter 2

Evening Faces

On his way from court to pay one of his calls at Rokujō, Genji stopped to inquire after his old nurse, Koremitsu's mother, at her house in Gojō. Gravely ill, she had become a nun. The carriage entrance was closed. He sent for Koremitsu and while he was waiting looked up and down the dirty, cluttered street. Beside the nurse's house was a new fence of plaited cypress. The four or five narrow shutters above had been raised, and new blinds, white and clean, hung in the apertures. He caught outlines of pretty foreheads beyond. He would have judged, as they moved about, that they belonged to rather tall women. What sort of women might they be? His carriage was simple and unadorned and he had no outrunners. Quite certain that he would not be recognized, he leaned out for a closer look. The hanging gate, of something like trelliswork, was propped on a pole, and he could see that the house was tiny and flimsy. He felt a little sorry for the occupants of such a place—and then asked himself who in this world had more than a temporary shelter.* A hut, a jeweled pavilion, they were the same. A pleasantly green vine was climbing a board wall. The white flowers, he thought, had a rather self-satisfied look about them.

" 'I needs must ask the lady far off yonder,' "† he said, as if to himself.

*Anonymous, *Kokinshū* 987:

> Where in all this world shall I call home?
> A temporary shelter is my home.

†Anonymous, *Kokinshū* 1007:

> I needs must ask the lady far off yonder
> What flower it is off there that blooms so white.

An attendant came up, bowing deeply. "The white flowers far off yonder are known as 'evening faces,'"* he said. "A very human sort of name—and what a shabby place they have picked to bloom in."

It was as the man said. The neighborhood was a poor one, chiefly of small houses. Some were leaning precariously, and there were "evening faces" at the sagging eaves.

"A hapless sort of flower. Pick one off for me, would you?"

The man went inside the raised gate and broke off a flower. A pretty little girl in long, unlined yellow trousers of raw silk came out through a sliding door that seemed too good for the surroundings. Beckoning to the man, she handed him a heavily scented white fan.

"Put it on this. It isn't much of a fan, but then it isn't much of a flower either."

Koremitsu, coming out of the gate, passed it on to Genji.

"They lost the key, and I have had to keep you waiting. You aren't likely to be recognized in such a neighborhood, but it's not a very nice neighborhood to keep you waiting in."

---

* *Yūgao, Lagenaria siceraria,* a kind of gourd.

Genji's carriage was pulled in and he dismounted. Besides Koremitsu, a son and a daughter, the former an eminent cleric, and the daughter's husband, the governor of Mikawa, were in attendance upon the old woman. They thanked him profusely for his visit.

The old woman got up to receive him. "I did not at all mind leaving the world, except for the thought that I would no longer be able to see you as I am seeing you now. My vows seem to have given me a new lease on life, and this visit makes me certain that I shall receive the radiance of Lord Amitābha with a serene and tranquil heart." And she collapsed in tears.

Genji was near tears himself. "It has worried me enormously that you should be taking so long to recover, and I was very sad to learn that you have withdrawn from the world. You must live a long life and see the career I make for myself. I am sure that if you do you will be reborn upon the highest summits of the Pure Land. I am told that it is important to rid oneself of the smallest regret for this world."

Fond of the child she has reared, a nurse tends to look upon him as a paragon even if he is a half-wit. How much prouder was the old woman, who somehow gained stature, who thought of herself as eminent in her own right for having been permitted to serve him. The tears flowed on.

Her children were ashamed for her. They exchanged glances. It would not do to have these contortions taken as signs of a lingering affection for the world.

Genji was deeply touched. "The people who were fond of me left me when I was very young. Others have come along, it is true, to take care of me, but you are the only one I am really attached to. In recent years there have been restrictions upon my movements, and I have not been able to look in upon you morning and evening as I would have wished, or indeed to have a good visit with you. Yet I become very depressed when the days go by and I do not see you. 'Would that there were on this earth no final partings.' "* He spoke with great solemnity, and the scent of his sleeve, as he brushed away a tear, quite flooded the room.

Yes, thought the children, who had been silently reproaching their mother for her want of control, the fates had been kind to her. They too were now in tears.

Genji left orders that prayers and services be resumed. As he went out he asked for a torch, and in its light examined the fan on which the "evening face" had rested. It was permeated with a lady's perfume, elegant and alluring. On it was a poem in a disguised cursive hand that suggested breeding and taste. He was interested.

"I think I need not ask whose face it is,
    So bright, this evening face, in the shining dew."

*Ariwara Narihira, *Kokinshū* 901 and *Tales of Ise* 84:

    Would that my mother might live a thousand years
    Would there were on this earth no final partings.

"Who is living in the house to the west?" he asked Koremitsu. "Have you perhaps had occasion to inquire?"

At it again, thought Koremitsu. He spoke somewhat tartly. "I must confess that these last few days I have been too busy with my mother to think about her neighbors."

"You are annoyed with me. But this fan has the appearance of something it might be interesting to look into. Make inquiries, if you will, please, of someone who knows the neighborhood."

Koremitsu went in to ask his mother's steward, and emerged with the information that the house belonged to a certain honorary vice-governor.* "The husband is away in the country, and the wife seems to be a young woman of taste. Her sisters are out in service here and there. They often come visiting. I suspect the fellow is too poorly placed to know the details."

His poetess would be one of the sisters, thought Genji. A rather practiced and forward young person, and, were he to meet her, perhaps vulgar as well—but the easy familiarity of the poem had not been at all

---

* *Yōmei no suke.* Once thought among the undecipherables in the *Genji*, it is now thought to refer to someone who has the title but not the perquisites of vice-governor.

unpleasant, not something to be pushed away in disdain. His amative
propensities, it will be seen, were having their way once more.

Carefully disguising his hand, he jotted down a reply on a piece of
notepaper and sent it in by the attendant who had earlier been of service.

"Come a bit nearer, please. Then might you know
Whose was the evening face so dim in the twilight."

Thinking it a familiar profile, the lady had not lost the opportunity
to surprise him with a letter, and when time passed and there was no
answer she was left feeling somewhat embarrassed and disconsolate. Now
came a poem by special messenger. Her women became quite giddy as they
turned their minds to the problem of replying. Rather bored with it all, the
messenger returned empty-handed. Genji made a quiet departure, lighted
by very few torches. The shutters next door had been lowered. There was
something sad about the light, dimmer than fireflies, that came through the
cracks.

At the Rokujō house, the trees and the plantings had a quiet dignity.
The lady herself was strangely cold and withdrawn. Thoughts of the
"evening faces" quite left him. He overslept, and the sun was rising when
he took his leave. He presented such a fine figure in the morning light that
the women of the place understood well enough why he should be so
universally admired. On his way he again passed those shutters, as he had
no doubt done many times before. Because of that small incident he now
looked at the house carefully, wondering who might be within.

"My mother is not doing at all well, and I have been with her," said
Koremitsu some days later. And, coming nearer: "Because you seemed so
interested, I called someone who knows about the house next door and had
him questioned. His story was not completely clear. He said that in the
Fifth Month or so someone came very quietly to live in the house, but that
not even the domestics had been told who she might be. I have looked
through the fence from time to time myself and had glimpses through
blinds of several young women. Something about their dress suggests that
they are in the service of someone of higher rank.* Yesterday, when the
evening light was coming directly through, I saw the lady herself writing
a letter. She is very beautiful. She seemed lost in thought, and the women
around her were weeping."

Genji had suspected something of the sort. He must find out more.

Koremitsu's view was that while Genji was undeniably someone the
whole world took seriously, his youth and the fact that women found him
attractive meant that to refrain from these little affairs would be less than
human. It was not realistic to hold that certain people were beyond temptation.

"Looking for a chance to do a bit of exploring, I found a small pretext

---

*They wear *shibira*, apparently a sort of apron or jacket indicating a small degree of formality.

for writing to her. She answered immediately, in a good, practiced hand. Some of her women do not seem at all beneath contempt."

"Explore very thoroughly, if you will. I will not be satisfied until you do."

The house was what the guardsman* would have described as the lowest of the low, but Genji was interested. What hidden charms might he not come upon!

He had thought the coldness of the governor's wife, the lady of "the locust shell," quite unique. Yet if she had proved amenable to his persuasions the affair would no doubt have been dropped as a sad mistake after that one encounter. As matters were, the resentment and the distinct possibility of final defeat never left his mind. The discussion that rainy night would seem to have made him curious about the several ranks. There had been a time when such a lady would not have been worth his notice. Yes, it had been broadening, that discussion! He had not found the willing and available one, the governor of Iyo's daughter, entirely uninteresting, but the thought that the stepmother must have been listening coolly to the interview was excruciating. He must await some sign of her real intentions.

The governor of Iyo returned to the city. He came immediately to Genji's mansion. Somewhat sunburned, his travel robes rumpled from the sea voyage, he was a rather heavy and displeasing sort of person. He was of good lineage, however, and, though aging, he still had good manners. As they spoke of his province, Genji wanted to ask the full count of those hot springs, but he was somewhat confused to find memories chasing one another through his head. How foolish that he should be so uncomfortable before the honest old man! He remembered the guardsman's warning that such affairs are unwise, and he felt sorry for the governor. Though he resented the wife's coldness, he could see that from the husband's point of view it was admirable. He was upset to learn that the governor meant to find a suitable husband for his daughter and take his wife to the provinces. He consulted the lady's young brother upon the possibility of another meeting. It would have been difficult even with the lady's cooperation, however, and she was of the view that to receive a gentleman so far above her would be extremely unwise.

Yet she did not want him to forget her entirely. Her answers to his notes on this and that occasion were pleasant enough, and contained casual little touches that made him pause in admiration. He resented her chilliness, but she interested him. As for the stepdaughter, he was certain that she would receive him hospitably enough however formidable a husband she might acquire. Reports upon her arrangements disturbed him not at all.

Autumn came. He was kept busy and unhappy by affairs of his own making, and he visited Sanjō infrequently. There was resentment.

*This paragraph and the succeeding three paragraphs refer to a scene in a chapter which has been omitted. So do the references three pages later to "the rainy night" and "the woman"; and, two pages later yet, another reference to the rainy night. The "wild carnation" is the daughter of the lady of the evening faces.

As for the affair at Rokujō, he had overcome the lady's resistance and had his way, and, alas, he had cooled toward her. People thought it worthy of comment that his passions should seem so much more governable than before he had made her his. She was subject to fits of despondency, more intense on sleepless nights when she awaited him in vain. She feared that if rumors were to spread the gossips would make much of the difference in their ages.

On a morning of heavy mists, insistently roused by the lady, who was determined that he be on his way, Genji emerged yawning and sighing and looking very sleepy. Chūjō, one of her women, raised a shutter and pulled a curtain aside as if urging her lady to come forward and see him off. The lady lifted her head from her pillow. He was an incomparably handsome figure as he paused to admire the profusion of flowers below the veranda. Chūjō followed him down a gallery. In an aster robe that matched the season pleasantly and a gossamer train worn with clean elegance, she was a pretty, graceful woman. Glancing back, he asked her to sit with him for a time at the corner railing. The ceremonious precision of the seated figure and the hair flowing over her robes were very fine.

He took her hand.

"Though loath to be taxed with seeking fresher blooms,
    I feel impelled to pluck this morning glory.

"Why should it be?"

She answered with practiced alacrity, making it seem that she was speaking not for herself but for her lady:

"In haste to plunge into the morning mists,
    You seem to have no heart for the blossoms here."

A pretty little page boy, especially decked out for the occasion, it would seem, walked out among the flowers. His trousers wet with dew, he broke off a morning glory for Genji. He made a picture that called out to be painted.

Even persons to whom Genji was nothing were drawn to him. No doubt even rough mountain men wanted to pause for a time in the shade of the flowering tree,* and those who had basked even briefly in his radiance had thoughts, each in accordance with his rank, of a daughter who might be taken into his service, a not ill-formed sister who might perform some humble service for him. One need not be surprised, then, that people with a measure of sensibility among those who had on some occasion received a little poem from him or been treated to some little kindness found him much on their minds. No doubt it distressed them not to be always with him.

I had forgotten: Koremitsu gave a good account of the fence peeping to which he had been assigned. "I am unable to identify her. She seems

*In the preface to the *Kokinshū* one of the "poetic immortals" is likened to a woodcutter resting under a cherry in full bloom.

determined to hide herself from the world. In their boredom her women
and girls go out to the long gallery at the street, the one with the shutters,
and watch for carriages. Sometimes the lady who seems to be their mistress
comes quietly out to join them. I've not had a good look at her, but she
seems very pretty indeed. One day a carriage with outrunners went by.
The little girls shouted to a person named Ukon that she must come in a
hurry. The captain* was going by, they said. An older woman came out
and motioned to them to be quiet. How did they know? she asked, coming
out toward the gallery. The passage from the main house is by a sort of
makeshift bridge. She was hurrying and her skirt caught on something, and
she stumbled and almost fell off. 'The sort of thing the god of Katsuragi
might do,'† she said, and seems to have lost interest in sightseeing. They
told her that the man in the carriage was wearing casual court dress and
that he had a retinue. They mentioned several names, and all of them were
undeniably Lord Tō no Chūjō's guards and pages.''

"I wish you had made positive identification." Might she be the lady

*Tō no Chūjō.
†Tradition held that the god of Katsuragi, south of Nara, was very ugly, and built a bridge
which he used only at night.

of whom Tō no Chūjō had spoken so regretfully that rainy night?

Koremitsu went on, smiling at this open curiosity. "I have as a matter of fact made the proper overtures and learned all about the place. I come and go as if I did not know that they are not all equals. They think they are hiding the truth and try to insist that there is no one there but themselves when one of the little girls makes a slip."

"Let me have a peep for myself when I call on your mother."

Even if she was only in temporary lodgings, the woman would seem to be of the lower class for which his friend had indicated such contempt that rainy evening. Yet something might come of it all. Determined not to go against his master's wishes in the smallest detail and himself driven by very considerable excitement, Koremitsu searched diligently for a chance to let Genji into the house. But the details are tiresome, and I shall not go into them.

Genji did not know who the lady was and he did not want her to know who he was. In very shabby disguise, he set out to visit her on foot. He must be taking her very seriously, thought Koremitsu, who offered his horse and himself went on foot.

"Though I do not think that our gentleman will look very good with tramps for servants."

To make quite certain that the expedition remained secret, Genji took with him only the man who had been his intermediary in the matter of the "evening faces" and a page whom no one was likely to recognize. Lest he be found out even so, he did not stop to see his nurse.

The lady had his messengers followed to see how he made his way home and tried by every means to learn where he lived; but her efforts came to nothing. For all his secretiveness, Genji had grown fond of her and felt that he must go on seeing her. They were of such different ranks, he tried to tell himself, and it was altogether too frivolous. Yet his visits were frequent. In affairs of this sort, which can muddle the senses of the most serious and honest of men, he had always kept himself under tight control and avoided any occasion for censure. Now, to a most astonishing degree, he would be asking himself as he returned in the morning from a visit how he could wait through the day for the next. And then he would rebuke himself. It was madness, it was not an affair he should let disturb him. She was of an extraordinarily gentle and quiet nature. Though there was a certain vagueness about her, and indeed an almost childlike quality, it was clear that she knew something about men. She did not appear to be of very good family. What was there about her, he asked himself over and over again, that so drew him to her?

He took great pains to hide his rank and always wore travel dress, and he did not allow her to see his face. He came late at night when everyone was asleep. She was frightened, as if he were an apparition from an old story. She did not need to see his face to know that he was a fine gentleman. But who might he be? Her suspicions turned to Koremitsu. It was that

young gallant, surely, who had brought the strange visitor. But Koremitsu pursued his own little affairs unremittingly, careful to feign indifference to and ignorance of this other affair. What could it all mean? The lady was lost in unfamiliar speculations.

Genji had his own worries. If, having lowered his guard with an appearance of complete unreserve, she were to slip away and hide, where would he seek her? This seemed to be but a temporary residence, and he could not be sure when she would choose to change it, and for what other. He hoped that he might reconcile himself to what must be and forget the affair as just another dalliance; but he was not confident.

On days when, to avoid attracting notice, he refrained from visiting her, his fretfulness came near anguish. Suppose he were to move her in secret to Nijō. If troublesome rumors were to arise, well, he could say that they had been fated from the start. He wondered what bond in a former life might have produced an infatuation such as he had not known before.

"Let's have a good talk," he said to her, "where we can be quite at our ease."

"It's all so strange. What you say is reasonable enough, but what you do is so strange. And rather frightening."

Yes, she might well be frightened. Something childlike in her fright brought a smile to his lips. "Which of us is the mischievous fox spirit? I wonder. Just be quiet and give yourself up to its persuasions."

Won over by his gentle warmth, she was indeed inclined to let him have his way. She seemed such a pliant little creature, likely to submit absolutely to the most outrageous demands. He thought again of Tō no Chūjō's "wild carnation," of the equable nature his friend had described that rainy night. Fearing that it would be useless, he did not try very hard to question her. She did not seem likely to indulge in dramatics and suddenly run off and hide herself, and so the fault must have been Tō no Chūjō's. Genji himself would not be guilty of such negligence—though it did occur to him that a bit of infidelity* might make her more interesting.

The bright full moon of the Eighth Month came flooding in through chinks in the roof. It was not the sort of dwelling he was used to, and he was fascinated. Toward dawn he was awakened by plebeian voices in the shabby houses down the street.

"Freezing, that's what it is, freezing. There's not much business this year, and when you can't get out into the country you feel like giving up. Do you hear me, neighbor?"

He could make out every word. It embarrassed the woman that, so near at hand, there should be this clamor of preparation as people set forth on their sad little enterprises. Had she been one of the stylish ladies of the world, she would have wanted to shrivel up and disappear. She was a placid sort, however, and she seemed to take nothing, painful or embarrassing or unpleasant, too seriously. Her manner elegant and yet girlish, she did not seem to know what the rather awful clamor up and down the street might mean. He much preferred this easygoing bewilderment to a show of consternation, a face scarlet with embarrassment. As if at his very pillow, there came the booming of a foot pestle,† more fearsome than the stamping of the thunder god, genuinely earsplitting. He did not know what device the sound came from, but he did know that it was enough to awaken the dead. From this direction and that there came the faint thump of fulling hammers against coarse cloth; and mingled with it—these were sounds to call forth the deepest emotions—were the calls of geese flying overhead. He slid a door open and they looked out. They had been lying near the veranda. There were tasteful clumps of black bamboo just outside and the dew shone as in more familiar places. Autumn insects sang busily, as if only inches from an ear used to wall crickets at considerable distances. It was all very clamorous, and also rather wonderful. Countless details could be overlooked in the singleness of his affection for the girl. She was pretty and fragile in a soft, modest cloak of lavender and a lined white robe. She had no single feature that struck him as especially beautiful, and yet, slender and fragile, she seemed so delicately beautiful that he was

*On whose part, his or the girl's? The passage is obscure.

†*Karausu.* The mortar was sunk in the floor and the pestle raised by foot and allowed to fall.

almost afraid to hear her voice. He might have wished her to be a little more assertive, but he wanted only to be near her, and yet nearer.

"Let's go off somewhere and enjoy the rest of the night. This is too much."

"But how is that possible?" She spoke very quietly. "You keep taking me by surprise."

There was a newly confiding response to his offer of his services as guardian in this world and the next. She was a strange little thing. He found it hard to believe that she had had much experience of men. He no longer cared what people might think. He asked Ukon to summon his man, who got the carriage ready. The women of the house, though uneasy, sensed the depth of his feelings and were inclined to put their trust in him.

Dawn approached. No cocks were crowing. There was only the voice of an old man making deep obeisance to a Buddha, in preparation, it would seem, for a pilgrimage to Mitake.* He seemed to be prostrating himself repeatedly and with much difficulty. All very sad. In a life itself like the morning dew, what could he desire so earnestly?

"Praise to the Messiah to come," intoned the voice.

"Listen," said Genji. "He is thinking of another world."

> "This pious one shall lead us on our way
>   As we plight our troth for all the lives to come."

The vow exchanged by the Chinese emperor and Yang Kuei-fei seemed to bode ill, and so he preferred to invoke Lord Maitreya, the Buddha of the Future; but such promises are rash.

> "So heavy the burden I bring with me from the past,
>   I doubt that I should make these vows for the future."

It was a reply that suggested doubts about his "lives to come."

The moon was low over the western hills. She was reluctant to go with him. As he sought to persuade her, the moon suddenly disappeared behind clouds in a lovely dawn sky. Always in a hurry to be off before daylight exposed him, he lifted her easily into his carriage and took her to a nearby villa. Ukon was with them. Waiting for the caretaker to be summoned, Genji looked up at the rotting gate and the ferns that trailed thickly down over it. The groves beyond were still dark, and the mist and the dews were heavy. Genji's sleeve was soaking, for he had raised the blinds of the carriage.

"This is a novel adventure, and I must say that it seems like a lot of trouble.

> "And did it confuse them too, the men of old,
>   This road through the dawn, for me so new and strange?

*In the Yoshino Mountains south of Nara.

"How does it seem to you?"
She turned shyly away.

>"And is the moon, unsure of the hills it approaches,
>Foredoomed to lose its way in the empty skies?

"I am afraid."
She did seem frightened, and bewildered. She was so used to all those swarms of people, he thought with a smile.

The carriage was brought in and its traces propped against the veranda while a room was made ready in the west wing. Much excited, Ukon was thinking about earlier adventures. The furious energy with which the caretaker saw to preparations made her suspect who Genji was. It was almost daylight when they alighted from the carriage. The room was clean and pleasant, for all the haste with which it had been readied.

"There are unfortunately no women here to wait upon His Lordship." The man, who addressed him through Ukon, was a lesser steward who had served in the Sanjō mansion of Genji's father-in-law. "Shall I send for someone?"

"The last thing I want. I came here because I wanted to be in complete solitude, away from all possible visitors. You are not to tell a soul."

The man put together a hurried breakfast, but he was, as he had said, without serving women to help him.

Genji told the girl that he meant to show her a love as dependable as "the patient river of the loons."* He could do little else in these strange lodgings.

The sun was high when he arose. He opened the shutters. All through the badly neglected grounds not a person was to be seen. The groves were rank and overgrown. The flowers and grasses in the foreground were a drab monotone, an autumn moor. The pond was choked with weeds, and all in all it was a forbidding place. An outbuilding seemed to be fitted with rooms for the caretaker, but it was some distance away.

"It is a forbidding place,"† said Genji. "But I am sure that whatever devils emerge will pass me by."

He was still in disguise. She thought it unkind of him to be so secretive, and he had to agree that their relationship had gone beyond such furtiveness.

>"Because of one chance meeting by the wayside
>The flower now opens in the evening dew.

"And how does it look to you?"

---

*Umanofuhito Kunihito, *Manyōshū* 4458:

>The patient river of the patient loons
>Will not run dry. My love will still outlast it.

†The repetition in almost identical language suggests a miscopying.

"The face seemed quite to shine in the evening dew,
But I was dazzled by the evening light."

Her eyes turned away. She spoke in a whisper.

To him it may have seemed an interesting poem.

As a matter of fact, she found him handsomer than her poem suggested, indeed frighteningly handsome, given the setting.

"I hid my name from you because I thought it altogether too unkind of you to be keeping your name from me. Do please tell me now. This silence makes me feel that something awful might be coming."

"Call me the fisherman's daughter."* Still hiding her name, she was like a little child.

"I see. I brought it all on myself? A case of *warekara*?"†

And so, sometimes affectionately, sometimes reproachfully, they talked the hours away.

Koremitsu had found them out and brought provisions. Feeling a little guilty about the way he had treated Ukon, he did not come near. He thought it amusing that Genji should thus be wandering the streets, and concluded that the girl must provide sufficient cause. And he could have had her himself, had he not been so generous.

Genji and the girl looked out at an evening sky of the utmost calm. Because she found the darkness in the recesses of the house frightening, he raised the blinds at the veranda and they lay side by side. As they gazed at each other in the gathering dusk, it all seemed very strange to her, unbelievably strange. Memories of past wrongs quite left her. She was more at ease with him now, and he thought her charming. Beside him all through the day, starting up in fright at each little noise, she seemed delightfully childlike. He lowered the shutters early and had lights brought.

"You seem comfortable enough with me, and yet you raise difficulties."

At court everyone would be frantic. Where would the search be directed? He thought what a strange love it was, and he thought of the turmoil the Rokujō lady was certain to be in.‡ She had every right to be resentful, and yet her jealous ways were not pleasant. It was that sad lady to whom his thoughts first turned. Here was the girl beside him, so simple and undemanding; and the other was so impossibly forceful in her de-

---

*Anonymous, *Shinkokinshū* 1701, and "Courtesan's Song," *Wakan Rōeishū* 722:

> A fisherman's daughter, I spend my life by the waves,
> The waves that tell us nothing. I have no home.

†Fujiwara Naoiko, *Kokinshū* 807:

> In the grasses the fishermen take, the insects sing:
> "I did it myself." I weep but do not hate you.

‡We do not learn much about "the Rokujō lady" until Chapter 6. There is a theory that "Evening Faces" was written considerably later than the present succession of chapters has it.

mands. How he wished he might in some measure have his freedom.

It was past midnight. He had been asleep for a time when an exceed-ingly beautiful woman appeared by his pillow.

"You do not even think of visiting me, when you are so much on my mind. Instead you go running off with someone who has nothing to recom-mend her, and raise a great stir over her. It is cruel, intolerable." She seemed about to shake the girl from her sleep. He awoke, feeling as if he were in the power of some malign being. The light had gone out. In great alarm, he unsheathed his sword and awakened Ukon. She too seemed frightened.

"Go out to the gallery and wake the guard. Have him bring a light."

"It's much too dark."

He forced a smile. "You're behaving like a child."

He clapped his hands and a hollow echo answered. No one seemed to hear. The girl was trembling violently. She was bathed in sweat and as if in a trance, quite bereft of her senses.

"She is such a timid little thing," said Ukon, "frightened when there is nothing at all to be frightened of. This must be dreadful for her."

Yes, poor thing, thought Genji. She did seem so fragile, and she had spent the whole day gazing up at the sky.

"I'll go get someone. What a frightful echo. You stay here with her." He pulled Ukon to the girl's side.

The lights in the west gallery had gone out. There was a gentle wind. He had few people with him, and they were asleep. They were three in number: a young man who was one of his intimates and who was the son of the steward here, a court page, and the man who had been his intermedi-ary in the matter of the "evening faces." He called out. Someone answered and came up to him.

"Bring a light. Wake the other, and shout and twang your bowstrings. What do you mean, going to sleep in a deserted house? I believe Lord Koremitsu was here."

"He was. But he said he had no orders and would come again at dawn."

An elite guardsman, the man was very adept at bow twanging. He went off with a shouting as of a fire watch. At court, thought Genji, the courtiers on night duty would have announced themselves, and the guard would be changing. It was not so very late.

He felt his way back inside. The girl was as before, and Ukon lay face down at her side.

"What is this? You're a fool to let yourself be so frightened. Are you worried about the fox spirits that come out and play tricks in deserted houses? But you needn't worry. They won't come near me." He pulled her to her knees.

"I'm not feeling at all well. That's why I was lying down. My poor lady must be terrified."

"She is indeed. And I can't think why."

He reached for the girl. She was not breathing. He lifted her and she was limp in his arms. There was no sign of life. She had seemed as defenseless as a child, and no doubt some evil power had taken possession of her. He could think of nothing to do. A man came with a torch. Ukon was not prepared to move, and Genji himself pulled up curtain frames to hide the girl.

"Bring the light closer."

It was·most a unusual order. Not ordinarily permitted at Genji's side, the man hesitated to cross the threshold.

"Come, come, bring it here! There is a time and place for ceremony."

In the torchlight he had a fleeting glimpse of a figure by the girl's pillow. It was the woman in his dream. It faded away like an apparition in an old romance. In all the fright and horror, his confused thoughts centered upon the girl. There was no room for thoughts of himself.

He knelt over her and called out to her, but she was cold and had stopped breathing. It was too horrible. He had no confidant to whom he could turn for advice. It was the clergy one thought of first on such occasions. He had been so brave and confident, but he was young, and this was too much for him. He clung to the lifeless body.

"Come back, my dear, my dear. Don't do this awful thing to me." But she was cold and no longer seemed human.

The first paralyzing terror had left Ukon. Now she was writhing and wailing. Genji remembered a devil a certain minister had encountered in the Grand Hall.*

"She can't possibly be dead." He found the strength to speak sharply. "All this noise in the middle of the night—you must try to be a little quieter." But it had been too sudden.

He turned again to the torchbearer. "There is someone here who seems to have had a very strange seizure. Tell your friend to find out where Lord Koremitsu is spending the night and have him come immediately. If the holy man is still at his mother's house, give him word, very quietly, that he is to come too. His mother and the people with her are not to hear. She does not approve of this sort of adventure."

He spoke calmly enough, but his mind was in a turmoil. Added to grief at the loss of the girl was horror, quite beyond describing, at this desolate place. It would be past midnight. The wind was higher and whistled more dolefully in the pines. There came a strange, hollow call of a bird. Might it be an owl? All was silence, terrifying solitude. He should not have chosen such a place—but it was too late now. Trembling violently, Ukon clung to him. He held her in his arms, wondering if she might be about to follow her lady. He was the only rational one present, and he could think of nothing to do. The flickering light wandered here and there. The upper parts of the screens behind them were in darkness, the lower parts fitfully in the light. There was a persistent creaking, as of someone coming

*The *Okagami* tells how Fujiwara Tadahira met a devil in the Shishinden. It withdrew when informed that he was on the emperor's business.

up behind them. If only Koremitsu would come. But Koremitsu was a nocturnal wanderer without a fixed abode, and the man had to search for him in numerous places. The wait for dawn was like the passage of a thousand nights. Finally he heard a distant crowing. What legacy from a former life could have brought him to this mortal peril? He was being punished for a guilty love, his fault and no one else's, and his story would be remembered in infamy through all the ages to come. There were no secrets, strive though one might to have them. Soon everyone would know, from his royal father down, and the lowest court pages would be talking; and he would gain immortality as the model of the complete fool.

Finally Lord Koremitsu came. He was the perfect servant who did not go against his master's wishes in anything at any time; and Genji was angry that on this night of all nights he should have been away, and slow in answering the summons. Calling him inside even so, he could not immediately find the strength to say what must be said. Ukon burst into tears, the full horror of it all coming back to her at the sight of Koremitsu. Genji too lost control of himself. The only sane and rational one present, he had held Ukon in his arms, but now he gave himself up to his grief.

"Something very strange has happened," he said after a time. "Strange —'unbelievable' would not be too strong a word. I wanted a priest—one does when these things happen—and asked your reverend brother to come."

"He went back up the mountain yesterday. Yes, it is very strange indeed. Had there been anything wrong with her?"

"Nothing."

He was so handsome in his grief that Koremitsu wanted to weep. An older man who has had everything happen to him and knows what to expect can be depended upon in a crisis; but they were both young, and neither had anything to suggest.

Koremitsu finally spoke. "We must not let the caretaker know. He may be dependable enough himself, but he is sure to have relatives who will talk. We must get away from this place."

"You aren't suggesting that we could find a place where we would be less likely to be seen?"

"No, I suppose not. And the women at her house will scream and wail when they hear about it, and they live in a crowded neighborhood, and all the mob around will hear, and that will be that. But mountain temples are used to this sort of thing. There would not be much danger of attracting attention." He reflected on the problem for a time. "There is a woman I used to know. She has gone into a nunnery up in the eastern hills. A very old lady, my father's nurse, is living there. The district seems to be rather heavily populated, but the nunnery is off by itself."

In the stir as daylight came, Koremitsu had the carriage brought up. Since Genji seemed incapable of the task, he wrapped the body in a covering and lifted it into the carriage. It was very tiny and very pretty, and not at all repellent. The wrapping was loose and the hair streamed forth, as if to darken the world before Genji's eyes.

He wanted to see the last rites through to the end, but Koremitsu would not hear of it. "Take my horse and go back to Nijō, now while the streets are still quiet."

He helped Ukon into the carriage and himself proceeded on foot, the skirts of his robe hitched up. It was a strange, bedraggled sort of funeral procession, he thought, but in the face of such anguish he was prepared to risk his life. Barely conscious, Genji made his way back to Nijō.

"Where have you been?" asked the women. "You are not looking at all well."

He did not answer. Alone in his room, he pressed a hand to his heart. Why had he not gone with the others? What would she think if she were to come back to life? She would think that he had abandoned her. Self-reproach filled his heart to breaking. He had a headache and feared he had a fever. Might he too be dying? The sun was high and still he did not emerge. Thinking it all very strange, the women pressed breakfast upon him. He could not eat. A messenger reported that the emperor had been troubled by his failure to appear the day before.

His brothers-in-law came calling.

"Come in, please, just for a moment." He received only Tō no Chūjō and kept a blind between them. "My old nurse fell seriously ill and took her vows in the Fifth Month or so. Perhaps because of them, she seemed to recover. But recently she had a relapse. Someone came to ask if I would not call on her at least once more. I thought I really must go and see an old and dear servant who was on her deathbed, and so I went. One of her servants was ailing, and quite suddenly, before he had time to leave, he died. Out of deference to me they waited until night to take the body away. All this I learned later. It would be very improper of me to go to court with all these festivities coming up,* I thought, and so I stayed away. I have had a headache since early this morning—perhaps I have caught cold. I must apologize."

"I see. I shall so inform your father. He sent out a search party during the concert last night, and really seemed very upset." Tō no Chūjō turned to go, and abruptly turned back. "Come now. What sort of brush did you really have? I don't believe a word of it."

Genji was startled, but managed a show of nonchalance. "You needn't go into the details. Just say that I suffered an unexpected defilement. Very unexpected, really."

Despite his cool manner, he was not up to facing people. He asked a younger brother-in-law to explain in detail his reasons for not going to court. He got off a note to Sanjō with a similar explanation.

Koremitsu came in the evening. Having announced that he had suffered a defilement, Genji had callers remain outside, and there were few people in the house. He received Koremitsu immediately.

"Are you sure she is dead?" He pressed a sleeve to his eyes.

Koremitsu too was in tears. "Yes, I fear she is most certainly dead. I could not stay shut up in a temple indefinitely, and so I have made arrangements with a venerable priest whom I happen to know rather well. Tomorrow is a good day for funerals."

"And the other woman?"

"She has seemed on the point of death herself. She does not want to be left behind by her lady. I was afraid this morning that she might throw herself over a cliff. She wanted to tell the people at Gojō, but I persuaded her to let us have a little more time."

"I am feeling rather awful myself and almost fear the worst."

"Come, now. There is nothing to be done and no point in torturing yourself. You must tell yourself that what must be must be. I shall let absolutely no one know, and I am personally taking care of everything."

"Yes, to be sure. Everything is fated. So I tell myself. But it is terrible to think that I have sent a lady to her death. You are not to tell your sister, and you must be very sure that your mother does not hear. I would not survive the scolding I would get from her."

"And the priests too: I have told them a plausible story." Koremitsu exuded confidence.

*There were many Shinto rites during the Ninth Month.

The women had caught a hint of what was going on and were more puzzled than ever. He had said that he had suffered a defilement, and he was staying away from court; but why these muffled lamentations?

Genji gave instructions for the funeral. "You must make sure that nothing goes wrong."

"Of course. No great ceremony seems called for."

Koremitsu turned to leave.

"I know you won't approve," said Genji, a fresh wave of grief sweeping over him, "but I will regret it forever if I don't see her again. I'll go on horseback."

"Very well, if you must." In fact Koremitsu thought the proposal very ill advised. "Go immediately and be back while it is still early."

Genji set out in the travel robes he had kept ready for his recent amorous excursions. He was in the bleakest despair. He was on a strange mission and the terrors of the night before made him consider turning back. Grief urged him on. If he did not see her once more, when, in another world, might he hope to see her as she had been? He had with him only Koremitsu and the attendant of that first encounter. The road seemed a long one.

The moon came out, two nights past full. They reached the river. In the dim torchlight, the darkness off towards Mount Toribe was ominous and forbidding; but Genji was too dazed with grief to be frightened. And so they reached the temple.

It was a harsh, unfriendly region at best. The board hut and chapel where the nun pursued her austerities were lonely beyond description. The light at the altar came dimly through cracks. Inside the hut a woman was weeping. In the outer chamber two or three priests were conversing and invoking the holy name in low voices. Vespers seemed to have ended in several temples nearby. Everything was quiet. There were lights and there seemed to be clusters of people in the direction of Kiyomizu. The grand tones in which the worthy monk, the son of the nun, was reading a sutra brought on what Genji thought must be the full flood tide of his tears.

He went inside. The light was turned away from the corpse. Ukon lay behind a screen. It must be very terrible for her, thought Genji. The girl's face was unchanged and very pretty.

"Won't you let me hear your voice again?" He took her hand. "What was it that made me give you all my love, for so short a time, and then made you leave me to this misery?" He was weeping uncontrollably.

The priests did not know who he was. They sensed something remarkable, however, and felt their eyes mist over.

"Come with me to Nijō," he said to Ukon.

"We have been together since I was very young. I never left her side, not for a single moment. Where am I to go now? I will have to tell the others what has happened. As if this weren't enough, I will have to put up with their accusations." She was sobbing. "I want to go with her."

"That is only natural. But it is the way of the world. Parting is always sad. Our lives must end, early or late. Try to put your trust in me." He comforted her with the usual homilies, but presently his real feelings came out. "Put your trust in me—when I fear I have not long to live myself." He did not after all seem likely to be much help.

"It will soon be light," said Koremitsu. "We must be on our way."

Looking back and looking back again, his heart near breaking, Genji went out. The way was heavy with dew and the morning mists were thick. He scarcely knew where he was. The girl was exactly as she had been that night. They had exchanged robes and she had on a red singlet of his. What might it have been in other lives that had brought them together? He managed only with great difficulty to stay in his saddle. Koremitsu was at the reins. As they came to the river Genji fell from his horse and was unable to remount.

"So I am to die by the wayside? I doubt that I can go on."

Koremitsu was in a panic. He should not have permitted this expedition, however strong Genji's wishes. Dipping his hands in the river, he turned and made supplication to Kiyomizu. Genji somehow pulled himself together. Silently invoking the holy name, he was seen back to Nijō.

The women were much upset by these untimely wanderings. "Very bad, very bad. He has been so restless lately. And why should he have gone out again when he was not feeling well?"

Now genuinely ill, he took to his bed. Two or three days passed and he was visibly thinner. The emperor heard of the illness and was much alarmed. Continuous prayers were ordered in this shrine and that temple. The varied rites, Shinto and Confucian and Buddhist, were beyond counting. Genji's good looks had been such as to arouse forebodings. All through the court it was feared that he would not live much longer. Despite his illness, he summoned Ukon to Nijō and assigned her rooms near his own. Koremitsu composed himself sufficiently to be of service to her, for he could see that she had no one else to turn to. Choosing times when he was feeling better, Genji would summon her for a talk, and she soon was accustomed to life at Nijō. Dressed in deep mourning, she was a somewhat stern and forbidding young woman, but not without her good points.

"It lasted such a very little while. I fear that I will be taken too. It must be dreadful for you, losing your only support. I had thought that as long as I lived I would see to all your needs, and it seems sad and ironical that I should be on the point of following her." He spoke softly and there were tears in his eyes. For Ukon the old grief had been hard enough to bear, and now she feared that a new grief might be added to it.

All through the Nijō mansion there was a sense of helplessness. Emissaries from court were thicker than raindrops. Not wanting to worry his father, Genji fought to control himself. His father-in-law was extremely solicitous and came to Nijō every day. Perhaps because of all the prayers and rites the crisis passed—it had lasted some twenty days—and left no ill effects. Genji's full recovery coincided with the final cleansing of the defilement. With the unhappiness he had caused his father much on his mind, he set off for court. His father-in-law the minister then took him to Sanjō, with many an admonition along the way. He felt for a time as if he had come back from a different world.

lost weight, but emaciation only made him handsomer. He spent a great deal of time gazing into space, and sometimes he would weep aloud. He must be in the clutches of some malign spirit, thought the women. It was all most peculiar.

He would summon Ukon on quiet evenings. "I don't understand it at all. Why did she so insist on keeping her name from me? Even if she *was* a fisherman's daughter it was cruel of her to be so uncommunicative. It was as if she did not know how much I loved her."

"There was no reason for keeping it secret. But why should she tell you about her insignificant self? Your attitude seemed so strange from the beginning. She used to say that she hardly knew whether she was waking or dreaming. Your refusal to identify yourself, you know, helped her guess who you were. It hurt her that you should belittle her by keeping your name from her."

"An unfortunate contest of wills. I did not want anything to stand between us; but I must always be worrying about what people will say.

I must refrain from things my father and all the rest of them might take me to task for. I am not permitted the smallest indiscretion. Everything is exaggerated so. The little incident of the evening faces' affected me strangely and I went to very great trouble to see her. There must have been a bond between us. A love doomed from the start to be fleeting—why should it have taken such complete possession of me and made me find her so precious? You must tell me everything. What point is there in keeping secrets now? I mean to make offerings every week, and I want to know in whose name I am making them."

"Yes, of course—why have secrets now? It is only that I do not want to slight what she made so much of. Her parents are dead. Her father was a guards captain. She was his special pet, but his career did not go well and his life came to an early and disappointing end. She somehow got to know Lord Tō no Chūjō—it was when he was still a lieutenant. He was very attentive for three years or so, and then about last autumn there was a rather awful threat from his father-in-law's house. She was ridiculously timid and it frightened her beyond all reason. She ran off and hid herself at her nurse's in the western part of the city. It was a wretched little hovel of a place. She wanted to go off into the hills, but the direction she had in mind has been taboo since New Year's. So she moved to the odd place where she was so upset to have you find her. She was more reserved and withdrawn than most people, and I fear that her unwillingness to show her emotions may have seemed cold."

So it was true. Affection and pity welled up yet more strongly.

"He once told me of a lost child. Was there such a one?"

"Yes, a very pretty little girl, born two years ago last spring."

"Where is she? Bring her to me without letting anyone know. It would be such a comfort. I should tell my friend Tō no Chūjō, I suppose, but why invite criticism? I doubt that anyone could reprove me for taking in the child. You must think up a way to get around the nurse."

"It would make me very happy if you were to take the child. I would hate to have her left where she is. She is there because we had no competent nurses in the house where you found us."

The evening sky was serenely beautiful. The flowers below the veranda were withered, the songs of the insects were dying too, and autumn tints were coming over the maples. Looking out upon the scene, which might have been a painting, Ukon thought what a lovely asylum she had found herself. She wanted to avert her eyes at the thought of the house of the "evening faces." A pigeon called, somewhat discordantly, from a bamboo thicket. Remembering how the same call had frightened the girl in that deserted villa, Genji could see the little figure as if an apparition were there before him.

"How old was she? She seemed so delicate, because she was not long for this world, I suppose."

"Nineteen, perhaps? My mother, who was her nurse, died and left me

behind. Her father took a fancy to me, and so we grew up together, and I never once left her side. I wonder how I can go on without her. I am almost sorry that we were so close.* She seemed so weak, but I can see now that she was a source of strength."

"The weak ones do have a power over us. The clear, forceful ones I can do without. I am weak and indecisive by nature myself, and a woman who is quiet and withdrawn and follows the wishes of a man even to the point of letting herself be used has much the greater appeal. A man can shape and mold her as he wishes, and becomes fonder of her all the while."

"She was exactly what you would have wished, sir." Ukon was in tears. "That thought makes the loss seem greater."

The sky had clouded over and a chilly wind had come up. Gazing off into the distance, Genji said softly:

"One sees the clouds as smoke that rose from the pyre,
    And suddenly the evening sky seems nearer."

"In the Eighth Month, the Ninth Month, the nights are long,"* he whispered, and lay down.

*Po Chu-i, Collected Works, XIX, "The Fulling Blocks at Night."

Chapter 3

Lavender

Genji was suffering from repeated attacks of malaria. All manner of religious services were commissioned, but they did no good.

In a certain temple in the northern hills, someone reported, there lived a sage who was a most accomplished worker of cures. "During the epidemic last summer all sorts of people went to him. He was able to cure them immediately when all other treatment had failed. You must not let it have its way. You must summon him at once."

Genji sent off a messenger, but the sage replied that he was old and bent and unable to leave his cave.

There was no help for it, thought Genji: he must quietly visit the man. He set out before dawn, taking four or five trusted attendants with him.

The temple was fairly deep in the northern hills. Though the cherry blossoms had already fallen in the city, it being late in the Third Month, the mountain cherries were at their best. The deepening mist as the party entered the hills delighted him. He did not often go on such expeditions, for he was of such rank that freedom of movement was not permitted him.

The temple itself was a sad place. The old man's cave was surrounded by rocks, high in the hills behind. Making his way up to it, Genji did not at first reveal his identity. He was in rough disguise, but the holy man immediately saw that he was someone of importance.

"This is a very great honor. You will be the gentleman who sent for me? My mind has left the world, and I have so neglected the ritual that

it has quite gone out of my head. I fear that your journey has been in vain."
Yet he got busily to work, and he smiled his pleasure at the visit.

He prepared medicines and had Genji drink them, and as he went
through his spells and incantations the sun rose higher. Genji walked a few
steps from the cave and surveyed the scene. The cave was on a height with
priestly cells spread out below it. Down a winding path he saw a wattled fence
of better workmanship than similar fences nearby. The halls and galleries
within were nicely disposed and there were fine trees in the garden.

"Whose house might that be?"

"A certain bishop, I am told, has been living there in seclusion for the
last two years or so."

"Someone who calls for ceremony—and ceremony is hardly possible
in these clothes. He must not know that I am here."

Several pretty little girls had come out to draw water and cut flowers
for the altar.

"And I have been told that a lady is in residence too. The bishop can
hardly be keeping a mistress. I wonder who she might be."

Several of his men went down to investigate, and reported upon what they had seen. "Some very pretty young ladies and some older women too, and some little girls."

Despite the sage's ministrations, which still continued, Genji feared a new seizure as the sun rose higher.

"It is too much on your mind," said the sage. "You must try to think of something else."

Genji climbed the hill behind the temple and looked off toward the city. The forests receded into a spring haze.

"Like a painting," he said. "People who live in such a place can hardly want to be anywhere else."

"Oh, these are not mountains at all," said one of his men."The mountains and seas off in the far provinces, now—they would make a real picture. Fuji and those other mountains."

Another of his men set about diverting him with a description of the mountains and shores of the West Country. "In the nearer provinces the Akashi coast in Harima is the most beautiful. There is nothing especially grand about it, but the view out over the sea has a quiet all its own. The house of the former governor—he took his vows not long ago, and he worries a great deal about his only daughter—the house is rather splendid. He is the son or grandson of a minister and should have made his mark in the world, but he is an odd sort of man who does not get along well with people. He resigned his guards commission and asked for the Harima post. But unfortunately the people of the province do not seem to have taken him quite seriously. Not wanting to go back to the city a failure, he became a monk. You may ask why he should have chosen then to live by the sea and not in a mountain temple. The provinces are full of quiet retreats, but the mountains are really too remote, and the isolation would have been difficult for his wife and young daughter. He seems to have concluded that life by the sea might help him to forget his frustrations.

"I was in the province not long ago and I looked in on him. He may not have done well in the city, but he could hardly have done better in Akashi. The grounds and the buildings are really very splendid. He was, after all, the governor, and he did what he could to make sure that his last years would be comfortable. He does not neglect his prayers, and they would seem to have given him a certain mellowness."

"And the daughter?" asked Genji.

"Pretty and pleasant enough. Each successive governor has asked for her hand but the old man has turned them all away. He may have ended up an insignificant provincial governor himself, he says, but he has other plans for her. He is always giving her last instructions. If he dies with his grand ambitions unrealized she is to leap into the sea."

Genji smiled.

"A cloistered maiden, reserved for the king of the sea," laughed one of his men. "A very extravagant ambition."

The man who had told the story was the son of the present governor of Harima. He had this year been raised to the Fifth Rank for his services in the imperial secretariat.

"I know why you lurk around the premises," said another. "You're a lady's man, and you want to spoil the old governor's plans."

And another: "You haven't convinced me. She's a plain country girl, no more. She's lived in the country most of her life with an old father who knows nothing of the times and the fashions."

"The mother is the one. She has used her connections in the city to find girls and women from the best families and bring them to Akashi. It makes your head spin to watch her."

"If the wrong sort of governor were to take over,* the old man would have his worries."

Genji was amused. "Ambition wide and deep as the sea. But alas, we would not see her for the seaweed."

Knowing his fondness for oddities, his men had hoped that the story would interest him.

"It is rather late, sir, and seeing as you have not had another attack, suppose we start for home."

But the sage objected. "He has been possessed by a hostile power. We must continue our services quietly through the night."

Genji's men were persuaded, and for Genji it was a novel and amusing excursion.

"We will start back at daybreak."

The evening was long. He took advantage of a dense haze to have a look at the house behind the wattled fence. Sending back everyone except Koremitsu, he took up a position at the fence. In the west room sat a nun who had a holy image before her. The blinds were slightly raised and she seemed to be offering flowers. She was leaning against a pillar and had a text spread out on an armrest. The effort to read seemed to take all her strength. Perhaps in her forties, she had a fair, delicate skin and a pleasantly full face, though the effects of illness were apparent. The features suggested breeding and cultivation. Cut cleanly at the shoulders, her hair seemed to him far more pleasing than if it had been permitted to trail the usual length. Beside her were two attractive women, and little girls scampered in and out. Much the prettiest was a girl of perhaps ten in a soft white singlet and a russet robe. He saw how lovely she would one day be. Rich hair spread over her shoulders like a fan. Her face was flushed from weeping.

"What is it?" The nun looked up. "Another fight?" He thought he saw a resemblance. Perhaps they were mother and daughter.

"Inuki let my baby sparrows loose." The child was very angry. "I had them in a basket."

"That stupid child," said a rather handsome woman with rich hair who seemed to be called Shōnagon and was apparently the girl's nurse.

*Or, depending on the text, "If the girl were to become countrified."

"She always manages to do the wrong thing, and we are forever scolding her. Where will they have flown off to? They were getting to be such sweet little things too! How awful if the crows find them." She went out.

"What a silly child you are, really too silly," said the nun. "I can't be sure I will last out the day, and here you are worrying about sparrows. I've told you so many times that it's a sin to put birds in a cage. Come here."

The child knelt down beside her. She was charming, with rich, un-plucked eyebrows and hair pushed childishly back from the forehead. How he would like to see her in a few years! And a sudden realization brought him close to tears: the resemblance to Fujitsubo, for whom he so yearned, was astonishing.

The nun stroked the girl's hair. "You will not comb it and still it's so pretty. I worry about you, you do seem so very young. Others are much more grown up at your age. Your poor dead mother: she was only ten when her father died, and she understood everything. What will become of you when I am gone?"

She was weeping, and a vague sadness had come over Genji too. The girl gazed attentively at her and then looked down. The hair that fell over her forehead was thick and lustrous.

"Are these tender grasses to grow without the dew
Which holds itself back from the heavens that would receive it?"

There were tears in the nun's voice, and the other woman seemed also to be speaking through tears:

"It cannot be that the dew will vanish away
Ere summer comes to these early grasses of spring."

The bishop came in. "What is this? Your blinds up? And today of all days you are out at the veranda? I have just been told that General Genji is up at the hermitage being treated for malaria. He came in disguise and I was not told in time to pay a call."

"And what a sight we are. You don't suppose he saw us?" She lowered the blinds.

"The shining one of whom the whole world talks. Wouldn't you like to see him? Enough to make a saint throw off the last traces of the vulgar world, they say, and feel as if new years had been added to his life. I will get off a note."

He hurried away, and Genji too withdrew. What a discovery! It was for such unforeseen rewards that his amorous followers were so constantly on the prowl. Such a rare outing for him, and it had brought such a find! She was a perfectly beautiful child. Who might she be? He was beginning to make plans: the child must stand in the place of the one whom she so resembled.

As he lay down to sleep, an acolyte came asking for Koremitsu. The cell was a narrow one and Genji could hear everything that was said.

"Though somewhat startled to learn that your lord had passed us by, we should have come immediately. The fact is that his secrecy rather upset us. We might, you know, have been able to offer shabby accommodations."

Genji sent back that he had been suffering from malaria since about the middle of the month and had been persuaded to seek the services of the sage, of whom he had only recently heard. "Such is his reputation that I hated to risk marring it by failing to recover. That is the reason for my secrecy. We shall come down immediately."

The bishop himself appeared. He was a man of the cloth, to be sure, but an unusual one, of great courtliness and considerable fame. Genji was ashamed of his own rough disguise.

The bishop spoke of his secluded life in the hills. Again and again he urged Genji to honor his house. "It is a log hut, no better than this, but you may find the stream cool and pleasant."

Genji went with him, though somewhat embarrassed at the extravagant terms in which he had been described to women who had not seen him. He wanted to know more about the little girl. The flowers and grasses in the bishop's garden, though of the familiar varieties, had a charm all their own. The night being dark, flares had been set out along the brook, and there were lanterns at the eaves. A delicate fragrance drifted through the air, mixing with the stronger incense from the altar and the very special scent which had been burnt into Genji's robes. The ladies within must have found the blend unsettling.

The bishop talked of this ephemeral world and of the world to come. His own burden of sin was heavy, thought Genji, that he had been lured into an illicit and profitless affair. He would regret it all his life and suffer even more terribly in the life to come. What joy to withdraw to such a place as this! But with the thought came thoughts of the young face he had seen earlier in the evening.

"Do you have someone with you here? I had a dream that suddenly begins to make sense."

"How quick you are with your dreams, sir! I fear my answer will disappoint you. It has been a very long time since the Lord Inspector died. I don't suppose you will even have heard of him. He was my brother-in-law. His widow turned her back on the world and recently she has been ill, and since I do not go down to the city she has come to stay with me here. It was her thought that I might be able to help her."

"I have heard that your sister had a daughter. I ask from no more than idle curiosity, you must believe me."

"There was an only daughter. She too has been dead these ten years and more. He took very great pains with her education and hoped to send her to court; but he died before that ambition could be realized, and the nun, my sister, was left to look after her. I do not know through whose offices it was that Prince Hyōbu began visiting the daughter in secret. His wife is from a very proud family, you know, sir, and there were unpleasant incidents, which finally drove the poor thing into a fatal decline. I saw before my own eyes how worry can destroy a person."

So the child he had seen would be the daughter of Prince Hyōbu and the unfortunate lady; and it was Fujitsubo, the prince's sister, whom she so resembled. He wanted more than ever to meet her. She was an elegant child, and she did not seem at all spoiled. What a delight if he could take her into his house and make her his ideal!

"A very sad story." He wished to be completely sure. "Did she leave no one behind?"

"She had a child just before she died, a girl, a great source of worry for my poor sister in her declining years."

There could be no further doubt. "What I am about to say will, I fear, startle you—but might I have charge of the child? I have reasons. I am not alone, and yet my life is lonely. If you are telling yourself that she is too young—well, sir, you are doing me an injustice. Other men may have improper motives, but I do not."

"Your words quite fill me with delight. But she is indeed young, so very young that we could not possibly think even in jest of asking you to take responsibility for her. Only the man who is presently to be her husband can take that responsibility. In a matter of such import I am not competent to give an answer. I must discuss the matter with my sister." He was suddenly remote and chilly.

Genji had spoken with youthful impulsiveness and could not think what to do next.

"It is my practice to conduct services in the chapel of Lord Amitābha." The bishop got up to leave. "I have not yet said vespers. I shall come again when they are over."

Genji was not feeling well. A shower passed on a chilly mountain wind, and the sound of the waterfall was higher. Intermittently came a rather sleepy voice, solemn and somehow ominous, reading a sacred text. The most insensitive of men would have been aroused by the scene. Genji was unable to sleep. The vespers were very long and it was growing late. There was evidence that the women in the inner rooms were still up. They were being quiet, but he heard a rosary brush against an armrest and, to give him a sense of elegant companionship, a faint rustling of silk. Screens lined the inside wall, very near at hand. He pushed one of the center panels some inches aside and rustled his fan. Though they must have thought it odd, the women could not ignore it. One of them came forward, then retreated a step or two.

"This is very strange indeed. Is there some mistake?"

"The guiding hand of the Blessed One makes no mistakes on the darkest nights." His was an aristocratic young voice.

"And in what direction does it lead?" the woman replied hesitantly. "This is most confusing."

"Very sudden and confusing, I am sure.

"Since first the wanderer glimpsed the fresh young grasses
His sleeves have known no respite from the dew.

"Might I ask you to pass my words on to your lady?"

"There is no one in this house to whom such a message can possibly seem appropriate."

"I have my reasons. You must believe me."

The woman withdrew to the rear of the house.

The nun was of course rather startled. "How very forward of him. He must think the child older than she is. And he must have heard our poems about the grasses. What can they have meant to him?" She hesitated for rather a long time. Persuaded that too long a delay would be rude, she finally sent back:

"The dew of a night of travel—do not compare it
With the dew that soaks the sleeves of the mountain dweller.

It is this last that refuses to dry."

manipulating

"I am not used to communicating through messengers. I wish to speak to you directly and in all seriousness."

Again the old nun hesitated. "There has been a misunderstanding, surely. I can hardly be expected to converse with such a fine young gentleman."

But the women insisted that it would be rude and unfeeling not to reply.

"Yes, I suppose you youngsters are not up to addressing him. As for me, I am awed by his earnestness." And she came forward.

"You will think me headstrong and frivolous for having addressed you without warning, but the Blessed One knows that my intent is not frivolous at all." He found the nun's quiet dignity somewhat daunting.

"I quite agree with you. This unexpected conversation can hardly be called frivolous."

"I have heard the sad story, and wonder if I might offer myself as a substitute for your late daughter. I was very young when I lost the one who was dearest to me, and all through the years since I have had strange feelings of aimlessness and futility. We share the same fate, and I wonder if I might not ask that we be companions in it. The opportunity is not likely to come again. I have spoken, I am sure you see, quite without reserve."

"What you say would delight me did I not fear a mistake. It is true that there is someone here who is under my inadequate protection; but she is very young, and you could not possibly be asked to accept her deficiencies. I must decline your very kind proposal."

"I repeat that I have heard the whole story. Your admirable reticence does not permit you to understand that my feelings are of no ordinary sort."

But to her they seemed, though she did not say so, quite outrageous. The bishop came out.

"Very well, then. I have made a beginning, and it has given me strength." And Genji pushed the screen back in place.

In the Lotus Hall, voices raised in an act of contrition mingled solemnly with the roar of the waterfall and the wind that came down from the mountain. Dawn was approaching.

This was Genji's poem, addressed to the bishop:

"A wind strays down from the hills to end my dream,
And tears well forth at these voices upon the waters."

And this the bishop's reply:

"These waters wet your sleeves. Our own are dry,
And tranquil our hearts, washed clean by mountain waters.

"Such is the effect of familiarity with these scenes."

There were heavy mists in the dawn sky, and bird songs came from Genji knew not where. Flowering trees and grasses which he could not identify spread like a tapestry before him. The deer that now paused to feed by the house and now wandered on were for him a strange and wonderful sight. He quite forgot his illness. Though it was not easy for the sage to leave his retreat, he made his way down for final services. His husky voice, emerging uncertainly from a toothless mouth, had behind it long years of discipline, and the mystic incantations suggested deep and awesome powers.

An escort arrived from the city, delighted to see Genji so improved, and a message was delivered from his father. The bishop had a breakfast of unfamiliar fruits and berries brought from far down in the valley.

"I have vowed to stay in these mountains until the end of the year, and cannot see you home." He pressed wine upon Genji. "And so a holy vow has the perverse effect of inspiring regrets."

"I hate to leave your mountains and streams, but my father seems worried and I must obey his summons. I shall come again before the cherry blossoms have fallen.

"I shall say to my city friends: 'Make haste to see
Those mountain blossoms. The winds may see them first.' "

His manner and voice were beautiful beyond description.
The bishop replied:

"In thirty hundreds of years it blooms but once.
My eyes have seen it, and spurn these mountain cherries."*

"A very great rarity indeed," Genji said, smiling, "a blossom with so long and short a span."

The sage offered a verse of thanks as Genji filled his cup:

"My mountain door of pine has opened briefly
To see a radiant flower not seen before."

There were tears in his eyes. His farewell present was a sacred mace †
which had special protective powers. The bishop too gave farewell presents: a rosary of carved ebony‡ which Prince Shōtoku had obtained in Korea, still in the original Chinese box, wrapped in a netting and attached to a branch of cinquefoil pine; several medicine bottles of indigo decorated with sprays of cherry and wisteria and the like; and other gifts as well, all of them appropriate to the mountain setting. Genji's escort had brought

---

*The *udumbara* was believed to bloom only once in three thousand years, and announce the appearance of the Buddha or a king of like powers.
† *Toko,* a sort of double-pointed spike used in esoteric Shingon rites.
‡ *Kongōji,* literally "diamond seed," thought to be the seed of a tree of the fig family.

gifts for the priests who had helped with the services, the sage himself and the rest, and for all the mountain rustics too. And so Genji started out.

The bishop went to the inner apartments to tell his sister of Genji's proposal.

"It is very premature. If in four or five years he has not changed his mind we can perhaps give it some thought."

The bishop agreed, and passed her words on without comment.

Much disappointed, Genji sent in a poem through an acolyte:

> "Having come upon an evening blossom,
> The mist is loath to go with the morning sun."

She sent back:

> "Can we believe the mist to be so reluctant?
> We shall watch the morning sky for signs of truth."

It was in a casual, cursive style, but the hand was a distinguished one.

He was about to get into his carriage when a large party arrived from the house of his father-in-law, protesting the skill with which he had eluded them. Several of his brothers-in-law, including the oldest, Tō no Chūjō, were among them.

"You know very well that this is the sort of expedition we like best. You could at least have told us. Well, here we are, and we shall stay and enjoy the cherries you have discovered."

They took seats on the moss below the rocks and wine was brought out. It was a pleasant spot, beside cascading waters. Tō no Chūjō took out a flute, and one of his brothers, marking time with a fan, sang "To the West of the Toyora Temple."* They were handsome young men, all of them, but it was the ailing Genji whom everyone was looking at, so handsome a figure as he leaned against a rock that he brought a shudder of apprehension. Always in such a company there is an adept at the flageolet, and a fancier of the *shō* pipes† as well.

The bishop brought out a seven-stringed Chinese koto and pressed Genji to play it. "Just one tune, to give our mountain birds a pleasant surprise."

Genji protested that he was altogether too unwell, but he played a passable tune all the same. And so they set forth. The nameless priests and acolytes shed tears of regret, and the aged nuns within, who had never before seen such a fine gentleman, asked whether he might not be a visitor from another world.

---

*"Katsuragi," a Saibara:

> See, by the Temple of Katsuragi,
> To the west of the Toyora Temple,
> White jewels in the Cypress Well,
> Bring them forth and the land will prosper,
> And we will prosper too.

†A kind of mouth organ.

"How can it be," said the bishop, brushing away a tear, "that such a one has been born into the confusion and corruption in which we live?"

The little girl too thought him very grand. "Even handsomer than Father," she said.

"So why don't you be his little girl?"

She nodded, accepting the offer; and her favorite doll, the one with the finest wardrobe, and the handsomest gentleman in her pictures too were thereupon named "Genji."

Back in the city, Genji first reported to his father upon his excursion. The emperor was shocked. It had been no ordinary indisposition.

He asked about the qualifications of the sage, and Genji replied in great detail.

"I must see that he is promoted. Such a remarkable record and I had not even heard of him."

Genji's father-in-law, the Minister of the Left, chanced to be in attendance. "I thought of going for you, but you did after all go off in secret. Suppose you have a few days' rest at Sanjō. I will go with you, immediately."

Genji was not enthusiastic, but he left with his father-in-law all the same. The minister had his own carriage brought up and insisted that Genji get in first. This solicitude rather embarrassed him.

At the minister's Sanjō mansion everything was in readiness. It had been polished and refitted until it was a jeweled pavilion, perfect to the last detail. As always, Genji's wife secluded herself in her private apartments, and it was only at her father's urging that she came forth; and so Genji had her before him, immobile, like a princess in an illustration for a romance. It would have been a great pleasure, he was sure, to have pertinent remarks from her upon his account of the mountain journey. She seemed the stiffest, remotest person in the world. How odd that the aloofness seemed only to grow as time went by.

"It would be nice, I sometimes think, if you could be a little more wifely. I have been very ill, and I am hurt, but not really surprised, that you have not inquired after my health."

"Like the pain, perhaps, of awaiting a visitor who does not come?"*

She cast a sidelong glance at him as she spoke, and her cold beauty was very intimidating indeed.

"You so rarely speak to me, and when you do you say such unpleasant things. 'A visitor who does not come'—that is hardly an appropriate way to describe a husband, and indeed it is hardly civil. I try this approach and I try that, hoping to break through, but you seem intent on defending all the approaches. Well, one of these years, perhaps, if I live long enough."

He withdrew to the bedchamber. She did not follow. Though there were things he would have liked to say, he lay down with a sigh. He closed his eyes, but there was too much on his mind to permit sleep.

*A poetic allusion, apparently, not satisfactorily identified.

He thought of the little girl and how he would like to see her grown into a woman. Her grandmother was of course right when she said that the girl was still too young for him. He must not seem insistent. And yet—was there not some way to bring her quietly to Nijō and have her beside him, a comfort and a companion? Prince Hyōbu was a dashing and stylish man, but no one could have called him remarkably handsome. Why did the girl so take after her aunt? Perhaps because aunt and father were children of the same empress. These thoughts seemed to bring the girl closer, and he longed to have her for his own.

The next day he wrote to the nun. He would also seem to have communicated his thoughts in a casual way to the bishop. To the nun he said:

"I fear that, taken somewhat aback by your sternness, I did not express myself very well. I find strength in the hope that something of the resolve demanded of me to write this letter will have conveyed itself to you."

With it was a tightly folded note for the girl:

"The mountain blossoms are here beside me still.
All of myself I left behind with them.

"I am fearful of what the night winds might have done."*

The writing, of course, and even the informal elegance of the folding, quite dazzled the superannuated women who received the letter. Somewhat overpowering, thought the grandmother.

She finally sent back: "I did not take your farewell remarks seriously; and now so soon to have a letter from you—I scarcely know how to reply. She cannot even write 'Naniwa'† properly, and how are we to expect that she give you a proper answer?

"Brief as the time till the autumn tempests come
To scatter the flowers—so brief your thoughts of her.

"I am deeply troubled."

The bishop's answer was in the same vein. Two or three days later Genji sent Koremitsu off to the northern hills.

"There is her nurse, the woman called Shōnagon. Have a good talk with her."

How very farsighted, thought Koremitsu, smiling at the thought of the girl they had seen that evening.

The bishop said that he was much honored to be in correspondence

---

*Prince Mototoshi, *Shūishū* 29:

> Fearful of what the night winds might have done,
> I rose at dawn—were my plum trees yet in bloom?

†A poem said to have been composed by the Korean Wani upon the accession of the emperor Nintoku, making congratulatory reference to the cherry blossoms of Naniwa, seems to have been used as a beginning lesson in calligraphy.

with Genji. Koremitsu was received by Shōnagon, and described Genji's apparent state of mind in great detail. He was a persuasive young man and he made a convincing case, but to the nun and the others this suit for the hand of a mere child continued to seem merely capricious. Genji's letter was warm and earnest. There was a note too for the girl:
"Let me see your first exercises at the brush.

"No Shallow Spring, this heart of mine, believe me.*
And why must the mountain spring then seem so distant?"

This was the nun's reply:

"The shallow mountain spring but brings regrets.
Do you see something there, O shallow one?"

Koremitsu's report was no more encouraging. Shōnagon had said that they would be returning to the city when the nun was a little stronger and would answer him then.

Fujitsubo was ill and had gone home to her family. Genji managed a sympathetic thought or two for his lonely father, but his thoughts were chiefly on the possibility of seeing Fujitsubo. He quite halted his visits to other ladies. All through the day, at home and at court, he sat gazing off into space, and in the evening he would press Omyōbu to be his intermediary. How she did it I do not know; but she contrived a meeting. It is sad to have to say that his earlier attentions, so unwelcome, no longer seemed real, and the mere thought that they had been successful was for Fujitsubo a torment.† Determined that there would not be another meeting, she was shocked to find him in her presence again. She did not seek to hide her distress, and her efforts to turn him away delighted him even as they put him to shame. There was no one else quite like her. In that fact was his undoing: he would be less a prey to longing if he could find in her even a trace of the ordinary. And the tumult of thoughts and feelings that now assailed him—he would have liked to consign it to the Mountain of Obscurity.‡ It might have been better, he sighed, so short was the night, if he had not come at all.

"So few and scattered the nights, so few the dreams.
Would that the dream tonight might take me with it."

He was in tears, and she did, after all, have to feel sorry for him.

"Were I to disappear in the last of dreams
Would yet my name live on in infamy?"

*Anonymous, *Manyōshū* 3807:

Image of Shallow Mount upon Shallow Spring.
No such shallowness in this heart of mine.

†No earlier meeting has been described.
‡Kurabunoyama, thought to have been either in Yamashiro or in Omi.

She had every right to be unhappy, and he was sad for her. Omyōbu gathered his clothes and brought them out to him.

Back at Nijō he spent a tearful day in bed. He had word from Omyōbu that her lady had not read his letter. So it always was, and yet he was hurt. He remained in distraught seclusion for several days. The thought that his father might be wondering about his absence filled him with terror.

Lamenting the burden of sin that seemed to be hers, Fujitsubo was more and more unwell, and could not bestir herself, despite repeated messages summoning her back to court. She was not at all her usual self —and what was to become of her? She took to her bed as the weather turned warmer. Three months had now passed and her condition was clear; and the burden of sin now seemed to have made it necessary that she submit to curious and reproving stares. Her women thought her behavior very curious indeed. Why had she let so much time pass without informing the emperor? There was of course a crucial matter of which she spoke to no one. Ben, the daughter of her old nurse, and Omyōbu, both of whom were very close to her and attended her in the bath, had ample opportunity to observe her condition. Omyōbu was aghast. Her lady had been trapped by the harshest of fates. The emperor would seem to have been informed that a malign spirit had possession of her, and to have believed the story, as did the court in general. He sent a constant stream of messengers, which terrified her and allowed no pause in her sufferings.

Genji had a strange, rather awful dream. He consulted a soothsayer, who said that it portended events so extraordinary as to be almost unthinkable.

"It contains bad omens as well. You must be careful."

"It was not my own dream but a friend's. We will see whether it comes true, and in the meantime you must keep it to yourself."

What could it mean? He heard of Fujitsubo's condition, thought of their night together, and wondered whether the two might be related. He exhausted his stock of pleas for another meeting. Horrified that matters were so out of hand, Omyōbu could do nothing for him. He had on rare occasions had a brief note, no more than a line or two; but now even these messages ceased coming.

Fujitsubo returned to court in the Seventh Month. The emperor's affection for her had only grown in her absence. Her condition was now apparent to everyone. A slight emaciation made her beauty seem if anything nearer perfection, and the emperor kept her always at his side. The skies as autumn approached called more insistently for music. Keeping Genji too beside him, the emperor had him try his hand at this and that instrument. Genji struggled to control himself, but now and then a sign of his scarcely bearable feelings did show through, to remind the lady of what she wanted more than anything to forget.

Somewhat improved, the nun had returned to the city. Genji had someone make inquiry about her residence and wrote from time to time. It was natural that her replies should show no lessening of her opposition, but it did not worry Genji as it once had. He had more considerable worries. His gloom was deeper as autumn came to a close. One beautiful moonlit night he collected himself for a visit to a place he had been visiting in secret. A cold, wintry shower passed. The address was in Rokujō, near the eastern limits of the city, and since he had set out from the palace the way seemed a long one. He passed a badly neglected house, the garden dark with ancient trees.

"The inspector's house," said Koremitsu, who was always with him. "I called there with a message not long ago. The old lady has declined so shockingly that they can't think what to do for her."

"You should have told me. I should have looked in on her. Ask, please, if she will see me."

Koremitsu sent a man in with the message.

The women had not been expecting a caller, least of all such a grand one. For some days the old lady had seemed beyond helping, and they feared that she would be unable to receive him. But they could hardly turn such a gentleman away—and so a cushion was put out for him in the south room.

"My lady says that she fears you will find it cluttered and dirty, but she is determined at least to thank you for coming. You must find the darkness and gloom unlike anything you have known."

And indeed he could not have denied that he was used to something rather different.

"You have been constantly on my mind, but your reserve has made it difficult for me to call. I am sorry that I did not know sooner of your illness."

"I have been ill for a very long time, but in this last extremity—it was good of him to come." He caught the sad, faltering tones as she gave the message to one of her women. "I am sorry that I cannot receive him properly. As for the matter he has raised, I hope that he will still count the child among those important to him when she is no longer a child. The thought of leaving her uncared for must, I fear, create obstacles along the road I yearn to travel. But tell him, please, how good it was of him. I wish the child were old enough to thank him too."

"Can you believe," he sent back, "that I would put myself in this embarrassing position if I were less than serious? There must be a bond between us, that I should have been so drawn to her since I first heard of her. It all seems so strange. The beginnings of it must have been in a different world. I will feel that I have come in vain if I cannot hear the sound of her young voice."

"She is asleep. She did not of course know that you were coming."

But just then someone came scampering into the room. "Grandmother, they say the gentleman we saw at the temple is here. Why don't you go out and talk to him?"

The women tried to silence her.

"But why? She said the very sight of him made her feel better. I heard her." The girl seemed very pleased with the information she brought.

Though much amused, Genji pretended not to hear. After proper statements of sympathy he made his departure. Yes, she did seem little more than an infant. He would be her teacher.

The next day he sent a letter inquiring after the old lady, and with it a tightly folded note for the girl:

> "Seeking to follow the call of the nestling crane
> The open boat is lost among the reeds.

"And comes again and again to you?"*

He wrote it in a childish hand, which delighted the women. The child was to model her own hand upon it, no detail changed, they said.

Shōnagon sent a very sad answer: "It seems doubtful that my lady, after whom you were so kind as to inquire, will last the day. We are on

*Anonymous, *Kokinshū* 732:

> Like the open boat that plies the familiar canal,
> I find that I come again and again to you.

the point of sending her off to the mountains once more. I know that she will thank you from another world."

In the autumn evening, his thoughts on his unattainable love, he longed more than ever, unnatural though the wish may have seemed, for the company of the little girl who sprang from the same roots. The thought of the evening when the old nun had described herself as dew holding back from the heavens made him even more impatient—and at the same time he feared that if he were to bring the girl to Nijō he would be disappointed in her.

> "I long to have it, to bring it in from the moor,
> The lavender* that shares its roots with another."

In the Tenth Month the emperor was to visit the Suzaku Palace.† From all the great families and the middle and upper courtly ranks the most

---

*Murasaki, a gromwell from the roots of which a lavender dye is extracted. Lavender, in general the color of affinity or intimacy, suggests more specifically the fuji of Fujitsubo, "Wisteria Court." It is because of this poem that the girl is presently to be called Murasaki. The name Murasaki Shikibu also derives from it.
†South of the main palace.

accomplished musicians and dancers were selected to go with him, and grandees and princes of the blood were busy at the practice that best suited their talents. Caught up in the excitement, Genji was somewhat remiss in inquiring after the nun.

When, finally, he sent off a messenger to the northern hills, a sad reply came from the bishop: "We lost her toward the end of last month. It is the way of the world, I know, and yet I am sad."

If the news shocked even him into a new awareness of evanescence, thought Genji, how must it be for the little girl who had so occupied the nun's thoughts? Young though she was, she must feel utterly lost. He remembered, though dimly, how it had been when his mother died, and he sent off an earnest letter of sympathy. Shōnagon's answer seemed rather warmer. He went calling on an evening when he had nothing else to occupy him, some days after he learned that the girl had come out of mourning and returned to the city. The house was badly kept and almost deserted. The poor child must be terrified, he thought. He was shown to the same room as before. Sobbing, Shōnagon told him of the old lady's last days. Genji too was in tears.

"My young lady's father would seem to have indicated a willingness to take her in, but she is at such an uncomfortable age, not quite a child and still without the discernment of an adult; and the thought of having her in the custody of the lady who was so cruel to her mother is too awful. Her sisters will persecute her dreadfully, I know. The fear of it never left my lady's mind, and we have had too much evidence that the fear was not groundless. We have been grateful for your expressions of interest, though we have hesitated to take them seriously. I must emphasize that my young lady is not at all what you must think her to be. I fear that we have done badly by her, and that our methods have left her childish even for her years."

"Must you continue to be so reticent and apologetic? I have made my own feelings clear, over and over again. It is precisely the childlike quality that delights me most and makes me think I must have her for my own. You may think me complacent and self-satisfied for saying so, but I feel sure that we were joined in a former life. Let me speak to her, please.

"Rushes hide the sea grass at Wakanoura.
    Will the waves that seek it out turn back to sea?*

"That would be too much to ask of them."

"The grass at Wakanoura were rash indeed
    To follow waves that go it knows not whither.

"It would be far, far too much to ask."

The easy skill with which she turned her poem made it possible for

---

*There is a pun on *mirume,* "seeing" and "sea grass."

him to forgive its less than encouraging significance. "After so many years," he whispered, "the gate still holds me back."*

The girl lay weeping for her grandmother. Her playmates came to tell her that a gentleman in court dress was with Shōnagon. Perhaps it would be her father?

She came running in. "Where is the gentleman, Shōnagon? Is Father here?"

What a sweet voice she had!

"I'm not your father, but I'm someone just as important. Come here."

She saw that it was the other gentleman, and child though she was, she flushed at having spoken out of turn. "Let's go." She tugged at Shōnagon's sleeve. "Let's go. I'm sleepy."

"Do you have to keep hiding yourself from me? Come here. You can sleep on my knee."

"She is really very young, sir." But Shōnagon urged the child forward, and she knelt obediently just inside the blinds.

He ran his hand over a soft, rumpled robe, and, a delight to the touch, hair full and rich to its farthest ends. He took her hand. She pulled away —for he was, after all, a stranger.

"I said I'm sleepy." She went back to Shōnagon.

He slipped in after her. "I am the one you must look to now. You must not be shy with me."

"Please, sir. You forget yourself. You forget yourself completely. She is simply not old enough to understand what you have in mind."

"It is you who do not understand. I see how young she is, and I have nothing of the sort in mind. I must again ask you to be witness to the depth and purity of my feelings."

It was a stormy night. Sleet was pounding against the roof.

"How can she bear to live in such a lonely place? It must be awful for her." Tears came to his eyes. He could not leave her. "Close the shutters. I will be your watchman. You need one on a night like this. Come close to me, all of you."

Quite as if he belonged there, he slipped into the girl's bedroom. The women were astounded, Shōnagon more than the rest. He must be mad! But she was in no position to protest. Genji pulled a singlet over the girl, who was trembling like a leaf. Yes, he had to admit that his behavior must seem odd; but, trying very hard not to frighten her, he talked of things he thought would interest her.

"You must come to my house. I have all sorts of pictures, and there are dolls for you to play with."

She was less frightened than at first, but she still could not sleep. The storm blew all through the night, and Shōnagon quite refused to budge

*Fujiwara Koretada, *Gosenshū* 732:

> Alone, in secret, I hurry to Meeting Hill.
> After so many years, the gate still holds me back.

from their side. They would surely have perished of fright, whispered the women, if they had not had him with them. What a pity their lady was not a little older!

It was still dark when the wind began to subside and he made his departure, and all the appearances were as of an amorous expedition. "What I have seen makes me very sad and convinces me that she must not be out of my sight. She must come and live with me and share my lonely days. This place is quite impossible. You must be in constant terror."

"Her father has said that he will come for her. I believe it is to be after the memorial services."

"Yes, we must think of him. But they have lived apart, and he must be as much of a stranger as I am. I really do believe that in this very short time my feelings for her are stronger than his." He patted the girl on the head and looked back smiling as he left.

There was a heavy mist and the ground was white. Had he been on his way from a visit to a woman, he would have found the scene very affecting; but as it was he was vaguely depressed. Passing the house of a woman he had been seeing in secret, he had someone knock on the gate. There was no answer, and so he had someone else from his retinue, a man of very good voice, chant this poem twice in tones that could not fail to attract attention:

> "Lost though I seem to be in the mists of dawn,
> I see your gate, and cannot pass it by."

She sent out an ordinary maid who seemed, however, to be a woman of some sensibility:

> "So difficult to pass? Then do come in.
> No obstacle at all, this gate of grass."

Something more was needed to end the night, but dawn was approaching. Back at Nijō, he lay smiling at the memory of the girl. The sun was high when he arose and set about composing a letter. A rather special sort of poem seemed called for, but he laid his brush aside and deliberated for a time, and presently sent some pictures.

Looking in on his daughter that same day, Prince Hyōbu found the house vaster and more cavernous than he had remembered it, and the decay astonishingly advanced since the grandmother's death.

"How can you bear it for even a moment? You must come and live with me. I have plenty of room. And Nurse here can have a room of her own. There are other little girls, and I am sure you will get on beautifully together." Genji's perfume had been transferred to the child. "What a beautiful smell. But see how rumpled and ragged you are. I did not like the idea of having you with an ailing lady and wanted you to come and live with me. But you held back so, and I have to admit that the lady who is to be your mother has not been happy at the idea herself. It seems very sad that we should have waited for this to happen."

"Please, my lord. We may be lonely, but it will be better for us to remain as we are at least for a time. It will be better for us to wait until she is a little older and understands things better. She grieves for her grandmother and quite refuses to eat."

She was indeed thinner, but more graceful and elegant.

"Why must she go on grieving? Her grandmother is gone, and that is that. She still has me." It was growing dark. The girl wept to see him go, and he too was in tears. "You mustn't be sad. Please. You mustn't be sad. I will send for you tomorrow at the very latest."

She was inconsolable when he had gone, and beyond thinking about her own future. She was old enough to know what it meant, that the lady who had never left her was now gone. Her playmates no longer interested her. She somehow got through the daylight hours, but in the evening she gave herself up to tears, and Shōnagon and the others wept at their inability to comfort her. How, they asked one another, could they possibly go on?

Genji sent Koremitsu to make excuses. He wanted very much to call, but he had received an ill-timed summons from the palace.

"Has he quite forgotten his manners?" said Shōnagon. "I know very well that this is not as serious an affair for him as for us, but a man is expected to call regularly at the beginning of any affair. Her father, if he hears of it, will think that we have managed very badly indeed. You are young, my lady, but you must not speak of it to anyone." But the girl was not listening as attentively as Shōnagon would have wished.

Koremitsu was permitted a hint or two of their worries. "Perhaps when the time comes we will be able to tell ourselves that what must be must be, but at the moment the incompatibility overshadows everything. And your lord says and does such extraordinary things. Her father came today and did not improve matters by telling us that nothing must be permitted to happen. What could be worse than your lord's way of doing things?" She was keeping her objections to a minimum, however, for she did not want Koremitsu to think that anything of real importance had occurred.

Puzzled, Koremitsu returned to Nijō and reported upon what he had seen and heard. Genji was touched, though not moved to pay a visit. He was worried about rumors and the imputation of recklessness and frivolity that was certain to go with them. He must bring the girl to Nijō.

He sent several notes, and in the evening dispatched Koremitsu, his most faithful and reliable messenger. Certain obstacles prevented Genji's calling in person, said Koremitsu, but they must not be taken to suggest a want of seriousness.

"Her royal father has said that he will come for her tomorrow. We are feeling rather pressed. It is sad, after all, to leave a familiar place, however shabby and weedy it may be. You must forgive us. We are not entirely ourselves."

She gave him short shrift. He could see that they were busy at needle-work and other preparations.

Genji was at his father-in-law's house in Sanjō. His wife was as always slow to receive him. In his boredom and annoyance he took out a Japanese koto and pleasantly hummed "The Field in Hitachi."* Then came Kore-mitsu's unsettling report. He must act. If he were to take her from her father's house, he would be called a lecher and a child thief. He must swear the women to secrecy and bring her to Nijō immediately.

"I will go early in the morning. Have my carriage left as it is, and order a guard, no more than a man or two."

Koremitsu went to see that these instructions were carried out. Genji knew that he was taking risks. People would say that his appetites were altogether too varied. If the girl were a little older he would be credited with having made a conquest, and that would be that. Though Prince Hyōbu would be very upset indeed, Genji knew that he must not let the

---

*A Saibara:

> I plow my field in Hitachi.
> You have made your way, this rainy night,
> Over mountain and over moor,
> To see if I have a lover.

child go. It was still dark when he set out. His wife had no more than usual to say to him.

"I have just remembered some business at Nijō that absolutely has to be taken care of. I should not be long."

Her women did not even know that he had gone. He went to his own rooms and changed to informal court dress. Koremitsu alone was on horseback.

When they reached their destination one of his men pounded on the gate. Ignorant of what was afoot, the porter allowed Genji's carriage to be pulled inside. Koremitsu went to a corner door and knocked. Shōnagon came out.

"My lord is here."

"And my lady is asleep. You pick strange hours for your visits." Shōnagon suspected that he was on his way home from an amorous adventure.

Genji had joined Koremitsu.

"There is something I must say to her before she goes to her father's."

Shōnagon smiled. "And no doubt she will have many interesting things to say in reply."

He pushed his way inside.

"Please, sir. We were not expecting anyone. The old women are a dreadful sight."

"I will go wake her. The morning mist is too beautiful for sleep."

He went into her bedroom, where the women were too surprised to cry out. He took her in his arms and smoothed her hair. Her father had come for her, she thought, only half awake.

"Let's go. I have come from your father's." She was terrified when she saw that it was not after all her father. "You are not being nice. I have told you that you must think of me as your father." And he carried her out.

A chorus of protests now came from Shōnagon and the others.

"I have explained things quite well enough. I have told you how difficult it is for me to visit her and how I want to have her in a more comfortable and accessible spot; and your way of making things easier is to send her off to her father. One of you may come along, if you wish."

"Please, sir." Shōnagon was wringing her hands. "You could not have chosen a worse time. What are we to say when her father comes? If it is her fate to be your lady, then perhaps something can be done when the time comes. This is too sudden, and you put us in an extremely difficult position."

"You can come later if you wish."

His carriage had been brought up. The women were fluttering about helplessly and the child was sobbing. Seeing at last that there was nothing else to be done, Shōnagon took up several of the robes they had been at work on the night before, changed to presentable clothes of her own, and got into the carriage.

It was still dark when they reached Nijō, only a short distance away. Genji ordered the carriage brought up to the west wing and took the girl inside.

"It is like a nightmare," said Shōnagon. "What am I to do?"

"Whatever you like. I can have someone see you home if you wish."

A bitter smile on her lips, Shōnagon got out of the carriage. What would her lady's father think when he came for her? And what did they now have to look forward to? The saddest thing was to be left behind by one's protectors. But tears did not augur well for the new life. With an effort she pulled herself together.

Since no one was living in this west wing, there was no curtained bedchamber. Genji had Koremitsu put up screens and curtains, sent someone else to the east wing for bedding, and lay down. Though trembling violently, the girl managed to keep from sobbing aloud.

"I always sleep with Shōnagon," she said softly in childish accents.

"Imagine a big girl like you still sleeping with her nurse."

Weeping quietly, the girl lay down.

Shōnagon sat up beside them, looking out over the garden as dawn came on. The buildings and grounds were magnificent, and the sand in the garden was like jewels. Not used to such affluence, she was glad there were no other women in this west wing. It was here that Genji received occasional callers. A few guards beyond the blinds were the only attendants.

They were speculating on the identity of the lady he had brought with him. "Someone worth looking at, you can bet."

Water pitchers and breakfast were brought in. The sun was high when Genji arose. "You will need someone to take care of you. Suppose you send this evening for the ones you like best." He asked that children be sent from the east wing to play with her. "Pretty little girls, please." Four little girls came in, very pretty indeed.

The new girl, his Murasaki, still lay huddled under the singlet he had thrown over her.

"You are not to sulk, now, and make me unhappy. Would I have done all this for you if I were not a nice man? Young ladies should do as they are told." And so the lessons began.

She seemed even prettier here beside him than from afar. His manner warm and fatherly, he sought to amuse her with pictures and toys he had sent for from the east wing. Finally she came over to him. Her dark mourning robes were soft and unstarched, and when she smiled, innocently and unprotestingly, he had to smile back. She went out to look at the trees and pond after he had departed for the east wing. The flowers in the foreground, delicately touched by frost, were like a picture. Streams of courtiers, of the medium ranks and new to her experience, passed back and forth. Yes, it was an interesting place. She looked at the pictures on screens and elsewhere and (so it is with a child) soon forgot her troubles.

Staying away from court for several days, Genji worked hard to make her feel at home. He wrote down all manner of poems for her to copy, and drew all manner of pictures, some of them very good. "I sigh, though I have not seen Musashi,"* he wrote on a bit of lavender paper. She took it up, and thought the hand marvelous. In a tiny hand he wrote beside it:

> "Not yet mine, these grasses of Musashi,
>   So near to dew-drenched grasses I cannot have."

"Now you must write something."

"But I can't." She looked up at him, so completely without affectation that he had to smile.

"You can't write as well as you would like to, perhaps, but it would be wrong of you not to write at all. You must think of me as your teacher."

It was strange that even her awkward, childish way of holding the brush should so delight him. Afraid she had made a mistake, she sought to conceal what she had written. He took it from her.

> "I do not know what it is that makes you sigh.
>   And whatever grass can it be I am so near to?"

The hand was very immature indeed, and yet it had strength, and character. It was very much like her grandmother's. A touch of the modern and it would not be at all unacceptable. He ordered dollhouses and as the two of them played together he found himself for the first time neglecting his sorrows.

Prince Hyōbu went for his daughter on schedule. The women were acutely embarrassed, for there was next to nothing they could say to him. Genji wished to keep the girl's presence at Nijō secret, and Shōnagon had enjoined the strictest silence. They could only say that Shōnagon had spirited the girl away, they did not know where.

He was aghast. "Her grandmother did not want me to have her, and so I suppose Shōnagon took it upon herself, somewhat sneakily I must say, to hide her away rather than give her to me." In tears, he added: "Let me know if you hear anything."

Which request only intensified their confusion.

The prince inquired of the bishop in the northern hills and came away no better informed. By now he was beginning to feel some sense of loss (such a pretty child); and his wife had overcome her bitterness and, happy at the thought of a little girl to do with as she pleased, was similarly regretful.

Presently Murasaki had all her women with her. She was a bright, lively child, and the boys and girls who were to be her playmates felt quite at home with her. Sometimes on lonely nights when Genji was away she

*Anonymous, *Kokin Rokujō, Zoku Kokka Taikan* 34353:

> I sigh at its name, though I have not seen Musashi.
> And know that my sigh is for those lavender grasses.

would weep for her grandmother. She thought little of her father. They had lived apart and she scarcely knew him. She was by now extremely fond of her new father. She would be the first to run out and greet him when he came home, and she would climb on his lap, and they would talk happily together, without the least constraint or embarrassment. He was delighted with her. A clever and watchful woman can create all manner of difficulties. A man must be always on his guard, and jealousy can have the most unwelcome consequences. Murasaki was the perfect companion, a toy for him to play with. He could not have been so free and uninhibited with a daughter of his own. There are restraints upon paternal intimacy. Yes, he had come upon a remarkable little treasure.

This Chapter
seems to have
hints of "Lolita,"
A man sexually
obsessed w/ an underaged
girl

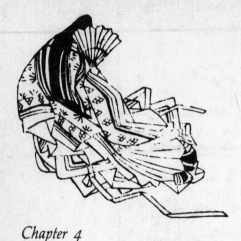

Chapter 4

An Autumn Excursion

The royal excursion to the Suzaku Palace took place toward the middle of the Tenth Month. The emperor's ladies lamented that they would not be present at what was certain to be a most remarkable concert. Distressed especially at the thought that Fujitsubo should be deprived of the pleasure, the emperor ordered a full rehearsal at the main palace. Genji and Tō no Chūjō danced "Waves of the Blue Ocean." Tō no Chūjō was a handsome youth who carried himself well, but beside Genji he was like a nondescript mountain shrub beside a blossoming cherry. In the bright evening light the music echoed yet more grandly through the palace and the excitement grew; and though the dance was a familiar one, Genji scarcely seemed of this world. As he intoned the lyrics his auditors could have believed they were listening to the Kalavinka bird of paradise. The emperor brushed away tears of delight, and there were tears in the eyes of all the princes and high courtiers as well. As Genji rearranged his dress at the end of his song and the orchestra took up again, he seemed to shine with an ever brighter light.

"Surely the gods above are struck dumb with admiration," Lady Kokiden, the mother of the crown prince, was heard to observe. "One is overpowered by such company."

Some of the young women thought her rather horrid.

To Fujitsubo it was all like a dream. How she wished that those unspeakable occurrences had not taken place. Then she might be as happy as the others.

She spent the night with the emperor.

"There was only one thing worth seeing," he said. " 'Waves of the Blue Ocean.' Do you not agree?"

"It was most unusual," she finally replied.

"Nor is Tō no Chūjō a mean dancer. There is something about the smallest gesture that tells of breeding. The professionals are very good in their way—one would certainly not wish to suggest otherwise—but they somehow lack freshness and spontaneity. When the rehearsals have been so fine one fears that the excursion itself will be a disappointment. But I would not for anything have wished you to miss it."

The next morning she had a letter from Genji. "And how did it all seem to you? I was in indescribable confusion. You will not welcome the question, I fear, but

> "Through the waving, dancing sleeves could you see a heart
>   So stormy that it wished but to be still?"

The image of the dancer was so vivid, it would seem, that she could not refuse to answer.

> "Of waving Chinese sleeves I cannot speak.
>   Each step, each motion, touched me to the heart.

"You may be sure that my thoughts were far from ordinary."

A rare treasure indeed. He smiled. With her knowledge of music and the dance and even, it would seem, things Chinese, she already spoke like an empress. He kept the letter spread before him as if it were a favorite sutra.

On the day of the excursion the emperor was attended by his whole court, the princes and the rest. The crown prince too was present. Music came from boats rowed out over the lake, and there was an infinite variety of Chinese and Korean dancing. Reed and string and drum echoed through the grounds. Because Genji's good looks had on the evening of the rehearsal filled him with foreboding, the emperor ordered sutras read in several temples. Most of the court understood and sympathized, but Kokiden thought it all rather ridiculous. The most renowned virtuosos from the high and middle court ranks were chosen for the flutists' circle. The director of the Chinese dances and the director of the Korean dances were both guards officers who held seats on the council of state. The dancers had for weeks been in monastic seclusion studying each motion under the direction of the most revered masters of the art.

The forty men in the flutists' circle played most marvelously. The sound of their flutes, mingled with the sighing of the pines, was like a wind coming down from deep mountains. "Waves of the Blue Ocean," among falling leaves of countless hues, had about it an almost frightening beauty. The maple branch in Genji's cap was somewhat bare and forlorn, most of the leaves having fallen, and seemed at odds with his handsome face. The

General of the Left* replaced it with several chrysanthemums which he brought from below the royal seat. The sun was about to set and a suspicion of an autumn shower rustled past as if the skies too were moved to tears. The chrysanthemums in Genji's cap, delicately touched by the frosts, gave new beauty to his form and his motions, no less remarkable today than on the day of the rehearsal. Then his dance was over, and a chill as if from another world passed over the assembly. Even unlettered menials, lost among deep branches and rocks, or those of them, in any event, who had some feeling for such things, were moved to tears. The Fourth Prince, still a child, son of Lady Shōkyōden,† danced "Autumn Winds," after "Waves of the Blue Ocean" the most interesting of the dances. All the others went almost unnoticed. Indeed complaints were heard that they marred what would otherwise have been a perfect day. Genji was that evening promoted to the First Order of the Third Rank, and Tō no Chūjō to the Second Order of the Fourth Rank, and other deserving courtiers were similarly rewarded, pulled upwards, it might be said, by Genji. He

---

*Otherwise unidentified.
†Neither mother nor son figures otherwise in the story.

brought pleasure to the eye and serenity to the heart, and made people wonder what bounty of grace might be his from former lives.

Fujitsubo had gone home to her family. Looking restlessly, as always, for a chance to see her, Genji was much criticized by his father-in-law's people at Sanjō. And rumors of the young Murasaki were out. Certain of the women at Sanjō let it be known that a new lady had been taken in at Nijō. Genji's wife was intensely displeased. It was most natural that she should be, for she did not of course know that the "lady" was a mere child. If she had complained to him openly, as most women would have done, he might have told her everything, and no doubt eased her jealousy. It was her arbitrary judgments that sent him wandering. She had no specific faults, no vices or blemishes, which he could point to. She had been the first lady in his life, and in an abstract way he admired and treasured her. Her feelings would change, he felt sure, once she was more familiar with his own. She was a perceptive woman, and the change was certain to come. She still occupied first place among his ladies.

Murasaki was by now thoroughly comfortable with him. She was maturing in appearance and manner, and yet there was artlessness in her way of clinging to him. Thinking it too early to let the people in the main hall know who she was, he kept her in one of the outer wings, which he had had fitted to perfection. He was constantly with her, tutoring her in the polite accomplishments and especially calligraphy. It was as if he had brought home a daughter who had spent her early years in another house. He had studied the qualifications of her stewards and assured himself that she would have everything she needed. Everyone in the house, save only Koremitsu, was consumed with curiosity. Her father still did not know of her whereabouts. Sometimes she would weep for her grandmother. Her mind was full of other things when Genji was with her, and often he stayed the night; but he had numerous other places to look in upon, and he was quite charmed by the wistfulness with which she would see him off in the evening. Sometimes he would spend two and three days at the palace and go from there to Sanjō. Finding a pensive Murasaki upon his return, he would feel as if he had taken in a little orphan. He no longer looked forward to his nocturnal wanderings with the same eagerness. Her granduncle the bishop kept himself informed of her affairs, and was pleased and puzzled. Genji sent most lavish offerings for memorial services.

Longing for news of Fujitsubo, still with her family, he paid a visit. Omyōbu, Chūnagon, Nakatsukasa, and others of her women received him, but the lady whom he really wanted to see kept him at a distance. He forced himself to make conversation. Prince Hyōbu, her brother and Murasaki's father, came in, having heard that Genji was on the premises. He was a man of great and gentle elegance, someone, thought Genji, who would interest him enormously were they of opposite sexes. Genji felt very near this prince so near the two ladies, and to the prince their conversation

seemed friendly and somehow significant as earlier conversations had not. How very handsome Genji was! Not dreaming that it was a prospective son-in-law he was addressing, he too was thinking how susceptible (for he was a susceptible man) he would be to Genji's charms if they were not of the same sex.

When, at dusk, the prince withdrew behind the blinds, Genji felt pangs of jealousy. In the old years he had followed his father behind those same blinds, and there addressed the lady. Now she was far away—though of course no one had wronged him, and he had no right to complain.

"I have not been good about visiting you," he said stiffly as he got up to leave. "Having no business with you, I have not wished to seem forward. It would give me great pleasure if you would let me know of any services I might perform for you."

Omyōbu could do nothing for him. Fujitsubo seemed to find his presence even more of a trial than before, and showed no sign of relenting. Sadly and uselessly the days went by. What a frail, fleeting union theirs had been!

Shōnagon, Murasaki's nurse, continued to marvel at the strange course their lives had taken. Perhaps some benign power had arranged it, the old nun having mentioned Murasaki in all her prayers. Not that everything was perfect. Genji's wife at Sanjō was a lady of the highest station, and other affairs, indeed too many of them, occupied him as well. Might not the girl face difficult times as she grew into womanhood? Yet he did seem fond of her as of none of the others, and her future seemed secure. The period of mourning for a maternal grandmother being set at three months, it was on New Year's Eve that Murasaki took off her mourning weeds. The old lady had been for her both mother and grandmother, however, and so she chose to limit herself to pale, unfigured pinks and lavenders and yellows. Pale colors seemed to suit her even better than rich ones.

"And do you feel all grown up, now that a new year has come?" Smiling, radiating youthful charm, Genji looked in upon her. He was on his way to the morning festivities at court.

She had already taken out her dolls and was busy seeing to their needs. All manner of furnishings and accessories were laid out on a yard-high shelf. Dollhouses threatened to overflow the room.

"Inuki knocked everything over chasing out devils last night and broke this." It was a serious matter. "I'm gluing it."

"Yes, she really is very clumsy, that Inuki. We'll ask someone to repair it for you. But today you must not cry. Crying is the worst way to begin a new year."

And he went out, his retinue so grand that it overflowed the wide grounds. The women watched from the veranda, the girl with them. She set out a Genji among her dolls and saw him off to court.

"This year you must try to be just a little more grown up," said Shōnagon. "Ten years old, no, even more, and still you play with dolls. It will not do. You have a nice husband, and you must try to calm down and be a little more wifely. Why, you fly into a tantrum even when we try to brush your hair." A proper shaming was among Shōnagon's methods.

So she had herself a nice husband, thought Murasaki. The husbands of these women were none of them handsome men, and hers was so very young and handsome. The thought came to her now for the first time, evidence that, for all this play with dolls, she was growing up. It sometimes puzzled her women that she should still be such a child. It did not occur to them that she was in fact not yet a wife.

From the palace Genji went to Sanjō. His wife, as always, showed no suggestion of warmth or affection; and as always he was uncomfortable.

"How pleasant if this year you could manage to be a little friendlier."

But since she had heard of his new lady she had become more distant than ever. She was convinced that the other was now first among his ladies, and no doubt she was as uncomfortable as he. But when he jokingly sought to make it seem that nothing was amiss, she had to answer, if reluctantly. Everything she said was uniquely, indefinably elegant. She was four years his senior and made him feel like a stripling. Where, he asked, was he to find a flaw in this perfection? Yet he seemed determined to anger her with his other affairs. She was a proud lady, the single and treasured daughter, by a princess, of a minister who overshadowed the other grandees, and she was not prepared to tolerate the smallest discourtesy. And here he was behaving as if these proud ways were his to make over. They were completely at cross purposes, he and she.

Though her father too resented Genji's other affairs, he forgot his annoyance when Genji was here beside him, and no service seemed too great or too small. As Genji prepared to leave for court the next day, the minister looked in upon him, bringing a famous belt for him to wear with his court dress, straightening his train, as much as helping him into his shoes. One almost felt something pathetic in this eagerness.

"I'll wear it to His Majesty's family dinner later in the month,"* said Genji.

"There are other belts that would do far more honor to such an occasion." The minister insisted that he wear it. "It is a little unusual, that is all."

Sometimes it was as if being of service to Genji were his whole life. There could be no greater pleasure than having such a son and brother, little though the Sanjō family saw of him.

Genji did not pay many New Year calls. He called upon his father, the crown prince, the old emperor,† and, finally, Fujitsubo, still with her family. Her women thought him handsomer than ever. Yes, each year, as he matured, his good looks produced a stronger shudder of delight and foreboding. Fujitsubo was assailed by innumerable conflicting thoughts.

The Twelfth Month, when she was to have been delivered of her child, had passed uneventfully. Surely it would be this month, said her women, and at court everything was in readiness; but the First Month too passed without event. She was greatly troubled by rumors that she had fallen under a malign influence. Her worries had made her physically ill and she began to wonder if the end was in sight. More and more certain as time passed that the child was his, Genji quietly commissioned services in various temples. More keenly aware than most of the evanescence of things, he now found added to his worries a fear that he would not see her again. Finally toward the end of the Second Month she bore a prince, and the jubilation was unbounded at court and at her family palace. She had not joined the emperor in praying that she be granted a long life, and yet she did not want to please Kokiden, an echo of whose curses had reached her. The will to live returned, and little by little she recovered.

The emperor wanted to see his little son the earliest day possible. Genji, filled with his own secret paternal solicitude, visited Fujitsubo at a time when he judged she would not have other visitors.

*The Naien, late in the First Month, graced by the composition of Chinese poetry.
†Perhaps the father of the reigning emperor, he is mentioned nowhere else. The reign of the present emperor seems to have been preceded by that of Fujitsubo's father, now dead.

guilty about affair

"Father is extremely anxious to see the child. Perhaps I might have a look at him first and present a report."

She refused his request, as of course she had every right to do. "He is still very shriveled and ugly."

There was no doubt that the child bore a marked, indeed a rather wonderful, resemblance to Genji. Fujitsubo was tormented by feelings of guilt and apprehension. Surely everyone who saw the child would guess the awful truth and damn her for it. People were always happy to seek out the smallest and most trivial of misdeeds. Hers had not been trivial, and dreadful rumors must surely be going the rounds. Had ever a woman been more sorely tried?

Genji occasionally saw Omyōbu and pleaded that she intercede for him; but there was nothing she could do.

"This insistence, my lord, is very trying," she said, at his constant and passionate pleas to see the child. "You will have chances enough later." Yet secretly she was as unhappy as he was.

"In what world, I wonder, will I again be allowed to see her?" The heart of the matter was too delicate to touch upon.

"What legacy do we bring from former lives
    That loneliness should be our lot in this one?

"I do not understand. I do not understand at all."

His tears brought her to the point of tears herself. Knowing how unhappy her lady was, she could not bring herself to turn him brusquely away.

"Sad at seeing the child, sad at not seeing.
    The heart of the father, the mother, lost in darkness."*

And she added softly: "There seems to be no lessening of the pain for either of you."

She saw him off, quite unable to help him. Her lady had said that because of the danger of gossip she could not receive him again, and she no longer behaved toward Omyōbu with the old affection. She behaved correctly, it was true, and did nothing that might attract attention, but Omyōbu had done things to displease her. Omyōbu was very sorry for them.

In the Fourth Month the little prince was brought to the palace. Advanced for his age both mentally and physically, he was already able to sit up and to right himself when he rolled over. He was strikingly like Genji. Unaware of the truth, the emperor would say to himself that people of remarkable good looks did have a way of looking alike. He doted upon the child. He had similarly doted upon Genji, but, because of strong opposition—and how deeply he regretted the fact—had been unable to

*See note‡, page 7.

make him crown prince. The regret increased as Genji, now a commoner, improved in looks and in accomplishments. And now a lady of the highest birth had borne the emperor another radiant son. The infant was for him an unflawed jewel, for Fujitsubo a source of boundless guilt and foreboding.

One day, as he often did, Genji was enjoying music in Fujitsubo's apartments. The emperor came out with the little boy in his arms.

"I have had many sons, but you were the only one I paid a great deal of attention to when you were this small. Perhaps it is the memory of those days that makes me think he looks like you. Is it that all children look alike when they are very young?" He made no attempt to hide his pleasure in the child.

Genji felt himself flushing crimson. He was frightened and awed and pleased and touched, all at the same time, and there were tears in his eyes. Laughing and babbling, the child was so beautiful as to arouse fears that he would not be long in this world. If indeed he resembled the child, thought Genji, then he must be very handsome. He must take better care of himself. (He seemed a little self-satisfied at times.) Fujitsubo was in such acute discomfort that she felt herself breaking into a cold sweat. Eager though he had been to see the child, Genji left in great agitation.

He returned to Nijō, thinking that when the agitation had subsided he would proceed to Sanjō and pay his wife a visit. In near the verandas the garden was a rich green, dotted with wild carnations. He broke a few off and sent them to Omyōbu, and it would seem that he also sent a long and detailed letter, including this message for her lady:

"I think of it as him, this wild carnation,
     And yet it is weighted with tears as with the dew.

" 'I know that when it blossoms at my hedge'*—but could any two be as much and as little to each other as we have been?"

Perhaps because the occasion seemed right, Omyōbu showed the letter to her lady.

"Do please answer him," she said, "if with something of no more weight than the dust on these petals."

Herself prey to violent emotions, Fujitsubo did send back an answer, a brief and fragmentary one, in a very faint hand:

"It serves you ill, the Japanese carnation,
     To make you weep. Yet I shall not forsake it."

Pleased with her success, Omyōbu delivered the note. Genji was looking forlornly out at the garden, certain that as always there would be

---

* Anonymous, *Gosenshū* 199:

> May it blossom quickly at my hedge,
> This wild carnation, that I may think of you.

silence. His heart jumped at the sight of Omyōbu and there were tears of joy in his eyes.

This moping, he decided, did no good. He went to the west wing in search of company. Rumpled and wild-haired, he played a soft strain on a flute as he came into Murasaki's room. She was leaning against an armrest, demure and pretty, like a wild carnation, he thought, with the dew fresh upon it. She was charming.

Annoyed that he had not come immediately, she turned away.

"Come here," he said, kneeling at the veranda.

She did not stir. "'Like the grasses at full tide,'"* she said softly, her sleeve over her mouth. He thought it very clever of her.

"That was unkind. So you have already learned to complain? I would not wish you to tire of me, you see, as they say the fishermen tire of the sea grasses at Ise."†

*Sakanoue no Iratsume, *Manyōshū* 1394:

> Are you hidden like the grasses at full tide,
> That so often I sigh for you, so seldom see you?

†Anonymous, *Kokinshū* 683:

> I might weary of you, so often would I see you.
> As at Ise they see each day the same sea grasses.

He had someone bring a thirteen-stringed koto.

"You must be careful. The second string breaks easily and we would not want to have to change it." And he lowered it to the *hyōjō* mode.*

After plucking a few notes to see that it was in tune, he pushed it toward her. No longer able to be angry, she played for him, briefly and very competently. He thought her delightful as she leaned forward to press a string with her left hand. He took out a flute and she had a music lesson. Very quick, she could repeat a difficult melody after but a single hearing. Yes, he thought, she was bright and amiable, everything he could have wished for. "Hosoroguseri" made a pretty duet, despite its outlandish name.† She was very young but she had a fine sense for music. Lamps were brought and they looked at pictures together. Since he had said that he would be going out, his men coughed nervously, to warn him of the time. If he did not hurry it would be raining, one of them said. Murasaki was suddenly a forlorn little figure. She put aside the pictures and lay with her face hidden in a pillow.

"Do you miss me when I am away?" He stroked the hair that fell luxuriantly over her shoulders.

She nodded a quick, emphatic nod.

"And I miss you. I can hardly bear to be away from you for a single day. But we must not make too much of these things. You are still a child, and there is a jealous and difficult lady whom I would rather not offend. I must go on visiting her, but when you are grown up I will not leave you ever. It is because I am thinking of all the years we will be together that I want to be on good terms with her."

His solemn manner dispelled her gloom but made her rather uncomfortable. She did not answer. Her head pillowed on his knee, she was presently asleep.

He told the women that he would not after all be going out. His retinue having departed, he ordered dinner and roused the girl.

"I am not going," he said.

She sat down beside him, happy again. She ate very little.

"Suppose we go to bed, then, if you aren't going out." She was still afraid he might leave her.

He already knew how difficult it would be when the time came for the final parting.

Everyone of course knew how many nights he was now spending at home. The intelligence reached his father-in-law's house at Sanjō.

"How very odd. Who might she be?" said the women. "We have not been able to find out. No one of very good breeding, you may be sure, to judge from the way she clings to him and presumes upon his affection. Probably someone he ran into at court and lost his senses over, and now he has hidden her away because he is ashamed to have people see her. But the oddest thing is that she's still a child."

*The tonic is E.
†It is the name of a plumed grass.

"I am sorry to learn that the Minister of the Left is unhappy with you," the emperor said to Genji. "You cannot be so young and innocent as to be unaware of all he has done for you since you were a very small boy. He has been completely devoted to you. Must you repay him by insulting him?"

It was an august reproach which Genji was unable to answer.

The emperor was suddenly sorry for him. It was clear that he was not happy with his wife. "I have heard no rumors, it is true, that you are promiscuous, that you have scattered your affections too liberally here at court and elsewhere. He must have stumbled upon some secret."

The emperor still enjoyed the company of pretty women. He preferred the pretty ones even among chambermaids and seamstresses, and all the ranks of his court were filled with the best-favored women to be found. Genji would joke with one and another of them, and few were of a mind to keep him at a distance. Someone among them would remark coyly that perhaps he did not like women; but, no doubt because she offered no novelty, he would answer so as not to give offense and refuse to be tempted. To some this moderation did not seem a virtue.

There was a lady of rather advanced years called Naishi. She was wellborn, talented, cultivated, and widely respected; but in matters of the heart she was not very discriminating. Genji had struck up relations, interested that her wanton ways should be so perdurable, and was taken somewhat aback at the warm welcome he received. He continued to be interested all the same and had arranged a rendezvous. Not wanting the world to see him as the boy lover of an aged lady, he had turned away further invitations. She was of course resentful.

One morning when she had finished dressing the emperor's hair and the emperor had withdrawn to change clothes, she found herself alone with Genji. She was bedecked and painted to allure, every detail urging him forward. Genji was dubious of this superannuated coquetry, but curious to see what she would do next. He tugged at her apron. She turned around, a gaudy fan hiding her face, a sidelong glance—alas, the eyelids were dark and muddy—emerging from above it. Her hair, which of course the fan could not hide, was rough and stringy. A very poorly chosen fan for an old lady, he thought, giving her his and taking it from her. So bright a red that his own face, he was sure, must be red from the reflection, it was decorated with a gold painting of a tall grove. In a corner, in a hand that was old-fashioned but not displeasingly so, was a line of poetry: "Withered is the grass of Oaraki."* Of all the poems she could have chosen!

"What you mean, I am sure, is that your grove is summer lodging for the cuckoo."†

They talked for a time. Genji was nervous lest they be seen, but Naishi was unperturbed.

> "Sere and withered though these grasses be,
> They are ready for your pony, should you come."

She was really too aggressive.

> "Were mine to part the low bamboo at your grove,
> It would fear to be driven away by other ponies.

"And that would not do at all."

He started to leave, but she caught at his sleeve. "No one has ever been so rude to me, no one. At my age I might expect a little courtesy."

These angry tears, he might have said, did not become an old lady.

"I will write. You have been on my mind a great deal." He tried to shake her off but she followed after.

" 'As the pillar of the bridge—' "‡ she said reproachfully.

*Anonymous, *Kokinshū* 892:

> Withered is the grass of Oaraki,
> No pony comes for it, no harvester.

†Saneakira, in his "private collection":

> The cuckoo calls, to tell us that the grove
> Of Oaraki is its summer lodging.

‡Anonymous, *Shinchokusenshū* 1285:

> Rotting as the pillar of the bridge,
> I think of you, and so the years go by.

Having finished dressing, the emperor looked in from the next room. He was amused. They were a most improbable couple.

"People complain that you show too little interest in romantic things," he laughed, "but I see that you have your ways."

Naishi, though much discommoded, did not protest with great vehemence. There are those who do not dislike wrong rumors if they are about the right men.

The ladies of the palace were beginning to talk of the affair, a most surprising one, they said. Tō no Chūjō heard of it. He had thought his own affairs varied, but the possibility of a liaison with an old woman had not occurred to him. An inexhaustibly amorous old woman might be rather fun. He arranged his own rendezvous. He too was very handsome, and Naishi thought him not at all poor consolation for the loss of Genji. Yet (one finds it hard to condone such greed) Genji was the one she really wanted.

Since Tō no Chūjō was secretive, Genji did not know that he had been replaced. Whenever Naishi caught sight of him she showered him with reproaches. He pitied her in her declining years and would have liked to do something for her, but was not inclined to trouble himself greatly.

One evening in the cool after a shower he was strolling past the Ummeiden Pavilion. Naishi was playing on her lute, most appealingly. She was a unique mistress of the instrument, invited sometimes to join men in concerts before the emperor. Unrequited love gave her playing tonight an especial poignancy.

"Shall I marry the melon farmer?"* she was singing, in very good voice.

Though not happy at the thought of having a melon farmer supplant him, he stopped to listen. Might the song of the maiden of E-chou, long ago, have had the same plaintive appeal?† Naishi seemed to have fallen into a meditative silence. Humming "The Eastern Cottage,"‡ he came up to her door. She joined in as he sang: "Open my door and come in." Few women would have been so bold.

> "No one waits in the rain at my eastern cottage.
> Wet are the sleeves of the one who waits within."

*"Yamashiro," a Saibara:

> The melon farmer wants me for his wife.
> Shall I marry the melon farmer
> Before the melons grow?

†Po Chü-i, Collected Works, X, "On Hearing a Song in the Night."
‡A Saibara:

> He: I am wet from the rain from the eaves of your eastern cottage.
> Will you not open the door and let me in?
> She: I would lock it if I had a bolt and lock.
> Open my door and come in. Am I anyone's wife?

It did not seem right, he thought, that he should be the victim of such reproaches. Why had she not yet, after all these years, learned patience?

"On closer terms with the eaves of your eastern cottage
I would not be, for someone is there before me."

He would have preferred to move on, but, remembering his manners, decided to accept her invitation. For a time they exchanged pleasant banter. All very novel, thought Genji.

Tō no Chūjō had long resented Genji's self-righteous way of chiding him for his own adventures. The proper face Genji showed the world seemed to hide rather a lot. Tō no Chūjō had been on the watch for an opportunity to give his friend a little of what he deserved. Now it had come. The sanctimonious one would now be taught a lesson.

It was late, and a chilly wind had come up. Genji had dozed off, it seemed. Tō no Chūjō slipped into the room. Too nervous to have more than dozed off, Genji heard him, but did not suspect who it would be. The superintendent of palace repairs, he guessed, was still visiting her. Not for the world would he have had the old man catch him in the company of the old woman.

"This is a fine thing. I'm going. The spider surely told you to expect him,* and you didn't tell me."

He hastily gathered his clothes and hid behind a screen. Fighting back laughter, Tō no Chūjō gave the screen an unnecessarily loud thump and folded it back. Naishi had indulged her amorous ways over long years and had had similarly disconcerting experiences often enough before. What did this person have in mind? What did he mean to do to her Genji? She fluttered about seeking to restrain the intruder. Still ignorant of the latter's identity, Genji thought of headlong flight; but then he thought of his own retreating figure, robes in disorder, cap all askew. Silently and wrathfully, Tō no Chūjō was brandishing a long sword.

"Please, sir, please."

Naishi knelt before him wringing her hands. He could hardly control the urge to laugh. Her youthful smartness had taken a great deal of contriving, but she was after all nearly sixty. She was ridiculous, hopping back and forth between two handsome young men. Tō no Chūjō was playing his role too energetically. Genji guessed who he was. He guessed too that this fury had to do with the fact that he was himself known. It all seemed very stupid and very funny. He gave the arm wielding the sword a stout pinch and Tō no Chūjō finally surrendered to laughter.

"You are insane," said Genji. "And these jokes of yours are dangerous. Let me have my clothes, if you will."

But Tō no Chūjō refused to surrender them.

"Well, then, let's be undressed together." Genji undid his friend's belt

---

*A busy spider was thought to give tidings of the approach of a lover.

and sought to pull off his clothes, and a seam was rent at the shoulder of a disputed robe.

> "You may not want the world to know of it,
> But forth it bursts from this connubial robe.

"It is not your wish, I am sure, that all the world should notice."*
Genji replied:

"You taunt me, sir, with being a spectacle
When you know full well that your own summer robes are showy."

Somewhat rumpled, they went off together, the best of friends. But as Genji went to bed he felt that he had been the loser, caught in such a very compromising position.

An outraged Naishi came the next morning to return a belt and a pair of trousers. She handed Genji a note:

*Anonymous, *Kokin Rokujō, Zoku Kokka Taikan* 34107:

> I keep them out of sight, my robes of crimson,
> It is not my wish that all the world should notice.

"I need not comment now upon my feelings.
The waves that came in together went out together,

leaving a dry river bed."

It was an inappropriate reproof after the predicament in which she
had placed him, thought Genji, and yet he could imagine how upset she
must be. This was his reply:

"I shall not complain of the wave that came raging in,
But of the welcoming strand I must complain."

The belt was Tō no Chūjō's, of a color too dark to go with Genji's robe.
He saw that he had lost a length of sleeve. A most unseemly performance.
People who wandered the way of love found themselves in mad situations.
With that thought he quelled his ardor.

On duty in the palace, Tō no Chūjō had the missing length of sleeve
wrapped and returned, with the suggestion that it be restored to its proper
place. Genji would have liked to know when he had succeeded in making off
with the sleeve. It was some comfort that he had the belt.

He returned it, wrapped in matching paper, with this poem:

"Not to be charged with having taken your take,
I return this belt of indigo undamaged."

An answer came immediately:

"I doubted not that you took my indigo belt,
And charge you now with taking the lady too.

You will pay for it, sir, one day."

Both were at court that afternoon. Tō no Chūjō had to smile at Genji's
cool aloofness as he sorted out petitions and orders, and his own businesslike efficiency was as amusing to Genji. They exchanged frequent smiles.

Tō no Chūjō came up to Genji when no one else was near. "You have
had enough, I hope," he said, with a fierce sidelong glance, "of these
clandestine adventures?"

"Why, pray, should I? The chief hurt was to you who were not invited
—and it matters a great deal, since you do so love each other."* And they
made a bond of silence, a vow that they would behave like the Know-
Nothing River.†

Tō no Chūjō lost no opportunity to remind Genji of the incident. And
it had all been because of that troublesome old woman, thought Genji. He

---

*Apparently a deliberate misquotation of a poem by Ise, *Kokin Rokujō, Zoku Kokka Taikan* 32960:

> The rumors are thick as the sea grass the fishermen gather.
> It matters not, for we do so love each other.

†Anonymous, *Kokinshū* 1108:

> If they should ask about us, O Know-Nothing River,
> Be true to your name, and merely say: "I wonder."

would not again make such a mistake. It was a trial to him that she continued, all girlishly, to make known her resentment. Tō no Chūjō did not tell his sister, Genji's wife, of the affair, but he did want to keep it in reserve. Because he was his father's favorite, Genji was treated respectfully even by princes whose mothers were of the highest rank, and only Tō no Chūjō refused to be awed by him. Indeed he was prepared to contest every small point. He and his sister, alone among the minister's children, had the emperor's sister for their mother. Genji belonged, it was true, to the royal family, but the son of the emperor's sister and of his favorite minister did not feel that he had to defer to anyone; and it was impossible to deny that he was a very splendid young gentleman. The rivalry between the two produced other amusing stories, I am sure, but it would be tedious to collect and recount them.

In the Seventh Month, Fujitsubo was made empress. Genji was given a seat on the council of state. Making plans for his abdication, the emperor wanted to name Fujitsubo's son crown prince. The child had no strong backing, however. His uncles were all princes of the blood, and it was not for them to take command of public affairs. The emperor therefore wanted Fujitsubo in an unassailable position from which to promote her son's career.

Kokiden's anger, most naturally, reached new peaks of intensity.

"You needn't be in such a stir," said the emperor. "Our son's day is coming, and no one will be in a position to challenge you."

As always, people talked. It was not an easy thing, in naming an empress, to pass over a lady who had for more than twenty years been the mother of the crown prince. Genji was in attendance the night Fujitsubo made her formal appearance as empress. Among His Majesty's ladies she alone was the daughter of an empress, and she was herself a flawless jewel; but for one man, at least, it was not an occasion for gladness. With anguish he thought of the lady inside the ceremonial palanquin. She would now be quite beyond his reach.

"I see her disappear behind the clouds
        And am left to grope my way through deepest darkness."

The days and months passed, and the little prince was becoming the mirror image of Genji. Though Fujitsubo was in constant terror, it appeared that no one had guessed the truth. How, people asked, could someone who was not Genji yet be as handsome as Genji? They were, Genji and the little prince, like the sun and moon side by side in the heavens.

Chapter 5

The Festival of the Cherry Blossoms

Towards the end of the Second Month, the festival of the cherry blossoms took place in the Grand Hall. The empress and the crown prince were seated to the left and right of the throne. This arrangement of course displeased Kokiden, but she put in an appearance all the same, unable to let such an occasion pass. It was a beautiful day. The sky was clear, birds were singing. Adepts at Chinese poetry, princes and high courtiers and others, drew lots to fix the rhyme schemes for their poems.

"I have drawn 'spring,'" said Genji, his voice finely resonant in even so brief a statement.

Tō no Chūjō might have been disconcerted at something in the eyes of the assembly as they turned from Genji to him, but he was calm and poised, and his voice as he announced his rhyme was almost as distinguished as Genji's. Several of the high courtiers seemed reluctant to follow the two, and the lesser courtiers were more reluctant still. They came stiffly out into the radiant garden, awed by the company in which they found themselves—for both the emperor and the crown prince were connoisseurs of poetry, and it was a time when superior poets were numerous. To produce a Chinese poem is never an easy task, but for them it seemed positive torture. Then there were the great professors who took such occasions in their stride, though their court dress may have been a little shabby. It was pleasant to observe the emperor's interest in all these varied sorts of people.

The emperor had of course ordered the concert to be planned with the greatest care. "Spring Warbler," which came as the sun was setting, was uncommonly fine. Remembering how Genji had danced at the autumn excursion, the crown prince himself presented a sprig of blossoms for his cap and pressed him so hard to dance that he could not refuse. Though he danced only a very brief passage, the quiet waving of his sleeves as he came to the climax was incomparable. The Minister of the Left forgot his anger at his negligent son-in-law. There were tears in his eyes.

"Where is Tō no Chūjō?" asked the emperor. "Have him come immediately."

Tō no Chūjō, whose dance was "Garden of Willows and Flowers," danced with more careful and deliberate art than had Genji, perhaps because he had been prepared for the royal summons. It was so interesting a performance that the emperor presented him with a robe—a most gratifying sign of royal approval, everyone agreed.

Other high courtiers danced, in no fixed order, but as it was growing dark one could not easily tell who were the better dancers. The poems were read. Genji's was so remarkable that the reader paused to comment upon each line. The professors were deeply moved. Since Genji was for the emperor a shining light, the poem could not fail to move him too. As for the empress, she wondered how Kokiden could so hate the youth—and reflected on her own misfortune in being so strangely drawn to him.

> "Could I see the blossom as other blossoms,
> Then would there be no dew to cloud my heart."

She recited it silently to herself. How then did it go the rounds and presently reach me?

The festivities ended late in the night.

The courtiers went their ways, the empress and the crown prince departed, all was quiet. The moon came out more brightly. It asked admiring, thought Genji, a trifle drunk. The ladies in night attendance upon the emperor would be asleep. Expecting no visitors, his own lady might have left a door open a crack. He went quietly up to her apartments, but the door of the one whom he might ask to show him in was tightly closed. He sighed. Still not ready to give up, he made his way to the gallery by Kokiden's pavilion. The third door from the north was open. Kokiden herself was with the emperor, and her rooms were almost deserted. The hinged door at the far corner was open too. All was silent. It was thus, he thought, that a lady invited her downfall. He slipped across the gallery and up to the door of the main room and looked inside. Everyone seemed to be asleep.

" 'What can compare with a misty moon of spring?' "* It was a sweet young voice, so delicate that its owner could be no ordinary serving woman.

She came (could he believe it?) to the door. Delighted, he caught at her sleeve.

"Who are you?" She was frightened.

"There is nothing to be afraid of.

> "Late in the night we enjoy a misty moon.
> There is nothing misty about the bond between us."

Quickly and lightly he lifted her down to the gallery and slid the door closed. Her surprise pleased him enormously.

Trembling, she called for help.

---

*Oe Chisato, *Shinkokinshū* 55:

> What can vie with a misty moon of spring,
> Shining dimly, yet not clouded over?

The poem has been misquoted, probably intentionally, to make it sound less Chinese and therefore more feminine.

"It will do you no good. I am always allowed my way. Just be quiet, if you will, please."

She recognized his voice and was somewhat reassured. Though of course upset, she evidently did not wish him to think her wanting in good manners. It may have been because he was still a little drunk that he could not admit the possibility of letting her go; and she, young and irresolute, did not know how to send him on his way. He was delighted with her, but also very nervous, for dawn was approaching. She was in an agony of apprehension lest they be seen.

"You must tell me who you are," he said. "How can I write to you if you do not? You surely don't think I mean to let matters stand as they are?"

> "Were the lonely one to vanish quite away,
> Would you go to the grassy moors to ask her name?"

Her voice had a softly plaintive quality.
"I did not express myself well.

> "I wish to know whose dewy lodge it is
> Ere winds blow past the bamboo-tangled moor.*

"Only one thing, a cold welcome, could destroy my eagerness to visit. Do you perhaps have some diversionary tactic in mind?"

They exchanged fans and he was on his way. Even as he spoke a stream of women was moving in and out of Kokiden's rooms. There were women in his own rooms too, some of them now awake. Pretending to be asleep, they poked one another and exchanged whispered remarks about the diligence with which he pursued these night adventures.

He was unable to sleep. What a beautiful girl! One of Kokiden's younger sisters, no doubt. Perhaps the fifth or sixth daughter of the family, since she had seemed to know so little about men? He had heard that both the fourth daughter, to whom Tō no Chūjō was uncomfortably married, and Prince Hotaru's wife were great beauties,† and thought that the encounter might have been more interesting had the lady been one of the older sisters. He rather hoped she was not the sixth daughter, whom the minister had thoughts of marrying to the crown prince. The trouble was that he had no way of being sure. It had not seemed that she wanted the affair to end with but the one meeting. Why then had she not told him how he might write to her? These thoughts and others suggest that he was much interested. He thought too of Fujitsubo's pavilion, and how much more mysterious and inaccessible it was, indeed how uniquely so.

He had a lesser spring banquet with which to amuse himself that day. He played the thirteen-stringed koto, his performance if anything subtler

---

*"I would like to know who you are now, before rumors spread abroad."
†The crown prince, Genji, and Prince Hotaru are all brothers.

and richer than that of the day before. Fujitsubo went to the emperor's apartments at dawn.

Genji was on tenterhooks, wondering whether the lady he had seen in the dawn moonlight would be leaving the palace. He sent Yoshikiyo and Koremitsu, who let nothing escape them, to keep watch; and when, as he was leaving the royal presence, he had their report, his agitation increased.

"Some carriages that had been kept out of sight left just now by the north gate. Two of Kokiden's brothers and several other members of the family saw them off; so we gathered that the ladies must be part of the family too. They were ladies of some importance, in any case—that much was clear. There were three carriages in all."

How might he learn which of the sisters he had become friends with? Supposing her father were to learn of the affair and welcome him gladly into the family—he had not seen enough of the lady to be sure that the prospect delighted him. Yet he did want very much to know who she was. He sat looking out at the garden.

Murasaki would be gloomy and bored, he feared, for he had not visited her in some days. He looked at the fan he had received in the dawn moonlight. It was a "three-ply cherry."* The painting on the more richly colored side, a misty moon reflected on water, was not remarkable, but the fan, well used, was a memento to stir longing. He remembered with especial tenderness the poem about the grassy moors.

He jotted down a poem beside the misty moon:

> "I had not known the sudden loneliness
> Of having it vanish, the moon in the sky of dawn."

He had been neglecting the Sanjō mansion of his father-in-law for rather a long time, but Murasaki was more on his mind. He must go comfort her. She pleased him more, she seemed prettier and cleverer and more amiable, each time he saw her. He was congratulating himself that his hopes of shaping her into his ideal might not prove entirely unrealistic. Yet he had misgivings—very unsettling ones, it must be said—lest by training her himself he put her too much at ease with men. He told her the latest court gossip and they had a music lesson. So he was going out again —she was sorry, as always, to see him go, but she no longer clung to him as she once had.

At Sanjō it was the usual thing: his wife kept him waiting. In his boredom he thought of this and that. Pulling a koto to him, he casually plucked out a tune. "No nights of soft sleep,"† he sang, to his own accompaniment.

---

*A somewhat mysterious object. One theory holds it to have had three-ply end ribs covered with pink paper.

†"The River Nuki," a Saibara:

> No nights of soft sleep,
> Soft as the reed pillow,
> The waves of the river Nuki.
> My father comes between us.

The minister came for a talk about the recent pleasurable events.

"I am very old, and I have served through four illustrious reigns, but never have I known an occasion that has added so many years to my life. Such clever, witty poems, such fine music and dancing—you are on good terms with the great performers who so abound in our day, and you arrange things with such marvelous skill. Even we aged ones felt like cutting a caper or two."

"The marvelous skill of which you speak, sir, amounts to nothing at all, only a word here and there. It is a matter of knowing where to ask. 'Garden of Willows and Flowers' was much the best thing, I thought, a performance to go down as a model for all the ages. And what a memorable day it would have been, what an honor for our age, if in the advancing spring of your life you had followed your impulse and danced for us."

Soon Tō no Chūjō and his brothers, leaning casually against the veranda railings, were in fine concert on their favorite instruments.

The lady of that dawn encounter, remembering the evanescent dream, was sunk in sad thoughts. Her father's plans to give her to the crown prince in the Fourth Month were a source of great distress. As for Genji, he was not without devices for searching her out, but he did not know which of Kokiden's sisters she was, and he did not wish to become involved with that unfriendly family.

Late in the Fourth Month the princes and high courtiers gathered at the mansion of the Minister of the Right, Kokiden's father, for an archery meet. It was followed immediately by a wisteria banquet. Though the cherry blossoms had for the most part fallen, two trees, perhaps having learned that mountain cherries do well to bloom late,* were at their belated best. The minister's mansion had been rebuilt and beautifully refurnished for the initiation ceremonies of the princesses his granddaughters. It was in the ornate style its owner preferred, everything in the latest fashion.

Seeing Genji in the palace one day, the minister had invited him to the festivities. Genji would have preferred to stay away, but the affair seemed certain to languish without him. The minister sent one of his sons, a guards officer, with a message:

"If these blossoms of mine were of the common sort,
    Would I press you so to come and look upon them?"

Genji showed the poem to his father.

"He seems very pleased with his flowers," laughed the emperor. "But you must go immediately. He has, after all, sent a special invitation. It is in his house that the princesses your sisters are being reared. You are scarcely a stranger."

Genji dressed with great care. It was almost dark when he finally presented himself. He wore a robe of a thin white Chinese damask with

*Ise, *Kokinshū* 68:

These mountain cherries with no one to look upon them:
Might they not bloom when all the others have fallen?

a red lining and under it a very long train of magenta. Altogether the dashing young prince, he added something new to the assembly that so cordially received him, for the other guests were more formally clad. He quite overwhelmed the blossoms, in a sense spoiling the party, and played beautifully on several instruments. Late in the evening he got up, pretending to be drunk. The first and third princesses were living in the main hall. He went to the east veranda and leaned against a door. The shutters were raised and women were gathered at the southwest corner, where the wisteria was in bloom. Their sleeves were pushed somewhat ostentatiously out from under blinds, as at a New Year's concert. All rather overdone, he thought, and he could not help thinking too of Fujitsubo's reticence.

"I was not feeling well in the first place, and they plied me with drink. I know I shouldn't, but might I ask you to hide me?" He raised the blind at the corner door.

"Please, dear sir, this will not do. It is for us beggars to ask such favors of you fine gentlemen." Though of no overwhelming dignity, the women were most certainly not common.

Incense hung heavily in the air and the rustling of silk was bright and lively. Because the princesses seemed to prefer modern things, the scene may perhaps have been wanting in mysterious shadows.

The time and place were hardly appropriate for a flirtation, and yet his interest was aroused. Which would be the lady of the misty moon?

"A most awful thing has happened," he said playfully. "Someone has stolen my fan."* He sat leaning against a pillar.

"What curious things that Korean does do." The lady who thus deftly returned his allusion did not seem to know about the exchange of fans.

Catching a sigh from another lady, he leaned forward and took her hand.

> "I wander lost on Arrow Mount and ask:
> May I not see the moon I saw so briefly?

"Or must I continue to wander?"
It seemed that she could not remain silent:

> "Only the flighty, the less than serious ones,
> Are left in the skies when the longbow moon is gone."†

It was the same voice. He was delighted. And yet—

---

*An oblique reference, the words for "fan" and "sash" being similar, to the Saibara "Ishikawa":

> A most awful thing has happened.
> Someone has stolen my sash.
> 'Tis the Korean of Ishikawa.

†Both poems contain elaborate allusions to archery.

Chapter 6

Heartvine

With the new reign Genji's career languished, and since he must be the more discreet about his romantic adventures as he rose in rank, he had less to amuse him. Everywhere there were complaints about his aloofness.

As if to punish him, there was one lady who continued to cause him pain with her own aloofness. Fujitsubo saw more of the old emperor, now abdicated, than ever. She was always at his side, almost as if she were a common housewife. Annoyed at this state of affairs, Kokiden did not follow the old emperor when he left the main palace. Fujitsubo was happy and secure. The concerts in the old emperor's palace attracted the attention of the whole court, and altogether life was happier for the two of them than while he had reigned. Only one thing was lacking: he greatly missed the crown prince, Fujitsubo's son, and worried that he had no strong backers. Genji, he said, must be the boy's adviser and guardian. Genji was both pleased and embarrassed.

And there was the matter of the lady at Rokujō. With the change of reigns, her daughter, who was also the daughter of the late crown prince, had been appointed high priestess of the Ise Shrine. No longer trusting Genji's affections, the Rokujō lady had been thinking that, making the girl's youth her excuse, she too would go to Ise.

The old emperor heard of her plans. "The crown prince was so very fond of her," he said to Genji, in open displeasure. "It is sad that you should have made light of her, as if she were any ordinary woman. I think of the high priestess as one of my own children, and you should be good to her mother, for my sake and for the sake of the dead prince. It does you no good to abandon yourself to these affairs quite as the impulse takes you."

It was perfectly true, thought Genji. He waited in silence.

"You should treat any woman with tact and courtesy, and be sure that you cause her no embarrassment. You should never have a woman angry with you."

What would his father think if he were to learn of Genji's worst indiscretion? The thought made Genji shudder. He bowed and withdrew.

The matter his father had thus reproved him for did no good for either of them, the woman or Genji himself. It was a scandal, and very sad for her. She continued to be very much on his mind, and yet he had no thought of making her his wife. She had grown cool toward him, worried about the difference in their ages. He made it seem that it was because of her wishes that he stayed away. Now that the old emperor knew of the affair the whole court knew of it. In spite of everything, the lady went on grieving that he had not loved her better.

There was another lady, his cousin Princess Asagao. Determined that she would not share the plight of the Rokujō lady, she refused even the briefest answer to his notes. Still, and he thought her most civil for it, she was careful to avoid giving open offense.

At Sanjō, his wife and her family were even unhappier about his infidelities, but, perhaps because he did not lie to them, they for the most part kept their displeasure to themselves. His wife was with child and in considerable distress mentally and physically. For Genji it was a strange and moving time. Everyone was delighted and at the same time filled with apprehension, and all manner of retreats and abstinences were prescribed for the lady. Genji had little time to himself. While he had no particular wish to avoid the Rokujō lady and the others, he rarely visited them.

At about this time the high priestess of Kamo resigned. She was replaced by the old emperor's third daughter, whose mother was Kokiden. The new priestess was a favorite of both her brother, the new emperor, and her mother, and it seemed a great pity that she should be shut off from court life; but no other princess was qualified for the position. The installation ceremonies, in the austere Shinto tradition, were of great dignity and solemnity. Many novel details were added to the Kamo festival in the Fourth Month, so that it was certain to be the finest of the season. Though the number of high courtiers attending the princess at the lustration* was limited by precedent, great care was taken to choose handsome men of good repute. Similar care was given to their uniforms and to the uniform trappings of their horses. Genji was among the attendants, by special command of the new emperor. Courtiers and ladies had readied their

---

*At the Kamo River, some days in advance of the festival.

carriages far in advance, and Ichijō was a frightening crush, without space for another vehicle. The stands along the way had been appointed most elaborately. The sleeves that showed beneath the curtains fulfilled in their brightness and variety all the festive promise.

Genji's wife seldom went forth on sightseeing expeditions and her pregnancy was another reason for staying at home.

But her young women protested. "Really, my lady, it won't be much fun sneaking off by ourselves. Why, even complete strangers—why, all the country folk have come in to see our lord! They've brought their wives and families from the farthest provinces. It will be too much if you make us stay away."

Her mother, Princess Omiya, agreed. "You seem to be feeling well enough, my dear, and they will be very disappointed if you don't take them."

And so carriages were hastily and unostentatiously decked out, and the sun was already high when they set forth. The waysides were by now too crowded to admit the elegant Sanjō procession. Coming upon several fine carriages not attended by grooms and footmen, the Sanjō men commenced clearing a space. Two palm-frond carriages remained, not new ones, obviously belonging to someone who did not wish to attract attention. The curtains and the sleeves and aprons to be glimpsed beneath them, some in the gay colors little girls wear, were in very good taste.

The men in attendance sought to defend their places against the Sanjō invaders. "We aren't the sort of people you push around."

There had been too much drink in both parties, and the drunken ones were not responsive to the efforts of their more mature and collected seniors to restrain them.

The palm-frond carriages were from the Rokujō house of the high priestess of Ise. The Rokujō lady had come quietly to see the procession, hoping that it might make her briefly forget her unhappiness. The men from Sanjō had recognized her, but preferred to make it seem otherwise.

"They can't tell us who to push and not to push," said the more intemperate ones to their fellows. "They have General Genji to make them feel important."

Among the newcomers were some of Genji's men. They recognized and felt a little sorry for the Rokujō lady, but, not wishing to become involved, they looked the other way. Presently all the Sanjō carriages were in place. The Rokujō lady, behind the lesser ones, could see almost nothing. Quite aside from her natural distress at the insult, she was filled with the bitterest chagrin that, having refrained from display, she had been recognized. The stools for her carriage shafts had been broken and the shafts propped on the hubs of perfectly strange carriages, a most undignified sight. It was no good asking herself why she had come. She thought of going home without seeing the procession, but there was no room for her to pass; and then came word that the procession was approaching, and she must, after all, see the man who had caused her such unhappiness.

How weak is the heart of a woman! Perhaps because this was not "the bamboo by the river Hinokuma,"* he passed without stopping his horse or looking her way; and the unhappiness was greater than if she had stayed at home.

Genji seemed indifferent to all the grandly decorated carriages and all the gay sleeves, such a flood of them that it was as if ladies were stacked in layers behind the carriage curtains. Now and again, however, he would have a smile and a glance for a carriage he recognized. His face was solemn and respectful as he passed his wife's carriage. His men bowed deeply, and the Rokujō lady was in misery. She had been utterly defeated.

She whispered to herself:

"A distant glimpse of the River of Lustration.
His coldness is the measure of my sorrow."

She was ashamed of her tears. Yet she thought how sorry she would have been if she had not seen that handsome figure set off to such advantage by the crowds.

*Anonymous, *Kokinshū* 1080:

In the bamboo by the river Hinokuma,
Stop that your horse may drink, and I may see you.

The high courtiers were, after their several ranks, impeccably dressed and caparisoned and many of them were very handsome; but Genji's radiance dimmed the strongest lights. Among his special attendants was a guards officer of the Sixth Rank, though attendants of such standing were usually reserved for the most splendid royal processions. His retinue made such a fine procession itself that every tree and blade of grass along the way seemed to bend forward in admiration.

It is not on the whole considered good form for veiled ladies of no mean rank and even nuns who have withdrawn from the world to be jostling and shoving one another in the struggle to see, but today no one thought it out of place. Hollow-mouthed women of the lower classes, their hair tucked under their robes, their hands brought respectfully to their foreheads, were hopping about in hopes of catching a glimpse. Plebeian faces were wreathed in smiles which their owners might not have enjoyed seeing in mirrors, and daughters of petty provincial officers of whose existence Genji would scarcely have been aware had set forth in carriages decked out with the most exhaustive care and taken up posts which seemed to offer a chance of being seen. There were almost as many things by the wayside as in the procession to attract one's attention.

And there were many ladies whom he had seen in secret and who now sighed more than ever that their station was so out of keeping with his. Prince Shikibu viewed the procession from a stand. Genji had matured and did indeed quite dazzle the eye, and the prince thought with foreboding that some god might have noticed, and was making plans to spirit the young man away. His daughter, Princess Asagao, having over the years found Genji a faithful correspondent, knew how remarkably steady his feelings were. She was aware that attentions moved ladies even when the donor was a most ordinary man; yet she had no wish for further intimacy. As for her women, their sighs of admiration were almost deafening.

No carriages set out from the Sanjō mansion on the day of the festival proper.

Genji presently heard the story of the competing carriages. He was sorry for the Rokujō lady and angry at his wife. It was a sad fact that, so deliberate and fastidious, she lacked ordinary compassion. There was indeed a tart, forbidding quality about her. She refused to see, though it was probably an unconscious refusal, that ladies who were to each other as she was to the Rokujō lady should behave with charity and forbearance. It was under her influence that the men in her service flung themselves so violently about. Genji sometimes felt uncomfortable before the proud dignity of the Rokujō lady, and he could imagine her rage and humiliation now.

He called upon her. The high priestess, her daughter, was still with her, however, and, making reverence for the sacred *sakaki* tree* her excuse, she declined to receive him.

She was right, of course. Yet he muttered to himself: "Why must it be so? Why cannot the two of them be a little less prickly?"

It was from his Nijō mansion, away from all this trouble, that he set forth to view the festival proper. Going over to Murasaki's rooms in the west wing, he gave Koremitsu instructions for the carriages.

"And are all our little ladies going too?" he asked. He smiled with pleasure at Murasaki, lovely in her festive dress. "We will watch it together." He stroked her hair, which seemed more lustrous than ever. "It hasn't been trimmed in a very long time. I wonder if today would be a good day for it." He summoned a soothsayer and while the man was investigating told the "little ladies" to go on ahead. They too were a delight, bright and fresh, their hair all sprucely trimmed and flowing over embroidered trousers.

He would trim Murasaki's hair himself, he said. "But see how thick it is. The scissors get all tangled up in it. Think how it will be when you grow up. Even ladies with very long hair usually cut it here at the forehead, and you've not a single lock of short hair. A person might even call it untidy."

The joy was more than a body deserved, said Shōnagon, her nurse.

*A glossy-leafed tree related to the camellia. Its branches are used in Shinto ritual.

"May it grow to a thousand fathoms," said Genji.

> "Mine it shall be, rich as the grasses beneath
> The fathomless sea, the thousand-fathomed sea."

Murasaki took out brush and paper and set down her answer:

> "It may indeed be a thousand fathoms deep.
> How can I know, when it restlessly comes and goes?"

She wrote well, but a pleasant girlishness remained.

Again the streets were lined in solid ranks. Genji's party pulled up near the cavalry grounds, unable to find a place.

"Very difficult," said Genji. "Too many of the great ones hereabouts."

A fan was thrust from beneath the blinds of an elegant ladies' carriage that was filled to overflowing.

"Suppose you pull in here," said a lady. "I would be happy to relinquish my place."

What sort of adventuress might she be? The place was indeed a good one. He had his carriage pulled in.

"How did you find it? I am consumed with envy."

She wrote her reply at the bent edge of a pretty little fan:

> "Ah, the fickleness! It summoned me
> To a meeting, the heartvine now worn by another.*

"The gods themselves seemed to summon me, though of course I am not admitted to the sacred precincts."

He recognized the hand: that of old Naishi,† still youthfully resisting the years.

Frowning, he sent back:

> "Yes, fickleness, this vine of the day of meeting,
> Available to all the eighty clans."

It was her turn to reply, this time in much chagrin:

> "Vine of meeting indeed! A useless weed,
> A mouthing, its name, of empty promises."

Many ladies along the way bemoaned the fact that, apparently in feminine company, he did not even raise the blinds of his carriage. Such

---

*The *aoi*, a vine the heart-shaped leaves of which are a common decorative motif, was a symbol of the Kamo festival. Because of its sound, *aoi* being also "day of meeting," it was much used in poetry to signify a rendezvous. This exchange of poems gives the chapter its title, and from the chapter title, in turn, comes the name Aoi, by which Genji's wife has traditionally been known.

†See Chapter 4.

a stately figure on the day of the lustration—and just see him today, quite at his ease, for everyone to see. The lady with him must surely be a beauty.

A tasteless exchange, thought Genji. A more proper lady would have kept the strictest silence, out of deference to the lady with him.

For the Rokujō lady the pain was unrelieved. She knew that she could expect no lessening of his coldness, and yet to steel herself and go off to Ise with her daughter—she would be lonely, she knew, and people would laugh at her. They would laugh just as heartily if she stayed in the city. Her thoughts were as the fisherman's bob at Ise.* Her very soul seemed to jump wildly about, and at last she fell physically ill.

Genji discounted the possibility of her going to Ise. "It is natural that you should have little use for a reprobate like myself and think of discarding me. But to stay with me would be to show admirable depths of feeling."

These remarks did not seem very helpful. Her anger and sorrow increased. A hope of relief from this agony of indecision had sent her to the river of lustration, and there she had been subjected to violence.

At Sanjō, Genji's wife seemed to be in the grip of a malign spirit. It was no time for nocturnal wanderings. Genji paid only an occasional visit to his own Nijō mansion. His marriage had not been happy, but his wife was important to him and now she was carrying his child. He had prayers read in his Sanjō rooms. Several malign spirits were transferred to the medium and identified themselves, but there was one which quite refused to move. Though it did not cause great pain, it refused to leave her for so much as an instant. There was something very sinister about a spirit that eluded the powers of the most skilled exorcists. The Sanjō people went over the list of Genji's ladies one by one. Among them all, it came to be whispered, only the Rokujō lady and the lady at Nijō seemed to have been singled out for special attentions, and no doubt they were jealous. The exorcists were asked about the possibility, but they gave no very informative answers. Of the spirits that did announce themselves, none seemed to feel any deep enmity toward the lady. Their behavior seemed random and purposeless. There was the spirit of her dead nurse, for instance, and there were spirits that had been with the family for generations and had taken advantage of her weakness.

The confusion and worry continued. The lady would sometimes weep in loud wailing sobs, and sometimes be tormented by nausea and shortness of breath.

The old emperor sent repeated inquiries and ordered religious services. That the lady should be worthy of these august attentions made the possibility of her death seem even more lamentable. Reports that they quite monopolized the attention of court reached the Rokujō mansion, to

*Anonymous, *Kokinshū* 509:

> Has my heart become the fisherman's bob at Ise?
> It jumps and bobs and knows not calm or resolve.

further embitter its lady. No one can have guessed that the trivial incident of the carriages had so angered a lady whose sense of rivalry had not until then been strong.

Not at all herself, she left her house to her daughter and moved to one where Buddhist rites would not be out of place.* Sorry to hear of the move, Genji bestirred himself to call on her. The neighborhood was a strange one and he was in careful disguise. He explained his negligence in terms likely to make it seem involuntary and to bring her forgiveness, and he told her of Aoi's† illness and the worry it was causing him.

"I have not been so very worried myself, but her parents are beside themselves. It has seemed best to stay with her. It would relieve me enormously if I thought you might take a generous view of it all." He knew why she was unwell, and pitied her.

They passed a tense night. As she saw him off in the dawn she found that her plans for quitting the city were not as firm as on the day before. Her rival was of the highest rank and there was this important new consid-

---

*They were out of place in the house of a Shinto priestess.
†Genji's wife's. See note*, page 102.

eration; no doubt his affections would finally settle on her. She herself would be left in solitude, wondering when he might call. The visit had only made her unhappier. In upon her gloom, in the evening, came a letter.

"Though she had seemed to be improving, she has taken a sudden and drastic turn for the worse. I cannot leave her."

The usual excuses, she thought. Yet she answered:

> "I go down the way of love and dampen my sleeves,
> And go yet further, into the muddy fields.

A pity the well is so shallow."*

The hand was the very best he knew. It was a difficult world, which refused to give satisfaction. Among his ladies there was none who could be dismissed as completely beneath consideration and none to whom he could give his whole love.

Despite the lateness of the hour, he got off an answer: "You only wet your sleeves—what can this mean? That your feelings are not of the deepest, I should think.

> "You only dip into the shallow waters,
> And I quite disappear into the slough?

"Do you think I would answer by letter and not in person if she were merely indisposed?"

The malign spirit was more insistent, and Aoi was in great distress. Unpleasant rumors reached the Rokujō lady, to the effect that it might be her spirit or that of her father, the late minister. Though she had felt sorry enough for herself, she had not wished ill to anyone; and might it be that the soul of one so lost in sad thoughts went wandering off by itself? She had, over the years, known the full range of sorrows, but never before had she felt so utterly miserable. There had been no release from the anger since the other lady had so insulted her, indeed behaved as if she did not exist. More than once she had the same dream: in the beautifully appointed apartments of a lady who seemed to be a rival she would push and shake the lady, and flail at her blindly and savagely. It was too terrible. Sometimes in a daze she would ask herself if her soul had indeed gone wandering off. The world was not given to speaking well of people whose transgressions had been far slighter. She would be notorious. It was common enough for the spirits of the angry dead to linger on in this world. She had thought them hateful, and it was her own lot to set a hateful example while she still lived. She must think no more about the man who had been so cruel to her. But so to think was, after all, to think.†

---

*Anonymous, *Kokin Rokujō, Zoku Kokka Taikan* 31863:

> A pity the mountain well should be so shallow.
> I seek to take water and only wet my sleeves.

†A poetic allusion, apparently, but none has been satisfactorily identified.

The high priestess, her daughter, was to have been presented at court the year before, but complications had required postponement. It was finally decided that in the Ninth Month she would go from court to her temporary shrine. The Rokujō house was thus busy preparing for two lustrations, but its lady, lost in thought, seemed strangely indifferent. A most serious state of affairs—the priestess's attendants ordered prayers. There were no really alarming symptoms. She was vaguely unwell, no more. The days passed. Genji sent repeated inquiries, but there was no relief from his worries about another invalid, a more important one.

It was still too early for Aoi to be delivered of her child. Her women were less than fully alert; and then, suddenly, she was seized with labor pains. More priests were put to more strenuous prayers. The malign spirit refused to move. The most eminent of exorcists found this stubbornness extraordinary, and could not think what to do. Then, after renewed efforts at exorcism, more intense than before, it commenced sobbing as if in pain.

"Stop for a moment, please. I want to speak to General Genji."

It was as they had thought. The women showed Genji to a place at Aoi's curtains. Thinking—for she did seem on the point of death—that Aoi had last words for Genji, her parents withdrew. The effect was grandly solemn as priests read from the Lotus Sutra in hushed voices. Genji drew the curtains back and looked down at his wife. She was heavy with child, and very beautiful. Even a man who was nothing to her would have been saddened to look at her. Long, heavy hair, bound at one side, was set off by white robes, and he thought her lovelier than when she was most carefully dressed and groomed.

He took her hand. "How awful. How awful for all of us." He could say no more.

Usually so haughty and forbidding, she now gazed up at him with languid eyes that were presently filled with tears. How could he fail to be moved? This violent weeping, he thought, would be for her parents, soon to be left behind, and perhaps, at this last leave-taking, for him too.

"You mustn't fret so. It can't be as bad as you think. And even if the worst comes, we will meet again. And your good mother and father: the bond between parents and children lasts through many lives. You must tell yourself that you will see them again."

"No, no. I was hurting so, I asked them to stop for a while. I had not dreamed that I would come to you like this. It is true: a troubled soul will sometimes go wandering off." The voice was gentle and affectionate.

"Bind the hem of my robe, to keep it within,
    The grieving soul that has wandered through the skies."*

It was not Aoi's voice, nor was the manner hers. Extraordinary—and then he knew that it was the voice of the Rokujō lady. He was aghast. He

*Tying the skirt of a robe was a device for keeping an errant spirit at home.

had dismissed the talk as vulgar and ignorant fabrication, and here before his eyes he had proof that such things did actually happen. He was horrified and repelled.

"You may say so. But I don't know who you are. Identify yourself."

It was indeed she. "Aghast"—is there no stronger word? He waved the women back.

Thinking that these calmer tones meant a respite from pain, her mother came with medicine; and even as she drank it down she gave birth to a baby boy. Everyone was delighted, save the spirits that had been transferred to mediums. Chagrined at their failure, they were raising a great stir, and all in all it was a noisy and untidy scene. There was still the afterbirth to worry about. Then, perhaps because of all the prayers, it too was delivered. The grand abbot of Hiei and all the other eminent clerics departed, looking rather pleased with themselves as they mopped their foreheads. Sure that the worst was past after all the anxious days, the women allowed themselves a rest.

The prayers went on as noisily as ever, but the house was now caught up in the happy business of ministering to a pretty baby. It hummed with excitement on each of the festive nights.* Fine and unusual gifts came from the old emperor and from all the princes and high courtiers. Ceremonies honoring a boy baby are always interesting.

The Rokujō lady received the news with mixed feelings. She had heard that her rival was critically ill, and now the crisis had passed. She was not herself. The strangest thing was that her robes were permeated with the scent of the poppy seeds burned at exorcisms. She changed clothes repeatedly and even washed her hair, but the odor persisted. She was overcome with self-loathing. And what would others be thinking? It was a matter she could discuss with no one. She could only suffer in distraught silence.

Somewhat calmer, Genji was still horrified at the unsolicited remarks he had had from the possessive spirit. He really must get off a note to the Rokujō lady. Or should he have a talk with her? He would find it hard to be civil, and he did not wish to hurt her. In the end he made do with a note.

Aoi's illness had been critical, and the strictest vigil must be continued. Genji had been persuaded to stop his nocturnal wanderings. He still had not really talked to his wife, for she was still far from normal. The child was so beautiful as to arouse forebodings, and preparations were already under way for a most careful and elaborate education. The minister was pleased with everything save the fact that his daughter had still not recovered. But he told himself that he need not worry. A slow convalescence was to be expected after so serious an illness.

Especially around the eyes, the baby bore a strong resemblance to the

---

*There were celebrations on the third, fifth, seventh, and ninth nights.

crown prince, whom Genji suddenly felt an intense longing to see. He could not sit still. He had to be off to court.

"I have been neglecting my duties," he said to the women, "and am feeling rather guilty. I think today I will venture out. It would be good if I might see her before I go. I am not a stranger, you know."

"Quite true, sir. You of all people should be allowed near. She is badly emaciated, I fear, but that is scarcely a reason for her to hide herself from you."

And so a place was set out for him at her bedside. She answered from time to time, but in a very weak voice. Even so little, from a lady who had been given up for dead, was like a dream. He told her of those terrible days. Then he remembered how, as if pulling back from a brink, she had begun talking to him so volubly and so eagerly. A shudder of revulsion passed over him.

"There are many things I would like to say to you, but you still seem very tired."

He even prepared medicine for her. The women were filled with admiration. When had he learned to be so useful?

She was sadly worn and lay as if on the border of death, pathetic and still lovely. There was not a tangle in her lustrous hair. The thick tresses that poured over her pillows seemed to him quite beyond compare. He gazed down at her, thinking it odd that he should have felt so dissatisfied with her over the years.

"I must see my father, but I am sure I will not be needed long. How nice if we could always be like this. But your mother is with you so much, I have not wanted to seem insistent. You must get back your strength and move back to your own rooms. Your mother pampers you too much. That may be one reason why you are so slow getting well."

As he withdrew in grand court dress she lay looking after him as she had not been in the habit of doing.

There was to be a conference on promotions and appointments. The minister too set off for court, in procession with all his sons, each of them with a case to plead and determined not to leave his side.

The Sanjō mansion was almost deserted. Aoi was again seized with a strangling shortness of breath; and very soon after a messenger had been sent to court she was dead. Genji and the others left court, scarcely aware of where their feet were taking them. Appointments and promotions no longer concerned them. Since the crisis had come at about midnight there was no possibility of summoning the grand abbot and his suffragans. Everyone had thought that the worst was over, and now of course everyone was stunned, dazed, wandering aimlessly from room to room, hardly knowing a door from a wall. Messengers crowded in with condolences, but the house was in such confusion that there was no one to receive them. The intensity of the grief was almost frightening. Since malign spirits had more than once attacked the lady, her father ordered the body left as it was for two or three days in hopes that she might revive. The signs of death were more and more pronounced, however, and, in great anguish, the family at length accepted the truth. Genji, who had private distress to add to the general grief, thought he knew as well as anyone ever would what unhappiness love can bring. Condolences even from the people most important to him brought no comfort. The old emperor, himself much grieved, sent a personal message; and so for the minister there was new honor, happiness to temper the sorrow. Yet there was no relief from tears.

Every reasonable suggestion was accepted toward reviving the lady, but, the ravages of death being ever more apparent, there was finally no recourse but to see her to Toribe Moor. There were many heartrending scenes along the way. The crowds of mourners and priests invoking the holy name quite overflowed the wide moor. Messages continued to pour in, from the old emperor, of course, and from the empress and crown prince and all the great houses as well.

The minister was desolate. "Now in my last years to be left behind by a daughter who should have had so many years before her." No one could see him without sharing his sorrow.

Grandly the services went on through the night, and as dawn came over the sky the mourners turned back to the city, taking with them only a handful of ashes. Funerals are common enough, but Genji, who had not been present at many, was shaken as never before. Since it was late in the Eighth Month a quarter moon still hung in a sky that would have brought melancholy thoughts in any case; and the figure of his father-in-law, as if groping in pitch darkness, seemed proper to the occasion and at the same time indescribably sad.

A poem came to his lips as he gazed up into the morning sky:

"Might these clouds be the smoke that mounts from her pyre?
They fill my heart with feelings too deep for words."

Back at Sanjō, he was unable to sleep. He thought over their years together. Why had he so carelessly told himself that she would one day understand? Why had he allowed himself silly flirtations, the smallest of them sure to anger her? He had let her carry her hostility to the grave. The regrets were strong, but useless.

It was as if in a trance that he put on the dull gray mourning robes. Had she outlived him, it occurred to him, hers would have been darker gray.[*]

"Weeds obey rules. Mine are the shallower hue.
But tears plunge my sleeves into the deepest wells."

He closed his eyes in prayer, a handsomer man in sorrow than in happiness. He intoned softly: "Hail, Samantabhadra, in whose serene

[*] A widow wore darker mourning than a widower.

thoughts all is contained."* The invocation seemed more powerful than from the mouth of the most reverent priest.

There were tears in his eyes as he took the little boy up in his arms. "What would we have to remember her by?"† he whispered to himself. The sorrow would be worse if he did not have this child.

Princess Omiya took to her bed in such a sad state that services were now commenced for her. The preparations for memorial rites were the sadder for the fact that there had been so little warning. Parents grieve at the loss of the most ill-favored child, and the intensity of the grief in this case was not to be wondered at. The family had no other daughters. It was as if—it was worse than if the jewels upon the silken sleeve had been shattered to bits.‡

Genji did not venture forth even to Nijō. He passed his days in tears and in earnest prayer. He did, it is true, send off a few notes. The high

*The source of the invocation is unknown.
†The nurse of Kanetada's mother, *Gosenshū* 1188:

> What would we have to remember our lady by
> Were it not for this keepsake, this child she left behind?

‡Apparently a quotation, but the source has not been identified.

priestess of Ise had moved to a temporary shrine in the guards' quarters of the palace. Making the girl's ritual purity her excuse, the Rokujō lady refused to answer. The world had not been kind to him, and now, gloomier than ever, he thought that if he had not had this new bond with the world he would have liked to follow what had for so long been his deepest inclinations and leave it entirely behind. But then he would think of the girl Murasaki at Nijō. He slept alone. Women were on duty nearby, but still he was lonely. Unable to sleep, he would say to himself: "In autumn, of all the seasons."* Summoning priests of good voice, he would have them chant the holy name; and the dawn sky would be almost more than he could bear.

In one of those late-autumn dawns when the very sound of the wind seems to sink to one's bones, he arose from a lonely, sleepless bed to see the garden enshrouded in mist. A letter was brought in, on dark blue-gray paper attached to a half-opened bud of chrysanthemum. In the best of taste, he thought. The hand was that of the Rokujō lady.

"Do you know why I have been so negligent?

> "I too am in tears, at the thought of her sad, short life.
> Moist the sleeves of you whom she left behind.

"These autumn skies make it impossible for me to be silent."

The hand was more beautiful than ever. He wanted to fling the note away from him, but could not. It seemed to him altogether too disingenuous. Yet he could not bring himself to sever relations. Poor woman, she seemed marked for notoriety. No doubt Aoi had been fated to die. But anger rose again. Why had he seen and heard it all so clearly, why had it been paraded before him? Try though he might, he could not put his feelings toward the woman in order. He debated at great length, remembering too that perhaps he should hold his tongue out of respect for the high priestess.

But he finally decided that the last thing he wanted was to seem cold and insensitive. His answer was on soft, quiet purple. "You for your part will understand, I am sure, the reasons for this inexcusably long silence. You have been much on my mind, but I have thought it best to keep my distance.

> "We go, we stay, alike of this world of dew.
> We should not let it have such a hold upon us.

"You too should try to shake loose. I shall be brief, for perhaps you will not welcome a letter from a house of mourning."

Now back at Rokujō, she waited until she was alone to read the letter. Her conscience told her his meaning all too clearly. So he knew. It was too

*Mibu Tadamine, *Kokinshū* 839:

> Why did he die in autumn, of all the seasons?
> In autumn one grieves for those who yet remain.

awful. Surely no one had been more cruelly treated by fate than herself.
What would the old emperor be thinking? He and her late husband, the
crown prince, were brothers by the same mother, and they had been very
close. The prince had asked his protection for their daughter, and he had
replied that he would look upon himself as taking the place of her father.
He had repeatedly invited the lady and her daughter to go on living in the
palace, but she held to a demanding view of the proprieties. And so she
had found herself in this childish entanglement, and had succeeded in
making a very bad name for herself. She was still not feeling well.

In fact, the name she had made for herself was rather different. She
had long been famous for her subtlety and refinement, and when her
daughter moved to another temporary shrine, this one to the west of the
city, all the details were tasteful and in the latest fashion. Genji was not
surprised to hear that the more cultivated of the courtiers were making it
their main business to part the dew-drenched grasses before the shrine.
She was a lady of almost too good taste. If, wanting no more of love, she
were to go with her daughter to Ise, he would, after all, miss her.

The memorial services were over, but Genji remained in seclusion for
seven weeks. Pitying him in the unaccustomed tedium, Tō no Chūjō would
come and divert him with the latest talk, serious and trivial; and it seems
likely that old Naishi was cause for a good laugh now and then.

"You mustn't make fun of dear old Granny," said Genji; but he found
stories of the old lady unfailingly amusing.

They would go over the list of their little adventures, on the night of
a misty autumn moon, just past full, and others; and their talk would come
around to the evanescence of things and they would shed a few tears.

On an evening of chilly autumn rains, Tō no Chūjō again came calling.
He had changed to lighter mourning and presented a fine, manly figure
indeed, enough to put most men to shame. Genji was at the railing of the
west veranda, looking out over the frostbitten garden. The wind was high
and it was as if his tears sought to compete with the driven rain.

"Is she the rain, is she the clouds? Alas, I cannot say."*

He sat chin in hand. Were he himself the dead lady, thought Tō no
Chūjō, his soul would certainly remain bound to this world. He came up
to his friend. Genji, who had not expected callers, quietly smoothed his
robes, a finely glossed red singlet under a robe of a deeper gray than Tō
no Chūjō's. It was the modest, conservative sort of dress that never seems
merely dull.

Tō no Chūjō too looked up at the sky.

"Is she the rain? Where in these stormy skies,
    To which of these brooding clouds may I look to find her?

Neither can I say," he added, as if to himself.

*More than one Chinese source has been averred.

"It is a time of storms when even the clouds
To which my lady has risen are blotted away."

Genji's grief was clearly unfeigned. Very odd, thought Tō no Chūjō. Genji had so often been reproved by his father for not being a better husband, and the attentions of his father-in-law had made him very uncomfortable. There were circumstances, having largely to do with his nearness to Princess Omiya, which kept him from leaving Aoi completely; and so he had continued to wait upon her, making little attempt to hide his dissatisfaction. Tō no Chūjō had more than once been moved to pity him in this unhappy predicament. And now it seemed that she had after all had a place in his affections, that he had loved and honored her. Tō no Chūjō's own sorrow was more intense for the knowledge. It was as if a light had gone out.

Gentians and wild carnations peeped from the frosty tangles. After Tō no Chūjō had left, Genji sent a small bouquet by the little boy's nurse, Saishō, to Princess Omiya, with this message:

"Carnations at the wintry hedge remind me
Of an autumn which we leave too far behind.

You do not, I hope, think the color inferior.''

Yes, the smiling little "wild carnation" he now had with him was a treasure.

The princess, less resistant to tears than the autumn leaves to the winds, had to have someone read Genji's note to her.

She sent this answer:

"I see them, and my sleeves are drenched afresh,
The wild carnations at the wasted hedge."

It was a dull time. He was sure that his cousin Princess Asagao, despite her past coolness, would understand his feelings on such an evening. He had not written in a long time, but their letters had always been irregularly spaced. His note was on azure Chinese paper.

"Many a desolate autumn have I known,
But never have my tears flowed as tonight.

Each year brings rains of autumn."*

His writing was more beautiful all the time, said her women, and see what pains he had taken. She must not leave the note unanswered.

She agreed. "I knew how things must be on Mount Ouchi,† but what was I to say?

"I knew that the autumn mists had faded away,
And looked for you in the stormy autumn skies."

That was all. It was in a faint hand which seemed to him—his imagination, perhaps—to suggest deep, mysterious things. We do not often find in this world that the actuality is better than the anticipation, but it was Genji's nature to be drawn to retiring women. A woman might be icy cold, he thought, but her affections, once awakened, were likely to be strengthened by the memory of the occasions that had called for reluctant sympathy. The affected, overrefined sort of woman might draw attention to herself, but it had a way of revealing flaws she was herself unaware of. He did not wish to rear his Murasaki after such a model. He had not forgotten to ask himself whether she would be bored and lonely without him, but he thought of her as an orphan he had taken in and did not worry himself greatly about what she might be thinking or doing, or whether she might be resentful of his outside activities. This was pleasant for him.

Ordering a lamp, he summoned several of the worthier women to keep him company. He had for some time had his eye on one Chūnagon, but for the period of mourning had put away amorous thoughts. It seemed most civilized of him.

He addressed them affectionately, though with careful politeness. "I have felt closer to you through these sad days. If I had not had you with

*Probably a poetic allusion.
†Why Genji's abode should be called Mt. Ouchi, which usually signifies the palace, is unclear.

me I would have been lonelier than I can think. We need not brood over what is finished, but I fear that difficult problems lie ahead of us."

They were in tears. "It has left us in the blackest darkness," said one of them, "and the thought of how things will be when you are gone is almost too much to bear." She could say no more.

Deeply touched, Genji looked from one to another. "When I am gone —how can that be? You must think me heartless. Be patient, and you will see that you are wrong. Though of course life is very uncertain." Tears came to his eyes as he looked into the lamplight. They made him if anything handsomer, thought the women.

Among them was a little girl, an orphan, of whom Aoi had been especially fond. He quite understood why the child should now be sadder than any of the others. "You must let me take care of you, Ateki." She broke into a violent sobbing. In her tiny singlet, a very dark gray, and her black cloak and straw-colored trousers, she was a very pretty little thing indeed.

Over and over again he asked the women to be patient. "Those of you who have not forgotten—you must bear the loneliness and do what you can for the boy. I would find it difficult to come visiting if you were all to run off."

They had their doubts. His visits, they feared, would be few and far between. Life would indeed be lonely.

Avoiding ostentation, the minister distributed certain of Aoi's belongings to her women, after their several ranks: little baubles and trinkets, and more considerable mementos as well.

Genji could not remain forever in seclusion. He went first to his father's palace. His carriage was brought up, and as his retinue gathered an autumn shower swept past, as if it knew its time, and the wind that summons the leaves blew a great confusion of them to the ground; and for the sorrowing women the sleeves that had barely had time to dry were damp all over again. Genji would go that night from his father's palace to Nijō. Thinking to await him there, his aides and equerries went off one by one. Though this would not of course be his last visit, the gloom was intense.

For the minister and Princess Omiya, all the old sorrow came back. Genji left a note for the princess: "My father has asked to see me, and I shall call upon him today. When I so much as set foot outside this house, I feel new pangs of grief, and I ask myself how I have survived so long. I should come in person to take my leave, I know, but I fear that I would quite lose control of myself. I must be satisfied with this note."

Blinded with tears, the princess did not answer.

The minister came immediately. He dabbed at his eyes, and the women were weeping too. There seemed nothing in the least false about Genji's own tears, which gave an added elegance and fineness of feature. At length controlling himself, the minister said: "An old man's tears have a way of gushing forth at the smallest provocation, and I am unable to stanch the flow. Sure that I must seem hopelessly senile and incontinent, I have been reluctant to visit your royal father. If the subject arises, perhaps you can explain to him how matters are. It is painful, at the end of your life, to be left behind by a child." He spoke with great difficulty.

Genji was weeping only less openly. "We all of course know the way of the world, that we cannot be sure who will go first and who will remain behind, but the shock of the specific instance is all the same hard to bear. I am sure that my father will understand."

"Well, then, perhaps you should go before it is too dark. There seems to be no letting up of the rain."

Genji looked around at the rooms he was about to leave. Behind curtains, through open doors, he could see some thirty women in various shades of gray, all weeping piteously.

"I have consoled myself," said the minister, "with the thought that you are leaving someone behind in this house whom you cannot abandon, and that you will therefore find occasion to visit in spite of what has happened; but these not very imaginative women are morbid in their insistence that you are leaving your old home for good. It is natural that they should grieve for the passing of the years when they have seen you on such intimate and congenial terms, indeed that they should grieve more than for the loss of their lady. You were never really happy with her, but I was sure that things would one day improve, and asked them to hope for the not perhaps very hopeful. This is a sad evening."

"They have chosen inadequate grounds for lamenting, sir. I may once have neglected you and your good lady, in the days when I too thought that a not very happy situation would improve. What could persuade me to neglect you now? You will see presently that I am telling you the truth."

He left. The minister came back into the house. All the furnishings and decorations were as they had been, and yet everything seemed lifeless and empty. At the bed curtains were an inkstone which Genji had left behind and some bits of paper on which he had practiced his calligraphy. Struggling to hold back the tears, the minister looked at them. There were, it seemed, some among the younger women who were smiling through their tears. Genji had copied and thrown away highly charged passages from old poems, Chinese and Japanese, in both formal and cursive scripts. Magnificent writing, thought the minister, looking off into space. It was cruel that Genji should now be a stranger.

"The old pillow, the old bed: with whom shall I share them now?" It was a verse from Po Chü-i.* Below it Genji had written a verse of his own:

> "Sad at the thought of her who sadly left it,
> I do not wish to leave the pillow she left."

"The flower is white with frost." It was another phrase from the same poem, and Genji had set down another of his own:

*From a Japanized version of "The Song of Everlasting Sorrow."

> "The dust piles on the now abandoned bed.
> How many dew-drenched nights have I slept alone!"

With these jottings were several withered carnations, probably from the day he had sent flowers to Princess Omiya.

The minister took them to her. "The terrible fact, of course, is that she is gone, but I tell myself that sad stories are far from unheard of in this world. The bond between us held for such a short time that I find myself thinking of the destinies we bring with us into this world. Hers was to stay a short time and to cause great sorrow. I have somehow taken comfort in the thought. But I have missed her more each day, and now the thought that he will be no more than a stranger is almost too much to bear. A day or two without him was too much, and now he has left us for good. How am I to go on?"

He could not control the quaver in his voice. The older of the women had broken into unrestrained sobbing. It was in more ways than one a cold evening.

The younger women were gathered in clusters, talking of things which had somehow moved them. No doubt, they said, Genji was right in seeking to persuade them of the comfort they would find in looking after the boy. What a very fragile little keepsake he was, all the same. Some said they would go home for just a few days and come again, and there were many emotional scenes as they said goodbye.

Genji called upon his father, the old emperor.

"You have lost a great deal of weight," said the emperor, with a look of deep concern. "Because you have been fasting, I should imagine." He pressed food on Genji and otherwise tried to be of service. Genji was much moved by these august ministrations.

He then called upon the empress, to the great excitement of her women.

"There are so many things about it that still make me weep," she sent out through Omyōbu. "I can only imagine how sad a time it has been for you."

"One knows, of course," he sent back, "that life is uncertain; but one does not really know until the fact is present and clear. Your several messages have given me strength." He seemed in great anguish, the sorrow of bereavement compounded by the sorrow he always felt in her presence. His dress, an unpatterned robe and a gray singlet, the ribbons of his cap tied up in mourning, seemed more elegant for its want of color.

He had been neglecting the crown prince. Sending in apologies, he made his departure late in the night.

The Nijō mansion had been cleaned and polished for his return. The whole household assembled to receive him. The higher-ranking ladies had sought to outdo one another in dress and grooming. The sight of them made him think of the sadly dejected ladies at Sanjō. Changing to less doleful clothes, he went to the west wing. The fittings, changed to welcome the autumn, were fresh and bright, and the young women and little girls were all very pretty in autumn dress. Shōnagon had taken care of everything.

Murasaki too was dressed to perfection. "You have grown," he said, lifting a low curtain back over its frame.

She looked shyly aside. Her hair and profile seemed in the lamplight even more like those of the lady he so longed for.

He had worried about her, he said, coming nearer. "I would like to tell you everything, but it is not a very lucky sort of story. Maybe I should rest awhile in the other wing. I won't be long. From now on you will never be rid of me. I am sure you will get very bored with me."

Shōnagon was pleased but not confident. He had so many wellborn ladies, another demanding one was certain to take the place of the one who was gone. She was a dry, unsentimental sort.

Genji returned to his room. Asking Chūjō to massage his legs, he lay down to rest. The next morning he sent off a note for his baby son. He gazed on and on at the answer, from one of the women, and all the old sadness came back.

It was a tedious time. He no longer had any enthusiasm for the careless night wanderings that had once kept him busy. Murasaki was much on his mind. She seemed peerless, the nearest he could imagine to his ideal. Thinking that she was no longer too young for marriage, he had occasionally made amorous overtures; but she had not seemed to understand. They had passed their time in games of Go and *hentsugi*.* She was clever and she had many delicate ways of pleasing him in the most trivial diversions. He had not seriously thought of her as a wife. Now he could not restrain himself. It would be a shock, of course.

What had happened? Her women had no way of knowing when the line had been crossed. One morning Genji was up early and Murasaki stayed on and on in bed. It was not at all like her to sleep so late. Might she be unwell? As he left for his own rooms, Genji pushed an inkstone inside her bed curtains.

At length, when no one else was near, she raised herself from her pillow and saw beside it a tightly folded bit of paper. Listlessly she opened it. There was only this verse, in a casual hand:

> "Many have been the nights we have spent together
> Purposelessly, these coverlets between us."

She had not dreamed he had anything of the sort on his mind. What a fool she had been, to repose her whole confidence in so gross and unscrupulous a man.

It was almost noon when Genji returned. "They say you're not feeling well. What can be the trouble? I was hoping for a game of Go."

*Or *hentsuki*. Guessing concealed parts of Chinese characters.

She pulled the covers over her head. Her women discreetly withdrew. He came up beside her.

"What a way to behave, what a very unpleasant way to behave. Try to imagine, please, what these women are thinking."

He drew back the covers. She was bathed in perspiration and the hair at her forehead was matted from weeping.

"Dear me. This does not augur well at all." He tried in every way he could think of to comfort her, but she seemed genuinely upset and did not offer so much as a word in reply.

"Very well. You will see no more of me. I do have my pride."

He opened her writing box but found no note inside. Very childish of her—and he had to smile at the childishness. He stayed with her the whole day, and he thought the stubbornness with which she refused to be comforted most charming.

Boar-day sweets* were served in the evening. Since he was still in mourning, no great ceremony attended upon the observance. Glancing over the varied and tastefully arranged foods that had been brought in

*Eaten on the first Day of the Boar in the Tenth Month, to insure good health, and perhaps too by way of prayer for a fruitful marriage, the wild boar being a symbol of fertility.

cypress boxes to Murasaki's rooms only, Genji went out to the south
veranda and called Koremitsu.

"We will have more of the same tomorrow night," he said, smiling,
"though not in quite such mountains. This is not the most propitious day."

Koremitsu had a quick mind. "Yes, we must be careful to choose lucky
days for our beginnings." And, solemnly and deliberately: "How many
rat-day sweets am I asked to provide?"*

"Oh, I should think one for every three that we have here."†

Koremitsu went off with an air of having informed himself ade-
quately. A clever and practical young fellow, thought Genji.

Koremitsu had the nuptial sweets prepared at his own house. He told
no one what they signified.

Genji felt like a child thief. The role amused him and the affection he
now felt for the girl seemed to reduce his earlier affection to the tiniest
mote. A man's heart is a very strange amalgam indeed! He now thought
that he could not bear to be away from her for a single night.

The sweets he had ordered were delivered stealthily, very late in the
night. A man of tact, Koremitsu saw that Shōnagon, an older woman,
might make Murasaki uncomfortable, and so he called her daughter.

"Slip this inside her curtains, if you will," he said, handing her an
incense box.‡ "You must see that it gets to her and to no one else. A solemn
celebration. No carelessness permitted."

She thought it odd. "Carelessness? Of that quality I have had no
experience."

"The very word demands care. Use it sparingly."

Young and somewhat puzzled, she did as she was told. It would seem
that Genji had explained the significance of the incense box to Murasaki.

The women had no warning. When the box emerged from the curtains
the next morning, the pieces of the puzzle began to fall into place. Such
numbers of dishes—when might they have been assembled?—and stands
with festooned legs, bearing sweets of a most especial sort. All in all, a
splendid array. How very nice that he had gone to such pains, thought
Shōnagon. He had overlooked nothing. She wept tears of pleasure and
gratitude.

"But he really could have let us in on the secret," the women whispered to one another. "What can the gentleman who brought them have
thought?"

When he paid the most fleeting call on his father or put in a brief

*There were no "rat-day sweets." The words for "rat" and "sleep" being homophonous, and
the Day of the Rat following the Day of the Boar, Koremitsu refers obliquely to the nuptial
bed.
†This statement was treated by early commentators as one of the "great *Genji* riddles." The
number three seems to be crucial, since the bridegroom ate three ritual cakes on the third
night of a marriage.
‡Probably to disguise the contents.

appearance at court, he would be impossibly restless, overcome with longing for the girl. Even to Genji himself it seemed excessive. He had resentful letters from women with whom he had been friendly. He was sorry, but he did not wish to be separated from his bride for even a night. He had no wish to be with these others and let it seem that he was indisposed.

"I shall hope to see you when this very difficult time has passed."

Kokiden took note of the fact that her sister Oborozukiyo, the lady of the misty moon, seemed to have fond thoughts of Genji.

"Well, after all," said her father, the Minister of the Right, "he has lost the lady most important to him. If what you suggest with such displeasure comes to pass, I for one will not be desolate."

"She must go to court," thought Kokiden. "If she works hard, she can make a life for herself there."

Genji had reciprocated the fond thoughts and was sorry to hear that she might be going to court; but he no longer had any wish to divide his affections. Life was short, he would settle them upon one lady. He had aroused quite enough resentment in his time.

As for the Rokujō lady, he pitied her, but she would not make a satisfactory wife. And yet, after all, he did not wish a final break. He told himself that if she could put up with him as he had been over the years, they might be of comfort to each other.

No one even knew who Murasaki was. It was as if she were without place or identity. He must inform her father, he told himself. Though avoiding display, he took great pains with her initiation ceremonies. She found this solicitude, though remarkable, very distasteful. She had trusted him, she had quite entwined herself about him. It had been inexcusably careless of her. She now refused to look at him, and his jokes only sent her into a more sullen silence. She was not the old Murasaki. He found the change both sad and interesting.

"My efforts over the years seem to have been wasted. I had hoped that familiarity would bring greater affection, and I was wrong."

On New Year's Day he visited his father and the crown prince. He went from the palace to the Sanjō mansion. His father-in-law, for whom the New Year had not brought a renewal of spirits, had been talking sadly of things gone by. He did not want this kind and rare visit to be marred by tears, but he was perilously near weeping. Perhaps because he was now a year older, Genji seemed more dignified and mature, and handsomer as well. In Aoi's rooms the unexpected visit reduced her women to tears. The little boy had grown. He sat babbling and laughing happily, the resemblance to the crown prince especially strong around the eyes and mouth. All the old fears came back which his own resemblance to the crown prince had occasioned. Nothing in the rooms had been changed. On a clothes rack, as always, robes were laid out for Genji; but there were none for Aoi.

A note came from Princess Omiya. "I had become rather better at controlling my tears, but this visit has quite unsettled me. Here are your

New Year robes. I have been so blinded with tears these last months that I fear the colors will not please you. Do, today at least, put them on, inadequate though they may be."

Yet others were brought in. A good deal of care had clearly gone into the weaving and dyeing of the singlets which she wished him to wear today. Not wanting to seem ungrateful, he changed into them. He feared that she would have been very disappointed if he had not come.

"I am here," he sent back, "that you may see for yourself whether or not spring has come. I find myself reduced to silence by all the memories.

"Yet once again I put on robes for the new,
    And tears are falling for all that went with the old.

I cannot contain them."

She sent back:

"The New Year brings renewal, I know, and yet
    The same old tears still flow from the same old woman."

The grief was still intense for both of them.

Chapter 7

The Sacred Tree

The Rokujō lady was more and more despondent as the time neared for her daughter's departure. Since the death of Aoi, who had caused her such pain, Genji's visits, never frequent, had stopped altogether. They had aroused great excitement among her women, who hoped that now he would marry her. Genji must have very specific reasons for having turned against her—there was no explaining his extreme coldness otherwise. She would think no more about him. She would go with her daughter. There were no precedents for a mother's accompanying a high priestess to Ise, but she had as her excuse that her daughter would be helpless without her. The real reason, of course, was that she wanted to flee these painful associations.

In spite of everything, Genji was sorry when he heard of her decision. He now wrote often and almost pleadingly, but she thought a meeting out of the question at this late date. She would risk disappointing him rather than have it all begin again.

She occasionally went from the priestess's temporary shrine to her Rokujō house, but so briefly and in such secrecy that Genji did not hear of the visits. The temporary shrine did not, he thought, invite casual visits. Although she was much on his mind, he let the days and months go by. His father, the old emperor, had begun to suffer from recurrent aches and cramps, and Genji had little time for himself. Yet he did not want the lady to go off to Ise thinking him completely heartless, nor did he wish to have a name at court for insensitivity. He gathered his resolve and set off for the shrine.

It was on about the seventh of the Ninth Month. The lady was under great tension, for their departure was imminent, possibly only a day or two away. He had several times asked for a word with her. He need not go inside, he said, but could wait on the veranda. She was in a torment of uncertainty but at length reached a secret decision: she did not want to seem like a complete recluse and so she would receive him through curtains.

It was over a reed plain of melancholy beauty that he made his way to the shrine. The flowers were gone and insects hummed sadly in the wintry tangles. A wind whistling through the pines brought snatches of music to most wonderful effect, though so distant that he could not tell what was being played. Not wishing to attract attention, he had some ten outrunners, men who had long been in his service, and his guards were in subdued livery. He had dressed with great care. His more perceptive men saw how beautifully the melancholy scene set him off, and he was having regrets that he had not made the journey often. A low wattle fence, scarcely more than a suggestion of an enclosure, surrounded a complex of board-roofed buildings, as rough and insubstantial as temporary shelters.

The shrine gates, of unfinished logs, had a grand and awesome dignity for all their simplicity, and the somewhat forbidding austerity of the place was accentuated by clusters of priests talking among themselves and coughing and clearing their throats as if in warning. It was a scene quite unlike any Genji had seen before. The fire lodge* glowed faintly. It was all in all a lonely, quiet place, and here away from the world a lady already deep in sorrow had passed these weeks and months. Concealing himself outside the north wing, he sent in word of his arrival. The music abruptly stopped and the silence was broken only by a rustling of silken robes.

Though several messages were passed back and forth, the lady herself did not come out.

"You surely know that these expeditions are frowned upon. I find it very curious that I should be required to wait outside the sacred paling. I want to tell you everything, all my sorrows and worries."

He was right, said the women. It was more than a person could bear, seeing him out there without even a place to sit down. What was she to do? thought the lady. There were all these people about, and her daughter would expect more mature and sober conduct. No, to receive him at this late date would be altogether too undignified. Yet she could not bring herself to send him briskly on his way. She sighed and hesitated and hesitated again, and it was with great excitement that he finally heard her come forward.

"May I at least come up to the veranda?" he asked, starting up the stairs.

*There are several theories about the use of this building. The most likely are that it was for preparing offerings and that it was for lighting torches and flares.

The evening moon burst forth and the figure she saw in its light was handsome beyond describing.

Not wishing to apologize for all the weeks of neglect, he pushed a branch of the sacred tree* in under the blinds.

"I come through the sacred gate," he said, "because I obey the urgings of a heart as constant as this evergreen. You do not respond as I had hoped you would."

She replied:

> "You err with your sacred tree and sacred gate.
> No beckoning cedars stand before my house."†

And he:

> "Thinking to find you here with the holy maidens,
> I followed the scent of the leaf of the sacred tree."

Though the scene did not encourage familiarity, he made bold to lean inside the blinds.

Sakaki, related to the camellia. See note, page 101.
†Anonymous, Kokinshū 982:

> Should you seek my house at the foot of Mount Miwa,
> You need only look for the cedars by the gate.

He had complacently wasted the days when he could have visited her and perhaps made her happy. He had begun to have misgivings about her, his ardor had cooled, and they had become the near strangers they were now. But she was here before him, and memories flooded back. He thought of what had been and what was to be, and he was weeping like a child.

She did not wish him to see her following his example. He felt even sadder for her as she fought to control herself, and it would seem that even now he urged her to change her plans. Gazing up into a sky even more beautiful now that the moon was setting, he poured forth all his pleas and complaints, and no doubt they were enough to erase the accumulated bitterness. She had resigned herself to what must be, and it was as she had feared. Now that she was with him again she found her resolve wavering.

Groups of young courtiers came up. It was a garden which aroused romantic urges and which a young man was reluctant to leave.

Their feelings for each other, Genji's and the lady's, had run the whole range of sorrows and irritations, and no words could suffice for all they wanted to say to each other. The dawn sky was as if made for the occasion. Not wanting to go quite yet, Genji took her hand, very gently.

"A dawn farewell is always drenched in dew,
But sad is the autumn sky as never before."

A cold wind was blowing, and a pine cricket* seemed to recognize the occasion. It was a serenade to which a happy lover would not have been deaf. Perhaps because their feelings were in such tumult, they found that the poems they might have exchanged were eluding them.

At length the lady replied:

"An autumn farewell needs nothing to make it sadder.
Enough of your songs, O crickets on the moors!"

It would do no good to pour forth all the regrets again. He made his departure, not wanting to be seen in the broadening daylight. His sleeves were made wet along the way with dew and with tears.

The lady, not as strong as she would have wished, was sunk in a sad reverie. The shadowy figure in the moonlight and the perfume he left behind had the younger women in a state only just short of swooning. "What kind of journey could be important enough, I ask you," said one of them, choking with tears, "to make her leave such a man?"

His letter the next day was so warm and tender that again she was tempted to reconsider. But it was too late: a return to the old indecision would accomplish nothing. Genji could be very persuasive even when he did not care a great deal for a woman, and this was no ordinary parting. He sent the finest travel robes and supplies, for the lady and for her women as well. They were no longer enough to move her. It was as if the thought

---

Matsumushi. It seems to have been what is today called "bell cricket," *suzumushi*. See note†, page 8.

had only now come to her of the ugly name she seemed fated to leave behind.

The high priestess was delighted that plans were now clear. The novel fact that she was taking her mother with her gave rise to talk, some sympathetic and some hostile. Happy are they whose place in the world puts them beneath such notice! The great ones of the world live sadly constricted lives.

On the sixteenth there was a lustration at the Katsura River, splendid as never before. Perhaps because the old emperor was so fond of the high priestess, the present emperor appointed a retinue of unusually grand rank and good repute to escort her to Ise. Genji sent a long letter (but not long enough) as the procession left the temporary shrine. For the princess there was a note tied with a ritual cord.* "To her whom it would be blasphemy to address in person," he wrote on the envelope.

"I would have thought not even the heavenly thunderer strong enough.†

"If my lady the priestess, surveying her manifold realms,
Has feelings for those below, let her feel for me.

"I tell myself that it must be, but remain unconvinced."

There was an answer despite the confusion, in the hand of the priestess's lady of honor:

"If a lord of the land is watching from above,
This pretense of sorrow will not have escaped his notice."

Genji would have liked to be present at the final audience with the emperor, but did not relish the role of rejected suitor. He spent the day in gloomy seclusion. He had to smile, however, at the priestess's rather knowing poem. She was clever for her age, and she interested him. Difficult and unconventional relationships always interested him. He could have done a great deal for her in earlier years and he was sorry now that he had not. But perhaps they would meet again—one never knew in this world.‡

A great many carriages had gathered, for an entourage presided over by ladies of such taste was sure to be worth seeing. It entered the palace in midafternoon. As the priestess's mother got into her state palanquin, she thought of her late father, who had had ambitious plans for her and prepared her with the greatest care for the position that was to be hers; and things could not have gone more disastrously wrong. Now, after all these years, she came to the palace again. She had entered the late crown prince's

---

* *Yū*, a cord of paper mulberry used by Shinto priests and priestesses to tie up their sleeves.
†Anonymous, *Kokinshū* 701:

> Is even the rage of the heavenly thunderer,
> Stamping and storming, enough to keep us apart?

‡It was common for a high priestess to be replaced at the beginning of a new reign.

household at sixteen and at twenty he had left her behind; and now, at thirty, she saw the palace once more.

> "The things of the past are always of the past.
> I would not think of them. Yet sad is my heart."

The priestess was a charming, delicate girl of fourteen, dressed by her mother with very great care. She was so compelling a little figure, indeed, that one wondered if she could be long for this world. The emperor was near tears as he put the farewell comb in her hair.

The carriages of their ladies were lined up before the eight ministries to await their withdrawal from the royal presence. The sleeves that flowed from beneath the blinds were of many and marvelous hues, and no doubt there were courtiers who were making their own silent, regretful farewells.

The procession left the palace in the evening. It was before Genji's mansion as it turned south from Nijō to Dōin. Unable to let it pass without a word, Genji sent out a poem attached to a sacred branch:

> "You throw me off; but will they not wet your sleeves,
> The eighty waves of the river Suzuka?"*

It was dark and there was great confusion, and her answer, brief and to the point, came the next morning from beyond Osaka Gate.

> "And who will watch us all the way to Ise,
> To see if those eighty waves have done their work?"

Her hand had lost none of its elegance, though it was a rather cold and austere elegance.

The morning was an unusually sad one of heavy mists. Absently he whispered to himself:

> "I see her on her way. Do not, O mists,
> This autumn close off the Gate of the Hill of Meeting."†

He spent the day alone, sunk in a sad reverie entirely of his own making, not even visiting Murasaki. And how much sadder must have been the thoughts of the lady on the road!

From the Tenth Month alarm for the old emperor spread through the whole court. The new emperor called to inquire after him. Weak though he was, the old emperor asked over and over again that his son be good to the crown prince. And he spoke too of Genji:

"Look to him for advice in large things and in small, just as you have until now. He is young but quite capable of ordering the most complicated public affairs. There is no office of which he need feel unworthy and no task in all the land that is beyond his powers. I reduced him to common rank so that you might make full use of his services. Do not, I beg of you, ignore my last wishes."

*In Ise. *Suzu* means "bell" and the swinging of a bell suggests rejection or shaking off.
†Osaka means "hill of meeting."

He made many other moving requests, but it is not a woman's place
to report upon them. Indeed I feel rather apologetic for having set down
these fragments.

Deeply moved, the emperor assured his father over and over again
that all of his wishes would be respected. The old emperor was pleased to
see that he had matured into a man of such regal dignity. The interview
was necessarily a short one, and the old emperor was if anything sadder
than had it not taken place.

The crown prince had wanted to come too, but had been persuaded
that unnecessary excitement was to be avoided and had chosen another
day. He was a handsome boy, advanced for his years. He had longed to
see his father, and now that they were together there were no bounds to
his boyish delight. Countless emotions assailed the old emperor as he saw
the tears in Fujitsubo's eyes. He had many things to say, but the boy
seemed so very young and helpless. Over and over again he told Genji
what he must do, and the well-being of the crown prince dominated his
remarks. It was late in the night when the crown prince made his departure. With virtually the whole court in attendance, the ceremony was in no
degree less grand than for the emperor's visit. The old emperor looked sadly
after the departing procession. The visit had been too short.

Kokiden too wanted to see him, but she did not want to see Fujitsubo. She hesitated, and then, peacefully, he died. The court was caught quite by surprise. He had, it was true, left the throne, but his influence had remained considerable. The emperor was young and his maternal grandfather, the Minister of the Right, was an impulsive, vindictive sort of man. What would the world be like, asked courtiers high and low, with such a man in control?

For Genji and Fujitsubo, the question was even crueler. At the funeral no one thought it odd that Genji should stand out among the old emperor's sons, and somehow people felt sadder for him than for his brothers. The dull mourning robes became him and seemed to make him more deserving of sympathy than the others. Two bereavements in successive years had informed him of the futility of human affairs. He thought once more of leaving the world. Alas, too many bonds still tied him to it.

The old emperor's ladies remained in his palace until the forty-ninth-day services were over. Then they went their several ways. It was the twentieth of the Twelfth Month, and skies which would in any case have seemed to mark the end of things were for Fujitsubo without a ray of sunlight. She was quite aware of Kokiden's feelings and knew that a world at the service of the other lady would be difficult to live in. But her thoughts were less of the future than of the past. Memories of her years with the old emperor never left her. His palace was no longer a home for his ladies, however, and presently all were gone.

Fujitsubo returned to her family palace in Sanjō. Her brother, Prince Hyōbu, came for her. There were flurries of snow, driven by a sharp wind. The old emperor's palace was almost deserted. Genji came to see them off and they talked of old times. The branches of the pine in the garden were brown and weighed down by snow.

The prince's poem was not an especially good one, but it suited the occasion and brought tears to Genji's eyes:

"Withered the pine whose branches gave us shelter?
    Now at the end of the year its needles fall."

The pond was frozen over. Genji's poem was impromptu and not, perhaps, among his best:

"Clear as a mirror, these frozen winter waters.
    The figure they once reflected is no more."

This was Omyōbu's poem:

"At the end of the year the springs are silenced by ice.
    And gone are they whom we saw among the rocks."

There were other poems, but I see no point in setting them down. The procession was as grand as in other years. Perhaps it was only in

the imagination that there was something forlorn and dejected about it Fujitsubo's own Sanjō palace now seemed like a wayside inn. Her thoughts were on the years she had spent away from it.

The New Year came, bringing no renewal. Life was sad and subdued. Sadder than all the others, Genji was in seclusion. During his father's reign, of course, and no less during the years since, the New Year appointments had brought such streams of horses and carriages to his gates that there had been room for no more. Now they were deserted. Only a few listless guards and secretaries occupied the offices. His favorite retainers did come calling, but it was as if they had time on their hands. So, he thought, life was to be.

In the Second Month, Kokiden's sister Oborozukiyo, she of the misty moon, was appointed wardress of the ladies' apartments, replacing a lady who in grief at the old emperor's death had become a nun. The new wardress was amiable and cultivated, and the emperor was very fond of her.

Kokiden now spent most of her time with her own family. When she was at court she occupied the Plum Pavilion. She had turned her old Kokiden Pavilion over to Oborozukiyo, who found it a happy change from her rather gloomy and secluded rooms to the north. Indeed it quite swarmed with ladies-in-waiting. Yet she could not forget that strange encounter with Genji, and it was on her initiative that they still kept up a secret correspondence. He was very nervous about it, but excited (for such was his nature) by the challenge which her new position seemed to offer.

Kokiden had bided her time while the old emperor lived, but she was a willful, headstrong woman, and now it seemed that she meant to have her revenge. Genji's life became a series of defeats and annoyances. He was not surprised, and yet, accustomed to being the darling of the court, he found the new chilliness painful and preferred to stay at home. The Minister of the Left, his father-in-law, was also unhappy with the new reign and seldom went to court. Kokiden remembered all too well how he had refused his daughter to the then crown prince and offered her to Genji instead. The two ministers had never been on good terms. The Minister of the Left had had his way while the old emperor lived, and he was of course unhappy now that the Minister of the Right was in control. Genji still visited Sanjō and was more civil and attentive than ever to the women there, and more attentive to the details of his son's education. He went far beyond the call of ordinary duty and courtesy, thought the minister, to whom he was as important as ever. His father's favorite son, he had had little time to himself while his father lived; but it was now that he began neglecting ladies with whom he had been friendly. These flirtations no longer interested him. He was soberer and quieter, altogether a model young man.

The good fortune of the new lady at Nijō was by now well known at court. Her nurse and others of her women attributed it to the prayers of the old nun, her grandmother. Her father now corresponded with her as he wished. He had had high hopes for his daughters by his principal wife, and they were not doing well, to the considerable chagrin and envy, it seems, of the wife. It was a situation made to order for the romancers.

In mourning for her father, the old emperor, the high priestess of Kamo resigned and Princess Asagao took her place. It was not usual for the granddaughter rather than the daughter of an emperor to hold the position, but it would seem that there were no completely suitable candidates for the position. The princess had continued over the years to interest Genji, who now regretted that she should be leaving his world. He still saw Chūjō, her woman, and he still wrote to the princess. Not letting his changed circumstances worry him unnecessarily, he sought to beguile the tedium by sending off notes here and there.

The emperor would have liked to follow his father's last injunctions and look to Genji for support, but he was young and docile and unable to impose his will. His mother and grandfather had their way, and it was not at all to his liking.

For Genji one distasteful incident followed another. Oborozukiyo relieved the gloom by letting him know that she was still fond of him. Though fraught with danger, a meeting was not difficult to arrange. Homage to the Five Lords* was to begin and the emperor would be in retreat. Genji paid his visit, which was like a dream. Chūnagon contrived to admit him to the gallery of the earlier meeting. There were many people about and the fact that he was nearer the veranda than usual was unfortunate. Since women who saw him morning and night never tired of him, how could it be an ordinary meeting for one who had seen so little of him? Oborozukiyo was at her youthful best. It may be that she was not as calm and dignified as she might have been, but her young charms were enough to please him all the same.

It was near dawn. Almost at Genji's elbow a guardsman announced himself in loud, vibrant tones. Another guardsman had apparently slipped in with one of the ladies hereabouts and this one had been dispatched to surprise him. Genji was both amused and annoyed. "The first hour of the tiger!"† There were calls here and there as guardsmen flushed out intruders.

The lady was sad, and more beautiful for the sadness, as she recited a poem:

> "They say that it is dawn, that you grow weary.
> I weep, my sorrows wrought by myself alone."

He answered:

> "You tell me that these sorrows must not cease?
> My sorrows, my love will neither have an ending."

He made his stealthy way out. The moon was cold in the faint beginnings of dawn, softened by delicate tracings of mist. Though in rough disguise, he was far too handsome not to attract attention. A guards officer, brother of Lady Shōkyōden,‡ had emerged from the Wisteria Court and was standing in the shadow of a latticed fence. If Genji failed to notice him, it was unfortunate. Hostile reports would spread.

Always when he had been with another lady he would think of the lady who was so cold to him. Though her aloofness was in its way admirable, he could not help resenting it. Visits to court being painful, Fujitsubo had to worry from afar about her son the crown prince. Though she had no one to turn to except Genji, whom she depended on for everything, she was tormented by evidence that his unwelcome affections were unchanged. Even the thought that the old emperor had died without suspecting the truth filled her with terror, which was intensified by the thought that if rumors were to get abroad, the results, quite aside from what they might mean for Fujitsubo herself, would be very unhappy for the crown prince. She even commissioned religious services in hopes of freeing herself from Genji's attentions and she exhausted every device to avoid him.

---

*Vidhyārāja, Japanese Myō-ō. Their blessings were invoked on such special occasions as the beginning of a new reign.
†About four in the morning.
‡One of the emperor's concubines, and an ally of the Minister of the Right.

She was appalled, then, when one day he found a way to approach her. He had made his plans carefully and no one in her household was aware of them. The result was for her an unrelieved nightmare.

The words with which he sought to comfort her were so subtle and clever that I am unable to transcribe them, but she was unmoved. After a time she was seized with sharp chest pains. Omyōbu and Ben hurried to her side. Genji was reeling from the grim determination with which she had repulsed him. Everything, past and future, seemed to fall away into darkness. Scarcely aware of what he was doing, he stayed on in her apartments even though day was breaking. Several other women, alerted to the crisis, were now up and about. Omyōbu and Ben bundled a half-conscious Genji into a closet. They were beside themselves as they pushed his clothes in after him. Fujitsubo was now taken with fainting spells. Prince Hyōbu and her chamberlain were sent for, and priests as well. A dazed Genji listened to the excitement from his closet.

Towards evening Fujitsubo began to feel rather more herself again. She had not the smallest suspicion that Genji was still in the house, her women having thought it best to keep the information from her. She came out to her sitting room. Much relieved, Prince Hyōbu departed. The room was almost empty. There were not many women whom she liked to have in her immediate presence and the others kept out of sight. Omyōbu and Ben were wondering how they might contrive to spirit Genji away. He must not be allowed to bring on another attack.

The closet door being open a few inches, he slipped out and made his way between a screen and the wall. He looked with wonder at the lady and tears came to his eyes. Still in some pain, she was gazing out at the garden. Might it be the end? she was asking herself. Her profile was lovely beyond description. The women sought to tempt her with sweets, which were indeed most temptingly laid out on the lid of a decorative box, but she did not look at them. To Genji she was a complete delight as she sat in silence, lost in deeply troubled meditations. Her hair as it cascaded over her shoulders, the lines of her head and face, the glow of her skin, were to Genji irresistibly beautiful. They were very much like each other, she and Murasaki. Memories had dimmed over the years, but now the astonishing resemblance did a little to dispel his gloom. The dignity that quite put one to shame also reminded him of Murasaki. He could hardly think of them as two persons, and yet, perhaps because Fujitsubo had been so much in his thoughts over the years, there did after all seem to be a difference. Fujitsubo's was the calmer and more mature dignity. No longer in control of himself, he slipped inside her curtains and pulled at her sleeve. So distinctive was the fragrance that she recognized him immediately. In sheer terror she sank to the floor.

If she would only look at him! He pulled her towards him. She turned to flee, but her hair became entangled in her cloak as she tried to slip out of it. It seemed to be her fate that everything should go against her!

Deliriously, Genji poured forth all the resentment he had kept to himself; but it only revolted her.

"I am not feeling well. Perhaps on another occasion I will be better able to receive you."

Yet he talked on. Mixed in with the flow were details which did, after all, seem to move her. This was not of course their first meeting, but she had been determined that there would not be another. Though avoiding explicit rejoinder, she held him off until morning. He could not force himself upon her. In her quiet dignity, she left him feeling very much ashamed of himself.

"If I may see you from time to time and so drive away a little of the gloom, I promise you that I shall do nothing to offend you."

The most ordinary things have a way of moving people who are as they were to each other, and this was no ordinary meeting. It was daylight. Omyōbu and Ben were insistent and Fujitsubo seemed barely conscious.

"I think I must die," he said in a final burst of passion. "I cannot bear the thought of having you know that I still exist. And if I die my love for you will be an obstacle on my way to salvation.

"If other days must be as this has been,
    I still shall be weeping two and three lives hence.

And the sin will be yours as well."

She sighed.

> "Remember that the cause is in yourself
> Of a sin which you say I must bear through lives to come."

She managed an appearance of resignation which tore at his heart. It was no good trying her patience further. Half distraught, he departed. He would only invite another defeat if he tried to see her again. She must be made to feel sorry for him. He would not even write to her. He remained shut up at Nijō, seeing neither the emperor nor the crown prince, his gloom spreading discomfort through the house and making it almost seem that he had lost the will to live. "I am in this world but to see my woes increase."* He must leave it behind—but there was the dear girl who so needed him. He could not abandon her.

Fujitsubo had been left a near invalid by the encounter. Omyōbu and Ben were saddened at Genji's withdrawal and refusal to write. Fujitsubo too was disturbed: it would serve the crown prince badly if Genji were to turn against her, and it would be a disaster if, having had enough of the world, he were to take holy orders. A repetition of the recent incident would certainly give rise to rumors which would make visits to the palace even more distasteful. She was becoming convinced that she must relinquish the title that had aroused the implacable hostility of Kokiden. She remembered the detailed and emphatic instructions which the old emperor had left behind. Everything was changed, no shadow remained of the past. She might not suffer quite as cruel a fate as Lady Ch'i,† but she must doubtless look forward to contempt and derision. She resolved to become a nun. But she must see the crown prince again before she did. Quietly, she paid him a visit.

Though Genji had seen to all her needs in much more complicated matters than this one, he pleaded illness and did not accompany her to court. He still made routine inquiries as civility demanded. The women who shared his secret knew that he was very unhappy, and pitied him.

Her little son was even prettier than when she had last seen him. He clung to her, his pleasure in her company so touching that she knew how difficult it would be to carry through her resolve. But this glimpse of court life told her more clearly than ever that it was no place for her, that the things she had known had vanished utterly away. She must always worry about Kokiden, and these visits would be increasingly uncomfortable; and in sum everything caused her pain. She feared for her son's future if she continued to let herself be called empress.

---

*Anonymous, *Kokinshū* 951:

> I am in this world but to see my woes increase.
> I shall go beyond the crags of Yoshino.

†A concubine of the emperor Kao-tsu who was murdered by his widow.

"What will you think of me if I do not see you for a very long time and become very unpleasant to look at?"

He gazed up at her. "Like Shikibu?" He laughed. "But why should you ever look like her?"

She wanted to weep. "Ah, but Shikibu is old and wrinkled. That is not what I had in mind. I meant that my hair would be shorter and I would wear black clothes and look like one of the priests that say prayers at night. And I would see you much less often."

"I would miss you," he said solemnly, turning away to hide his tears. The hair that fell over his shoulders was wonderfully lustrous and the glow in his eyes, warmer as he grew up, was almost enough to make one think he had taken Genji's face for a mask. Because his teeth were slightly decayed, his mouth was charmingly dark when he smiled. One almost wished that he had been born a girl. But the resemblance to Genji was for her like the flaw in the gem. All the old fears came back.

Genji too wanted to see the crown prince, but he wanted also to make Fujitsubo aware of her cruelty. He kept to himself at Nijō. Fearing that his indolence would be talked about and thinking that the autumn leaves would be at their best, he went off to the Ujii Temple, to the north of the city, over which an older brother of his late mother presided. Borrowing the uncle's cell for fasting and meditation, he stayed for several days.

The fields, splashed with autumn color, were enough to make him forget the city. He gathered erudite monks and listened attentively to their discussions of the scriptures. Though he would pass the night in the thoughts of the evanescence of things to which the setting was so conducive, he would still, in the dawn moonlight, remember the lady who was being so cruel to him. There would be a clattering as the priests put new flowers before the images, and the chrysanthemums and the falling leaves of varied tints, though the scene was in no way dramatic, seemed to offer asylum in this life and hope for the life to come. And what a purposeless life was his!

"All who invoke the holy name shall be taken unto Lord Amitābha and none shall be abandoned,"* proclaimed Genji's uncle in grand, lingering tones, and Genji was filled with envy. Why did he not embrace the religious life? He knew (for the workings of his heart were complex) that the chief reason was the girl at Nijō.

He had been away from her now for an unusually long time. She was much on his mind and he wrote frequently. "I have come here," he said in one of his letters, "to see whether I am capable of leaving the world. The serenity I had hoped for eludes me and my loneliness only grows. There are things I have yet to learn. And have you missed me?" It was on heavy Michinoku paper. The hand, though casual, was strong and distinguished.

> "In lodgings frail as the dew upon the reeds
> I left you, and the four winds tear at me."

*From what was to become one of the main texts of the Pure Land Sect.

It brought tears to her eyes. Her answer was a verse on a bit of white paper:

"Weak as the spider's thread upon the reeds,
    The dew-drenched reeds of autumn, I blow with the winds."

He smiled. Her writing had improved. It had come to resemble his, though it was gentler and more ladylike. He congratulated himself on having such a perfect subject for his pedagogical endeavors.

The Kamo Shrines were not far away. He got off a letter to Princess Asagao, the high priestess. He sent it through Chūjō, with this message for Chūjō herself: "A traveler, I feel my heart traveling yet further afield; but your lady will not have taken note of it, I suppose."

This was his message for the princess herself:

"The gods will not wish me to speak of them, perhaps,
    But I think of sacred cords of another autumn.

'Is there no way to make the past the present?' "*

He wrote as if their relations might permit a certain intimacy. His note was on azure Chinese paper attached most solemnly to a sacred branch from which streamed ritual cords.

Chūjō's answer was courteous and leisurely. "We live a quiet life here, and I have time for many stray thoughts, among them thoughts of you and my lady."

There was a note from the princess herself, tied with a ritual cord:

"Another autumn—what can this refer to?
    A secret hoard of thoughts of sacred cords?

And in more recent times?"†

The hand was not perhaps the subtlest he had seen, but it showed an admirable mastery of the cursive style, and interested him. His heart leaped (most blasphemously) at the thought of a beauty of feature that would doubtless have outstripped the beauty of her handwriting.

He remembered that just a year had passed since that memorable night at the temporary shrine of the other high priestess, and (blasphemously again) he found himself berating the gods, that the fates of his two cousins should have been so strangely similar. He had had a chance of successfully wooing at least one of the ladies who were the subjects of these improper thoughts, and he had procrastinated; and it was odd that he should now have these regrets. When, occasionally, Princess Asagao answered, her tone was not at all unfriendly, though one might have taxed her with a certain inconsistency.

---

* *Tales of Ise* 32:

    Is there no way to make the past the present,
        To wind and unwind it like a ball of yarn?

†Very cryptic. Apparently a poetic allusion.

He read the sixty Tendai fascicles and asked the priests for explanations of difficult passages. Their prayers had brought this wondrous radiance upon their monastery, said even the lowliest of them, and indeed Genji's presence seemed to bring honor to the Blessed One himself. Though he quietly thought over the affairs of the world and was reluctant to return to it, thoughts of the lady at Nijō interfered with his meditations and made it seem useless to stay longer. His gifts were lavish to all the several ranks in the monastery and to the mountain people as well; and so, having exhausted the possibilities of pious works, he made his departure. The woodcutters came down from the hills and knelt by the road to see him off. Still in mourning, his carriage draped in black, he was not easy to pick out, but from the glimpses they had they thought him a fine figure of a man indeed.

Even after this short absence Murasaki was more beautiful and more sedately mature. She seemed to be thinking about the future and what they would be to each other. Perhaps it was because she knew all about his errant ways that she had written of the "reeds of autumn." She pleased him more and more and it was with deeper affection thàn ever that he greeted her.

He had brought back autumn leaves more deeply tinted by the dews than the leaves in his garden. Fearing that people might be remarking upon his neglect of Fujitsubo, he sent a few branches as a routine gift, and with them a message for Omyōbu:

"The news, which I received with some wonder, of your lady's visit to the palace had the effect of making me want to be in retreat for a time. I have rather neglected you, I fear. Having made my plans, I did not think it proper to change them. I must share my harvest with you. A sheaf of autumn leaves admired in solitude is like 'damasks worn in the darkness of the night.'* Show them to your lady, please, when an occasion presents itself."

They were magnificent. Looking more closely, Fujitsubo saw hidden in them a tightly folded bit of paper. She flushed, for her women were watching. The same thing all over again! So much more prudent and careful now, he was still capable of unpleasant surprises. Her women would think it most peculiar. She had one of them put the leaves in a vase out near the veranda.

Genji was her support in private matters and in the far more important matter of the crown prince's well-being. Her clipped, businesslike notes left him filled with bitter admiration at the watchfulness with which she eluded his advances. People would notice if he were suddenly to terminate his services, and so he went to the palace on the day she was to return to her family.

He first called on the emperor, whom he found free from court business and happy to talk about recent and ancient events. He bore a strong resemblance to their father, though he was perhaps handsomer, and there was a gentler, more amiable cast to his features. The two brothers exchanged fond glances from time to time. The emperor had heard, and himself had had reason to suspect, that Genji and Oborozukiyo were still seeing each other. He told himself, however, that the matter would have been worth thinking about if it had only now burst upon the world, but that it was not at all strange or improper that old friends should be interested in each other. He saw no reason to caution Genji. He asked Genji's opinion about certain puzzling Chinese texts, and as the talk naturally turned to little poems they had sent and received he remarked on the departure of the high priestess for Ise. How pretty she had been that day! Genji told of the dawn meeting at the temporary shrine.

It was a beautiful time, late in the month. A quarter moon hung in the sky. One wanted music on nights like this, said the emperor.†

"Her Majesty is leaving the palace this evening," said Genji, "and I

*Ki no Tsurayuki, *Kokinshū* 297:

> Autumn leaves which fall in distant mountains
> Are damasks worn in the darkness of the night.

†Music is forbidden because the court is in mourning.

was thinking of calling on her. Father left such detailed instructions and there is no one to look after her. And then of course there is the crown prince."

"Yes, Father did worry a great deal about the crown prince. Indeed one of his last requests was that I adopt him as my own son. He is, I assure you, much on my mind, but one must worry about seeming partial and setting a precedent. He writes remarkably well for his age, making up for my own awkward scrawl and general incompetence."

"He is a clever child, clever beyond his years. But he is very young."

As he withdrew, a nephew of Kokiden happened to be on his way to visit a younger sister. He was on the winning side and saw no reason to hide his light. He stopped to watch Genji's modest retinue go by.

"A white rainbow crosses the sun," he grandly intoned. "The crown prince trembles."*

Genji was startled but let the matter pass. He was aware that Kokiden's hostility had if anything increased, and her relatives had their ways of making it known. It was unpleasant, but one was wise to look the other way.

"It is very late, I fear," he sent in to Fujitsubo. "I have been with the emperor."

On such nights his father's palace would have been filled with music. The setting was the same, but there was very little left by which to remember the old reign.

Omyōbu brought a poem from Fujitsubo:

"Ninefold mists have risen and come between us.
I am left to imagine the moon beyond the clouds."

She was so near that he could feel her presence. His bitterness quite left him and he was in tears as he replied:

"The autumn moon is the autumn moon of old.
How cruel the mists that will not let me see it.

The poet has told us that mists are as unkind as people, and so I suppose that I am not the first one so troubled."†

She had numerous instructions for her son with which to delay her farewell. He was too young to pay a great deal of attention, however, and she drew little comfort from this last interview. Though he usually went to bed very early, tonight he seemed determined to stay up for her departure. He longed to go with her, but of course it was impossible.

That objectionable nephew of Kokiden's had made Genji wonder what people really thought of him. Life at court was more and more trying.

---

*A treasonous prince in the *Shih Chi* was persuaded by a white rainbow passing through the sun that a plot against Ch'in Shih-huang-ti would not succeed. The implication seems to be that Genji, an ally of the crown prince, is disloyal to the emperor.
†The poet has not been identified.

Days went by and he did not get off a note to Oborozukiyo. The late-autumn skies warned of the approach of winter rains. A note came from her, whatever she may have meant by thus taking the initiative:

"Anxious, restless days. A gust of wind,
  And yet another, bringing no word from you."

It was a melancholy season. He was touched that she should have ventured to write. Asking the messenger to wait, he selected a particularly fine bit of paper from a supply he kept in a cabinet and then turned to selecting brush and ink. All very suggestive, thought the women. Who might the lady be?

"I had grown thoroughly weary of a one-sided correspondence, and now—'So long it has been that you have been waiting too?'*

"Deceive yourself not into thinking them autumn showers,
  The tears I weep in hopeless longing to see you.

"Let our thoughts of each other drive the dismal rains from our minds."

One may imagine that she was not the only lady who tried to move him, but his answers to the others were polite and perfunctory.

Fujitsubo was making preparations for a solemn reading of the Lotus Sutra, to follow memorial services on the anniversary of the old emperor's death. There was a heavy snowfall on the anniversary, early in the Eleventh Month.

This poem came from Genji:

"We greet once more the day of the last farewell,
  And when, in what snows, may we hope for a day of meeting?"

It was a sad day for everyone.
This was her reply:

"To live these months without him has been sorrow.
  But today seems to bring a return of the days of old."

The hand was a casual one, and yet—perhaps he wished it so—it was uniquely graceful and dignified. Though he could not expect from her the bright, modern sort of elegance, there were few who could be called her rivals. But today, with its snow and its memories, he could not think of her. He lost himself in prayer.

The reading took place toward the middle of the Twelfth Month. All the details were perfection, the scrolls to be dedicated on each of the several days, the jade spindles, the mountings of delicate silk, the brocade covers. No one was surprised, for she was a lady who on far less important

---

*Anonymous, *Gosenshū* 1261:

    Sadly I wait, so far beneath your notice.
    So long it has been that you have been waiting too?

occasions thought no detail too trivial for her attention. The wreaths and flowers, the cloths for the gracefully carved lecterns—they could not have been outdone in paradise itself. The reading on the first day was dedicated to her father, the late emperor, on the second to her mother, the empress, and on the third to her husband. The third day brought the reading of the climactic fifth scroll. High courtiers gathered in large numbers, though aware that the dominant faction at court would not approve. The reader had been chosen with particular care, and though the words themselves, about firewood and the like,* were familiar, they seemed grander and more awesome than ever before. The princes made offerings and Genji seemed far handsomer than any of his brothers. It may be that I remark too frequently upon the fact, but what am I to do when it strikes me afresh each time I see him?

On the last day, Fujitsubo offered prayers and vows of her own. In the course of them she announced her intention of becoming a nun. The assembly was incredulous. Prince Hyōbu and Genji were visibly shaken. The prince went into his sister's room even before the services were over.

---

*Among the menial tasks which the Buddha in a former incarnation performed that he might receive the Lotus Sutra was the cutting of firewood.

She made it very clear, however, that her decision was final. In the quiet at the end of the reading she summoned the grand abbot of Hiei and asked that he administer the vows. As her uncle, the bishop of Yokawa, approached to trim her hair, a stir spread through the hall, and there were unpropitious sounds of weeping. It is strangely sad even when old and unremarkable people leave the world, and how much sadder the sudden departure of a lady so young and beautiful. Her brother was sobbing openly. Saddened and awed by what had just taken place, the assembly dispersed. The old emperor's sons, remembering what Fujitsubo had been to their father, offered words of sympathy as they left. For Genji it was as if darkness had settled over the land. Still in his place, he could think of nothing to say. He struggled to control himself, for an excess of sorrow was certain to arouse curiosity. When Prince Hyōbu had left he went in to speak to Fujitsubo. The turmoil was subsiding and the women, in little clusters, were sniffling and dabbing at their eyes. The light from a cloudless moon flooded in, silver from the snow in the garden.

Genji somehow managed to fight back the tears that welled up at the memories the scene brought back. "What are you thinking of, taking us so by surprise?"

She replied, as always, through Omyōbu: "It is something on which I deliberated for a very long time. I did not want to attract attention. It might have weakened my resolve."

From her retreat came poignant evidence of sorrow. There was a soft rustling of silk as her women moved diffidently about. The wind had risen. The mysterious scent of "dark incense"* drifted through the blinds, to mingle with the fainter incense from the altars and Genji's own perfume and bring thoughts of the Western Paradise.

A messenger came from the crown prince. At the memory of their last interview her carefully maintained composure quite left her, and she was unable to answer. Genji set down an answer in her place. It was a difficult time, and he was afraid that he did not express himself well.

> "My heart is with her in the moonlight above the clouds,
>   And yet it stays with you in this darker world.

"I am making excuses. Such resolve leaves me infinitely dissatisfied with myself."

That was all. There were people about, and he could not even begin to describe his turbulent thoughts.

Fujitsubo sent out a note:

> "Though I leave behind a world I cannot endure,
>   My heart remains with him, still of that world.

And will be muddied by it."

---

*A mixture of cloves, aloes, and other perfumes.

It would seem to have been largely the work of her sensitive women. Numb with sorrow, Genji made his way out.

Back at Nijō he withdrew to his own rooms, where he spent a sleepless night. In a world that had become in every way distasteful, he too still thought of the crown prince. The old emperor had hoped that at least the boy's mother would stay with him, and now, driven away, she would probably feel constrained to relinquish her title as well. What if Genji were to abandon the boy? All night the question chased itself through his mind.

He turned to the work of fitting out the nunnery and hurried to have everything ready by the end of the year. Omyōbu had followed her lady in taking vows. To her too, most feelingly, he sent gifts and assurances of his continuing esteem.

A complete description of such an event has a way of seeming overdone, and much has no doubt been left out; which is a pity, since many fine poems are sure to be exchanged at such times.

He felt more at liberty now to call on her, and sometimes she would come out and receive him herself. The old passions were not dead, but there was little that could be done to satisfy them now.

The New Year came. The court was busy with festive observances, the emperor's poetry banquet and the carols.* Fujitsubo devoted herself to her beads and prayers and tried to ignore the echoes that reached her. Thoughts of the life to come were her strength. She put aside all the old comforts and sorrows. Leaving her old chapel as it was, she built a new one some distance to the south of the west wing, and there she took up residence, and lost herself in prayer and meditation.

Genji came calling and saw little sign that the New Year had brought new life. Her palace was silent and almost deserted. Only her nearest confidantes were still with her, and even they (or perhaps it was his imagination) seemed downcast and subdued. The white horses,† which her entire household came out to see, brought a brief flurry of the old excitement. High courtiers had once gathered in such numbers that there had seemed room for no more, and it was sad though understandable that today they gathered instead at the mansion of the Minister of the Right, across the street. Genji was as kind and attentive as ever, and to the women, shedding unnoticed tears, he seemed worth a thousand of the others.

Looking about him at these melancholy precincts, Genji was at first unable to speak. They had become in every way a nunnery: the blinds and curtains, all a drab gray-green, glimpses of gray and yellow sleeves— melancholy and at the same time quietly, mysteriously beautiful. He looked out into the garden. The ice was melting from the brook and pond, and the willow on the bank, as if it alone were advancing boldly into

The Naien and the Otokotōka respectively. See note, page 76.
†After being reviewed by the emperor, on the seventh day of the First Month, ceremonial horses were reviewed by other members of the royal family.

spring, had already sent out shoots. "Uncommonly elegant fisherfolk,"* he whispered, himself an uncommonly handsome figure.

> "Briny my sleeves at the pines of Urashima
> As those of the fisherfolk who take the sea grass."

Her reply was faint and low, from very near at hand, for the chapel was small and crowded with holy objects:

> "How strange that waves yet come to Urashima,
> When all the things of old have gone their way."

He tried not to weep. He would have preferred not to show his tears to nuns who had awakened to the folly of human affairs. He said little more.

"What a splendid gentleman he has become," sobbed one of the old women. "Back in the days when everything was going his way, when the whole world seemed to be his, we used to hope that something would come along to jar him just a little from his smugness. But now look at him, so calm and sober and collected. There is something about him when he does the smallest little thing that tugs at a person's heart. It's all too sad."

Fujitsubo too thought a great deal about the old days.

The spring promotions were announced, and they brought no happiness to Fujitsubo's household. Promotions that should have come in the natural order of things or because of her position were withheld. It was unreasonable to argue that because she had become a nun she was no longer entitled to the old emoluments; but that was the argument all the same. For her people, the world was a changed place. Though there were times when she still had regrets, not for herself but for those who depended upon her, she turned ever more fervently to her prayers, telling herself that the security of her son was the important thing. Her secret worries sometimes approached real terror. She would pray that by way of recompense for her own sufferings his burden of guilt be lightened, and in the prayer she would find comfort.

Genji understood and sympathized. The spring lists had been no more satisfying for his people than for hers. He remained in seclusion at Nijō.

And it was a difficult time for the Minister of the Left. Everything was changed, private and public. He handed in his resignation, but the emperor, remembering how his father had looked to the minister as one of the men on whom the stability of the reign depended and how just before his death he had asked especially that the minister's services be retained, said that he could not dispense with such estimable services. He declined to accept the resignation, though it was tendered more than once. Finally

*Sosei, *Gosenshū* 1094:

> Long have I heard of the pines of Urashima.
> Uncommonly elegant fisherfolk dwell among them.

Ama means both "fisherman" and "nun." The pun is repeated in Genji's poem.

the minister withdrew to the seclusion of his Sanjō mansion, and the Minister of the Right was more powerful and prosperous every day. With the retirement of a man who should have been a source of strength, the emperor was helpless. People of feeling all through the court joined him in his laments.

Genji's brothers-in-law, the sons of the Minister of the Left, were all personable and popular young men, and life had been pleasant for them. Now they too were in eclipse. On Tō no Chūjō's rare visits to his wife, the fourth daughter of the Minister of the Right, he was made to feel all too clearly that she was less than delighted with him and that he was not the minister's favorite son-in-law. As if to emphasize the point, he too was omitted from the spring lists. But he was not one to fret over the injustice. Genji's setbacks seemed to him evidence enough that public life was insecure, and he was philosophic about his own career. He and Genji were constant companions in their studies and in such diversions as music. Now and then something of their madcap boyhood rivalry seemed almost to come back.

Genji paid more attention than in other years to the semiannual readings of holy scriptures and commissioned several unscheduled readings as well. He would summon learned professors who did not have much else to do and beguile the tedium of his days composing Chinese poetry and joining in contests of rhyme guessing and the like. He seldom went to court. This indolent life seems to have aroused a certain amount of criticism.

On an evening of quiet summer rain when the boredom was very great, Tō no Chūjō came calling and brought with him several of the better collections of Chinese poetry. Going into his library, Genji opened cases he had not looked into before and chose several unusual and venerable collections. Quietly he sent out invitations to connoisseurs of Chinese poetry at court and in the university. Dividing them into teams of the right and of the left, he set them to a rhyme-guessing contest. The prizes were lavish. As the rhymes became more difficult even the erudite professors were sometimes at a loss, and Genji would dazzle the assembly by coming up with a solution which had eluded them. The meeting of so many talents in one person—it was the wonder of the day, and it told of great merits accumulated in previous lives.

Two days later Tō no Chūjō gave a banquet for the victors. Though it was a quiet, unostentatious affair, the food was beautifully arranged in cypress boxes. There were numerous gifts and there were the usual diversions, Chinese poetry and the like. Here and there below the veranda a solitary rose was coming into bloom, more effective, in a quiet way, than the full bloom of spring or autumn. Several of the guests presently took up instruments and began an impromptu concert. One of Tō no Chūjō's little sons, a boy of eight or nine who had just this year been admitted to the royal presence, sang for them in fine voice and played on the *shō* pipes.

A favorite of Genji, who often joined him in a duet, the boy was Tō no Chūjō's second son and a grandson of the Minister of the Right. He was gifted and intelligent and very handsome as well, and great care had gone into his education. As the proceedings grew noisier he sang "Takasago"* in a high, clear voice. Delighted, Genji took off a singlet and presented it to him. A slight flush from drink made Genji even handsomer than usual. His skin glowed through his light summer robes. The learned guests looked up at him from the lower tables with eyes that had misted over. "I might have met the first lily of spring"—the boy had come to the end of his song. Tō no Chūjō offered Genji a cup of wine and with it a verse:

> "I might have met the first lily of spring, he says.
> I look upon a flower no less pleasing."

Smiling, Genji took the cup:

> "The plant of which you speak bloomed very briefly.
> It opened at dawn to wilt in the summer rains,

and is not what it used to be."

Though Tō no Chūjō did not entirely approve of this garrulity, he continued to press wine upon his guest.

There seem to have been numerous other poems; but Tsurayuki has warned that it is in bad taste to compose under the influence of alcohol and that the results are not likely to have much merit,† and so I did not trouble myself to write them down. All the poems, Chinese and Japanese alike, were in praise of Genji. In fine form, he said as if to himself: "I am the son of King Wen, the brother of King Wu." It was magnificent. And what might he have meant to add about King Ch'eng?‡ At that point, it seems, he thought it better to hold his tongue. Prince Sochi,** who could always be counted upon to enliven these gatherings, was an accomplished musician and a witty and good-humored adversary for Genji.

Oborozukiyo was spending some time with her family. She had had several attacks of malaria and hoped that rest and the services of priests might be beneficial. Everyone was pleased that this treatment did indeed prove effective. It was a rare opportunity. She made certain arrangements with Genji and, though they were complicated, saw him almost every night. She was a bright, cheerful girl, at her youthful best, and a small loss of weight had made her very beautiful indeed. Because her sister, Kokiden, also happened to be at home, Genji was in great apprehension lest his presence be detected. It was his nature to be quickened by danger, how-

---

*A congratulatory Saibara.

†The warning is not to be found in Tsurayuki's surviving works.

‡"I am the son of King Wen, the brother of King Wu, and the uncle of King Ch'eng," says the Duke of Chou in the *Shih Chi*.

**Both Murasaki's father and one of Genji's brothers, Prince Hotaru. are sometimes called Prince Sochi. This could be either.

ever, and with elaborate stealth he continued his visits. Although it would seem that, as the number increased, several women of the house began to suspect what was happening, they were reluctant to play informer to the august lady. The minister had no suspicions.

Then one night toward dawn there came a furious thunderstorm. The minister's sons and Kokiden's women were rushing about in confusion. Several women gathered trembling near Oborozukiyo's bed curtains. Genji was almost as frightened, for other reasons, and unable to escape. Daylight came. He was in a fever, for a crowd of women had by now gathered outside the curtains. The two women who were privy to the secret could think of nothing to do.

The thunder stopped, the rain quieted to showers. The minister went first to Kokiden's wing and then, his approach undetected because of the rain on the roof, to Oborozukiyo's. He marched jauntily up the gallery and lifted a blind.

"How did you come through it all? I was worried about you and meant to look in on you. Have the lieutenant* and Her Majesty's vice-chamberlain been here?"

*One of his sons.

A cascade of words poured forth. Despite the precariousness of his situation, Genji could not help smiling at the difference between the two ministers. The man could at least have come inside before he commenced his speech.

Flushed and trembling, Oborozukiyo slipped through the bed curtains. The minister feared that she had had a relapse.

"My, but you do look strange. It's not just malaria, it's some sort of evil spirit, I'm sure of it, a very stubborn one. We should have kept those priests at it."

He caught sight of a pale magenta sash entwined in her skirts. And something beside the curtain too, a wadded bit of paper on which he could see traces of writing.

"What might *this* be?" he asked in very great surprise. "Not at all something that I would have expected to find here. Let me have it. Give it to me, now. Let me see what it is."

The lady glanced over her shoulder and saw the incriminating objects. And now what was she to do? One might have expected a little more tact and forbearance from a man of parts. It was an exceedingly difficult moment, even if she was his own daughter. But he was a headstrong and not very thoughtful man, and all sense of proportion deserted him. Snatching at the paper, he lifted the bed curtains. A gentleman was lying there in dishabille. He hid his face and sought to pull his clothes together. Though dizzy with anger, the minister pulled back from a direct confrontation. He took the bit of paper off to the main hall.

Oborozukiyo was afraid she would faint and wished she might expire on the spot. Genji was of course upset too. He had gone on permitting himself these heedless diversions and now he faced a proper scandal. But the immediate business was to comfort the lady.

It had always been the minister's way to keep nothing to himself, and now the crotchetiness of old age had been added in ample measure to this effusiveness. Why should he hold back? He poured out for Kokiden the full list of his complaints.

"It is Genji's handwriting," he said, after describing what he had just seen. "I was careless and I let it all get started several years ago. But Genji is Genji, and I forgave everything and even hoped I might have him as a son-in-law. I was not happy of course that he did not seem to take her very seriously, and sometimes he did things that seemed completely outrageous; but I told myself that these things happen. I was sure that His Majesty would overlook a little blemish or two and take her in, and so I went back to my original plan and sent her off to court. I wasn't happy —who would have been?—that the affair had made him feel a little odd about her and kept her from being one of his favorites. And now I really do think I've been misused. Boys will do this sort of thing, I know, but it's really too much. They say he's still after the high priestess of Kamo and gets off secret letters to her, and something must be going on there too. He is a disgrace to his brother's reign and a disgrace in general, to himself and everyone else too. But I would have expected him to be cleverer about it. One of the brighter and more talented people of our day, everyone says. I simply would not have expected it of him."

Of an even more choleric nature, Kokiden spoke in even stronger terms. "My son is emperor, to be sure, but no one has ever taken him seriously. The old Minister of the Left refused to let him have that prize daughter of his and then gave her to a brother who was hardly out of swaddling clothes and wasn't even a prince any more. And my sister: we had thought of letting His Majesty have her, and did anyone say anything at all to Genji when he had everyone laughing at the poor thing? Oh, no —he was to be just everyone's son-in-law, it seemed. Well, we had to make do and found a place for her. I was sorry, of course, but I hoped she might work hard and still make a decent career, and someday teach that awful boy a lesson. And now see what she has done. She has let him get the better of her. I think it very likely indeed that something is going on between him and the high priestess. The sum and substance of it all is that we must be careful. He is waiting very eagerly for the next reign to come."

The minister was beginning to feel a little sorry for Genji and to regret that he had come to her with his story. "Well, be that as it may, I mean to speak to no one else of what has happened. You would be wise not to tell His Majesty. I imagine she is presuming on his kindness and is sure he will forgive even this. Tell her to be more careful, and if she isn't, well, I suppose I'll have to take responsibility."

But it did not seem that he had quieted her anger. "That awful boy" had come into a house where she and her sister were living side by side. It was a deliberate insult. She was angrier and angrier. It would seem that the time had come for her to lay certain plans.

Chapter 8

The Orange Blossoms

Genji's troubles, which he had brought upon himself, were nothing new. There was already gloom enough in his public and private life, and more seemed to be added each day. Yet there were affairs from which he could not withdraw.

Among the old emperor's ladies had been one Reikeiden. She had no children, and after his death her life was sadly straitened. It would seem that only Genji remembered her. A chance encounter at court, for such was his nature, had left him with persistent thoughts of her younger sister. He paid no great attention to her, however, and it would seem that life was as difficult for her as for her sister. Now, in his own despondency, his thoughts turned more fondly to the girl, a victim if ever there was one of evanescence and hostile change. Taking advantage of a rare break in the early-summer rains, he went to call on her.

He had no outrunners and his carriage and livery were unobtrusive. As he crossed the Inner River and left the city he passed a small house with tasteful plantings. Inside someone was playing a lively strain on a Japanese koto accompanied by a thirteen-stringed Chinese koto of good quality. The house being just inside the gate, he leaned from his carriage to survey the scene. The fragrance that came on the breeze from a great laurel tree* made him think of the Kamo festival. It was a pleasant scene. And yes—he had seen it once before, a very long time ago. Would he be

*Katsura, Cercidiphyllum japonicum, more properly a Judas tree.

remembered? Just then a cuckoo called from a nearby tree, as if to urge him on. He had the carriage turned so that he might alight. Koremitsu, as always, was his messenger.

> "Back at the fence where once it sang so briefly,
> The cuckoo is impelled to sing again."

The women seemed to be near the west veranda of the main building. Having heard the same voices on that earlier occasion, Koremitsu coughed to attract attention and handed in his message. There seemed to be numbers of young women inside and they at first seemed puzzled to know who the sender might be.

This was the answer:

> "It seems to be a cuckoo we knew long ago.
> But alas, under rainy skies we cannot be sure."

Koremitsu saw that the bewilderment was only pretended. "Very well. The wrong trees, the wrong fence."* And he went out.

*Apparently a reference to a poem or proverb.

And so the women were left to nurse their regrets. It would not have been proper to pursue the matter, and that was the end of it. Among women of their station in life, he thought first of the Gosechi dancer, a charming girl, daughter of the assistant viceroy of Kyushu.* He went on thinking about whatever woman he encountered. A perverse concomitant was that the women he went on thinking about went on thinking about him.

The house of the lady he had set out to visit was, as he had expected, lonely and quiet. He first went to Reikeiden's apartments and they talked far into the night. The tall trees in the garden were a dark wall in the light of the quarter moon. The scent of orange blossoms drifted in, to call back the past. Though no longer young, Reikeiden was a sensitive, accomplished lady. The old emperor had not, it is true, included her among his particular favorites, but he had found her gentle and sympathetic. Memory following memory, Genji was in tears. There came the call of a cuckoo— might it have been the same one? A pleasant thought, that it had come following him. "How did it know?"† he whispered to himself.

"It catches the scent of memory, and favors
The village where the orange blossoms fall.‡

"I should come to you often, when I am unable to forget those years. You are a very great comfort, and at the same time I feel a new sadness coming over me. People change with the times. There are not many with whom I can exchange memories, and I should imagine that for you there are even fewer."

He knew how useless it was to complain about the times, but perhaps he found something in her, an awareness and a sensitivity, that set off a chain of responses in himself.

"The orange blossoms at the eaves have brought you
To a dwelling quite forgotten by the world."

She may not have been one of his father's great loves, but there was no doubt that she was different from the others.

Quietly he went to the west front and looked in on the younger sister. He was a rare visitor and one of unsurpassed good looks, and it would seem that such resentment as had been hers quite faded away. His manner as

---

*The episode dangles curiously. The Gosechi dancer appears in the next chapter and is not to be identified with this lady.

†Anonymous, *Kokin Rokujō, Zoku Kokka Taikan* 33650:

> We talk of things of old and—how did it know?—
> The cuckoo calls in a voice known long ago.

‡Anonymous, *Kokinshū* 139:

> At the scent of orange blossoms, awaiting the Fifth Month,
> One thinks of a scented sleeve of long ago.

always gentle and persuasive, it is doubtful that he said anything he did not mean. There were no ordinary, common women among those with whom he had had even fleeting affairs, nor were there any among them in whom he could find no merit; and so it was, perhaps, that an easy, casual relationship often proved durable. There were some who changed their minds and went on to other things, but he saw no point in lamenting what was after all the way of the world. The lady behind that earlier fence would seem to have been among the changeable ones.

Chapter 9

Suma

For Genji life had become an unbroken succession of reverses and afflictions. He must consider what to do next. If he went on pretending that nothing was amiss, then even worse things might lie ahead. He thought of the Suma coast. People of worth had once lived there, he was told, but now it was deserted save for the huts of fishermen, and even they were few. The alternative was worse, to go on living this public life, so to speak, with people streaming in and out of his house. Yet he would hate to leave, and affairs at court would continue to be much on his mind if he did leave. This irresolution was making life difficult for his people.

Unsettling thoughts of the past and the future chased one another through his mind. The thought of leaving the city aroused a train of regrets, led by the image of a grieving Murasaki. It was very well to tell himself that somehow, someday, by some route they would come together again. Even when they were separated for a day or two Genji was beside himself with worry and Murasaki's gloom was beyond describing. It was not as if they would be parting for a fixed span of years; and if they had only the possibility of a reunion on some unnamed day with which to comfort themselves, well, life is uncertain, and they might be parting forever. He thought of consulting no one and taking her with him, but the inappropriateness of subjecting such a fragile lady to the rigors of life on that harsh coast, where the only callers would be the wind and the waves, was too obvious. Having her with him would only add to his worries. She guessed his thoughts and was unhappy. She let it be known that she did not want to be left behind, however forbidding the journey and life at the end of it.

Then there was the lady of the orange blossoms. He did not visit her often, it is true, but he was her only support and comfort, and she would have every right to feel lonely and insecure. And there were women who, after the most fleeting affairs with him, went on nursing their various secret sorrows.

Fujitsubo, though always worried about rumors, wrote frequently. It struck him as bitterly ironical that she had not returned his affection earlier, but he told himself that a fate which they had shared from other lives must require that they know the full range of sorrows.

He left the city late in the Third Month. He made no announcement of his departure, which was very inconspicuous, and had only seven or eight trusted retainers with him. He did write to certain people who should know of the event. I have no doubt that there were many fine passages in the letters with which he saddened the lives of his many ladies, but, grief-stricken myself, I did not listen as carefully as I might have.

Two or three days before his departure he visited his father-in-law. It was sad, indeed rather eerie, to see the care he took not to attract notice. His carriage, a humble one covered with cypress basketwork, might have been mistaken for a woman's. The apartments of his late wife wore a lonely, neglected aspect. At the arrival of this wondrous and unexpected guest, the little boy's nurse and all the other women who had not taken positions elsewhere gathered for a last look. Even the shallowest of the younger women were moved to tears at the awareness he brought of transience and mutability. Yūgiri, the little boy, was very pretty indeed, and indefatigably noisy.

"It has been so long. I am touched that he has not forgotten me." He took the boy on his knee and seemed about to weep.

The minister, his father-in-law, came in. "I know that you are shut up at home with little to occupy you, and I had been thinking I would like to call on you and have a good talk. I talk on and on when once I let myself get started. But I have told them I am ill and have been staying away from court, and I have even resigned my offices; and I know what they would say if I were to stretch my twisted old legs for my own pleasure. I hardly need to worry about such things any more, of course, but I am still capable of being upset by false accusations. When I see how things are with you, I know all too painfully what a sad day I have come on at the end of too long a life. I would have expected the world to end before this was allowed to happen, and I see not a ray of light in it all."

"Dear sir, we must accept the disabilities we bring from other lives. Everything that has happened to me is a result of my own inadequacy. I

have heard that in other lands as well as our own an offense which does not, like mine, call for dismissal from office is thought to become far graver if the culprit goes on happily living his old life. And when exile is considered, as I believe it is in my case, the offense must have been thought more serious. Though I know I am innocent, I know too what insults I may look forward to if I stay, and so I think that I will forestall them by leaving."

Brushing away tears, the minister talked of old times, of Genji's father, and all he had said and thought. Genji too was weeping. The little boy scrambled and rolled about the room, now pouncing upon his father and now making demands upon his grandfather.

"I have gone on grieving for my daughter. And then I think what agony all this would have been to her, and am grateful that she lived such a short life and was spared the nightmare. So I try to tell myself, in any event. My chief sorrows and worries are for our little man here. He must grow up among us dotards, and the days and months will go by without the advantage of your company. It used to be that even people who were guilty of serious crimes escaped this sort of punishment; and I suppose we must call it fate, in our land and other lands too, that punishment should come all the same. But one does want to know what the charges are. In your case they quite defy the imagination."

Tō no Chūjō came in. They drank until very late, and Genji was induced to stay the night. He summoned Aoi's various women. Chūnagon was the one whom he had most admired, albeit in secret. He went on talking to her after everything was quiet, and it would seem to have been because of her that he was prevailed upon to spend the night. Dawn was at hand when he got up to leave. The moon in the first suggestions of daylight was very beautiful. The cherry blossoms were past their prime, and the light through the few that remained flooded the garden silver. Everything faded together into a gentle mist, sadder and more moving than on a night in autumn. He sat for a time leaning against the railing at a corner of the veranda. Chūnagon was waiting at the door as if to see him off.

"I wonder when we will be permitted to meet again." He paused. She was in tears. "Never did I dream that this would happen, and I neglected you in the days when it would have been so easy to see you."

Saishō, Yūgiri's nurse, came with a message from Princess Omiya. "I would have liked to say goodbye in person, but I have waited in hope that the turmoil of my thoughts might quiet a little. And now I hear that you are leaving, and it is still so early. Everything seems changed, completely wrong. It is a pity that you cannot at least wait until our little sleepyhead is up and about."

Weeping softly, Genji whispered to himself, not precisely by way of reply:

"There on the shore, the salt burners' fires await me.
Will their smoke be as the smoke over Toribe Moor?

Is this the parting at dawn we are always hearing of? No doubt there are those who know."

"I have always hated the word 'farewell,'" said Saishō, whose grief seemed quite unfeigned. "And our farewells today are unlike any others."

"Over and over again," he sent back to Princess Omiya, "I have thought of all the things I would have liked to say to you; and I hope you will understand and forgive my muteness. As for our little sleepyhead, I fear that if I were to see him I would wish to stay on even in this hostile city, and so I shall collect myself and be on my way."

All the women were there to see him go. He looked more elegant and handsome than ever in the light of the setting moon, and his dejection would have reduced tigers and wolves to tears. These were women who had served him since he was very young. It was a sad day for them.

There was a poem from Princess Omiya:

"Farther retreats the day when we bade her goodbye,
For now you depart the skies that received the smoke."

Sorrow was added to sorrow, and the tears almost seemed to invite further misfortunes.

He returned to Nijō. The women, awake the whole night through, it seemed, were gathered in sad clusters. There was no one in the guardroom. The men closest to him, reconciled to going with him, were making their own personal farewells. As for other court functionaries, there had been ominous hints of sanctions were they to come calling, and so the grounds, once crowded with horses and carriages, were empty and silent. He knew again what a hostile world it had become. There was dust on the tables, cushions had been put away. And what would be the extremes of waste and the neglect when he was gone?

He went to Murasaki's wing of the house. She had been up all night, not even lowering the shutters. Out near the verandas little girls were noisily bestirring themselves. They were so pretty in their night dress— and presently, no doubt, they would find the loneliness too much, and go their various ways. Such thoughts had not before been a part of his life.

He told Murasaki what had kept him at Sanjō. "And I suppose you are filled with the usual odd suspicions. I have wanted to be with you every moment I am still in the city, but there are things that force me to go out. Life is uncertain enough at best, and I would not want to seem cold and unfeeling."

"And what should be 'odd' now except that you are going away?"

That she should feel these sad events more cruelly than any of the others was not surprising. From her childhood she had been closer to Genji than to her own father, who now bowed to public opinion and had not offered a word of sympathy. His coldness had caused talk among her women. She was beginning to wish that they had kept him in ignorance of her whereabouts.

Someone reported what her stepmother was saying: "She had a sudden stroke of good luck, and now just as suddenly everything goes wrong. It makes a person shiver. One after another, each in his own way, they all run out on her."

This was too much. There was nothing more she wished to say to them. Henceforth she would have only Genji.

"If the years go by and I am still an outcast," he continued, "I will come for you and bring you to my 'cave among the rocks.'* But we must not be hasty. A man who is out of favor at court is not permitted the light of the sun and the moon, and it is thought a great crime, I am told, for him to go on being happy. The cause of it all is a great mystery to me, but I must accept it as fate. There seems to be no precedent for sharing exile with a lady, and I am sure that to suggest it would be to invite worse insanity from an insane world."

He slept until almost noon.

Tō no Chūjō and Genji's brother, Prince Hotaru, came calling. Since he was now without rank and office, he changed to informal dress of unfigured silk, more elegant, and even somehow grand, for its simplicity. As he combed his hair he could not help noticing that loss of weight had made him even handsomer.

"I am skin and bones," he said to Murasaki, who sat gazing at him, tears in her eyes. "Can I really be as emaciated as this mirror makes me? I am a little sorry for myself.

"I now must go into exile. In this mirror
An image of me will yet remain beside you."

Huddling against a pillar to hide her tears, she replied as if to herself:

"If when we part an image yet remains,
Then will I find some comfort in my sorrow."

Yes, she was unique—a new awareness of that fact stabbed at his heart.

Prince Hotaru kept him affectionate company through the day and left in the evening.

It was not hard to imagine the loneliness that brought frequent notes

---

*Anonymous, *Kokinshū* 952:

Where shall I go, to what cave among the rocks,
To be free of tidings of this gloomy world?

from the house of the falling orange blossoms. Fearing that he would seem
unkind if he did not visit the ladies again, he resigned himself to spending
yet another night away from home. It was very late before he gathered
himself for the effort.

"We are honored that you should consider us worth a visit," said Lady
Reikeiden—and it would be difficult to record the rest of the interview.

They lived precarious lives, completely dependent on Genji. So lonely
indeed was their mansion that he could imagine the desolation awaiting
it once he himself was gone; and the heavily wooded hill rising dimly
beyond the wide pond in misty moonlight made him wonder whether the
"cave among the rocks" at Suma would be such a place.

He went to the younger sister's room, at the west side of the house.
She had been in deep despondency, almost certain that he would not find
time for a visit. Then, in the soft, sad light of the moon, his robes giving
off an indescribable fragrance, he made his way in. She came to the veranda
and looked up at the moon. They talked until dawn.

"What a short night it has been. I think how difficult it will be for us
to meet again, and I am filled with regrets for the days I wasted. I fear I
worried too much about the precedents I might be setting."

A cock was crowing busily as he talked on about the past. He made
a hasty departure, fearful of attracting notice. The setting moon is always
sad, and he was prompted to think its situation rather like his own. Catching the deep purple of the lady's robe, the moon itself seemed to be
weeping.*

> "Narrow these sleeves, now lodging for the moonlight.
> Would they might keep a light which I do not tire of."

Sad himself, Genji sought to comfort her.

> "The moon will shine upon this house once more.
> Do not look at the clouds which now conceal it.

"I wish I were really sure it is so, and find the unknown future
clouding my heart."

He left as dawn was coming over the sky.

His affairs were in order. He assigned all the greater and lesser affairs
of the Nijō mansion to trusted retainers who had not been swept up in the
currents of the times, and he selected others to go with him to Suma. He
would take only the simplest essentials for a rustic life, among them a book
chest, selected writings of Po Chü-i and other poets, and a seven-stringed
Chinese koto. He carefully refrained from anything which in its ostentation might not become a nameless rustic.

Assigning all the women to Murasaki's west wing, he left behind

---

*Ise, *Kokinshū* 756:

> Catching the drops on my sleeves as I lay in thought,
> The moonlight seemed to be shedding tears of its own.

deeds to pastures and manors and the like and made provision for all his various warehouses and storerooms. Confident of Shōnagon's perspicacity, he gave her careful instructions and put stewards at her disposal. He had been somewhat brisk and businesslike toward his own serving women, but they had had security—and now what was to become of them?

"I shall be back, I know, if I live long enough. Do what you can in the west wing, please, those of you who are prepared to wait."

And so they all began a new life.

To Yūgiri's nurse and maids and to the lady of the orange blossoms he sent elegant parting gifts and plain, useful everyday provisions as well.

He even wrote to Oborozukiyo. "I know that I have no right to expect a letter from you; but I am not up to describing the gloom and the bitterness of leaving this life behind.

"I was snagged upon a shoal of a river of tears.
Was that the start of this drift to deeper waters?

"Remembering is the crime to which I cannot plead innocent."

He wrote nothing more, for there was a danger that his letter would be intercepted.

Though she fought to maintain her composure, there was nothing she could do about the tears that wet her sleeves.

"The foam on the river of tears will disappear
Short of the shoals of meeting that wait downstream."

There was something very fine about the hand disordered by grief.

He longed to see her again, but she had too many relatives who wished him ill. Discretion forbade further correspondence.

On the night before his departure he visited his father's grave in the northern hills. Since the moon would be coming up shortly before dawn, he went first to take leave of Fujitsubo. Receiving him in person, she spoke of her worries for the crown prince. It cannot have been, so complicated were matters between them, a less than deeply felt interview. Her dignity and beauty were as always. He would have liked to hint at old resentments; but why, at this late date, invite further unpleasantness, and risk adding to his own agitation?

He only said, and it was reasonable enough: "I can think of a single offense for which I must undergo this strange, sad punishment, and because of it I tremble before the heavens. Though I would not care in the least if my own unworthy self were to vanish away, I only hope that the crown prince's reign is without unhappy event."

She knew too well what he meant, and was unable to reply. He was almost too handsome as at last he succumbed to tears.

"I am going to pay my respects at His Majesty's grave. Do you have a message?"

She was silent for a time, seeking to control herself.

"The one whom I served is gone, the other must go.
Farewell to the world was no farewell to its sorrows."

But for both of them the sorrow was beyond words.
He replied:

"The worst of grief for him should long have passed.
And now I must leave the world where dwells the child."*

The moon had risen and he set out. He was on horseback and had only
five or six attendants, all of them trusted friends. I need scarcely say that
it was a far different procession from those of old. Among his men was that
guards officer who had been his special attendant at the Kamo lustration
services.† The promotion he might have expected had long since passed
him by, and now his right of access to the royal presence and his offices
had been taken away. Remembering that day as they came in sight of the
Lower Kamo Shrine, he dismounted and took Genji's bridle.

*Konoyo means both "this world" and "the world of the child."
†See Chapter 6.

"There was heartvine in our caps. I led your horse.
And now at this jeweled fence I berate the gods."

Yes, the memory must be painful, for the young man had been the most resplendent in Genji's retinue. Dismounting, Genji bowed toward the shrine and said as if by way of farewell:

"I leave this world of gloom. I leave my name
To the offices of the god who rectifies."*

The guards officer, an impressionable young man, gazed at him in wonder and admiration.

Coming to the grave, Genji almost thought he could see his father before him. Power and position were nothing once a man was gone. He wept and silently told his story, but there came no answer, no judgment upon it. And all those careful instructions and admonitions had served no purpose at all?

Grasses overgrew the path to the grave, the dew seemed to gather weight as he made his way through. The moon had gone behind a cloud and the groves were dark and somehow terrible. It was as if he might lose his way upon turning back. As he bowed in farewell, a chill came over him, for he seemed to see his father as he once had been.

"And how does he look upon me? I raise my eyes,
And the moon now vanishes behind the clouds."

Back at Nijō at daybreak, he sent a last message to the crown prince. Tying it to a cherry branch from which the blossoms had fallen, he addressed it to Omyōbu, whom Fujitsubo had put in charge of her son's affairs. "Today I must leave. I regret more than anything that I cannot see you again. Imagine my feelings, if you will, and pass them on to the prince.

"When shall I, a ragged, rustic outcast,
See again the blossoms of the city?"

She explained everything to the crown prince. He gazed at her solemnly.

"How shall I answer?" Omyōbu asked.

"I am sad when he is away for a little, and he is going so far, and how —tell him that, please."

A sad little answer, thought Omyōbu.†

All the details of that unhappy love came back to her. The two of them should have led placid, tranquil lives, and she felt as if she and she alone had been the cause of all the troubles.

"I can think of nothing to say." It was clear to him that her answer

---

*Tadasu no kami, "the god who rectifies," has his abode in the Lower Kamo Shrine.
†The crown prince's answer breaks into seven-syllable lines, as if he were trying to compose a poem.

had indeed been composed with great difficulty. "I passed your message on to the prince, and was sadder than ever to see how sad it made him.

"Quickly the blossoms fall. Though spring departs,
   You will come again, I know, to a city of flowers."

There was sad talk all through the crown prince's apartments in the wake of the letter, and there were sounds of weeping. Even people who scarcely knew him were caught up in the sorrow. As for people in his regular service, even scullery maids of whose existence he can hardly have been aware were sad at the thought that they must for a time do without his presence.

So it was all through the court. Deep sorrow prevailed. He had been with his father day and night from his seventh year, and, since nothing he had said to his father had failed to have an effect, almost everyone was in his debt. A cheerful sense of gratitude should have been common in the upper ranks of the court and the ministries, and omnipresent in the lower ranks. It was there, no doubt; but the world had become a place of quick punishments. A pity, people said, silently reproving the great ones whose power was now absolute; but what was to be accomplished by playing the martyr? Not that everyone was satisfied with passive acceptance. If he had not known before, Genji knew now that the human race is not perfect.

He spent a quiet day with Murasaki and late in the night set out in rough travel dress.

"The moon is coming up. Do please come out and see me off. I know that later I will think of any number of things I wanted to say to you. My gloom strikes me as ridiculous when I am away from you for even a day or two."

He raised the blinds and urged her to come forward. Trying not to weep, she at length obeyed. She was very beautiful in the moonlight. What sort of home would this unkind, inconstant city be for her now? But she was sad enough already, and these thoughts were best kept to himself.

He said with forced lightness:

"At least for this life we might make our vows, we thought.
   And so we vowed that nothing would ever part us.

How silly we were!"
This was her answer:

"I would give a life for which I have no regrets
   If it might postpone for a little the time of parting."

They were not empty words, he knew; but he must be off, for he did not want the city to see him in broad daylight.

Her face was with him the whole of the journey. In great sorrow he boarded the boat that would take him to Suma. It was a long spring day and there was a tail wind, and by late afternoon he had reached the strand

where he was to live. He had never before been on such a journey, however short. All the sad, exotic things along the way were new to him. The Oe station* was in ruins, with only a grove of pines to show where it had stood.

> "More remote, I fear, my place of exile
>   Than storied ones in lands beyond the seas."

The surf came in and went out again. "I envy the waves," he whispered to himself.† It was a familiar poem, but it seemed new to those who heard him, and sad as never before. Looking back toward the city, he saw that the mountains were enshrouded in mist. It was as though he had indeed come "three thousand leagues."‡ The spray from the oars brought thoughts scarcely to be borne.

*In the heart of the present Osaka. It was used by high priestesses on their way to and from Ise.

†*Tales of Ise* 7, attributed to Ariwara Narihira:

> Strong my yearning for what I have left behind.
> I envy the waves that go back whence they came.

‡Po Chü-i, Collected Works, XIII, "Lines Written on the Winter Solstice, in the Arbutus Hall."

"Mountain mists cut off that ancient village.
Is the sky I see the sky that shelters it?"

Not far away Yukihira had lived in exile, "dripping brine from the sea grass."* Genji's new house was some distance from the coast, in mountains utterly lonely and desolate. The fences and everything within were new and strange. The grass-roofed cottages, the reed-roofed galleries—or so they seemed—were interesting enough in their way. It was a dwelling proper to a remote littoral, and different from any he had known. Having once had a taste for out-of-the-way places, he might have enjoyed this Suma had the occasion been different.

Yoshikiyo had appointed himself a sort of confidential steward. He summoned the overseers of Genji's several manors in the region and assigned them to necessary tasks. Genji watched admiringly. In very quick order he had a rather charming new house. A deep brook flowed through the garden with a pleasing murmur, new plantings were set out; and when finally he was beginning to feel a little at home he could scarcely believe that it all was real. The governor of the province, an old retainer, discreetly performed numerous services. All in all it was a brighter and livelier place than he had a right to expect, although the fact that there was no one whom he could really talk to kept him from forgetting that it was a house of exile, strange and alien. How was he to get through the months and years ahead?

The rainy season came. His thoughts traveled back to the distant city. There were people whom he longed to see, chief among them the lady at Nijō, whose forlorn figure was still before him. He thought too of the crown prince, and of little Yūgiri, running so happily, that last day, from father to grandfather and back again. He sent off letters to the city. Some of them, especially those to Murasaki and to Fujitsubo, took a great deal of time, for his eyes clouded over repeatedly.

This is what he wrote to Fujitsubo:

"Briny our sleeves on the Suma strand; and yours
In the fisher cots of thatch at Matsushima?†

"My eyes are dark as I think of what is gone and what is to come, and 'the waters rise.' "‡

His letter to Oborozukiyo he sent as always to Chūnagon, as if it were a private matter between the two of them. "With nothing else to occupy me, I find memories of the past coming back.

*Ariwara Yukihira, *Kokinshū* 962:

> If someone should inquire for me, reply:
> "He idles at Suma, dripping brine from the sea grass."

†A very common pun makes Matsushima "the isle of the one who waits."
‡Ki no Tsurayuki, *Kokin Rokujō, Zoku Kokka Taikan* 33193:

> The sorrow of parting brings such floods of tears
> That the waters of this river must surely rise.

"At Suma, unchastened, one longs for the deep-lying sea pine.
And she, the fisher lady burning salt?"

I shall leave the others, among them letters to his father-in-law and
Yūgiri's nurse, to the reader's imagination. They reached their several
destinations and gave rise to many sad and troubled thoughts.

Murasaki had taken to her bed. Her women, doing everything they
could think of to comfort her, feared that in her grief and longing she might
fall into a fatal decline. Brooding over the familiar things he had left
behind, the koto, the perfumed robes, she almost seemed on the point of
departing the world. Her women were beside themselves. Shōnagon sent
asking that the bishop, her uncle, pray for her. He did so, and to double
purpose, that she be relieved of her present sorrows and that she one day
be permitted a tranquil life with Genji.

She sent bedding and other supplies to Suma. The robes and trousers
of stiff, unfigured white silk brought new pangs of sorrow, for they were
unlike anything he had worn before. She kept always with her the mirror
to which he had addressed his farewell poem, though it was not acquitting
itself of the duty he had assigned to it. The door through which he had
come and gone, the cypress pillar at his favorite seat—everything brought
sad memories. So it is even for people hardened and seasoned by trials, and
how much more for her, to whom he had been father and mother! "Grasses
of forgetfulness"* might have sprung up had he quite vanished from the
earth; but he was at Suma, not so very far away, she had heard. She could
not know when he would return.

For Fujitsubo, sorrow was added to uncertainty about her son. And
how, at the thought of the fate that had joined them, could her feelings
for Genji be of a bland and ordinary kind? Fearful of gossips, she had
coldly turned away each small show of affection, she had become more and
more cautious and secretive, and she had given him little sign that she
sensed the depth of his affection. He had been uncommonly careful himself. Gossips are cruelly attentive people (it was a fact she knew too well),
but they seemed to have caught no suspicion of the affair. He had kept
himself under tight control and preserved the most careful appearances.
How then could she not, in this extremity, have fond thoughts for him?

Her reply was more affectionate than usual.

"The nun of Matsushima burns the brine
And fuels the fires with the logs of her lamenting,

now more than ever."

Enclosed with Chūnagon's letter was a brief reply from Oborozukiyo:

"The fisherwife burns salt and hides her fires
And strangles, for the smoke has no escape."

*Wasuregusa, day lilies.

"I shall not write of things which at this late date need no saying."

Chūnagon wrote in detail of her lady's sorrows. There were tears in his eyes as he read her letter.

And Murasaki's reply was of course deeply moving. There was this poem:

"Taking brine on that strand, let him compare
His dripping sleeves with these night sleeves of mine."

The robes that came with it were beautifully dyed and tailored. She did everything so well. At Suma there were no silly and frivolous distractions, and it seemed a pity that they could not enjoy the quiet life together. Thoughts of her, day and night, became next to unbearable. Should he send for her in secret? But no: his task in this gloomy situation must be to make amends for past misdoings. He began a fast and spent his days in prayer and meditation.

There were also messages about his little boy, Yūgiri. They of course filled him with longing; but he would see the boy again one day, and in the meantime he was in good hands. Yet a father must, however he tries, "wander lost in thoughts upon his child."*

In the confusion I had forgotten: he had sent off a message to the Rokujō lady, and she on her own initiative had sent a messenger to seek out his place of exile. Her letter was replete with statements of the deepest affection. The style and the calligraphy, superior to those of anyone else he knew, showed unique breeding and cultivation.

"Having been told of the unthinkable place in which you find yourself, I feel as if I were wandering in an endless nightmare. I should imagine that you will be returning to the city before long, but it will be a very long time before I, so lost in sin, will be permitted to see you.

"Imagine, at Suma of the dripping brine,
The woman of Ise, gathering briny sea grass.

And what is to become of one, in a world where everything conspires to bring new sorrow?" It was a long letter.

"The tide recedes along the coast of Ise.
No hope, no promise in the empty shells."

Laying down her brush as emotion overcame her and then beginning again, she finally sent off some four or five sheets of white Chinese paper. The gradations of ink were marvelous. He had been fond of her, and it had been wrong to make so much of that one incident. She had turned against him and presently left him. It all seemed such a waste. The letter itself and the occasion for it so moved him that he even felt a certain affection for the messenger, an intelligent young man in her daughter's service. Detaining him for several days, he heard about life at Ise. The house being

*See note‡, page 7.

rather small, the messenger was able to observe Genji at close range. He was moved to tears of admiration by what he saw.

The reader may be left to imagine Genji's reply. He said among other things: "Had I known I was destined to leave the city, it would have been better, I tell myself in the tedium and loneliness here, to go off with you to Ise.

> "With the lady of Ise I might have ridden small boats
> That row the waves, and avoided dark sea tangles.*

> "How long, dripping brine on driftwood logs,
> On logs of lament, must I gaze at this Suma coast?

"I cannot know when I will see you again."

But at least his letters brought the comfort of knowing that he was well.

*"Men of Ise," a "vulgar song" (*fūzokuuta*):

> Oh, the men of Ise are strange ones.
> How so? How are they strange?
> They ride small boats that row the waves,
> That row the waves, they do.

There came letters, comforting and yet sad, from the lady of the orange blossoms and her sister.

"Ferns of remembrance weigh our eaves ever more,
And heavily falls the dew upon our sleeves."

There was no one, he feared, whom they might now ask to clear away the rank growth. Hearing that the long rains had damaged their garden walls, he sent off orders to the city that people from nearby manors see to repairs.

Oborozukiyo had delighted the scandalmongers, and she was now in very deep gloom. Her father, the minister, for she was his favorite daughter, sought to intercede on her behalf with the emperor and Kokiden. The emperor was moved to forgive her. She had been severely punished, it was true, for her grave offense, but not as severely as if she had been one of the companions of the royal bedchamber. In the Seventh Month she was permitted to return to court. She continued to long for Genji. Much of the emperor's old love remained, and he chose to ignore criticism and keep her near him, now berating her and now making impassioned vows. He was a handsome man and he groomed himself well, and it was something of an affront that old memories should be so much with her.

"Things do not seem right now that he is gone," he said one evening when they were at music together. "I am sure that there are many who feel the loss even more strongly than I do. I cannot put away the fear that I have gone against Father's last wishes and that it is a dereliction for which I must one day suffer." There were tears in his eyes and she too was weeping. "I have awakened to the stupidity of the world and I do not feel that I wish to remain in it much longer. And how would you feel if I were to die? I hate to think that you would grieve less for me gone forever than for him gone so briefly such a short distance away. The poet who said that we love while we live did not know a great deal about love."* Tears were streaming from Oborozukiyo's eyes. "And whom might you be weeping for? It is sad that we have no children. I would like to follow Father's instructions and adopt the crown prince, but people will raise innumerable objections. It all seems very sad."

There were some whose ideas of government did not accord with his own, but he was too young to impose his will. He passed his days in helpless anger and sorrow.

At Suma, melancholy autumn winds were blowing. Genji's house was some distance from the sea, but at night the wind that blew over the barriers, now as in Yukihira's day, seemed to bring the surf to his bedside. Autumn was hushed and lonely at a place of exile. He had few companions. One night when they were all asleep he raised his head from his pillow and listened to the roar of the wind and of the waves, as if at his

*The poet has not been satisfactorily identified.

ear. Though he was unaware that he wept, his tears were enough to set his pillow afloat.* He plucked a few notes on his koto, but the sound only made him sadder.

"The waves on the strand, like moans of helpless longing.
The winds—like messengers from those who grieve?"

He had awakened the others. They sat up, and one by one they were in tears.

This would not do. Because of him they had been swept into exile, leaving families from whom they had never before been parted. It must be very difficult for them, and his own gloom could scarcely be making things easier. So he set about cheering them. During the day he would invent games and make jokes, and set down this and that poem on multicolored patchwork, and paint pictures on fine specimens of figured Chinese silk. Some of his larger paintings were masterpieces. He had long ago been told of this Suma coast and these hills and had formed a picture of them in his mind, and he found now that his imagination had fallen short of the

*This extravagant figure of speech is to be found in *Kokin Rokujō, Zoku Kokka Taikan* 34087.

actuality. What a pity, said his men, that they could not summon Tsunenori and Chieda* and other famous painters of the day to add colors to Genji's monochromes. This resolute cheerfulness had the proper effect. His men, four or five of whom were always with him, would not have dreamed of leaving him.

There was a profusion of flowers in the garden. Genji came out, when the evening colors were at their best, to a gallery from which he had a good view of the coast. His men felt chills of apprehension as they watched him, for the loneliness of the setting made him seem like a visitor from another world. In a dark robe tied loosely over singlets of figured white and aster-colored trousers, he announced himself as "a disciple of the Buddha" and slowly intoned a sutra, and his men thought that they had never heard a finer voice. From offshore came the voices of fishermen raised in song. The barely visible boats were like little seafowl on an utterly lonely sea, and as he brushed away a tear induced by the sound of the oars, so like the calls of geese winging overhead, the white of his hand against the jet black of his rosary was enough to bring comfort to men who had left their families behind.

*Tsunenori seems to have been active some three quarters of a century before; so too, presumably, was Chieda.

"Might they be companions of those I long for?
Their cries ring sadly through the sky of their journey."

This was Yoshikiyo's reply:

"I know not why they bring these thoughts of old,
These wandering geese. They were not then my comrades."

And Koremitsu's:

"No colleagues of mine, these geese beyond the clouds,
So I had thought. They chose to leave their homes."

And that of the guards officer who had cut such a proud figure on the
day of the Kamo lustration:

"Sad are their cries as they wing their way from home.
They still find solace, for they still have comrades.

It is cruel to lose one's comrades."

His father had been posted to Hitachi, but he himself had come with
Genji. He contrived, for all that must have been on his mind, to seem
cheerful.

A radiant moon had come out. They were reminded that it was the
harvest full moon. Genji could not take his eyes from it. On other such
nights there had been concerts at court, and perhaps they of whom he was
thinking would be gazing at this same moon and thinking of him.

"My thoughts are of you, old friend," he sang, "two thousand leagues
away."* His men were in tears.

His longing was intense at the memory of Fujitsubo's poem about the
ninefold mists. Other memories came back, and he turned away to hide his
tears. It was very late, said his men, but still he did not come inside.

"So long as I look upon it I find comfort,
The moon which comes again to the distant city."

He thought of the emperor and how much he had resembled their
father, that last night when they had talked so fondly of old times. "I still
have with me the robe which my lord gave me,"† he whispered, going
inside. He did in fact have a robe that was a gift from the emperor, and
he kept it always beside him.

"Not bitter thoughts alone does this singlet bring.
Its sleeves are damp with tears of affection too."

The assistant viceroy of Kyushu was returning to the capital. He had
a large family and was especially well provided with daughters, and since
progress by land would have been difficult he had sent his wife and the

---

*Po Chü-i, Collected Works, XIV, "On the Evening of the Full Moon of the Eighth Month."
†Sugawara Michizane, "The Tenth of the Ninth Month," in Last Poems (Kanke Kōsō).

daughters by boat. They proceeded by easy stages, putting in here and there along the coast. The scenery at Suma was especially pleasing, and the news that Genji was in residence produced blushes and sighs far out at sea. The Gosechi dancer* would have liked to cut the tow rope and drift ashore. The sound of a koto came faint from the distance, the sadness of it joined to a sad setting and sad memories. The more sensitive members of the party were in tears.

The assistant viceroy sent a message. "I had hoped to call on you immediately upon returning to the city from my distant post, and when, to my surprise, I found myself passing your house, I was filled with the most intense feelings of sorrow and regret. Various acquaintances who might have been expected to come from the city have done so, and our party has become so numerous that it would be out of the question to call on you. I shall hope to do so soon."

His son, the governor of Chikuzen, brought the message. Genji had taken notice of the youth and obtained an appointment for him in the imperial secretariat. He was sad to see his patron in such straits, but people were watching and had a way of talking, and he stayed only briefly.

"It was kind of you to come," said Genji. "I do not often see old friends these days."

His reply to the assistant viceroy was in a similar vein. Everyone in the Kyushu party and in the party newly arrived from the city as well was deeply moved by the governor's description of what he had seen. The tears of sympathy almost seemed to invite worse misfortunes.

The Gosechi dancer contrived to send him a note.

"Now taut, now slack, like my unruly heart,
The tow rope is suddenly still at the sound of a koto.

"Scolding will not improve me."†
He smiled, so handsome a smile that his men felt rather inadequate.

"Why, if indeed your heart is like the tow rope,
Unheeding must you pass this strand of Suma?

"I had not expected to leave you for these wilds."‡
There once was a man who, passing Akashi on his way into exile, brought pleasure into an innkeeper's life with an impromptu Chinese poem.** For the Gosechi dancer the pleasure was such that she would have liked to make Suma her home.

---

*See Chapter 8.
†Anonymous, *Kokinshū* 508:

> My heart is like a ship upon the seas.
> I am easily moved. Scolding will not improve me.

‡Ono no Takamura, *Kokinshū* 961:

> I had not expected to leave you for these wilds.
> A fisherman's net is mine, an angler's line.

**The exile was Sugawara Michizane. The incident is recorded in the *Okagami*.

As time passed, the people back in the city, and even the emperor himself, found that Genji was more and more in their thoughts. The crown prince was the saddest of all. His nurse and Omyōbu would find him weeping in a corner and search helplessly for ways to comfort him. Once so fearful of rumors and their possible effect on this child of hers and Genji's, Fujitsubo now grieved that Genji must be away.

In the early days of his exile he corresponded with his brothers and with important friends at court. Some of his Chinese poems were widely praised.

Kokiden flew into a rage. "A man out of favor with His Majesty is expected to have trouble feeding himself. And here he is living in a fine stylish house and saying awful things about all of us. No doubt the grovelers around him are assuring him that a deer is a horse.*

And so writing to Genji came to be rather too much to ask of people, and letters stopped coming.

The months went by, and Murasaki was never really happy. All the women from the other wings of the house were now in her service. They had been of the view that she was beneath their notice, but as they came to observe her gentleness, her magnanimity in household matters, her thoughtfulness, they changed their minds, and not one of them departed her service. Among them were women of good family. A glimpse of her was enough to make them admit that she deserved Genji's altogether remarkable affection.

And as time went by at Suma, Genji began to feel that he could bear to be away from her no longer. But he dismissed the thought of sending for her: this cruel punishment was for himself alone. He was seeing a little of plebeian life, and he thought it very odd and, he must say, rather dirty. The smoke near at hand would, he supposed, be the smoke of the salt burners' fires. In fact, someone was trying to light wet kindling just behind the house.

"Over and over the rural ones light fires.
    Not so unflagging the urban ones with their inquiries."

It was winter, and the snowy skies were wild. He beguiled the tedium with music, playing the koto himself and setting Koremitsu to the flute, with Yoshikiyo to sing for them. When he lost himself in a particularly moving strain the others would fall silent, tears in their eyes.

He thought of the lady the Chinese emperor sent off to the Huns.† How must the emperor have felt, how would Genji himself feel, in so

---

*It is recorded in the *Shih Chi* chronicle of the reign of Ch'in Shih-huang-ti that a eunuch planning rebellion showed the high courtiers a deer and required them to call it a horse, and so assured himself that they feared him.

†Wang Chao-chün was dispatched to the Huns from the harem of the Han emperor Yüan-ti because she had failed to bribe the artists who did portraits of court ladies, and the emperor therefore thought her ill favored.

disposing of a beautiful lady? He shuddered, as if some such task might be approaching, "at the end of a frosty night's dream."*

A bright moon flooded in, lighting the shallow-eaved cottage to the farthest corners. He was able to imitate the poet's feat of looking up at the night sky without going to the veranda.† There was a weird sadness in the setting moon. "The moon goes always to the west,"‡ he whispered.

"All aimless is my journey through the clouds.
  It shames me that the unswerving moon should see me."

He recited it silently to himself. Sleepless as always, he heard the sad calls of the plovers in the dawn and (the others were not yet awake) repeated several times to himself:

"Cries of plovers in the dawn bring comfort
  To one who awakens in a lonely bed."

His practice of going through his prayers and ablutions in the deep of

*From a Chinese poem about Miss Wang in the *Wakan Rōeishū*, by Oe no Asatsuna.
†In another Chinese poem in the *Wakan Rōeishū*, Miyoshi Kiyoyuki so describes a view of the night sky from within a ruined palace.
‡Sugawara Michizane, "To the Moon," in *Last Poems*.

night seemed strange and wonderful to his men. Far from being tempted to leave him, they did not return even for brief visits to their families.

The Akashi coast was a very short distance away. Yoshikiyo remembered the daughter of the former governor, now a monk, and wrote to her. She did not answer.

"I would like to see you for a few moments sometime at your convenience," came a note from her father. "There is something I want to ask you."

Yoshikiyo was not encouraged. He would look very silly if he went to Akashi only to be turned away. He did not go.

The former governor was an extremely proud and intractable man. The incumbent governor was all-powerful in the province, but the eccentric old man had no wish to marry his daughter to such an upstart. He learned of Genji's presence at Suma.

"I hear that the shining Genji is out of favor," he said to his wife, "and that he has come to Suma. What a rare stroke of luck—the chance we have been waiting for. We must offer our girl."

"Completely out of the question. People from the city tell me that he has any number of fine ladies of his own and that he has reached out for one of the emperor's. That is why the scandal. What interest can he possibly take in a country lump like her?"

"You don't understand the first thing about it. My own views couldn't be more different. We must make our plans. We must watch for a chance to bring him here." His mind was quite made up, and he had the look of someone whose plans were not easily changed. The finery which he had lavished upon house and daughter quite dazzled the eye.

"He may be ever so grand a grand gentleman," persisted the mother, "but it hardly seems the right and sensible thing to choose of all people a man who has been sent into exile for a serious crime. It might just possibly be different if he were likely to look at her—but no. You must be joking."

"A serious crime! Why in China too exactly this sort of thing happens to every single person who has remarkable talents and stands out from the crowd. And who do you think he is? His late mother was the daughter of my uncle, the Lord Inspector. She had talent and made a name for herself, and when there wasn't enough of the royal love to go around, the others were jealous, and finally they killed her. But she left behind a son who was a royal joy and comfort. Ladies should have pride and high ambitions. I may be a bumpkin myself, but I doubt that he will think her entirely beneath contempt."

Though the girl was no great beauty, she was intelligent and sensitive and had a gentle grace of which someone of far higher rank would have been proud. She was reconciled to her sad lot. No one among the great persons of the land was likely to think her worth a glance. The prospect of marrying someone nearer her station in life revolted her. If she was left behind by those on whom she depended, she would become a nun, or perhaps throw herself into the sea.

Her father had done everything for her. He sent her twice a year to the Sumiyoshi Shrine, hoping that the god might be persuaded to notice her.

The New Year came to Suma, the days were longer, and time went by slowly. The sapling cherry Genji had planted the year before sent out a scattering of blossoms, the air was soft and warm, and memories flooded back, bringing him often to tears. He thought longingly of the ladies for whom he had wept when, toward the end of the Second Month the year before, he had prepared to depart the city. The cherries would now be in bloom before the Grand Hall. He thought of that memorable cherry-blossom festival, and his father, and the extraordinarily handsome figure his brother, now the emperor, had presented, and he remembered how his brother had favored him by reciting his Chinese poem.*

A Japanese poem formed in his mind:

"Fond thoughts I have of the noble ones on high,
    And the day of the flowered caps has come again."

Tō no Chūjō was now a councillor. He was a man of such fine charac-

*See Chapter 5, in which, however, there is no mention of this mark of the royal favor. Seven years have passed.

ter that everyone wished him well, but he was not happy. Everything made him think of Genji. Finally he decided that he did not care what rumors might arise and what misdeeds he might be accused of and hurried off to Suma. The sight of Genji brought tears of joy and sadness. Genji's house seemed very strange and exotic. The surroundings were such that he would have liked to paint them. The fence was of plaited bamboo and the pillars were of pine and the stairs of stone.* It was a rustic, provincial sort of dwelling, and very interesting.

Genji's dress too was somewhat rustic. Over a singlet dyed lightly in a yellowish color denoting no rank or office† he wore a hunting robe and trousers of greenish gray. It was plain garb and intentionally countrified, but it so became the wearer as to bring an immediate smile of pleasure to his friend's lips. Genji's personal utensils and accessories were of a makeshift nature, and his room was open to anyone who wished to look in. The gaming boards and stones were also of rustic make. The religious objects that lay about told of earnest devotion. The food was very palatable and very much in the local taste. For his friend's amusement, Genji had fishermen bring fish and shells. Tō no Chūjō had them questioned about their maritime life, and learned of perils and tribulations. Their speech was as incomprehensible as the chirping of birds, but no doubt their feelings were like his own. He brightened their lives with clothes and other gifts. The stables being nearby, fodder was brought from a granary or something of the sort beyond, and the feeding process was as novel and interesting as everything else. Tō no Chūjō hummed the passage from "The Well of Asuka"‡ about the well-fed horses.

Weeping and laughing, they talked of all that had happened over the months.

"Yūgiri quite rips the house to pieces, and Father worries and worries about him."

Genji was of course sorry to hear it; but since I am not capable of recording the whole of the long conversation, I should perhaps refrain from recording any part of it. They composed Chinese poetry all through the night. Tō no Chūjō had come in defiance of the gossips and slanderers, but they intimidated him all the same. His stay was a brief one.

Wine was brought in, and their toast was from Po Chü-i:**

"Sad topers we. Our springtime cups flow with tears."

The tears were general, for it had been too brief a meeting.
A line of geese flew over in the dawn sky.

"In what spring tide will I see again my old village?
    I envy the geese, returning whence they came."

*Giving the house a Chinese aspect.
†Probably a pink touched with yellow.
‡A Saibara (a sort of folk song taken up by the Heian nobility).
**Recollections of meetings with Yüan Chen, Collected Works, XVII.

Sorrier than ever that he must go, Tō no Chūjō replied:

> "Sad are the geese to leave their winter's lodging.
> Dark my way of return to the flowery city."

He had brought gifts from the city, both elegant and practical. Genji gave him in return a black pony, a proper gift for a traveler.

"Considering its origins, you may fear that it will bring bad luck; but you will find that it neighs into the northern winds."*

It was a fine beast.

"To remember me by," said Tō no Chūjō, giving in return what was recognized to be a very fine flute. The situation demanded a certain reticence in the giving of gifts.

The sun was high, and Tō no Chūjō's men were becoming restive. He looked back and looked back, and Genji almost felt that no visit at all would have been better than such a brief one.

"And when will we meet again? It is impossible to believe that you will be here forever."

> "Look down upon me, cranes who skim the clouds,
> And see me unsullied as this cloudless day.

"Yes, I do hope to go back, someday. But when I think how difficult it has been for even the most remarkable men to pick up their old lives, I am no longer sure that I want to see the city again."

> "Lonely the voice of the crane among the clouds.
> Gone the comrade that once flew at its side.

"I have been closer to you than ever I have deserved. My regrets for what has happened are bitter."

They scarcely felt that they had had time to renew their friendship. For Genji the loneliness was unrelieved after his friend's departure.

It was the day of the serpent, the first such day in the Third Month.

"The day when a man who has worries goes down and washes them away," said one of his men, admirably informed, it would seem, in all the annual observances.

Wishing to have a look at the seashore, Genji set forth. Plain, rough curtains were strung up among the trees, and a soothsayer who was doing the circuit of the province was summoned to perform the lustration.

Genji thought he could see something of himself in the rather large doll being cast off to sea, bearing away sins and tribulations.

> "Cast away to drift on an alien vastness,
> I grieve for more than a doll cast out to sea."

---

*"Old Poem," *Wen-hsüan:*

> The Tartar pony faces towards the north.
> The Annamese bird nests on the southern branch.

The bright, open seashore showed him to wonderful advantage. The sea stretched placid into measureless distances. He thought of all that had happened to him, and all that was still to come.

"You eight hundred myriad gods must surely help me,
For well you know that blameless I stand before you."

Suddenly a wind came up and even before the services were finished the sky was black. Genji's men rushed about in confusion. Rain came pouring down, completely without warning. Though the obvious course would have been to return straightway to the house, there had been no time to send for umbrellas. The wind was now a howling tempest, everything that had not been tied down was scuttling off across the beach. The surf was biting at their feet. The sea was white, as if spread over with white linen. Lightning flashed and thunder roared. Fearful every moment of being struck down, they finally made their way back to the house.

"I've never seen anything like it," said one of the men. "Winds do come up from time to time, but not without warning. It is all very strange and very terrible."

The lightning and thunder seemed to announce the end of the world, and the rain to beat its way into the ground; and Genji sat calmly reading a sutra. The thunder subsided in the evening, but the wind went on through the night.

"Our prayers seem to have been answered. A little more and we would have been carried off. I've heard that tidal waves do carry people off before they know what is happening to them, but I've not seen anything like this."

Towards dawn sleep was at length possible. A man whom he did not recognize came to Genji in a dream.

"The court summons you." He seemed to be reaching for Genji. "Why do you not go?"

It would be the king of the sea, who was known to have a partiality for handsome men. Genji decided that he could stay no longer at Suma.

Chapter 10

Akashi

The days went by and the thunder and rain continued. What was Genji to do? People would laugh if, in this extremity, out of favor at court, he were to return to the city. Should he then seek a mountain retreat? But if it were to be noised about that a storm had driven him away, then he would cut a ridiculous figure in history.

His dreams were haunted by that same apparition. Messages from the city almost entirely ceased coming as the days went by without a break in the storms. Might he end his days at Suma? No one was likely to come calling in these tempests.

A messenger did come from Murasaki, a sad, sodden creature. Had they passed in the street, Genji would scarcely have known whether he was man or beast, and of course would not have thought of inviting him to come near. Now the man brought a surge of pleasure and affection—though Genji could not help asking himself whether the storm had weakened his moorings.

Murasaki's letter, long and melancholy, said in part: "The terrifying deluge goes on without a break, day after day. Even the skies are closed off, and I am denied the comfort of gazing in your direction.

"What do they work, the sea winds down at Suma?
At home, my sleeves are assaulted by wave after wave."

Tears so darkened his eyes that it was as if they were inviting the waters to rise higher.

The man said that the storms had been fierce in the city too, and that a special reading of the Prajñāpāramitā Sutra had been ordered. "The streets are all closed and the great gentlemen can't get to court, and everything has closed down."

The man spoke clumsily and haltingly, but he did bring news. Genji summoned him near and had him questioned.

"It's not the way it usually is. You don't usually have rain going on for days without a break and the wind howling on and on. Everyone is terrified. But it's worse here. They haven't had this hail bearing right through the ground and thunder going on and on and not letting a body think." The terror written so plainly on his face did nothing to improve the spirits of the people at Suma.

Might it be the end of the world? From dawn the next day the wind was so fierce and the tide so high and the surf so loud that it was as if the crags and the mountains must fall. The horror of the thunder and lightning was beyond description. Panic spread at each new flash. For what sins, Genji's men asked, were they being punished? Were they to perish without another glimpse of their mothers and fathers, their dear wives and children?

Genji tried to tell himself that he had been guilty of no misdeed for which he must perish here on the seashore. Such were the panic and confusion around him, however, that he bolstered his confidence with special offerings to the god of Sumiyoshi.

"O you of Sumiyoshi who protect the lands about: if indeed you are an avatar of the Blessed One, then you must save us."

His men were of course fearful for their lives; but the thought that so fine a gentleman (and in these deplorable circumstances) might be swept beneath the waters seemed altogether too tragic. The less distraught among them prayed in loud voices to this and that favored deity, Buddhist and Shinto, that their own lives be taken if it meant that his might be spared.

They faced Sumiyoshi and prayed and made vows: "Our lord was reared deep in the fastnesses of the palace, and all blessings were his; and yet, in the abundance of his goodness, he has brought strength through these lands to all who have sunk beneath the weight of their troubles. In punishment for what crimes do you call forth these howling waves? Judge his case if you will, you gods of heaven and earth. Guiltless, he is accused of a crime, stripped of his offices, driven from his house and city, left as you see him with no relief from the torture and the lamentation. And now these horrors, and even his life seems threatened. Why? we must ask. Because of sins in some other life, because of crimes in this one? If your vision is clear, O you gods, then take all this away."

Genji offered prayers to the king of the sea and countless other gods as well. The thunder was increasingly more terrible, and finally the gallery adjoining his rooms was struck by lightning. Flames sprang up and the gallery was destroyed. The confusion was immense; the whole world seemed to have gone mad. Genji was moved to a building out in back, a kitchen or something of the sort it seemed to be. It was crowded with people of every station and rank. The clamor was almost enough to drown out the lightning and thunder. Night descended over a sky already as black as ink.

Presently the wind and rain subsided and stars began to come out. The kitchen being altogether too mean a place, a move back to the main hall was suggested. The charred remains of the gallery were an ugly sight, however, and the hall had been badly muddied and all the blinds and curtains blown away. Perhaps, Genji's men suggested somewhat tentatively, it might be better to wait until dawn. Genji sought to concentrate upon the holy name, but his agitation continued to be very great.

He opened a wattled door and looked out. The moon had come up. The line left by the waves was white and dangerously near, and the surf was still high. There was no one here whom he could turn to, no student of the deeper truths who could discourse upon past and present and perhaps explain these wild events. All the fisherfolk had gathered at what they had heard was the house of a great gentleman from the city. They were as noisy and impossible to communicate with as a flock of birds, but no one thought of telling them to leave.

"If the wind had kept up just a little longer," someone said, "absolutely everything would have been swept under. The gods did well by us."

There are no words—"lonely" and "forlorn" seem much too weak—to describe his feelings.

"Without the staying hand of the king of the sea
The roar of the eight hundred waves would have taken us under."

Genji was as exhausted as if all the buffets and fires of the tempest had been aimed at him personally. He dozed off, his head against some nondescript piece of furniture.

The old emperor came to him, quite as when he had lived. "And why are you in this wretched place?" He took Genji's hand and pulled him to his feet. "You must do as the god of Sumiyoshi tells you. You must put out to sea immediately. You must leave this shore behind."

"Since I last saw you, sir," said Genji, overjoyed, "I have suffered an unbroken series of misfortunes. I had thought of throwing myself into the sea."

"That you must not do. You are undergoing brief punishment for certain sins. I myself did not commit any conscious crimes while I reigned, but a person is guilty of transgressions and oversights without his being aware of them. I am doing penance and have no time to look back towards this world. But an echo of your troubles came to me and I could not stand idle. I fought my way through the sea and up to this shore and I am very tired; but now that I am here I must see to a matter in the city." And he disappeared.

Genji called after him, begging to be taken along. He looked around him. There was only the bright face of the moon. His father's presence had been too real for a dream, so real that he must still be here. Clouds traced sad lines across the sky. It had been clear and palpable, the figure he had so longed to see even in a dream, so clear that he could almost catch an afterimage. His father had come through the skies to help him in what had seemed the last extremity of his sufferings. He was deeply grateful, even to the tempests; and in the aftermath of the dream he was happy.

Quite different emotions now ruffled his serenity. He forgot his immediate troubles and only regretted that his father had not stayed longer. Perhaps he would come again. Genji would have liked to go back to sleep, but he lay wakeful until daylight.

A little boat had pulled in at the shore and two or three men came up.

"The revered monk who was once governor of Harima has come from Akashi. If the former Minamoto councillor, Lord Yoshikiyo, is here, we wonder if we might trouble him to come down and hear the details of our mission."

Yoshikiyo pretended to be surprised and puzzled. "He was once among my closer acquaintances here in Harima, but we had a falling out and it has been some time since we last exchanged letters. What can have brought him through such seas in that little boat?"

Genji's dream had given intimations. He sent Yoshikiyo down to the boat immediately. Yoshikiyo marveled that it could even have been launched upon such a sea.

These were the details of the mission, from the mouth of the old governor: "Early this month a strange figure came to me in a dream. I listened, though somewhat incredulously, and was told that on the thirteenth there would be a clear and present sign. I was to ready a boat and make for this shore when the waves subsided. I did ready a boat, and then came this savage wind and lightning. I thought of numerous foreign sovereigns who have received instructions in dreams on how to save their lands, and I concluded that even at the risk of incurring his ridicule I must on the day appointed inform your lord of the import of the dream. And so I did indeed put out to sea. A strange jet blew all the way and brought us to this shore. I cannot think of it except as divine intervention. And might I ask whether there have been corresponding manifestations here? I do hate to trouble you, but might I ask you to communicate all of this to your lord?"

Yoshikiyo quietly relayed the message, which brought new considerations. There had been these various unsettling signs conveyed to Genji dreaming and waking. The possibility of being laughed at for having departed these shores under threat now seemed the lesser risk. To turn his back on what might be a real offer of help from the gods would be to ask for still worse misfortunes. It was not easy to reject ordinary advice, and personal reservations counted for little when the advice came from great eminences. "Defer to them; they will cause you no reproaches," a wise man of old once said.* He could scarcely face worse misfortunes by deferring than by not deferring, and he did not seem likely to gain great merit and profit by hesitating out of concern for his brave name. Had not his own father come to him? What room was there for doubts?

He sent back his answer: "I have been through a great deal in this strange place, and I hear nothing at all from the city. I but gaze upon a sun and moon going I know not where as comrades from my old home; and now comes this angler's boat, happy tidings on an angry wind.† Might there be a place along your Akashi coast where I can hide myself?"

The old man was delighted. Genji's men pressed him to set out even before sunrise. Taking along only four or five of his closest attendants, he boarded the boat. That strange wind came up again and they were at Akashi as if they had flown. It was very near, within crawling distance, so to speak; but still the workings of the wind were strange and marvelous.

The Akashi coast was every bit as beautiful as he had been told it was. He would have preferred fewer people, but on the whole he was pleased. Along the coast and in the hills the old monk had put up numerous

*Lao-tze, say early commentaries; but the advice is not to be found in his extant writings.
†Ki no Tsurayuki, *Gosenshū* 1225:

> An angler's boat upon the waves that pound us,
> Happy tidings on an angry wind.

buildings with which to take advantage of the four seasons: a reed-roofed beach cottage with fine seasonal vistas; beside a mountain stream a chapel of some grandeur and dignity, suitable for rites and meditation and invocation of the holy name; and rows of storehouses where the harvest was put away and a bountiful life assured for the years that remained. Fearful of the high tides, the old monk had sent his daughter and her women off to the hills. The house on the beach was at Genji's disposal.

The sun was rising as Genji left the boat and got into a carriage. This first look by daylight at his new guest brought a happy smile to the old man's lips. He felt as if the accumulated years were falling away and as if new years had been granted him. He gave silent thanks to the god of Sumiyoshi. He might have seemed ridiculous as he bustled around seeing to Genji's needs, as if the radiance of the sun and the moon had become his private property; but no one laughed at him.

I need not describe the beauty of the Akashi coast. The careful attention that had gone into the house and the rocks and plantings of the garden, the graceful line of the coast—it was infinitely pleasanter than Suma, and one would not have wished to ask a less than profoundly sensitive painter to paint it. The house was in quiet good taste. The old man's way of life was as Genji had heard it described, hardly more rustic than that of the grandees at court. In sheer luxury, indeed, he rather outdid them.

When Genji had rested for a time he got off messages to the city. He summoned Murasaki's messenger, who was still at Suma recovering from the horrors of his journey. Loaded with rewards for his services, he now set out again for the city. It would seem that Genji sent off a description of his perils to priests and others of whose services he regularly made use,* but he told only Fujitsubo how narrow his escape had in fact been. He repeatedly laid down his brush as he sought to answer that very affectionate letter from Murasaki.

''I feel that I have run the whole gamut of horrors and then run it again, and more than ever I would like to renounce the world; but though everything else has fled away, the image which you entrusted to the mirror has not left me. I hate the thought that I might not see you again.

>"Yet farther away, upon the beach at Akashi,
>   My thoughts of a distant city, and of you.

"I am still half dazed, which fact will I fear be too apparent in the confusion and disorder of this letter.''

Though it was true that his letter was somewhat disordered, his men thought it splendid. How very fond he must be of their lady! It would seem that they sent off descriptions of their own perils.

The apparently interminable rains had at last stopped and the sky was bright far into the distance. The fishermen radiated good spirits. Suma had been a lonely place with only a few huts scattered among the rocks. It was true that the crowds here at Akashi were not entirely to Genji's liking, but it was a pleasant spot with much to interest him and take his mind from his troubles.

The old man's devotion to the religious life was rather wonderful. Only one matter interfered with it: worry about his daughter. He told Genji a little of his concern for the girl. Genji was sympathetic. He had heard that she was very handsome and wondered if there might not be some bond between them, that he should have come upon her in this strange place. But no; here he was in the remote provinces, and he must think of nothing but his own prayers. He would be unable to face Murasaki if he were to depart from the promises he had made her. Yet he continued to be interested in the girl. Everything suggested that her nature and appearance were very far from ordinary.

Reluctant to intrude himself, the old man had moved to an outbuilding. He was restless and unhappy when away from Genji, however, and he prayed more fervently than ever to the gods and Buddhas that his unlikely hope might be realized. Though in his sixties he had taken good

*The commentators inform us that these men are probably a part of Genji's spy system.

care of himself and was young for his age. The religious life and the fact
that he was of proud lineage may have had something to do with the
matter. He was stubborn and intractable, as old people often are, but he
was well versed in antiquities and not without a certain subtlety. His
stories of old times did a great deal to dispel Genji's boredom. Genji had
been too busy himself for the sort of erudition, the lore about customs and
precedents, which he now had in bits and installments, and he told himself
that it would have been a great loss if he had not known Akashi and its
venerable master.

In a sense they were friends, but Genji rather overawed the old man.
Though he had seemed so confident when he told his wife of his hopes,
he hesitated, unable to broach the matter, now that the time for action had
come, and seemed capable only of bemoaning his weakness and inadequacy. As for the daughter, she rarely saw a passable man here in the
country among people of her own rank; and now she had had a glimpse
of a man the like of whom she had not suspected to exist. She was a shy,
modest girl, and she thought him quite beyond her reach. She had had
hints of her father's ambitions and thought them wildly inappropriate, and
her discomfort was greater for having Genji near.

It was the Fourth Month. The old man had all the curtains and fixtures
of Genji's rooms changed for fresh summery ones. Genji was touched and
a little embarrassed, feeling that the old man's attentions were perhaps a
bit overdone; but he would not have wished for the world to offend so
proud a nature.

A great many messages now came from the city inquiring after his
safety. On a quiet moonlit night when the sea stretched off into the
distance under a cloudless sky, he almost felt that he was looking at the
familiar waters of his own garden. Overcome with longing, he was like a
solitary, nameless wanderer. "Awaji, distant foam,"* he whispered to himself.

> "Awaji: in your name is all my sadness,
>   And clear you stand in the light of the moon tonight."

He took out the seven-stringed koto, long neglected, which he had
brought from the city and spread a train of sad thoughts through the house
as he plucked out a few tentative notes. He exhausted all his skills on "The
Wide Barrow,"† and the sound reached the house in the hills on a sighing
of wind and waves. Sensitive young ladies heard it and were moved. Lowly
rustics, though they could not have identified the music, were lured out
into the sea winds, there to catch cold.

*The name Awaji suggests both *awa*, "foam," and *aware*, an ejaculation of vague and unde-
fined sadness. Oshikōchi Mitsune, *Shinkokinshū* 1513:

> The moon seemed ah so distant at Awaji.
> From these cloudly sovereign heights it seems so near.

†A Chinese composition, apparently, which does not survive.

The old man could not sit still. Casting aside his beads, he came running over to the main house.

"I feel as if a world I had thrown away were coming back," he said, breathless and tearful. "It is a night such as to make one feel that the blessed world for which one longs must be even so."

Genji played on in a reverie, a flood of memories of concerts over the years, of this gentleman and that lady on flute and koto, of voices raised in song, of times when he and they had been the center of attention, recipients of praise and favors from the emperor himself. Sending to the house on the hill for a lute and a thirteen-stringed koto, the old man now seemed to change roles and become one of these priestly mendicants who make their living by the lute. He played a most interesting and affecting strain. Genji played a few notes on the thirteen-stringed koto which the old man pressed on him and was thought an uncommonly impressive performer on both sorts of koto. Even the most ordinary music can seem remarkable if the time and place are right; and here on the wide seacoast, open far into the distance, the groves seemed to come alive in colors richer than the bloom of spring or the change of autumn, and the calls of the water rails were as if they were pounding on the door and demanding to be admitted.

The old man had a delicate style to which the instruments were beautifully suited and which delighted Genji. "One likes to see a gentle lady quite at her ease with a koto," said Genji, as if with nothing specific in mind.

The old man smiled. "And where, sir, is one likely to find a gentler, more refined musician than yourself? On the koto I am in the third generation from the emperor Daigo. I have left the great world for the rustic surroundings in which you have found me, and sometimes when I have been more gloomy than usual I have taken out a koto and picked away at it; and, curiously, there has been someone who has imitated me. Her playing has come quite naturally to resemble my master's. Or perhaps it has only seemed so to the degenerate ear of the mountain monk who has only the pine winds for company. I wonder if it might be possible to let you hear a strain, in the greatest secrecy of course." He brushed away a tear.

"I have been rash and impertinent. My playing must have sounded like no playing at all." Genji turned away from the koto. "I do not know why, but it has always been the case that ladies have taken especially well to the koto. One hears that with her father to teach her the fifth daughter of the emperor Saga was a great master of the instrument, but it would seem that she had no successors. The people who set themselves up as masters these days are quite ordinary performers with no real grounding at all. How fascinating that someone who still holds to the grand style should be hidden away on this coast. Do let me hear her."

"No difficulty at all, if that is what you wish. If you really wish it, I can summon her. There was once a poet, you will remember, who was much pleased at the lute of a tradesman's wife.* While we are on the subject of lutes, there were not many even in the old days who could bring out the best in the instrument. Yet it would seem that the person of whom I speak plays with a certain sureness and manages to affect a rather pleasing delicacy. I have no idea where she might have acquired these skills. It seems wrong that she should be asked to compete with the wild waves, but sometimes in my gloom I do have her strike up a tune."

He spoke with such spirit that Genji, much interested, pushed the lute toward him.

He did indeed play beautifully, adding decorations that have gone out of fashion. There was a Chinese elegance in his touch, and he was able to induce a particularly solemn tremolo from the instrument. Though it might have been argued that the setting was wrong, an adept among his retainers was persuaded to sing for them about the clean shore of Ise.† Tapping out the rhythm, Genji would join in from time to time, and the old man would pause to offer a word of praise. Refreshments were brought in, very prettily arranged. The old man was most assiduous in seeing that the cups were kept full, and it became the sort of evening when troubles are forgotten.

Late in the night the sea breezes were cool and the moon seemed brighter and clearer as it sank towards the west. All was quiet. In pieces and fragments the old man told about himself, from his feelings upon taking up residence on this Akashi coast to his hopes for the future life and the prospects which his devotions seemed to be opening. He added, unsolicited, an account of his daughter. Genji listened with interest and sympathy.

"It is not easy for me to say it, sir, but the fact that you are here even briefly in what must be for you strange and quite unexpected surroundings, and the fact that you are being asked to undergo trials new to your experience—I wonder if it might not be that the powers to whom an aged monk has so fervently prayed for so many years have taken pity on him. It is now eighteen years since I first prayed and made vows to the god of Sumiyoshi.‡ I have had certain hopes for my daughter since she was very young, and every spring and autumn I have taken her to Sumiyoshi. At each of my six daily services, three of them in the daytime and three at night, I have put aside my own wishes for salvation and ventured a suggestion that my hopes for the girl be noticed. I have sunk to this provincial

*Po Chü-i, Collected Works, XII, "The Lutist."
†"The Sea of Ise," a Saibara:

> On the clean shore of Ise,
> Let us gather shells in the tide.
> Let us gather shells and jewels.

‡There is a chronological difficulty, since by this account the girl would be about nine when, in Chapter 3, she is reported to be turning away suitors.

obscurity because I brought an unhappy destiny with me into this life. My father was a minister, and you see what I have become. If my family is to follow the same road in the future, I ask myself, then where will it end? But I have had high hopes for her since she was born. I have been determined that she go to some noble gentleman in the city. I have been accused of arrogance and unworthy ambitions and subjected to some rather unpleasant treatment. I have not let it worry me. I have said to her that while I live I will do what I can for her, limited though my resources may be; and that if I die before my hopes are realized she is to throw herself into the sea." He was weeping. It had taken great resolve for him to speak so openly.

Genji wept easily these days. "I had been feeling put upon, bundled off to this strange place because of crimes I was not aware of having committed. Your story makes me feel that there is a bond between us. Why did you not tell me earlier? Nothing has seemed quite real since I came here, and I have given myself up to prayers to the exclusion of everything else, and so I fear that I will have struck you as spiritless. Though reports had reached me of the lady of whom you have spoken, I had feared that she would want to have nothing to do with an outcast

like myself. You will be my guide and intermediary? May I look forward
to company these lonely evenings?"

The old man was thoroughly delighted.

"Do you too know the sadness of the nights
  On the shore of Akashi with only thoughts for companions?

"Imagine, if you will, how it has been for us through the long months
and years." He faltered, though with no loss of dignity, and his voice was
trembling.

"But you, sir, are used to this seacoast.

"The traveler passes fretful nights at Akashi.
  The grass which he reaps for his pillow reaps no dreams."

His openness delighted the old man, who talked on and on—and
became rather tiresome, I fear. In my impatience I may have allowed
inaccuracies to creep in, and exaggerated his eccentricities.

In any event, he felt a clean happiness sweep over him. A beginning
had been made.

At about noon the next day Genji got off a note to the house on the
hill. A real treasure might lie buried in this unlikely spot. He took a great
deal of trouble with his note, which was on a fine saffron-colored Korean
paper.

"I catch, as I gaze into unresponsive skies,
  A glimpse of a grove of which I have had certain tidings.

"My resolve has been quite dissipated."*
And was that all? one wonders.

The old man had been waiting. Genji's messenger came staggering
back down the hill, for he had been hospitably received.

But the girl was taking time with her reply. The old man rushed to
her rooms and urged haste, but to no avail. She thought her hand quite
unequal to the task, and awareness of the difference in their stations
dismayed her. She was not feeling well, she said, and lay down.

Though he would certainly have wished it otherwise, the old man
finally answered in her place. "Her rustic sleeves are too narrow to encom-
pass such awesome tidings, it would seem, and indeed she seems to have
found herself incapable of even reading your letter.

"She gazes into the skies into which you gaze.
  May they bring your thoughts and hers into some accord.

"But I fear that I will seem impertinent and forward."

*Anonymous, *Kokinshū* 503:

    Resolve that I would keep them to myself,
    These thoughts of you, has been quite dissipated.

It was in a most uncompromisingly old-fashioned hand, on sturdy Michinoku paper; but there was something spruce and dashing about it too. Yes, "forward" was the proper word. Indeed, Genji was rather startled. The old man had given the messenger a "bejeweled apron," an appropriate gift from a beach cottage.*

He got off another message the next day, beautifully written on soft, delicate paper. "I am not accustomed to receiving letters from ladies' secretaries.

"Unwillingly reticent about my sorrows
I still must be—for no one makes inquiry.

"Though it is difficult to say just what I mean."

There would have been something unnatural about a girl who refused to be interested in such a letter. She thought it splendid, but she also thought it impossibly out of her reach. Notice from such supreme heights had the perverse effect of reducing her to tears and inaction.

She was finally badgered into setting something down. She chose delicately perfumed lavender paper and took great care with the gradations of her ink.

"Unwillingly reticent—how can it be so?
How can you sorrow for someone you have not met?"

The diction and the handwriting would have done credit to any of the fine ladies at court. He fell into a deep reverie, for he was reminded of days back in the city. But he did not want to attract attention, and presently shook it off.

Every other day or so, choosing times when he was not likely to be noticed, and when he imagined that her thoughts might be similar to his —a quiet, uneventful evening, a lonely dawn—he would get off a note to her. There was a proud reserve in her answers which made him want more than ever to meet her. But there was Yoshikiyo to think of. He had spoken of the lady as if he thought her his property, and Genji did not wish to contravene these long-standing claims. If her parents persisted in offering her to him, he would make that fact his excuse, and seek to pursue the affair as quietly as possible. Not that she was making things easy for him. She seemed prouder and more aloof than the proudest lady at court; and so the days went by in a contest of wills.

The city was more than ever on his mind now that he had moved beyond the Suma barrier. He feared that not even in jest† could he do without Murasaki. Again he was asking himself if he might not bring her

---

*There is a pun on *tamamo*, "jeweled apron" (an elegant word for "apron") and a kind of seaweed.
†Anonymous, *Kokinshū* 1025:

> I thought to see whether I could do without you.
> I cannot tell of the longing, even in jest.

quietly to Akashi, and he was on the point of doing just that. But he did not expect to be here very much longer, and nothing was to be gained by inviting criticism at this late date.

In the city it had been a year of omens and disturbances. On the thirteenth day of the Third Month, as the thunder and winds mounted to new fury, the emperor had a dream. His father stood glowering at the stairs to the royal bedchamber and had a great deal to say, all of it, apparently, about Genji. Deeply troubled, the emperor described the dream to his mother.

"On stormy nights a person has a way of dreaming about the things that are on his mind," she said. "If I were you I would not give it a second thought."

Perhaps because his eyes had met the angry eyes of his father, he came down with a very painful eye ailment. Retreat and fasting were ordered for the whole court, even Kokiden's household. Then the minister, her father, died. He was of such years that his death need have surprised no one, but Kokiden too was unwell, and worse as the days went by; and the emperor had a great deal to worry about. So long as an innocent Genji was off in the wilderness, he feared, he must suffer. He ventured from time to time a suggestion that Genji be restored to his old rank and offices.

His mother sternly advised against it. "People will tax you with shallowness and indecision. Can you really think of having a man go into exile and then bringing him back before the minimum three years have gone by?"

And so he hesitated, and he and his mother were in increasingly poor health.

At Akashi it was the season when cold winds blow from the sea to make a lonely bed even lonelier.

Genji sometimes spoke to the old man. "If you were perhaps to bring her here when no one is looking?"

He thought that he could hardly be expected to visit her. She had her own ideas. She knew that rustic maidens should come running at a word from a city gentleman who happened to be briefly in the vicinity. No, she did not belong to his world, and she would only be inviting grief if she pretended that she did. Her parents had impossible hopes, it seemed, and were asking the unthinkable and building a future on nothing. What they were really doing was inviting endless trouble. It was good fortune enough to exchange notes with him for so long as he stayed on this shore. Her own prayers had been modest: that she be permitted a glimpse of the gentleman of whom she had heard so much. She had had her glimpse, from a distance, to be sure, and, brought in on the wind, she had also caught hints of his unmatched skill (of this too she had heard) on the koto. She had learned rather a great deal about him these past days, and she was satisfied. Indeed a nameless woman lost among the fishermen's huts had no right to expect even this. She was acutely embarrassed at any suggestion that he be invited nearer.

Her father too was uneasy. Now that his prayers were being answered he began to have thoughts of failure. It would be very sad for the girl, offered heedlessly to Genji, to learn that he did not want her. Rejection was painful at the hands of the finest gentleman. His unquestioning faith in all the invisible gods had perhaps led him to overlook human inclinations and probabilities.

"How pleasant," Genji kept saying, "if I could hear that koto to the singing of the waves. It is the season for such things. We should not let it pass."

Dismissing his wife's reservations and saying nothing to his disciples, the old man selected an auspicious day. He bustled around making preparations, the results of which were dazzling. The moon was near full. He sent off a note which said only: "This night that should not be wasted."* It seemed a bit arch, but Genji changed to informal court dress and set forth late in the night. He had a carriage decked out most resplendently, and then, deciding that it might seem ostentatious, went on horseback instead. The lady's house was some distance back in the hills. The coast

*Minamoto Nobuakira, *Gosenshū* 103:

> If only I could show them to someone who knows,
> This moon, these flowers, this night that should not be wasted.

lay in full view below, the bay silver in the moonlight. He would have liked to show it to Murasaki. The temptation was strong to turn his horse's head and gallop on to the city.

"Race on through the moonlit sky, O roan-colored horse,
And let me be briefly with her for whom I long."*

The house was a fine one, set in a grove of trees. Careful attention had gone into all the details. In contrast to the solid dignity of the house on the beach, this house in the hills had a certain fragility about it, and he could imagine the melancholy thoughts that must come to one who lived here. There was sadness in the sound of the temple bells borne in on pine breezes from a hall of meditation nearby. Even the pines seemed to be asking for something as they sent their roots out over the crags. All manner of autumn insects were singing in the garden. He looked about him and saw a pavilion finer than the others. The cypress door upon which the moonlight seemed to focus was slightly open.

He hesitated and then spoke. There was no answer. She had resolved

*A play on words gives a roan horse a special affinity with moonlight.

to admit him no nearer. All very aristocratic, thought Genji. Even ladies so wellborn that they were sheltered from sudden visitors usually tried to make conversation when the visitor was Genji. Perhaps she was letting him know that he was under a cloud. He was annoyed and thought of leaving. It would run against the mood of things to force himself upon her, and on the other hand he would look rather silly if it were to seem that she had bested him at this contest of wills. One would indeed have wished to show him, the picture of dejection, "to someone who knows."

A curtain string brushed against a koto, to tell him that she had been passing a quiet evening at her music.

"And will you not play for me on the koto of which I have heard so much?

"Would there were someone with whom I might share my thoughts
And so dispel some part of these sad dreams."

"You speak to one for whom the night has no end.
How can she tell the dreaming from the waking?"

The almost inaudible whisper reminded him strongly of the Rokujō lady.

This lady had not been prepared for an incursion and could not cope with it. She fled to an inner room. How she could have contrived to bar it he could not tell, but it was very firmly barred indeed. Though he did not exactly force his way through, it is not to be imagined that he left matters as they were. Delicate, slender—she was almost too beautiful. Pleasure was mingled with pity at the thought that he was imposing himself upon her. She was even more pleasing than reports from afar had had her. The autumn night, usually so long, was over in a trice. Not wishing to be seen, he hurried out, leaving affectionate assurances behind.

He got off an unobtrusive note later in the morning. Perhaps he was feeling twinges of conscience. The old monk was equally intent upon secrecy, and sorry that he was impelled to treat the messenger rather coolly.

Genji called in secret from time to time. The two houses being some distance apart, he feared being seen by fishermen, who were known to relish a good rumor, and sometimes several days would elapse between his visits. Exactly as she had expected, thought the girl. Her father, forgetting that enlightenment was his goal, quite gave his prayers over to silent queries as to when Genji might be expected to come again; and so (and it seems a pity) a tranquillity very laboriously attained was disturbed at a very late date.

Genji dreaded having Murasaki learn of the affair. He still loved her more than anyone, and he did not want her to make even joking reference to it. She was a quiet, docile lady, but she had more than once been unhappy with him. Why, for the sake of brief pleasure, had he caused her pain? He wished it were all his to do over again. The sight of the Akashi lady only brought new longing for the other lady.

He got off a more earnest and affectionate letter than usual, at the end of which he said: "I am in anguish at the thought that, because of foolish occurrences for which I have been responsible but have had little heart, I might appear in a guise distasteful to you. There has been a strange, fleeting encounter. That I should volunteer this story will make you see, I hope, how little I wish to have secrets from you. Let the gods be my judges.

> "It was but the fisherman's brush with the salty sea pine
> Followed by a tide of tears of longing."

Her reply was gentle and unreproachful, and at the end of it she said: "That you should have deigned to tell me a dreamlike story which you could not keep to yourself calls to mind numbers of earlier instances.

> "Naïve of me, perhaps; yet we did make our vows.
> And now see the waves that wash the Mountain of Waiting!"*

It was the one note of reproach in a quiet, undemanding letter. He found it hard to put down, and for some nights he stayed away from the house in the hills.

The Akashi lady was convinced once more that her fears had become actuality. Now seemed the time to throw herself into the sea. She had only her parents to turn to and they were very old. She had had no ambitions for herself, no thought of making a respectable marriage. Yet the years had gone by happily enough, without storms or tears. Now she saw that the world can be very cruel. She managed to conceal her worries, however, and to do nothing that might annoy Genji. He was more and more pleased with her as time went by.

But there was the other, the lady in the city, waiting and waiting for his return. He did not want to do anything that would make her unhappy, and he spent his nights alone. He sent sketchbooks off to her, adding poems calculated to provoke replies. No doubt her women were delighted with them; and when the sorrow was too much for her (and as if by thought transference) she too would make sketches and set down notes which came to resemble a journal.

And what did the future have in store for the two of them?

The New Year came, the emperor was ill, and a pall settled over court life. There was a son, by Lady Shōkyōden, daughter of the Minister of the

---

*Anonymous, *Kokinshū* 1093:

> On the day that I am unfaithful to my vows,
> May the waves break over the Mountain of Waiting of Sué.

A very common pun makes Matsuyama, "Mount of the Pines," also "Mountain of Waiting."

Right,* but the child was only two, far too young for the throne. The obvious course was to abdicate in favor of the crown prince. As the emperor turned over in his mind the problem of advice and counsel for his successor, he thought it more than ever a pity that Genji should be off in the provinces. Finally he went against Kokiden's injunctions and issued an amnesty. Kokiden had been ill from the previous year, the victim of a malign spirit, it seemed, and numerous other dire omens had disturbed the court. Though the emperor's eye ailment had for a time improved, perhaps because of strict fasting, it was worse again. Late in the Seventh Month, in deep despondency, he issued a second order, summoning Genji back to the city.

Genji had been sure that a pardon would presently come, but he also knew that life is uncertain. That it should come so soon was of course pleasing. At the same time the thought of leaving this Akashi coast filled him with regret. The old monk, though granting that it was most proper and just, was upset at the news. He managed all the same to tell himself that Genji's prosperity was in his own best interest. Genji visited the lady every night and sought to console her. From about the Sixth Month she had shown symptoms such as to make their relations more complex. A sad, ironical affair seemed at the same time to come to a climax and to disintegrate. He wondered at the perverseness of fates that seemed always to be bringing new surprises. The lady, and one could scarcely have blamed her, was sunk in the deepest gloom. Genji had set forth on a strange, dark journey with a comforting certainty that he would one day return to the city; and he now lamented that he would not see this Akashi again.

His men, in their several ways, were delighted. An escort came from the city, there was a joyous stir of preparation, and the master of the house was lost in tears. So the month came to an end. It was a season for sadness in any case, and sad thoughts accosted Genji. Why, now and long ago, had he abandoned himself, heedlessly but of his own accord, to random, profitless affairs of the heart?

"What a great deal of trouble he does cause," said those who knew the secret. "The same thing all over again. For almost a year he didn't tell anyone and he didn't seem to care the first thing about her. And now just when he ought to be letting well enough alone he makes things worse."

Yoshikiyo was the uncomfortable one. He knew what his fellows were saying: that he had talked too much and started it all.

Two days before his departure Genji visited his lady, setting out earlier than usual. This first really careful look at her revealed an astonishingly proud beauty. He comforted her with promises that he would choose an opportune time to bring her to the city. I shall not comment again upon his own good looks. He was thinner from fasting, and emaciation seemed to add the final touches to the picture. He made tearful vows. The lady

*Later to be the father-in-law of Tamakazura.

replied in her heart that this small measure of affection was all she wanted and deserved, and that his radiance only emphasized her own dullness. The waves moaned in the autumn winds, the smoke from the salt burners' fires drew faint lines across the sky, and all the symbols of loneliness seemed to gather together.

"Even though we now must part for a time,
   The smoke from these briny fires will follow me."

"Smoldering thoughts like the sea grass burned on these shores.
   And what good now to ask for anything more?"

She fell silent, weeping softly, and a rather conventional poem seemed to say a great deal.

She had not, through it all, played for him on the koto of which he had heard so much.

"Do let me hear it. Let it be a memento."

Sending for the seven-stringed koto he had brought from the city, he played an unusual strain, quiet but wonderfully clear on the midnight air. Unable to restrain himself, the old man pushed a thirteen-stringed koto toward his daughter. She was apparently in a mood for music. Softly she tuned the instrument, and her touch suggested very great polish and elegance. He had thought Fujitsubo's playing quite incomparable. It was in the modern style, and enough to bring cries of wonder from anyone who knew a little about music. For him it was like Fujitsubo herself, the essence of all her delicate awareness. The koto of the lady before him was quiet and calm, and so rich in overtones as almost to arouse envy. She left off playing just as the connoisseur who was her listener had passed the first stages of surprise and become eager attention. Disappointment and regret succeeded pleasure. He had been here for nearly a year. Why had he not insisted that she play for him, time after time? All he could do now was repeat the old vows.

"Take this koto," he said, "to remember me by Someday we will play together."

Her reply was soft and almost casual:

"One heedless word, one koto, to set me at rest.
   In the sound of it the sound of my weeping, forever."

He could not let it pass.

"Do not change the middle string* of this koto.
   Unchanging I shall be till we meet again.

"And we will meet again before it has slipped out of tune."

Yet it was not unnatural that the parting should seem more real than the reunion.

*There are several theories as to what the expression might mean. The most likely of them has it referring not to the seven-stringed but to the thirteen-stringed koto.

On the last morning Genji was up and ready before daybreak. Though he had little time to himself in all the stir, he contrived to write to her:

"Sad the retreating waves at leaving this shore.
Sad I am for you, remaining after."

"You leave, my reed-roofed hut will fall to ruin.
Would that I might go out with these waves."

It was an honest poem, and in spite of himself he was weeping. One could, after all, become fond of a hostile place, said those who did not know the secret. Those who did, Yoshikiyo and others, were a little jealous, concluding that it must have been a rather successful affair.

There were tears, for all the joy; but I shall not dwell upon them.

The old man had arranged the grandest of farewell ceremonies. He had splendid travel robes for everyone, even the lowliest footmen. One marveled that he had found time to collect them all. The gifts for Genji himself were of course the finest, chests and chests of them, borne by a retinue which he attached to Genji's. Some of them would make very suitable gifts in the city. He had overlooked nothing.

The lady had pinned a poem to a travel robe:

"I made it for you, but the surging brine has wet it.
And might you find it unpleasant and cast it off?"

Despite the confusion, he sent one of his own robes in return, and with it a note:
"It was very thoughtful of you.

"Take it, this middle robe, let it be the symbol
Of days uncounted but few between now and then."

Something else, no doubt, to put in her chest of memories. It was a fine robe and it bore a most remarkable fragrance. How could it fail to move her?

The old monk, his face like one of the twisted shells on the beach, was meanwhile making some of the younger people smile. "I have quite renounced the world," he said, "but the thought that I may not see you back to the city—

"Though weary of life, seasoned by salty winds,
I am not able to leave this shore behind,

and I wander lost in thoughts upon my child.* Do let me see you at least as far as the border. It may seem forward of me, but if something should from time to time call up thoughts of her, do please let her hear from you."

"It is an impossibility, sir, for very particular reasons, that I can ever forget her. You will very quickly be made to see my real intentions. If I seem dispirited, it is only because I am sad to leave all this behind.

*See note‡, page 7.

"I wept upon leaving the city in the spring.
I weep in the autumn on leaving this home by the sea.

"What else can I do?" And he brushed away a tear.

The old man seemed on the point of expiring.

The lady did not want anyone to guess the intensity of her grief, but it was there, and with it sorrow at the lowly rank (she knew that she could not complain) that had made this parting inevitable. His image remained before her, and she seemed capable only of weeping.

Her mother tried everything to console her. "What could we have been thinking of? You have such odd ideas," she said to her husband, "and I should have been more careful."

"Enough, enough. There are reasons why he cannot abandon her. I have no doubt that he has already made his plans. Stop worrying, mix yourself a dose of something or other. This wailing will do no good." But he was sitting disconsolate in a corner.

The women of the house, the mother and the nurse and the rest, went on charging him with unreasonable methods. "We had hoped and prayed over the years that she might have the sort of life any girl wants, and things finally seemed to be going well—and now see what has happened."

It was true. Old age suddenly advanced and subdued him, and he spent his days in bed. But when night came he was up and alert.

"What can have happened to my beads?"

Unable to find them, he brought empty hands together in supplication. His disciples giggled. They giggled again when he set forth on a moonlight peregrination and managed to fall into the brook and bruise his hip on one of the garden stones he had chosen so carefully. For a time pain drove away, or at least obscured, his worries.

Genji went through lustration ceremonies at Naniwa and sent a messenger to Sumiyoshi with thanks that he had come thus far and a promise to visit at a later date in fulfillment of his vows. His retinue had grown to an army and did not permit side excursions. He made his way directly back to the city. At Nijō the reunion was like a dream. Tears of joy flowed so freely as almost to seem inauspicious. Murasaki, for whom life had come to seem of as little value as her farewell poem had suggested it to be, shared in the joy. She had matured and was more beautiful than ever. Her hair had been almost too rich and thick. Worry and sorrow had thinned it somewhat and thereby improved it. And now, thought Genji, a deep peace coming over him, they would be together. And in that instant there came to him the image of the one whom he had not been ready to leave. It seemed that his life must go on being complicated.

He told Murasaki about the other lady. A pensive, dreamy look passed over his face, and she whispered, as if to dismiss the matter: "For myself I do not worry."*

He smiled. It was a charmingly gentle reproof. Unable to take his eyes from her now that he had her before him, he could not think how he had survived so many months and years without her. All the old bitterness came back. He was restored to his former rank and made a supernumerary councillor. All his followers were similarly rehabilitated. It was as if spring had come to a withered tree.

The emperor summoned him and as they made their formal greetings thought how exile had improved him. Courtiers looked on with curiosity, wondering what the years in the provinces would have done to him. For the elderly women who had been in service since the reign of his late father, regret gave way to noisy rejoicing. The emperor had felt rather shy at the prospect of receiving Genji and had taken great pains with his dress. He seemed pale and sickly, though he had felt somewhat better these last few days. They talked fondly of this and that, and presently it was night. A full moon flooded the tranquil scene. There were tears in the emperor's eyes.

"We have not had music here of late," he said, "and it has been a very long time since I last heard any of the old songs."

*Ukon, *Shūishū* 870:

> For myself, who am forgotten, I do not worry,
> But for him who vowed fidelity while he lived.

Genji replied:

> "Cast out upon the sea, I passed the years
>   As useless as the leech child of the gods."*

The emperor was touched and embarrassed.

> "The leech child's parents met beyond the pillar.
>   We meet again to forget the spring of parting."

He was a man of delicate grace and charm.

Genji's first task was to commission a grand reading of the Lotus Sutra in his father's memory. He called on the crown prince, who had grown in his absence, and was touched that the boy should be so pleased to see him. He had done so well with his studies that there need be no misgivings about his competence to rule. It would seem that Genji also called on Fujitsubo, and managed to control himself sufficiently for a quiet and affectionate conversation.

I had forgotten: he sent a note with the retinue which, like a returning wave, returned to Akashi. Very tender, it had been composed when no one was watching.

"And how is it with you these nights when the waves roll in?

> "I wonder, do the morning mists yet rise,
>   There at Akashi of the lonely nights?"

The Kyushu Gosechi dancer had had fond thoughts of the exiled Genji, and she was vaguely disappointed to learn that he was back in the city and once more in the emperor's good graces. She sent a note, with instructions that the messenger was to say nothing of its origin:

> "There once came tidings from a boat at Suma,
>   From one who now might show you sodden sleeves."

Her hand had improved, though not enough to keep him from guessing whose it was.

> "It is I, not you, from whom the complaints should come.
>   My sleeves have refused to dry since last you wrote."

He had not seen enough of her, and her letter brought fond memories. But he was not going to embark upon new adventures.

To the lady of the orange blossoms he sent only a note, cause more for disappointment than for pleasure.

---

*In one of the *Nihongi* versions of the creation myth, the leech child, among the Sun Goddess's siblings, lives approximately the period of Genji's exile before being cast out to sea. It is at a pillar (see the emperor's answering poem) that both the leech and the Sun Goddess are conceived.

Chapter 11

Channel Buoys

Unable to forget that almost too vivid dream of his father and wanting somehow to lighten the penance, Genji immediately set about plans for a reading of the Lotus Sutra. It was to be in the Tenth Month. Everyone at court helped with the arrangements. The spirit of cooperation was as before Genji fell into disfavor.

Though seriously ill, Kokiden was still an enemy, angry that she had not succeeded in crushing him completely. The emperor had been convinced that he must pay the penalty for having gone against his father's wishes. Now that he had had Genji recalled, he was in greatly improved spirits, and the eye ailment that had so troubled him had quite gone away. Melancholy forebodings continued to be with him, however. He frequently sent for Genji, who was now in his complete confidence. Everyone thought it splendid that he was at last having his way.

The day appointed for his abdication drew near. It grieved him to think of the precarious position in which it would leave Oborozukiyo.

"Your father is dead," he said to her, "and my mother is in worse health all the time. I doubt that I have much longer to live and fear that everything will change once I am gone. I know that there is someone you have long preferred to me; but it has been a way of mine to concentrate upon one object, and I have thought only of you. Even if the man whom you prefer does as you wish him to, I doubt that his affection can match my own. The thought is too much for me." He was in tears.

She flushed and turned away. An irresistible charm seemed to flow from her, to make him forget his grievances.

"And why have you not had a child? It seems such a pity. No doubt you will shortly have one by the man with whom you seem to have the stronger bond, and that will scarcely be to my taste. He is a commoner, you know, and I suppose the child must be reared as a commoner."

These remarks about the past and about the future so shamed her that she could not bring herself to look at him. He was a handsome, civil man, and his behavior over the years had told of a deepening affection; and so she had come to understand, as she had become more alive to these subtleties, that Genji, for all his good looks and gallantry, had been less than ideally devoted to her. Why had she surrendered to childish impulses and permitted a scandal which had seriously damaged her name and done no good for his? These reminders of the past brought her untold pain.

In the Second Month of the following year initiation ceremonies were held for the crown prince. He was eleven, tall and mature for his age, and the very image of Genji. The world marveled at the almost blinding radiance, but it was a source of great trepidation for Fujitsubo. Very pleased with his successor, the emperor in a most gentle and friendly way discussed plans for his own abdication.

He abdicated that same month, so suddenly that Kokiden was taken by surprise.

"I know that it will be as a person of no importance," he said, seeking to calm her, "but I hope that I will see you rather more frequently and at my leisure."

His son by Lady Shōkyōden was made crown prince. Everything had changed overnight, causes for rejoicing were innumerable. Genji was made a minister. As the number of ministers is limited by the legal codes and there were at the time no vacancies, a supernumerary position was created for him. It was assumed that his would be the strongest hand in the direction of public affairs.

"I am not up to it," he said, deferring to his father-in-law, who was persuaded to come out of retirement and accept appointment as regent.

"I resigned because of poor health," protested the old man, "and now I am older and even more useless."

It was pointed out, however, that in foreign countries statesmen who in time of civil disorder have withdrawn to deep mountain retreats have thought it no shame, despite their white beards, to be of service once peace has been restored. Indeed they have been revered as the true saints and sages. The court and the world at large agreed that there need be no obstacle whatever to resuming upon recovery offices resigned because of illness. Unable to persist in his refusal, he was appointed chancellor. He was sixty-three. His retirement had been occasioned in part by the fact that affairs of state were not going as he wished, but now all was in order. His sons, whose careers had been in eclipse, were also brought back. Most striking was the case of Tō no Chūjō, who was made a supernumerary councillor. He had been especially careful about the training of his daughter, now twelve, by Kokiden's sister, and was hoping to send her to court. The boy who had sung "Takasago" so nicely* had come of age and was the sort of son every father wished for. Indeed Tō no Chūjō had a troop of sons by his various ladies which quite filled Genji with envy.

Genji's own Yūgiri was as handsome a boy as any of them. He served as page for both the emperor and the crown prince. His grandparents, Princess Omiya and the chancellor, continued to grieve for their daughter. But she was gone, and they had Genji's prosperity to take their minds from their sorrow; and it seemed that the gloomy years of Genji's exile had vanished without a trace. Genji's devotion to the family of his late wife was as it had always been. He overlooked no occasion that seemed to call for a visit, or for gifts to the nurse and the others who had remained faithful through the bad years. One may be sure that there were many happy women among them.

At Nijō too there were women who had awaited his return. He wished to do everything possible to make up for the sorrows that must have been theirs, and upon such women as Chūjō and Nakatsukasa, appropriately to their station in life, he bestowed a share of his affection. This left him no time for women outside the house. He had most splendidly remodeled the lodge to the east of his mansion. He had inherited it from his father, and his plan was that it be home for the lady of the orange blossoms and other neglected favorites.

I have said nothing about the Akashi lady, whom he had left in such uncertainty. Busy with public and private affairs, he had not been able to inquire after her as he would have wished. From about the beginning of the Third Month, though he told no one, she was much on his mind, for her time must be approaching. He sent off a messenger, who very soon returned.

"A girl was safely delivered on the sixteenth."

It was his first daughter. He was delighted—but why had he not brought the lady to have her child in the capital?

"You will have three children," a fortuneteller had once told him. "Two of them are certain to become emperor and empress. The least of the three will become chancellor, the most powerful man in the land." The whole of the oracle seemed by way of coming true.

He had consulted physiognomists in large numbers and they had been unanimous in telling him that he would rise to grand heights and have the world to do with as he wished; but through the unhappy days he had dismissed them from his thoughts. With the commencement of the new reign it seemed that his most extravagant hopes were being realized. The throne itself lay beyond his reach. He had been his father's favorite over

*See Chapter 7

his many brothers, but his father had determined to reduce him to common status, and that fact made it apparent that the throne must not be among his ambitions. Although the reasons were of course secret, the accession of the new emperor seemed evidence enough that the fortuneteller had not deceived him. As for future prospects, he thought that he could see the god of Sumiyoshi at work. Had it been foreordained that someone from Akashi was meant for remarkable things, and was it for that reason that her eccentric father had had what had seemed preposterous plans? Genji had done badly in letting his daughter be born in a corner of the provinces. He must send for mother and daughter as soon as the proprieties allowed, and he gave orders that the remodeling of the east lodge be hurried.

Capable nurses would be difficult to find, he was afraid, in Akashi. He remembered having heard the sad story of a woman whose mother had been among the old emperor's private secretaries and whose father had been a chamberlain and councillor. The parents both dead and the lady herself in straitened circumstances, she had struck up an unworthy liaison and had a child as a result. She was young and her prospects were poor, and she did not hesitate at the invitation to quit a deserted and ruinous mansion, and so the contract was made. By way of some errand or other, in the greatest secrecy, Genji visited her. Though she had made the commitment, she had been having second thoughts. The honor of the visit quite removed her doubts.

"I shall do entirely as you wish."

Since it was a propitious day, he sent her off immediately.

"You will think it selfish and unfeeling of me, I am sure; but I have rather special plans. Tell yourself that there is a precedent for being sent off to a hard life in a strange land, and put up with it for a time." And he told her in detail of her duties.

Since she had been at court, he had occasionally had a glimpse of her. She was thinner now. Her once fine mansion was sadly neglected, and the plantings in the garden were rank and overgrown. How, he wondered, had she endured such a life?

"Suppose we call it off," he said jokingly, "and keep you here." She was such a pretty young woman that he could not take his eyes from her.

She could not help thinking that, if it was all the same, she would prefer serving him from somewhat nearer at hand.

> "I have not been so fortunate as to know you,
>   But now I may say how sad it has been to part.

"And so perhaps I should go with you."
She smiled.

> "I do not trust regrets at so quick a farewell.
>   The truth has to do with someone you wish to visit."

It was nicely done.

She left the city by carriage. He assigned as escort men whom he trusted implicitly and enjoined them to the strictest secrecy. He sent with her a sword for the little girl and other appropriate gifts and provisions, in such quantities that the procession was in danger of falling behind schedule. His attentions to the newly appointed nurse could not have been more elaborate.

He smiled to think what this first grandchild would mean to the old man, how busy and self-important he would be. No doubt it told of events in a former life (and the thought brought twinges of conscience), that she meant so much to Genji himself. Over and over again he told the nurse that he would not be quick to forgive lapses and oversights.

> "One day this sleeve of mine shall be her shelter
>   Whose years shall be as the years of the angel's rock."*

They took a boat down the river and hurried onwards by horse. The old man was overjoyed and there was no end to his awed gratitude. He

---

*"May she live a *kalpa.*" Among the definitions of a *kalpa* is the time required for brushes of an angel's wing once a millennium to wear away a rock several billion cubic miles in volume.

made obeisance in the direction of the capital. At this evidence that the little girl was important to Genji he began to feel rather in awe of her too. She had an unearthly, almost ominous sort of beauty, to make the nurse see that the fuss and bother had not after all been overdone. There had been something horrible about this sudden removal to the countryside, but now it was as if she were awakening from a nightmare into broad sunlight. She already adored the little girl.

The Akashi lady had been in despair. She had decided as the months went by that life was without meaning. This evidence of Genji's good intentions was comforting. She bestirred herself to make the guests from the city feel welcome.

The escort was in a hurry to return. She set down something of her feelings in a letter to Genji, to which she added this poem:

"These sleeves are much too narrow to offer protection.
    The blossom awaits those all-encompassing ones."*

Genji was astonished at himself, that his daughter should be so much on his mind and that he should so long to see her.

He had said little to Murasaki of the events at Akashi, but he feared that she might have the story from someone else. "And that would seem to be the situation," he said, concluding his account. "Somehow everything has gone wrong. I don't have children where I really want them, and now there is a child in a very unlikely place. And it is a girl. I could of course simply disown her, but that is the sort of thing I do not seem capable of. I will bring her here one of these days and let you have a look at her. You are not to be jealous, now."

Murasaki flushed. "How strange you are. You make me dislike myself, constantly assigning traits which are not mine at all. When and by whom, I wonder, shall I begin to have lessons in jealousy?"

Genji smiled, and tears came to his eyes. "When indeed, pray. You are very odd, my dear. Things come into your mind that would not occur to anyone else."

She thought of their longing for each other through the years apart, of letters back and forth, and his delinquencies and her resentment seemed like a silly joke.

"There are very special reasons for it all," he continued, "that she should be so much on my mind, and that I should be so diligent in my inquiries. But I fear that it is too soon to tell you of them. You would not understand. I think that the setting may have been partly responsible."

He had told of her of the lines of smoke across the Akashi sky that last evening, and, though with some understatement, perhaps, of the lady's appearance and of her skill on the koto. And so while she herself had been

*Anonymous, *Gosenshū* 64:

They need, these blossoms of spring, assailed by the winds,
    An all-encompassing sleeve to close off the skies.

lost in infinite sadness, thought Murasaki, he had managed to keep himself entertained. It did not seem right that he should have allowed himself even a playful glance at another woman.

If he had his ways, she would have hers. She looked aside, whispering as if to herself: "There was a time when we seemed rather a nicely matched couple.

"I think I shall be the first to rise as smoke,
    And it may not go the direction of that other."

"What a very unpleasant thing to say.

"For whom, in mountains, upon unfriendly seas,
    Has the flow of my tears been such as to sweep me under?

"I wish you could understand me, but of course it is not the way of this world that we are ever completely understood. I would not care or complain except for the fact that I do so love you."

He took out a koto and tuned it and pushed it towards her; but, perhaps somewhat displeased at his account of the other lady's talents, she refused to touch it. She was a calmly, delightfully gentle lady, and these small outbursts of jealousy were interesting, these occasional shows of anger charming. Yes, he thought, she was someone he could be with always.

His daughter would be fifty days old on the fifth of the Fifth Month. He longed more than ever to see her. What a splendid affair the fiftieth-day celebrations would be if they might take place in the city! Why had he allowed the child to be born in so unseemly a place? If it had been a boy he would not have been so concerned, but for a girl it was a very great disability not to be born in the city. And she seemed especially important because his unhappiness had had so much to do with her destinies.

He sent off messengers with the strictest orders to arrive on that day and no other. They took with them all the gifts which the most fertile imagination could have thought of for such an occasion, and practical everyday supplies as well.

This was Genji's note:

"The sea grass, hidden among the rocks, unchanging,
    Competes this day for attention with the iris.*

"I am quite consumed with longing. You must be prepared to leave Akashi. It cannot be otherwise. I promise you that you have not the smallest thing to worry about."

The old man's face was a twisted shell once more, this time, most properly, with joy. Very elaborate preparations had been made for the

---

Ayame, "iris," also suggests "attention." The fifth of the Fifth Month is the day of the iris (more properly, sweet-flag) festival.

fiftieth-day ceremonies, but had these envoys not come from Genji they would have been like brocades worn in the night.*

The nurse had found the Akashi lady to her liking, a pleasant companion in a gloomy world. Among the women whom the lady's parents, through family connections, had brought from the city were several of no lower standing than the nurse; but they were all aged, tottering people who could no longer be used at court and who had in effect chanced upon Akashi in their search for a retreat among the crags. The nurse was at her elegant best. She gave this and that account, as her feminine sensibilities led her, of the great world, and she spoke too of Genji and how everyone admired him. The Akashi lady began to think herself important for having had something to do with the little memento he had left behind. The nurse saw Genji's letter. What extraordinary good fortune the lady did have, she had been thinking, and how unlucky she had been herself; and Genji's inquiries made her feel important too.

The lady's reply was honest and unaffected.

"The crane is lost on an insignificant isle.
  Not even today do you come to seek it out.

"I cannot be sure how long a life darkened by lonely reveries and brightened by occasional messages from outside can be expected to continue, and must beg of you that the child be freed of uncertainty the earliest day possible."

Genji read the letter over and over again, and sighed.

"The distant boat more distant."† Murasaki looked away as she spoke, as if to herself, and said no more.

"You do make a large thing of it. Myself, I make no more of it than this: sometimes a picture of that seacoast comes into my mind, and memories come back, and I sigh. You are very attentive, not to miss the sigh."

He let her see only the address. The hand would have done honor to the proudest lady at court. She could see why the Akashi lady had done so well.

It was sad that his preoccupation with Murasaki had left him no time for the lady of the orange blossoms. There were public affairs as well, and he was now too important to wander about as he would wish. It seemed that all was quiet in that sector, and so he gave little thought to it. Then came the long rains of early summer to lay a pall over things and bring a respite from his duties. He roused himself for a visit.

Though she saw little of him, the lady was completely dependent on him; but she was not of the modern sort, given to outpourings of resent-

*The *Shih Chi* informs us that to be rich and powerful and not to display that fact in one's native village is to wear brocades in pitch darkness. See also note*, page 140.
†Ise, *Shinkokinshū* 1048:

You seem more distant than the distant boat
More distant yet as it rows out from Kumano.

ment. He knew that she would not make him uncomfortable. Long neglected, her house now wore a weirdly ruinous aspect. As usual, he first
looked in on her sister, and late in the night moved on to the lady's own
rooms. He was himself weirdly beautiful in the misty moonlight. She felt
very inadequate, but she was waiting for him out near the veranda, in
meditative contemplation of the night. Her refusal to let anything upset
her was remarkable.

From nearby there came the metallic cry of a water rail.

"Did not this bird come knocking at my door,
    What cause would I have to admit the moon to these ruins?"

Her soft voice, trailing off into silence, was very pleasing. He sighed,
almost wishing it were not the case that each of his ladies had something
to recommend her. It made for a most complicated life.

"You respond to the call of every water rail?
    You must find yourself admitting peculiar moons.

"I am worried."

Not of course that he really suspected her of indiscretion. She had waited for him and she was very dear to him.

She reminded him of his farewell admonition not to look at the cloudy moon. "And why," she said, gently as always, "should I have thought then that I was unhappy? It is no better now."

He made the usual points (one wondered that they came so effortlessly) as he sought to comfort her.

He had not forgotten the Kyushu Gosechi dancer. He would have liked to see her again, but a clandestine meeting was altogether too difficult to arrange. He dominated her thoughts, so much so that she had turned away all the prospective bridegrooms who interested her father and had decided that she would not marry. Genji's plans were that once his east lodge had been redone, all cheerfully and pleasantly, he would gather just such ladies there, and, should a child be born who required careful upbringing, ask them to take charge of it. The new house compared very well indeed with the old, for he had assigned officials of intelligence and good taste to the work of remodeling.

He had not forgotten Oborozukiyo. He let her know that that unfortunate event had not stilled his ardor. She had learned her lesson, however, and so for Genji an affair that had never been really successful had become a complete failure.

Life was pleasant for the retired emperor, who had taken up residence in the Suzaku Palace. He had parties and concerts as the seasons went by and was in generally good spirits. Various ladies were still with him. The mother of the crown prince was the exception. Not especially conspicuous among them, she had been no match for Oborozukiyo. Now she had come into her own. She left the emperor's side to manage the crown prince's affairs. Genji now occupied his mother's rooms at the palace. The crown prince was in the Pear Pavilion, which adjoined them, and Genji was his companion and servant.

Though Fujitsubo could not resume her former titles, she was given the emoluments of a retired emperor. She maintained a full household and pursued her religious vocation with solemn grandeur. Factional politics had in recent years made it difficult for her to visit the palace, and she had grieved at not being able to see her son. Now everything was as she would have wished it, and the time had come for Kokiden to be unhappy with the world. Genji was scrupulously attentive to Kokiden's needs. This fact did nothing to change her feelings towards him, which were the subject of unfriendly criticism.

Prince Hyōbu, Murasaki's father, had sought during the bad years to please the dominant faction. Genji had not forgotten. Genji's conduct was on the whole not vengeful, but he was sometimes openly unfriendly to the prince. Fujitsubo saw and was unhappy.

The conduct of public affairs was now divided between Genji and his father-in-law, to pursue as they wished. The ceremonies when Tō no Chūjō's daughter entered court in the Eighth Month were magnificent, under the energetic direction of the chancellor himself. It was known that Prince Hyōbu had been putting all his time and wealth into preparing his second daughter for court service. Genji made it clear that the girl was not to be so honored, and what was the prince to do?

In the autumn Genji made a pilgrimage to Sumiyoshi. It was a brilliant progress, in thanks for the granting of his prayers. By the merest chance, it came on the day the Akashi lady had chosen for her own pilgrimage, a semiannual observance which this time had a special purpose, to apologize for her not having been able to present herself the year before or earlier this year. She came by ship. As the ship pulled in, a gorgeous array of offerings was being laid out on the beach. The shrine precincts rang with the shouts of bearers and there were uniformed dancers, all very good-looking.

"And whose party might it be?" asked one of her men.

The very inferior footman to whom the query was made laughed heartily. "You mean there is someone who does not know that the Genji minister has come because of his vows?"

The lady was stunned. To have chosen this day of all days, to be among the distant onlookers—her own inferiority could not have been emphasized more painfully. She was, in spite of it, tied to him by some bond or other, and here were these underlings, completely pleased with themselves, reflecting his glory. Why, because of what crimes and sins, should she, who never ceased thinking of him, have made this journey to Sumiyoshi on this day without catching an echo of it all? She could only turn away and try to hide her sorrow.

Genji's attendants were numberless, their robes of deep hues and brilliant hues like maple leaves and cherry blossoms against the deep green of the pine groves. Among the courtiers of the Sixth Rank, the yellow-green of the imperial secretariat stood out. The man who had on an earlier day had bitter words for the sacred fence of Kamo was among them. Also holding a guards commission, he had an imposing retinue of his own. Yoshikiyo too was a guards officer. He seemed especially proud of himself, and indeed his scarlet robe was very grand. All the men she had known at Akashi were scattered among the crowds, almost unrecognizable in their finery, the picture of prosperity. The young courtiers had even sought to outdo one another in caparisoning their horses, and for the rustics from Akashi it was a very fine show.

For the lady it was torment to see all the splendor and not to see Genji himself. Like the Kawara minister,* he had been granted a special honor guard of page boys, ten of them, all very pretty, of uniform height, and resplendently decked out, the cords that bound up their hair in the page-boy style a most elegant blending from white to deep purple. Yūgiri, whom Genji denied nothing, had put even his stableboys into livery.

---

*Minamoto Tōru. It is recorded that certain high courtiers received page-boy guards as a mark of special favor, but it is not recorded that Tōru was ever so honored.

The Akashi lady felt as if she were gazing at a realm beyond the clouds. Her own child seemed so utterly insignificant. She bowed to the shrine and prayed more fervently.

The governor of the province came to greet Genji, and no doubt the repast he had made ready was finer than for most ministers.

The lady could bear no more. "If I were to go up with my miserable little offerings, the god would scarcely notice, and would not think I had done much by way of keeping my promises. But the whole trip would be pointless if we were to turn and go home." She suggested that they put in at Naniwa and there commission lustration ceremonies.

Not dreaming what had happened, Genji passed the night in entertainments sure to please the god. He went beyond all his promises in the novelty and ingenuity of the dances. His nearest retainers, men like Koremitsu, knew how much the god had done for them. As Genji came unannounced from the shrine, Koremitsu handed him a poem:

"These pines of Sumiyoshi make me think
Of days when we were neighbors to this god."

Very apt, thought Genji.

"Remembering those fearful winds and waves,
Am I to forget the god of Sumiyoshi?

"Yes, it has without question been through his intervention." There
was solemn gratitude in the words.

Genji was greatly upset when Koremitsu told him that a boat had
come from Akashi and been turned away by the crowds on the beach.
Again the god of Sumiyoshi seemed to be at work. The lady would surely
regret having chosen this day. He must at least get off a note. Leaving
Sumiyoshi, he made excursions to other famous places in the region and
had grand and solemn lustrations performed on the seven strands of
Naniwa. "The waves of Naniwa,"* he said to himself (though with no real

*Prince Motoyoshi, *Shūishū* 766:

The waves of Naniwa: if I throw myself in,
As the channel buoys suggest, perhaps we shall meet.

Miotsukushi, "channel buoys," suggests bringing one's affairs to an end, being done with
it all. There were "seven strands" at which lustrations were performed in Kyoto, but the
meaning of "the seven strands of Naniwa" is unclear.

thought, one may imagine, of throwing himself in) as he looked out over the buoys that marked the Horie channel.

Koremitsu, who was among his mounted attendants, overheard. Always prepared for such an exigency, he took out a short writing brush and handed it to Genji.

A most estimable servant, thought Genji, jotting down a poem on a sheet of paper he had at hand.

> "Firm the bond that brings us to Naniwa,
>   Whose channel buoys invite me to throw myself in."

Koremitsu sent it to the lady by a messenger who was familiar with the events at Akashi. She wept tears of joy at even so small a favor. A line of horsemen was just then passing by.

This was her reply, to which she tied sacred cords for the lustration at Tamino:*

> "A lowly one whose place is not to demand,
>   To what purpose, at Naniwa, should I cast myself in?"

It was evening, and the scene was a lovely one, with the tide flooding in and cranes calling ceaselessly from the shallows. He longed to see her, whatever these crowds might think.

> "My sleeves are wet as when I wandered these shores.
>   The Isle of the Raincoat does not fend off the dews."†

To joyous music, he continued his round of the famous places, but his thoughts were with the Akashi lady.

Women of pleasure‡ were in evidence. It would seem that there were susceptible young men even among the highest ranks. Genji looked resolutely away. It was his view that one should be moved only by adequate forces, and that frivolous claims were to be rejected even in the most ordinary affairs. Their most seductive and studied poses had no effect upon him.

His party moved on. The next day being a propitious one, the Akashi lady made offerings at Sumiyoshi, and so, in keeping with her more modest station, acquitted herself of her vows. The incident had only served to intensify her gloom. A messenger came from Genji even before he could have returned to the city. He meant very shortly to send for her, he said. She was glad, and yet she hesitated, fearing the uncertainties of sailing off beyond the islands to a place she could not call home. Her father too was uneasy. But life in Akashi would be even more difficult than in earlier years. Her reply was obedient but indecisive.

I had forgotten: a new high priestess had been appointed for the Ise

---

*In the heart of Osaka, the Naniwa of the tale.
†Tamino means "field of the rain cloak." Genji's poem is an acrostic, with the name Naniwa buried in it.
‡*Asobi.* This is the only hint in the tale that such a class existed.

Shrine, and the Rokujō lady had returned to the city with her daughter. Genji's attentions, his inquiries as to her needs, were as always very thorough, but she remembered his coldness in other years and had no wish to call back the old sorrow and regret. She would treat him as a distant friend, no more. For his part, he made no special effort to see her. The truth was that he could not be sure of his own feelings, and his station in life was now such that he could not pursue sundry love affairs as he once had. He had no heart for importuning the lady. He would have liked all the same to see what the years had done to her daughter, the high priestess. The Rokujō house had been kept in good repair. As always, she selected only ladies of the finest taste and endowments to be with her, and the house was once more a literary and artistic salon. Though her life was in many ways lonely, there were ample pleasures and distractions.

Suddenly she fell ill. Troubled by feelings of guilt that she had spent those years in Ise, so remote from the Good Law, she became a nun.

Genji canceled all his appointments and rushed to her side. The old passion had departed, but she had been important to him. His commiserations were endless. She had had a place set out for him near her pillows. Raising herself to an armrest, she essayed her own answers. She seemed very weak, and he wept to think that she might die before he was able to let her know how fond he had been of her. It moved her deeply to think that now, when everything else seemed to be going, he should still care.

She spoke to him of her daughter. "She will have no one to turn to when I am gone. Please do count her among those who are important to you. She has been the unluckiest of girls, poor dear. I am a useless person and I have done her no good, but I tell myself that if my health will only hold out a little longer I may look after her until she is better able to look after herself." She was weeping, and life did indeed seem to be leaving her.

"You speak as if we might become strangers. It could not have happened, it would have been quite impossible, even if you had not said this to me. I mean to do everything I can for her. You must not worry."

"It is all so difficult. Even when a girl has a father to whom she can look with complete confidence, the worst thing is to lose her mother. Life can be dreadfully complicated when her guardian is found to have thoughts not becoming a parent. Unfortunate suspicions are sure to arise, and other women will see their chance to be ugly. These are distasteful forebodings, I know. But please do not let anything of the sort come into your relations with her. My life has been an object lesson in uncertainty, and my only hope now is that she be spared it all."

She need not be *quite* so outspoken, thought Genji; but he replied calmly enough. "I am a steadier and soberer person than I used to be, and it astonishes me that you still think me a trifler. One of these days the true state of affairs will be apparent even to you."

It was dark outside her curtains, through which came suggestions of lamplight. Was it just possible? He slid forward and looked through an

opening in the curtains. He saw her dimly, leaning against an armrest, so beautiful with her hair cut short that he wished he might ask someone to do her likeness. And the one beyond, to the east of the bed curtains, would be the priestess. Her curtain frames had been pushed casually to one side. She sat chin in hand, in an attitude of utter despondency. Though he could not see her well, she seemed very beautiful. There was great dignity in the flow of her hair down over her shoulders and in the shape of her head, and he could see that, for all the nobility, it was also a winsome and delicate sort of beauty. He felt certain stirrings of the heart, and remembered her mother's worries.

"I am feeling much worse," said the lady, "and fear I may be guilty of rudeness if you stay longer." A woman helped her into bed.

"How happy I would be if this visit might bring some sign of improvement. What exactly is the nature of the illness?"

She had sensed that she was being seen. "I must look like a witch. There is a very strong bond between us—it must be so—that you should have come to me now. I have been able to tell you a little of what has been on my mind, and I am no longer afraid to die."

"It moves me deeply that you should have thought me worthy. I have many brothers, but I have never felt close to them. My father looked upon the high priestess as one of his daughters, and to me she shall be a sister. I have no daughters of my own. She will fill an emptiness in my life."

His inquiries were warm and frequent, but a week or so later she died. Aware all over again of the uncertainty of life, Genji gave orders for the funeral and went into retreat. The priestess's stewards could have seen to them after a fashion, but he was her chief support.

He paid a visit. She replied, through her lady of honor, that she was feeling utterly lost and helpless.

"Your mother spoke about you, and left instructions, and it would be a great satisfaction if I might have your complete confidence."

Her women found him such a source of strength and comfort that they thought he could be forgiven earlier derelictions.

The services were very grand, with numerous people from Genji's house to help.

Still in retreat, he sent frequently to inquire after her. When presently she had regained a measure of composure, she sent her own replies. She was far from easy about being in correspondence with him, but her nurse and others insisted that it would be rude to use an intermediary.

It was a day of high winds and driving snow and sleet. He thought how much more miserable the weather must seem to her.

"I can imagine," he wrote, "what these hostile skies must do to you, and yet—

"From skies of wild, unceasing snow and sleet
    Her spirit watches over a house of sorrow."

He had chosen paper of a cloudy azure, and taken pains with all the details which he thought might interest a young girl.

She was hard put to reply, but her women again insisted that secretaries should have no part in these matters. She finally set down a poem on a richly perfumed gray paper, relying on the somber texture to modulate the shadings of her ink.

"I wish to go, but, blind with tears, am helpless
    As snows which were not asked where they would fall."

It was a calm, reserved hand, not remarkably skilled, but with a pleasantly youthful quality about it and much that told of good breeding. She had had a particular place in his thoughts ever since her departure for Ise, and now of course nothing stood in his way. But, as before, he reconsidered. Her mother had had good reason for her fears, which worried him less, it must be added, than the rumors that were even now going the rounds. He would behave in quite the opposite manner. He would be a model of propriety and parental solicitude, and when the emperor was a little older and better equipped to understand, he would bring her to court. With no daughters on hand to make life interesting, he would look after her as if she were his daughter. He was most attentive to her needs and, choosing his occasions well, sometimes visited her.

"You will think it forward of me to say so, but I would like nothing better than to be thought a substitute for your mother. Every sign that you trust me will please me enormously."

She was of a very shy and introspective nature, reluctant even to let him hear her voice. Her women were helpless to overcome this extreme reticence. She had in her service several minor princesses whose breeding and taste were such, he was sure, that she need not feel at all uncomfortable or awkward at court. He wanted very much to have a look at her and see whether his plans were well grounded—evidence, perhaps, that his fatherly impulses were not unmixed. He could not himself be sure when his feelings would change, and he let fall no hint of his plans. The princess's household felt greatly in his debt for his careful attention to the funeral and memorial services.

The days went by in dark procession. Her retainers began to take their leave. Her house, near the lower eastern limits of the city, was in a lonely district of fields and temples where the vesper bells often rang an accompaniment to her sobs. She and her mother had been close as parent and child seldom are. They had not been separated even briefly, and it had been without precedent for a mother to accompany a high priestess to Ise. She would have begged to be taken on this last journey as well, had it been possible.

There were men of various ranks who sought to pay court through her women. Quite as if he were her father, Genji told the women that none of them, not even the nurse, should presume to take matters into her own hands. They were very careful, for they would not want damaging reports to reach the ears of so grand a gentleman.

The Suzaku emperor still had vivid memories of the rites in the Grand Hall upon her departure for Ise, and of a beauty that had seemed almost frightening.

"Have her come to me," he had said to her mother. "She shall live exactly as my sisters, the high priestess of Kamo and the others."

But the Rokujō lady had misgivings and managed to evade the august invitation. The Suzaku emperor already had several wellborn consorts, and her daughter would be without strong backing. He was not in good health, moreover, and she feared that to her own misfortune might be added her daughter's. With the Rokujō lady gone, the priestess's women were more acutely aware than ever of the need for strong backing. The Suzaku emperor repeated his invitation.

Genji learned of his brother's hopes. It would be altogether too high-handed to spirit the princess away, and on the other hand Genji would have strong regrets at letting such a beautiful lady go. He decided that he must consult Fujitsubo, the mother of the new emperor.

He told her of all that was troubling him. "Her mother was a careful, thoughtful lady. My loose ways were responsible for all the trouble. I cannot tell you how it hurts me to think that she came to hate me. She died hating me; but as she lay dying she spoke to me about her daughter. Enough had been said about me, I gather, to convince her that I was the one to turn to, and so she controlled her anger and confided in me. The thought of it makes me want to start weeping again. I would find it difficult to ignore such a sad case even if it were not my personal concern, and I want to do all I can to put the poor lady's soul at rest and persuade her to forgive me. His Majesty is mature for his age, but he is still very young, and I often think how good it would be if he had someone with him who knew a little about the world. But of course the decision must be yours."

"This is very thoughtful and understanding of you. One does not wish to be unkind to the Suzaku emperor, of course, but perhaps, taking advantage of the Rokujō lady's instructions, you could pretend to be unaware of his wishes. He seems in any case to have given himself over to his prayers, and such concerns can scarcely matter very much any more. I am sure that if you explain the situation to him he will not harbor any deep resentment."

"If you agree, then, and are kind enough to number her among the acceptable candidates, I shall say a word to her of your decision. I have thought a great deal about her interests and have at length come to the conclusion I have just described to you. The gossips do upset me, of course."

He would do as she suggested. Pretending to be unaware of the Suzaku emperor's hopes, he would take the girl into the Nijō mansion.

He told Murasaki of this decision. "And," he added, "she is just the right age to be a good companion."

She was delighted. He pushed ahead with his plans.

Fujitsubo was concerned about her brother, Prince Hyōbu, who was in a fever, it seemed, to have his own daughter received at court. He and Genji were not on good terms. What did Genji propose to do in the matter?

Tō no Chūjō's daughter, now a royal consort, occupied the Kokiden apartments, and made a good playmate for the emperor. She had been adopted by her grandfather, the chancellor, who denied her nothing. Prince Hyōbu's daughter was about the same age as the emperor, and Fujitsubo feared that they would make a rather ridiculous couple, as if they were playing house together. She was delighted at the prospect of having an older lady with him, and she said as much. Genji was untiring in his services, advising him in public matters, of course, to the great satisfaction of Fujitsubo, and managing his private life as well. Fujitsubo was ill much of the time. Even when she was at the palace she found it difficult to be with her son as much as she wished. It was quite imperative that he have an older lady to look after him.

Chapter 12

A Picture Contest

Fujitsubo was most eager that Akikonomu, the former high priestess of Ise, be received at court. Genji knew that Akikonomu had no strong and reliable backer but, not wanting to alienate the Suzaku emperor, had decided not to bring her to Nijō. Making every effort to appear withdrawn and impartial, he took general responsibility for the proceedings and stood in the place of the girl's father.

The Suzaku emperor knew of course that it would not do to write to her of his disappointment. On the day of her presentation at court he sent magnificent robes and other gifts as well, wonderfully wrought cases and vanity chests and incense coffers, and incomparable incenses and sachets, so remarkable that they could be detected even beyond the legendary hundred paces. It may have been that the very special attention he gave to his gifts had to do with the fact that Genji would see them.

Akikonomu's lady of honor showed them to Genji. He took up a comb box of the most remarkable workmanship, endlessly fascinating in its detail. Among the rosettes on the box of decorative combs was a poem in the Suzaku emperor's own hand:

"I gave you combs and sent you far away.
The god now sends me far away from you?"

Genji almost felt as if he were guilty of sacrilege and blasphemy. From his own way of letting his emotions run wild, he could imagine Suzaku's

feelings when the priestess had departed for Ise, and his disappointment when, after years of waiting, she had returned to the city and everything had seemed in order, and this new obstacle had intervened. Would bitterness and resentment mar the serenity of his retirement? Genji knew that he himself would have been very much upset indeed. And it was he who had brought Akikonomu to the new emperor at the cost of hurting the retired emperor. There had been a time, of course, when he had felt bitter and angry at Suzaku; but he had known through it all that his brother was of a gentle, sensitive nature. He sat lost in thought.

"And how does she mean to answer? Have there been other letters? What have they said?"

But the lady of honor showed no disposition to let him see them.

Akikonomu was not feeling well and would have preferred not to answer.

"But you must, my lady." Genji could hear the discussion through blinds and curtains. "You know that you owe him a little respect."

"They are quite right," said Genji. "It will not do at all. You must let him have something, if only a line or two."

Though the inclination not to answer was very strong, Akikonomu

remembered her departure for Ise. Gently, softly handsome, the emperor
had wept that she must leave. Though only a child, she had been deeply
touched. And she remembered her dead mother, then and on other occasions. This (and only this?) was the poem which she finally set down:

> "Long ago, one word you said: Away!
> Sorry now am I that I paid no heed."

She rewarded Suzaku's messenger lavishly. Genji would have liked to
see her reply, but could hardly say so. He was genuinely troubled. Suzaku
was so handsome a man that one could imagine falling in love with him
were he a woman, and Akikonomu was by no means an ill match for him.
Indeed they would have been a perfect couple. And the present emperor
was still a boy. Genji wondered whether Akikonomu herself might not feel
uneasy at so incongruous a match. But it was too late now to halt the
proceedings.

He gave careful instructions to the superintendent of palace repairs.
Not wishing the Suzaku emperor to think that he was managing the girl's
affairs, he paid only a brief courtesy call upon her arrival at court. She had
always been surrounded by gifted and accomplished women, and now that
the ones who had gone home were back with her she had easily the finest
retinue at court. Genji thought of the Rokujō lady, her dead mother. With
what feelings of pride would she now be overseeing her daughter's affairs!
He would have thought her death a great loss even if he had not loved her.
She had had few rivals. Her tastes had been genuinely superior, and she
was much in his thoughts these days.

Fujitsubo was also at court. The emperor had heard that a fine new
lady had arrived, and his eagerness was most charming.

"Yes, she is splendid," said his mother. "You must be on your best
behavior when you meet her."

He feared that a lady of such advanced years might not be easy to talk
to. It was late in the night when she made her appearance. She was small
and delicately molded, and she seemed quiet and very much in control of
herself, and in general made a very good impression on the emperor. His
favorite companion was Tō no Chūjō's little daughter, who occupied the
Kokiden apartments. The new arrival, so calm and self-possessed, did
make him feel on the defensive, and then Genji behaved towards her with
such solemnity that the emperor was lured into rather solemn devoirs.
Though he distributed his nights impartially between the two ladies, he
preferred the Kokiden apartments for diurnal amusements. Tō no Chūjō
had ambitious plans for his daughter and was worried about this new
competitor.

The Suzaku emperor had difficulty resigning himself to what had
happened. Genji came calling one day and they had a long and affectionate
talk. The Suzaku emperor, who had more than once spoken to Genji of the
priestess's departure for Ise, mentioned it again, though somewhat circum-

spectly. Genji gave no open indication that he knew what had happened, but he did discuss it in a manner which he hoped would elicit further remarks from his brother. It was clear that the Suzaku emperor had not ceased to love the girl, and Genji was very sorry for him indeed. He knew and regretted that he could not see for himself the beauty which seemed to have such a powerful effect upon everyone who did see it. Akikonomu permitted not the briefest glimpse. And so of course he was fascinated. He saw enough to convince him that she must be very near perfection.

The emperor had two ladies and there was no room for a third. Prince Hyōbu's plans for sending his daughter to court had foundered. He could only hope that as the emperor grew older he would be in a more receptive mood. The competition between the two ladies was warm.

The emperor loved art more than anything else. He loved to look at paintings and he painted beautifully. Akikonomu was also an accomplished artist. He went more and more frequently to her apartments, where the two of them would paint for each other. His favorites among the young courtiers were painters and students of painting. It delighted him to watch this new lady, so beautiful and so elegant, casually sketching a scene, now and again pulling back to think the matter over. He liked her much better now.

Tō no Chūjō kept himself well informed. A man of affairs who had strong competitive instincts, he was determined not to lose this competition. He assembled master painters and he told them exactly what he wanted, and gave them the best materials to work with. Of the opinion that illustrations for the works of established authors could always be counted on, he chose his favorites and set his painters to illustrating them. He also commissioned paintings of the seasons and showed considerable flair with the captions. The emperor liked them all and wanted to share his pleasure with Akikonomu; but Tō no Chūjō objected. The paintings were not to leave the Kokiden apartments.

Genji smiled. "He was that way when he was a boy, and in many ways he still is a boy. I do not think it a very deft way to manage His Majesty. I'll send off my whole collection and let him do with it as he pleases."

All the chests and bookcases at Nijō were ransacked for old paintings and new, and Genji and Murasaki sorted out the ones that best suited current fancies. There were interesting and moving pictures of those sad Chinese ladies Yang Kuei-fei and Wang Chao-chün.* Genji feared, however, that the subjects were inauspicious.

Thinking this a good occasion to show them to Murasaki, he took out the sketchbooks and journals of his exile. Any moderately sensitive lady would have found tears coming to her eyes. For Murasaki those days had been unrelieved pain, not easily forgotten. Why, she asked, had he not let her see them before?

*See note†, page 178.

"Better to see these strands where the fishermen dwell
Than far away to weep, all, all alone.

"I think the uncertainty might have been less cruel."
It was true.

"Now more than in those painful days I weep
As tracings of them bring them back to me."

He must let Fujitsubo see them. Choosing the more presentable
scrolls, the ones in which life upon those shores came forward most viv-
idly, he found his thoughts returning to Akashi.

Hearing of Genji's activities, Tō no Chūjō redoubled his own efforts.
He quite outdid himself with all the accessories, spindles and mountings
and cords and the like. It was now the middle of the Third Month, a time
of soft, delicious air, when everyone somehow seemed happy and at peace.
It was also a quiet time at court, when people had leisure for these avoca-
tions. Tō no Chūjō saw a chance to bring the young emperor to new
raptures. He would offer his collection for the royal review.

Both in the Kokiden apartments and in Akikonomu's Plum Pavilion
there were paintings in endless variety. Illustrations for old romances
seemed to interest both painter and viewer. Akikonomu rather preferred
secure and established classics, while the Kokiden girl chose the romances
that were the rage of the day. To the casual observer it might have seemed
perhaps that her collection was the brighter and the more stylish. Connoisseurs among the court ladies had made the appraisal of art their principal
work.

Fujitsubo was among them. She had had no trouble giving up most
pleasures, but a fondness for art had refused to be shaken off. Listening
to the aesthetic debates, she hit upon an idea: the ladies must divide into
two sides.

On the left was the Plum Pavilion or Akikonomu faction, led by
Heinaishinosuke, Jijū no Naishi, and Shōshō no Myōbu; and in the right
or Kokiden faction, Daini no Naishinosuke, Chūjō no Myōbu, and Hyōe
no Myōbu. Fujitsubo listened with great interest as each gave forth with
her opinions. They were all of them gifted students of art.

The first match was between an illustration for *The Bamboo Cutter*, the
ancestor of all romances, and a scene centering upon Toshikage from *The
Tale of the Hollow Tree*.

From the left came this view: "The story has been with us for a very
long time, as familiar as the bamboo growing before us, joint upon joint.
There is not much in it that is likely to take us by surprise. Yet the moon
princess did avoid sullying herself with the affairs of this world, and her
proud fate took her back to the far heavens; and so perhaps we must accept
something august and godly in it, far beyond the reach of silly, superficial
women."

And this from the right: "It may be as you say, that she returned to a realm beyond our sight and so beyond our understanding. But this too must be said: that in our world she lived in a stalk of bamboo, which fact suggests rather dubious lineage. She exuded a radiance, we are told, which flooded her stepfather's house with light; but what is that to the light which suffuses these many-fenced halls and pavilions? Lord Abe threw away a thousand pieces of gold and another thousand in a desperate attempt to purchase the fire rat's skin, and in an instant it was up in flames —a rather disappointing conclusion. Nor is it very edifying, really, that Prince Kuramochi, who should have known how well informed the princess was in these matters, should have forged a jeweled branch and so made of himself a forgery too."

The *Bamboo Cutter* illustration, by Kose no Omi* with a caption by Ki no Tsurayuki, was mounted on Chinese silk and had a cerise cover and a spindle of sandalwood—rather uninteresting, all in all.

"Now let us look at the other. Toshikage was battered by tempests and waves and swept off to foreign parts, but he finally came home, whence his musical activities sent his fame back across the waters and down through the centuries. This painting successfully blends the Chinese and the Japanese and the new and the old, and I say that it is without rival."

On stiff white paper with a blue mounting and a spindle of yellow jade, it was the work of Tsunenori and bore a caption by Michikaze.† The effect was dazzlingly modern. The left had to admit defeat.

The Tales of Ise was pitted against *The Tale of Jōsammi.*‡ No decision was forthcoming. The picture offered by the right was again a bright, lively painting of contemporary life with much, including details of the palace itself, to recommend it.

"Shall we forget how deep is the sea of Ise
Because the waves have washed away old tracks?"

It was Heinaishinosuke, pleading the cause of the left, though without great fire or eloquence. "Are the grand accomplishments of Lord Narihira to be dwarfed by a little love story done with a certain cleverness and plausibility?"

"To this Jōsammi, high above august clouds,
The thousand-fathomed sea seems very shallow."

It was Daini, speaking for the right.

*A son of Kose no Kanaoka, active early in the tenth century.
†For Tsunenori, see note*, page 175. Ono no Michikaze, or Tōfū, active in the early and middle tenth century, is commonly called one of the three great calligraphers of the Heian Period. Murasaki Shikibu seems to be setting the episode some three quarters of a century before the time of writing.
‡The latter has been lost.

Fujitsubo offered an opinion. "However one may admire the proud spirit of Lady Hyōe, one certainly would not wish to malign Lord Narihira.

"At first the strands of sea grass may seem old,
But the fisherfolk of Ise are with us yet."

And so poem answered poem in an endless feminine dispute. The younger and less practiced women hung upon the debate as if for their very lives; but security precautions had been elaborate, and even the grand ladies were permitted to see only the smallest part of the riches.

Genji stopped by and was much diverted. If it was all the same, he said, why not make the final judgments in the emperor's presence? He had had a royal inspection in mind from the start, and so had taken very great pains with his selections, which included a scroll of his own Suma and of his Akashi paintings. Nor was Tō no Chūjō to be given low marks for effort. The chief business at court these days had become the collecting of evocative paintings.

"I think it spoils the fun to have them painted specially," said Genji. "I think we should limit ourselves to the ones we have had all along."

He was of course referring to Tō no Chūjō and his secret studio.

The Suzaku emperor heard of the stir and gave Akikonomu paintings of his own, among them representations of court festivals for which the emperor Daigo had done the captions; and on a scroll depicting events from his own reign was the scene, for him unforgettable, of Akikonomu's departure for Ise. He himself had carefully gone over the sketches, and the finished painting, by Kose no Kimmochi,* quite lived up to his hopes. It was in a box, completely modern, of pierced aloeswood with rosettes that quietly enhanced its beauty. He sent a verbal message through a guards captain on special assignment to Suzaku, setting down only this verse, beside a painting of the solemn arrival at the Grand Hall:

"Though now I dwell beyond the sacred confines,
My heart is there committing you to the gods."

It required an answer. Bending a corner of one of the sacred combs, she tied a poem to it and wrapped it in azure Chinese paper:

"Within these sacred precincts all has changed.
Fondly I think of the days when I served the gods."

She rewarded the messenger very elegantly.

The Suzaku emperor was deeply moved and longed to return to his days on the throne. He was annoyed at Genji, who perhaps was now having a gentle sort of revenge. It would seem that the Suzaku emperor sent large numbers of pictures through his mother to the Kokiden lady. Oborozukiyo, another fancier of painting, had also put together a distinguished collection.

*A grandson of Kanaoka.

The day was appointed. The careful casualness of all the details would have done justice to far more leisurely preparations. The royal seat was put out in the ladies' withdrawing rooms, and the ladies were ranged to the north and south. The seats of the courtiers faced them on the west. The paintings of the left were in boxes of red sandalwood on sappanwood stands with flaring legs. Purple Chinese brocades were spread under the stands, which were covered with delicate lavender Chinese embroidery. Six little girls sat behind them, their robes of red and their jackets of white lined with red, from under which peeped red and lavender. As for the right or Kokiden side, the boxes were of heavy aloes and the stands of lighter aloes. Green Korean brocades covered the stands, and the streamers and the flaring legs were all in the latest style. The little page girls wore green robes and over them white jackets with green linings, and their singlets were of a grayish green lined with yellow. Most solemnly they lined up their treasures. The emperor's own women were in the uniforms of the two sides.

Genji and Tō no Chūjō were present, upon royal invitation. Prince Hotaru, a man of taste and cultivation and especially a connoisseur of painting, had taken an inconspicuous place among the courtiers. Perhaps Genji had suggested inviting him. It was the emperor's wish that he act as umpire. He found it almost impossible to hand down decisions. Old masters had painted cycles of the four seasons with uncommon power, fluency, and grace, and a rather wonderful sense of unity; but they sometimes seemed to run out of space, so that the observer was left to imagine the grandeur of nature for himself. Some of the more superficial pictures of our own day, their telling points in the dexterity and ingenuity of the strokes and in a certain impressionism, did not seem markedly their inferior, and sometimes indeed seemed ahead of them in brightness and good spirits. Several interesting points were made in favor of both.

The doors to the breakfast suite, north of the ladies' withdrawing rooms, had been slid open so that Fujitsubo might observe the proceedings. Having long admired her taste in painting, Genji was hoping that she might be persuaded to give her views. When, though infrequently, he was not entirely satisfied with something Prince Hotaru said and offered an opinion of his own, he had a way of sweeping everything before him.

Evening came, and still Prince Hotaru had not reached a final decision. As its very last offering Akikonomu's side brought out a scroll depicting life at Suma. Tō no Chūjō was startled. Knowing that the final inning had come, the Kokiden faction too brought out a very remarkable scroll, but there was no describing the sure delicacy with which Genji had quietly set down the moods of those years. The assembly, Prince Hotaru and the rest, fell silent, trying to hold back tears. They had pitied him and thought of themselves as suffering with him; and now they saw how it had really been. They had before their eyes the bleakness of those nameless strands and inlets. Here and there, not so much open description as poetic impressions, were captions in cursive Chinese and Japanese. There was no point

now in turning to the painting offered by the right. The Suma scroll had blocked everything else from view. The triumph of the left was complete.

Dawn approached and Genji was vaguely melancholy. As the wine flagons went the rounds he fell into reminiscence.

"I worked very hard at my Chinese studies when I was a boy, so hard that Father seemed to fear I might become a scholar. He thought it might be because scholarship seldom attracts wide acclaim, he said, that he had rarely seen it succeed in combining happiness with long life. In any event, he thought it rather pointless in my case, because people would notice me whether I knew anything or not. He himself undertook to tutor me in pursuits not related to the classics. I don't suppose I would have been called remarkably inept in any of them, but I did not really excel in any of them either. But there was painting. I was the merest dabbler, and yet there were times when I felt a strange urge to do something really good. Then came my years in the provinces and leisure to examine that remarkable seacoast. All that was wanting was the power to express what I saw and felt, and that is why I have kept my inadequate efforts from you until now. I wonder," he said, turning to Prince Hotaru, "if my presuming to bring them out might set some sort of precedent for impertinence and conceit."

"It is true of every art," said the prince, "that real mastery requires concentrated effort, and it is true too that in every art worth mastering (though of course that word 'mastering' contains all manner of degrees and stages) the evidences of effort are apparent in the results. There are two mysterious exceptions, painting* and the game of Go, in which natural ability seems to be the only thing that really counts. Modest ability can of course be put to modest use. A rather ordinary person who has neither worked nor studied so very hard can paint a decent picture or play a decent game of Go. Sometimes the best families will suddenly produce someone who seems to do everything well." He was now speaking to Genji. "Father was tutor for all of us, but I thought he took himself seriously only when you were his pupil. There was poetry, of course, and there was music, the flute and the koto. Painting seemed less study than play, something you let your brush have its way with when poetry had worn you out. And now see the results. See all of our professionals running off and hiding their faces."

The prince may have been in his cups. In any event, the thought of the old emperor brought a new flood of tears.

A quarter moon having risen, the western sky was silver. Musical instruments were ordered from the royal collection. Tō no Chūjō chose a Japanese koto. Genji was generally thought the finest musician in court, but Tō no Chūjō was well above the ordinary. Genji chose a Chinese koto, as did Prince Hotaru, and Shōshō no Myōbu took up a lute. Courtiers with a good sense of rhythm were set to marking time, and all in all it was a very good concert indeed. Faces and flowers emerged dimly in the morning twilight, and birds were singing in a clear sky. Gifts were brought from Fujitsubo's apartments. The emperor himself bestowed a robe on Prince Hotaru.

Examination and criticism of Genji's journals had become the main business of the court. He asked that his paintings of the seacoast be given to Fujitsubo. She longed to see what went before and came after, but he said only that he would in due course show her everything. The pleasure which he had given the emperor was pleasure for Genji himself. It worried Tō no Chūjō that Genji should so favor Akikonomu. Was her triumph to be complete? He comforted himself with the thought that the emperor would not have forgotten his own early partiality for the Kokiden girl. Surely she would not be cast aside.

Genji had a strong sense of history and wanted this to be one of the ages when things begin. Very great care therefore went into all the fetes and observances. It was an exciting time.

But he was also obsessed with evanescence. He was determined to withdraw from public affairs when the emperor was a little older. Every precedent told him that men who rise to rank and power beyond their years cannot expect long lives. Now, in this benign reign, perhaps by way of compensation for the years of sorrow and disgrace, Genji had an abun-

---

*"The taking of the brush," which also covers calligraphy.

dance, indeed a plethora, of rank and honor. Further glory could only bring uncertainty. He wanted to withdraw quietly and make preparations for the next life, and so add to his years in this one. He had purchased a quiet tract off in a mountain village and was putting up a chapel and collecting images and scriptures. But first he must see that no mistake was made in educating his children. So it was that his intentions remained in some doubt.

A Note About the Translator

Edward G. Seidensticker is professor of Japanese at Columbia University and a noted translator. Among his translations have been a number of works by Tanizaki Junichiro and Kawabata Yasunari, one of which—Kawabata's *The Sound of the Mountain*—won the National Book Award for Translation in 1970. He is also the author of several books in English and Japanese. The Japanese government recently awarded him one of its highest honors, the third-class Order of the Rising Sun, for his part in introducing Japanese novels abroad. Mr. Seidensticker teaches in New York for six months of the year and lives the rest of the time in Tokyo and Honolulu.